WORST-KEPT SECRET

Sienna Cash

NOT THE CRITIC PRESS LLC

www.siennacash.com

Cover Design by Julie Jones
Cover Illustration Copyright © 2016 by Julie Jones

Lyrics from "Accidental Man" © 2006 Bearded Emperor Music. Used with permission from Alex Dezen.

Published by Not the Critic Press LLC
www.notthecriticpress.com
First Printing, 2016

Library of Congress Control Number: 2016903409
ISBN 978-1-945070-00-6 (Print)
ISBN 978-1-945070-01-3 (Kindle eBook)
ASIN B01C22CSTY

All characters appearing in this work are fictitious. Any resemblance to real persons, living or dead, is purely coincidental. While locations may be based in reality, details are the product of the author's imagination. Any factual errors are purely the fault (or intent) of the author.

Soundtrack

Elderly Woman Behind the Counter in a Small Town *by Pearl Jam*
Left of Center *by Suzanne Vega*
Rio *by Duran Duran*
The First Day of My Life *by Bright Eyes*
El Paso *by Marty Robbins*
Keep Your Hands to Yourself *by the Georgia Satellites*
Hoodoo Voodoo *by Wilco and Billy Bragg*
Somebody that I Used to Know *by Gotye (feat. Kimbra)*
Happiness *by Elliott Smith*
If It's the Beaches *by the Avett Brothers*
Accidental Man *by the Damnwells*
One *by U2*
Nineteen *by Old 97's*
Stacy's Mom *by Fountains of Wayne*
Happy Boy *by the Beat Farmers*
Take It Easy *by Andy Taylor*

For Matto and the Wreckers,
which would probably make a cool band name.

PROLOGUE

Here I am, in the driveway, and I can't bring myself to get out of the damn car.

The weather feels like it was special-ordered from God. The kind of day mid-September is capable of bringing but often doesn't: cloudless blue sky, warm enough without being uncomfortable, not a trace of humidity, a light breeze making the trees tell secrets. Ideal moving weather. So why can't I move?

It's like I'm tethered to the boxes of my life. On the passenger seat. In the back seat. And the trunk. There's got to be some symbolism here.

It's residential limbo: don't want to go forward, can't go back. Whatever I carry over the threshold first will signify something. Something sucky.

I maneuver the driver's seat back and rest my bare feet on the dash, on either side of the steering wheel. A Pearl Jam song from forever ago comes on. Strangely fitting. I feel like my heart and thoughts are fading, too.

You see, I'd come up with a novel idea. Move back to my hometown to live with my mother. Just to get my bearings and recalibrate my life. My mom didn't talk about loneliness—she was much too independent for that—but the house is big. It has to feel empty without my dad.

Now all I have to do is tell her.

I planned to earlier, but the how and the why of how I ended up in the driveway of my childhood home was too long and embarrassing to share over the phone. I decided it would be simpler to just tell her in person. So I loaded everything into the car.

And maybe I wanted to see the look on her face. She'll be thrilled to have company. To have a daughter to dote on. Someone to cook for and hug. This will be one of the best surprises she's had in years.

But first I have to get myself out of the car.

My hand rests on the car door handle, poised for exit.

Maybe I'll hang here just till this song is over.

Unless the next song is good.

Eight minutes pass and a Prius slides in next to me, in my mom's spot. The driver is out and indicating I should roll down

1

the window before I've even registered it's her. Even through her sunglasses I can feel her taking in my reclining position, judging, dismissing.

"What are you doing here?"

This is my sister, asking me. Of course. Of *course* Marina would show up today of all days, and of course she would act as if I were the one invading her space. We stare down our reflections in each other's sunglasses, her showered and made up, in fancy-ass yoga pants and fitted North Face jacket, me all scruffy in a Katniss braid, the yoga pants I've slept in, an ancient tank top, and a hoodie. I'm hung over and look it. My flip-flops are somewhere on the floor below. I fidget slightly against the seat. Yup, not even wearing a bra.

I do what makes sense. I volley. "What are *you* doing here?"

"I live here?" she says pointedly, but with a question mark, like I'm daft. "Mom told you, right?" She vanishes into the house, holstering her stun gun as she goes.

My head pounds anew. I almost laugh. And then I do laugh, because, again, of course it's like this. I mean, why wouldn't it be? I veer hairpin-turn left and make a rash, last-minute decision to do something different and unexpected. Totally unlike me.

And here she is, my big sister, doing the exact same thing. And doing it first. Right on schedule.

PART 1:
before

Sienna Cash

one

"Charlotte! Why didn't you call?" My mother turns off the kitchen faucet. Her hug, as always, smells like lilacs, but I cringe at her voice. It's only been an hour since I washed down three ibuprofen with my iced coffee. It hasn't made a dent yet, but I guess that's not surprising. By the time Kendra and I stopped drinking last night, it was today.

Mom regards me apologetically, drying her hands on a dishtowel. She glances at the clock. "You just caught me before I left. It's Carol's daughter's baby shower. I was going to call you tonight." She adds words to a notepad on the wall as she speaks—her ongoing grocery list, no doubt. My mother will always multitask in analog.

Marina is nowhere in sight. "Mom," I say. I'm calm. My voice is at normal volume. On the stool, I wait for her to look at me. "Why is Marina here?"

"That's why I was going to call you. She has a big case in Danborn for the next few weeks. So she's staying here, at home!" She glances out the window, frowning. "What's all that in your car?"

One month. That's what I told Kendra last night. I can do anything for one month. We clinked our pint glasses to confirm it, then waved the bartender over for a refill.

I'd been trying to blame Cam, making Kendra recite in a monotone, "The breakup was a good thing. Cam was your placeholder. We know this. We need to move on from knowing this."

I was trying. I'd been dumped before, after all. I was familiar with the procedure. And it wasn't like I hadn't seen it coming or was even in love with him anymore. But it still sucked.

Especially since Cam didn't just leave me, he *replaced* me. While he was rolling in the happiness of a new relationship, I was still covering up holes. Deleting his profile from Netflix. Giving my clothes more breathing room in the closet. I started eating more takeout and began the arduous task of looking for a place to live when our lease ran out in November. It probably cost him plenty to pay double rent in the meantime, but I'm sure he felt too guilty to complain.

It wasn't until I had finally adjusted to singlehood, with tentative plans to move in with my friend Xanna, that he called me. Not texted. Called. That alone was startling. When I called him back (*as if* I would pick up), he insisted we meet in person. I tried to say no. But Cam wasn't an insister normally. He came over. In my (our) kitchen, he seemed nervous. He also looked a little different, and I was trying to figure out whether he'd actually gotten a new haircut or simply styled it another way when he said something about the lease. After he apologized for the third time, my mind backed up.

"Did you say I had to move out by the end of *this* month?"

"Yes," he choked, his face a map of his misery.

That was two days ago. He explained the whole thing, something about the guy he first sublet the place from, but I've forgotten it already. All that mattered was that I was screwed.

I could have stayed with Kendra. She offered. Just until Xanna's roommate left. So did Cam, for that matter, which I would have laughed at if he didn't look so wretched. Move in with him and his new girlfriend in their rehabbed duplex in a hipster neighborhood in Dorchester? I wasn't a masochist. But I let him sweat overnight, thinking I was considering it.

Kendra's studio was tiny enough. And I didn't want to make a hasty decision to become roommates with people I might end up hating after the first unwelcome discovery. I was twenty-six, for God's sake. Wasn't I done living with strangers?

I still had three weeks till my deadline, but knew I'd drive myself crazy with options. So I was done. I was moving home.

I've visited my parents' house in Danborn regularly over the years—holidays, birthdays—but I can't remember the last time I darkened the doorway of my bedroom. It's spooky. And the bed is way too small. Looking around I feel mentally disheveled and out of whack, and not just from last night's bender. Like there's something I haven't told myself and just need to remember.

Sitting on the foot of the bed, I slide through the camera roll on my phone. There it is, the last photo I took of Cam. I caught him with his tongue out of his mouth in concentration when he was putting together an IKEA bookcase. He looks effortlessly cute, in a way I hadn't seen in a while. Which is precisely why I pulled out my camera for the shot. I call Kendra. "Tell me again why I can't blame Cam."

"Blame him all you want," she says. "Are you at your house?"

"Look at him," I say. "He looks like a guy who shouldn't have done this to me."

"It's the IKEA photo, isn't it? I knew you sounded weird. Take me off speaker."

"If I could see him," Kendra continues, off speaker, "I'd say he looks like a guy who fulfilled his role in your life. He pulled you out of your slutty summer. He gave you a long, successful relationship."

"Successful relationships don't end." I know I sound bratty. It must be the room, stuffed with invisible highschoolery.

"Yes they do, or we'd all marry our high-school boyfriend."

We both go quiet, and I know she's already regretting what she's said.

I get off the bed, which creaks, and walk over to my bulletin board, homemade and painted blue and gold in the spirit of Danborn High (starting as a junior, I really got into the school-spirit thing) and decorated with photos, collage-style. My longtime friend Kelly, who's getting married in December, side-hugging Kendra on her eighteenth birthday. The three of us in sunglasses and baseball caps the day after prom. And of course, Dean, variously: looking over his shoulder in sunglasses; smiling from the driver's seat of his car; at the beach, with me swung up in his arms.

"Cam already has a new successful relationship," I point out, turning away from the photos.

"You *introduced* him to Katherine."

From the way she's drawing her breath in through her nose, I can tell Kendra's about ten seconds away from hanging up on me. "Okay. I'm sorry. I'm done. But I'm going a little crazy." I take my own deep breath and ask my best friend, "Do you know where I am right now? I'm in my old bedroom. I'm sitting at my high-school desk, next to my twin bed, staring at a Linkin Park poster and prom pictures. Everything I own that I could fit into

7

my car is outside, and I want to just leave it there and get back in my car and turn the fuck around, because guess who's down the hall, also in her old bedroom?"

"Marina?" Kendra's voice has a nose wrinkle.

"She's living here."

"Marina? But how—that doesn't make any sense!"

"I know."

"She lives in New Hampshire!"

"I know."

"She's married!"

"I *know*." I've been wondering about this myself. I hope she's not getting divorced. Her husband's the best part about her.

I open the windows, feeling all at once how stuffy the room is, and probably has been for years. Some kid is pushing a lawnmower past the Hunters' pool next door towards my mom's yard. He's dancing. Rather animatedly. Christ, he must be stoned. He's also shirtless, hair spilling out from a bandana tied around his head, do-rag style. Hippie stoner, perhaps. Cute hippie stoner, I determine, reserving an amendment for when I see him at eye level.

I exit to the hallway to hear better and lower my voice. "Kendra, come get me. I was going to spend today moving my shit, but I can't even. Come over and we'll go out. I'll stay at your place tonight and deal with this all tomorrow."

"Can't. I have a thing."

"With who?"

"First date." Kendra's a serial dater, and so picky she never shares the names of guys she dates until they've been out twice. No exceptions. "Plus I've seen how you pack. I'm not helping."

"Fine. I hope I get to find out this one's name."

Kendra emits a blowy exhale. "Don't we all."

Deleting the picture of Cam is an empty act—I can always retrieve it later—but for the moment it gratifies me.

I may as well admit that, yes, Cam and I stayed together about twice as long as we should have. But as your mid-twenties give way to your late twenties, even the most staunch feminist would admit that being half of a couple is infinitely easier than being single. Once everyone starts settling down, the plus-one reasons alone make it worthwhile.

It's also easier than sleeping around. Which was the state I was in when Cam found me, extra tan from my between-real-jobs gig at a golf course, extra thin from crash dieting all spring,

and extra highlighted, just because. That summer, for the first
and only time in my life, I couldn't step into a bar without men
offering to buy me a drink. I made a game of taking them up on
it. Until the night Cam and I were both in line at a bar near
Faneuil Hall, and he bent down to my ear to say, "The round's
on me. What are you drinking this time?" Only then did he
realize I wasn't his friend Liza. He did buy me that drink, out of
embarrassment, and I thought he was so cute I broke summer
protocol and didn't kiss him. Not that night, anyway. He texted
me the next day.

With our shared Catholic-school history and the discovery of
mutual confessed-and-confirmed friends, we eased into a
relationship, both thinking we found The One. By the time, a
few months in, I backed into the realization that I wasn't as in
love with him as I wanted to be, we were already on cruise
control. I genuinely liked him too much to pull over. More than
that, I liked *us*. We were friends. We got along better than a lot
of couples I knew. And who knew, that initial spark could come
back. He was cute, albeit in a bland, prep-school sort of way.
He'd gone to Dartmouth, graduated a couple years ahead of
me, had a good job in finance. He treated me well, which was
more than I could say for some of my friends' boyfriends. And
he came from a good family, which worked well for holidays.

But beyond that first, heady six-week period after we met,
I'd never risen above lukewarm with Cam. It was unsettling. I
always thought that real, grown-up love—the post-high school
kind—meant you felt it in your toes. But the warm pressure of
his hand on the small of my back felt safe, not exciting. Even
sex was vanilla—not even French vanilla. Sleeping with him felt
like rehearsing a PG-13 movie scene. On the rare occasions he
coaxed an orgasm out of me, he regarded himself with wonder,
like he didn't quite believe he had it in him.

Still, nothing was ever bad enough to force the breakup
hand. In the course of our three years together, we could have
easily gotten sick of one another or decided it was pointless to
commit any more time to someone who was secretly scared of
roller coasters (him) or who, when you came down to it, didn't
give a damn whether the Red Sox won or lost (me). If nothing
happened to shake things up, everything would go on as usual.
Politeness became us.

Eventually what happened was Katherine. Not Kathy, not
Katie, not Kate, *Katherine*. I'd known her in college—a friend of
a friend, really—and when I ran into her one night in the city I

introduced her to my friends, including Cam. She rendered him so immediately speechless I actually found myself feeling bad for him in a laboratory, stand-back-and-observe sort of way. I finally called him on his acting distant a few days later, out of curiosity more than anything, and he spilled everything, even though he hadn't done so much as call her. "I love you as much as I thought I was capable of," he told me later. "I didn't know there was more."

I didn't argue, because yeah. I did know.

t w o

C am will deliver the furniture I want to keep—like my bed and dresser—but everything else is on me. I borrow my mom's car to bring another load of my stuff from the apartment. At the last minute, I decide to stay over rather than hang out in Danborn with Marina. It's likely the last time I can.

On my way back the next morning, I stop at the Dunkin' Donuts in my mom's neighborhood. I'm adding sugar to my iced coffee when I see a guy come in who looks familiar. With a start I realize it's Steve Linstrom, albeit a little bigger, a little softer. I knew Steve in high school, but I didn't really *know* him. A year older than me, he was always—back then—the best-looking guy at Danborn High without trying, with a perpetual cheerleader or blond soccer/volleyball/field hockey star on his arm. I've probably spoken seven sentences to him in my life. But a quick glance around tells me laying low is not an option, so I paste a smile on my face and resign myself to the nice-to-see-you conversation. I'm pushing the lid back down on my cup when he turns to the people following him in. First is—oh my God—Keith Hunter. Even without him facing me I recognize my next-door neighbor's height and soldier-like posture instantly. And suddenly my heart is in my throat and I'm scurrying around a corner, almost tripping over a table-full of customers. Because if Keith's in Danborn, and he's not alone, there's only one person he could be with.

When you break up with someone, you always wonder about the moment you'll cross paths again. My predictions with Dean have usually involved dim but flattering light, professionally

11

done makeup (me), and miles of regret leading to a life-changing revelation (him). It definitely does not involve a stark, fluorescent Dunkin' Donuts, air-dried hair twisted up birds-nest style, and my glasses. All I can manage is the certainty that if that moment is now, I sure as hell am going to see him first.

Unlike Steve, to whom the ten years since high school have not been benevolent, and Keith, who's more clean-cut and rigid than ever, Dean looks the same. Gloriously unchanged, yet heightened in all the ways. He's easily twenty pounds lighter than Steve, with decidedly more hair. Although I've heard tell he's been sporting a goatee on and off, right now his face is beautifully bare. Steve says something to him, and Dean's answering laugh is a prayer I know by heart. I can't believe it gets to be the same.

The line moves forward and I, backward, inching my way to the exit. But a kid behind me has a reckless elbow, and I can't save my coffee. It thunks on the floor. A flying starburst of coffee goes everywhere, and all eyes shoot my way.

I see it happen on Dean's face. I've registered. But Keith speaks first. "Hey Charlie." He walks over, blocking my view. He looks as if he wants to hug me, then appears to think better of it. "How goes it?"

"Pretty good." I'm trying to smooth out my voice and both not look at Dean and look at him at the same time. I push my glasses up on my nose. Thank God I at least managed to shower today, but would it have killed me to put my contacts in?

Keith holds out a fistful of napkins. Mortification tickles my skin. "Thanks." Stiffly I blot at my shirt. "I'd give you a hello hug, but..." I look down. "Runaway kid."

"We'll get you another." He calls over to Dean, still in line, still watching me. "Throw in another iced coffee. Large." He turns back to me. "What kind?"

"Hazelnut. Light."

The two of us step aside so an employee can properly mop up my mess.

"So what's going on, Charlie? You visiting your parents?"

I press my lips together. He's officially on notice for forgetting about my dad. For Christ's sake, he lived *next door*. I debate how much to tell him. He may not be my favorite person, but his best friend is another matter entirely. "Actually, yeah. Just for a couple weeks while I'm between apartments. And switching jobs. Weren't you in...Chicago?"

Keith smiles, like he's impressed or glad I've remembered. "Yeah, for a few years now." My eyes must wander to Dean, because he adds, as if I've asked a question, "Dean was there too."

I keep my voice casual. "'Was?'"

He rolls his eyes. "He's decided to become a townie again. I couldn't talk him out of it." He glances at Dean, paying the cashier, before turning back to me. "So Charlie—"

"Where is he living?"

Keith blinks. "Who, Dean?"

But I don't answer, because here Dean comes, coffee in hand. He's holding it near the top, so I reach for the bottom. "Thanks. You didn't have to do that."

"Don't mention it. It's good to see you, Charlie." Dean holds my gaze for a minute, and I know I should leave—I smell like coffee and am generally not fit for public consumption—but I can't look away.

He starts to say something else, and that's when I find my voice. "It was great seeing you all," I say blandly, backing toward the door. "Thanks again."

I sit behind the wheel of my mom's car, sucking down coffee. My face starts to feel strange. I look in the rearview and see a grin. A big, stupid grin with a mind of its own.

"Mom? Is that you?"

Marina always manages to sound like she's exasperated, as if things already aren't quite up to standard. When I walk into the kitchen, she's visibly disappointed. "Where's Mom?" I shrug, but her attention is already elsewhere. "That's okay, I have to meet Todd for brunch anyway." She's talking to herself, or more accurately, to her phone. "I'll just see her later."

As if my presence finally registers fully, she glances at me for more than a millisecond. Her face is framed perfectly by her lawyerly blown-out hair, her features swept by that familiar air of defiance—proof positive that she doesn't like being around me any more than I like being around her.

"Mom said you're staying here for a while too," she says.

More like living. "Yup." I climb up on a stool and select a banana, marveling at its perfection. My mom's bananas are always perfectly yellow, while mine seem to spot on the drive home from the grocery store.

"For how long?"

"I don't know. A few weeks."

"Why do you open your bananas that way?"

"What?" I look down.

"From the bottom like that."

"It's actually the right way to open them." I learned this from YouTube, years ago, but I'm not about to tell her that.

She seems as if she's going to respond, then shakes her head, dismissing the subject. "I have a case in Danborn District Court that starts Monday." She redirects her focus to her phone. "I can probably work late now if I have to," she mutters. "That's one good thing about you being here."

A beat later Marina processes my silence. Her head snaps up. "I mean—"

"I'm going to unpack." I step past her to drop my half-eaten banana into the compost under the sink. (My mom is also the compost queen. Other people's parents are dragged kicking and screaming into the world of reducing and reusing; my mom was on the committee in favor of installing recycling bins in every trash pickup customer's yard, like, years ago.)

"Charlie," Marina begins, like I owe her something. But I don't. I never have.

Surveying the contents of the back seat of my car, I take deep breath after deep breath. After all this time, it's absurd that she can still make me cry. I try to concentrate on the task at hand, forcing some sort of order out of chaos. I take so long trying to form a game plan that when a voice calls to me, I jump three feet.

"Moving in?"

I wipe my eyes quickly, smudging my glasses. Approaching me is Lawn Boy from yesterday. I was right. He *is* cute. "Something like that," I offer vaguely as I give up on the backseat and pop the trunk. Jesus. Cam would never have let me pack this way. Maybe I'll choose a category. "Things with cords" sounds reasonable enough.

"Need a hand?" Lawn Boy asks. I gingerly reach under the pile of stuff. All at once my field of vision is full of jeans, then boots, worn black ones with thick soles. I stand back up. The kid is wearing a faded black T-shirt championing a band I've never heard of. Even tamed by the do-rag, he has a lot more hair than I realized. It's messy and wavy, the color of sand when the tide goes out. A toothpick is in his mouth. His jeans are well worn and stained with paint, and I can't help absorbing how finely muscled his legs are under the thinned denim.

14

I also can't stop staring at him. Not just because he is seriously good-looking, but because he looks so goddamn...familiar.

"You're the treehouse girl." He smiles at my shock and goes on. "Don't you know who I am, Charlie?"

He knows me? My mind searches back through jobs and parties and friends of friends. I step back slightly and scrutinize him through narrowed eyes, needing distance. He's definitely cute, but he clearly isn't old enough to have been in school with me, or to be friends (or a boyfriend) of any of my friends. I gather purchase on the lamps and cords, stuffing them in one of the empty boxes I've thrown on top of the mess. "Should I?"

"I've only known you all my life." He indicates that I should pass the box to him, and something about the way he turns to my house, walking with navigational confidence toward the basement door, kick-starts my brain. Wait a minute. Is it...no way. No *way*. But even as I'm denying it, a mental slideshow plays of a little boy with missing front teeth in a Superman cape, a kid off to the side as I pose for prom pictures.

"Oh my God."

His expression, thrown over his shoulder and clearly staged, has the air of *People*'s Sexiest Man Alive. "I get that a lot."

It's all crystallized: Lawn Boy is Wade Hunter, little brother of Keith. Thus also my next-door neighbor.

Holy shit. Wade Hunter. When's the last time I saw him? The summer before college? The year after, maybe, when my dad died, the last time I lived at home? My memory hiccups over different images of him, as a toddler, as a tree-climbing grade-schooler, as a gawky tween with orthodontia on the horizon. Since then, gawkiness seems to have given way to some strikingly good looks. Objectively speaking, of course. I want to take a Brillo pad to my thoughts of just a minute ago, rinse my brain with Listerine. It *is* pretty embarrassing, even in the privacy of my own head, to discover that I've been ogling a kid whose diapers I've actually changed. Gross.

But I'm also...what? A little discombobulated, like a third-grader who's caught her teacher examining the asparagus in the produce aisle at the Stop & Shop. I know what I'm seeing, but the context is all wrong.

For a distraction more than anything, I retrieve my iced coffee from the cup holder in the car, finishing the last watery remnants while willing other thoughts, any thoughts, to flow into my mind. Nevertheless, when he returns I hug him. It's true—I have known him his whole life. I remember the day he was born, how Keith stayed over our house waiting for his baby brother. We made pizza and had a pepperoni fight.

"The last time I saw you, you were..." I can't think of a way to finish without sounding insulting.

"Awkwardly adolescent?" he suggests.

"No," I say quickly, telling myself that just because he seems to read my mind doesn't mean he actually can. I'm also a little thrown. Is it weird that he's funny? It's definitely weird that he's taller than me. And that hugging him felt slightly better than it should have. "I meant more like..." I can't finish. I guess it's not crazy to think of him as an adult, sort of, and someone with a sense of humor. I do the math: If I'm twenty-six, that makes him—

"I'm nineteen," he says.

He has to stop that.

"So you're in college," I realize.

"I was."

"And now you're—?"

"Not."

"Allrighty." I have my own taboo subjects; I can certainly recognize others' when I hear them.

"And you're..." he prompts.

"In college?" God, he has a fabulous smile. Direct, happy, intentional. "Living here. Temporarily."

"And weren't you living in...?"

"Somerville," I confirm as he arrives at the same answer. How does he know this?

"And now you're...?"

"Not."

He nods gamely. Fair enough.

"I just saw your brother," I tell him.

"Yeah, he's in town for the weekend." He's inspecting the inside of the car. "I'm supposed to be cleaning gutters, but I could take time out to help a lady," he says, making me feel about ninety. I have a flash of how my stuffed car must look to an outsider. From a stranger's perspective I can see the haphazardness, how it probably looks as if it were packed by a schizophrenic. Nothing organized, an alarm clock peeking out from the top of a box that contains what looks like sweaters, stuffed animals pressed against the glass like a kid's face in the back window of the family station wagon, computer monitor teetering dangerously on the headrest of the back seat, propped up just barely by an equally precarious pile of small kitchen appliances. And that's just what I could fit in my own car. There's a whole other version of this in my mom's.

Wade looks at the mess, then back at me, then back at the mess. He begins to speak, then stops. I shrug. "I was in a hurry."

"I see that." He sighs, like he's bracing himself, and proceeds to efficiently build an armload of stuff that actually makes sense to move together. I let him. Why not? He wants to help. We spend the next hour—likely a twenty-minute job if I'd packed properly, using tape and boxes and Sharpied labels and all the normal, sane things you're supposed to—depositing armloads of loosely organized stuff into a semi-empty corner of the walk-out basement. As we do, we chat. He fills in the blanks. I learn that he hasn't been here permanently since he moved to Colorado to live with his dad, which explains why I can't remember seeing him around. Now that I think about it, it actually sounds a little bit familiar, like something I'd been told at some point and forgotten.

"Wow," I say when he's done, as we both survey the pile in the corner of the basement. "Clearly I needed you."

"Packing isn't your strong suit, Charlie Michaelsen."

"Not even close," I say amiably.

"You have more back at your place." It's not a question, and it sounds a little resigned.

"Yep. At least one more carload." Then I hear myself asking: "Wanna come?"

I pull into the drive-thru at the Dunkin' Donuts next to the highway. "What can I get you?"

"Iced hazelnut, cream, no sugar." I must look surprised because he says, "Is coffee okay?"

"Of course." I don't want to say what I'm thinking, which is that he's too young to drink coffee, never mind to take it exactly the same way I do. But that's ludicrous. He's nineteen, not nine.

"I'm old enough to drink coffee," he says, doing that thing again. He also sounds amused, and I can feel blood moving into my cheeks.

"I know," I say, my eyes on the menu display. How is it that he is able to make me blush? "You're an adult." As weird as that seems to me.

"Not only can I drive, I can vote and go to war."

17

I let myself smile as we pull forward. "And I have to respect that you're a DD fan," I say.

"I'm relieved to hear you're not one of those Starbucks people."

Now I really smile. I look at him like, *Be serious.*

On the highway, we lapse into silence. I steal a glance at him, not sure if I should stoke the conversation. But he seems okay, not nervous or fidgety, so I sink into myself instead. I still don't know if I did the right thing, moving home, and floating in uncertainty like this bothers me.

I'm actually pretty good with big decisions, as long as I have adequate time to make them, though "adequate time" usually equates to assuming the pace of, as Kendra says, a lazy snail. I make lists, I weigh options. I'm the master of the pro-con list. When I finally pull the trigger on a decision, I've usually been mentally there for a while. So far I've never regretted anything. Not quitting my job as the summer-camp lifeguard in mid-July for the nannying gig. Not buying my first car, the Civic with the improbable 150,000 miles on it that lasted till Christmas break of sophomore year in college. Not even losing my virginity on a living room floor at the now-young-sounding age of sixteen.

Sixteen. Wow. The nineteen-year-old next to me must have already had sex. And from the looks of him, likely lots of it.

I feel old.

This moving-home decision, though, left me none of my usual time to think. Beyond crowding Kendra out or becoming roommates with the first couple of Dorchester, I had no real options. No matter which way I turn the situation, I can't come up with any alternative that would have worked. Even now, the idea of trying to find housing last-minute in the college-heavy city of Boston makes me want to curl into a fetal position.

"Mind if I turn on the radio?" Wade asks me.

"Of course not. Have at it." As he's cruising through the presets, I ask him, "Why did you call me treehouse girl?"

"That's how I always thought of you, when I was a kid," he answers, rejecting station after station. "You were always in the treehouse."

I shake my head. "I wasn't."

"That wasn't you? Long brown hair, superior climbing skills?"

It used to be blond. White-blond, really, when I was a toddler, then darkening into its eventual mousy brown by middle school. Funny, thinking back to my childhood, I still think of myself as blond; sometimes the mirror surprises me.

"Nice of you to notice."

"I noticed a lot of things about you."

Poker face, I tell myself. Why is he baiting me? I reach behind for my messenger bag on the floor of the back seat. My fingers find my wallet, my sunblock, what seems to be the remnants of a melted Kind bar, and—there. I slide on my sunglasses.

"You had glasses on before," he says.

"I put my contacts in."

"You look good in glasses."

I have no idea how to respond to that, besides saying thanks. So I do. And then, idiotically, I say, "So tell me, Wade, what do you do for fun?" I sound like his visiting aunt.

He gives me a strange look, then appears to consider the question. "Fun."

"Like in your free time? Friday and Saturday nights? You bungee jump? Scale skyscrapers? Dig trenches?" I keep my voice light.

I feel rather than see him shrug. "Nothing exciting, I guess. I read. I ride my bike, though not here. I hike and camp with my dog, though again, not here. I listen to music. I see bands play."

"Where?" I ask, picturing someone's backyard.

"Clubs, usually."

"You can get in?"

"There are such things as eighteen-plus shows. Even all-ages."

"Ah. And fake IDs?"

"Those too." He tells me about the last show he saw, an eighties tribute band for a friend's birthday, which actually was in someone's backyard.

I smirk. "Everyone's retro."

"You don't like eighties music?"

I shrug. "You do?"

"I like all music."

"You can't like all music."

"I can't?"

I shake my head knowingly. "People say that, but they don't really mean it. Usually they mean all music except country, or all music except rap."

"I like country and rap. I even like Christian rock." I raise an eyebrow at him, which for some reason makes him laugh. "I'm a pop culture junkie," he says, like that should explain it all. "I like everything."

"What does that mean?"

He looks at me sideways. "You need me to define pop culture junkie?"

"No." I'm trying to change lanes, but I forget to signal and another car beeps at me. "Chill!" I yell to the Jeep now speeding up to get away from me. Great, I'm going to kill us both. "No," I repeat, "I don't need you to define it. I was just wondering if it means the same to you as it does to me."

"Why wouldn't it?"

He's right. Why wouldn't it? "Forget it. I take it back."

Amazingly, he drops it. Or at least is willing to change the subject. To me.

"So what about you?" he asks.

I blink. "I'm sorry?"

"What do you do for fun?"

I shrug. "I have no idea." He's skeptical. "What? I don't."

"Okay, how about: what music do *you* like? What bands to you go out of your way to pay money to see?"

I'm blank. I try to pull out the names of musicians from memory, but they're all infused with other people. Frat-boy bands from college. Cam's Jimmy Buffet (inherited from his dad) and emo. No one I can claim as my own.

"That's more my friend Xanna's life," I say finally. "You should talk to her."

"Is she single?" He sounds like he's teasing, but I don't look at him to verify.

"She's bi. And she's my age." I feel protective suddenly, though of exactly what I couldn't say.

"And that's a bad thing?"

I snort in lieu of a reply. I don't know which part of what I said he's referring to, and I'm not going to ask. What's a kosher conversational style with your friend's little brother? More specifically—fine, if I'm going to be honest—if your friend's little brother happens to have laughing eyes and jeans that fit like blue skin? I find myself somewhere between the way a babysitter talks to her charge and the way you talk to your best friend's boyfriend who happens to be extremely hot. Harmless on the surface but fraught underneath, because you never know what's going to get taken the wrong way. Nothing can be left to a chance interpretation out of context.

We settle back into silence, a surprisingly comfortable one, given the circumstances. Once off the highway and into Somerville, I orient him to the area. He pays polite attention, but as I'm turning down my street he says, "So you really don't do anything for fun."

I park on the street and turn the car off. One by one I stick out the fingers of my right hand, thumb first. "I'm twenty-six, I just got dumped"—fine, it was six weeks ago, but he doesn't know that—"I have no money saved, my job sucks, and I just moved back home with my mom." I don't say "Need I say more," but the phrase hangs in the air nonetheless.

On the landing to my building he holds the outside door open for me, and I fiddle to isolate the key I need. I can tell he's watching me. I feel slightly outside of my skin, an odd sense of... not quite déjà vu, but familiarity. Familiarity that doesn't seem earned.

"He must have been an idiot," he says.

My head jerks up. "Who?"

"The guy who dumped you."

The raise of his eyebrows is almost imperceptible. His gaze holds mine and for an instant I see not my friend's little brother or my next-door neighbor, but a guy on my doorstep. I feel flirted with. Still holding the door, the guy moves his hand, feather-light, to my lower back.

"After you."

I find escape in the pile of books in a corner of the now-bare living room, an impetus for something to say. "I do like to read. Behold the evidence. The very heavy evidence."

Together we regard the stacks of books and the empty boxes next to them. "Well," Wade says, with the tone of someone who is making every effort to look on the bright side, "at least they'll be easier to pack."

three

When my friend Kelly's family relocated during her sophomore year of college, they didn't quite count her when allocating space in the new house. Christmas and summers, she had to sleep on the pullout in the living room, which we tease her about to this day. No one could quite top that story, but for the most part, my friends pretty much lost their bedrooms by the time they reported for their first college class. Younger siblings invaded, guest rooms were created, sewing/crafting rooms sprang seemingly from nowhere.

But not mine. My mom kept my and Marina's bedrooms intact, unfortunate shrines to our high-school selves. Entering my room feels like the abandoned set of a long-canceled TV show, or one of those stores-turned-museums where people just locked up and left in the middle of the day, never to return, register receipts still marking that final purchase. All the Harry Potter books I didn't want to take to college, the CDs I owned before ripping them and switching over to an almost all-digital music library, the trendy-for-a-minute jewelry and clothes I couldn't bring myself to get rid of...everything then is now.

Maybe it's because other people are always more interesting than ourselves, but Marina's room, especially, has the feel of a museum. I used to sneak in and sift through her stuff, especially the year she was missing. I'd run my fingers over the titles of her books, study the pages she'd dog-eared to figure out if something, anything at all, would provide a clue as to who she was, why she was gone, or when she'd be back.

Sometimes I even fell asleep on the vast, empty expanse of her bed that I was always careful to smooth when I left.

One time, when I was thirteen and we still hadn't found her, rummaging under that bed revealed a treasure trove: a boot-shoebox of notebooks, journals, and half-written letters and poems. The poem that sticks with me had only a single line. *Way over there, across the room...* I considered it for days. Was it a boy over there? A friend? A window? It sounded like a poem that needed to be finished. I tried to do just that, channeling my big sister while sitting at her desk, after school or after dinner when my parents watched TV in the den. My words were never good enough. Marina was the writer in the family, always had been—at least before she gave it all up for the law. Even before I started I knew nothing I could come up with would come anywhere close to what she'd planned on.

It's beyond comprehension that she's there now, down the hall, door shut to the rest of the world, true to form. I can hear my mom moving around downstairs, the clink of the spoon in her last cup of tea. She'll be sitting in her chair in the den with the TV on as background while she reads her latest library book. I was there with her, for a while, in my dad's chair next to her. A Sunday night like nothing had changed, even though everything has. My dad could have been in the bathroom. Or refilling the Scotch he liked to sip. I feigned exhaustion and came up to bed.

Sleep isn't happening. Music isn't helping. The book I'm trying to read is stupid and cliché. Before I've acknowledged to myself what I'm doing I'm down the stairs and out the back door, carrying my shoes and a Diet Coke. I saw it yesterday, out the window, when Wade was mowing the lawn. The ladder seems weathered, and repaired at least once. But it feels solid. I slip on my Chucks and step up first one step, then another. I probably weigh twice what I did the last time I did this. I make it all the way up, like a girl with superior climbing skills would. The trap door above my head falls open silently when pushed, and I smile, remembering the thick felt my dad and I had thought to line the top edge with.

I get comfortable in the back corner of the "outside" part without the roof, and the moon moves across the charcoal blue sky through the black tree branches above. From this vantage point I can see one rectangle of light in the second floor next door. Wade's room? It faces my house. Is he in there right now? Do I want to know?

23

No. I do not. I shouldn't even be wondering that. God.
I let my eyes shut.
It's probably his room.
Who else's could it be?
Up until now, everything about my house has seemed small. The stairs to my bedroom, the formerly enormous backyard, even the length of the driveway is tinier than I remember, the way an adult's eyes put the remnants of a child's life back into perspective. But here, in the treehouse, even with my eyes closed, the world still feels just as big as it did when I was nine. Much bigger than me.

I'm searching for an extra stapler when I discover Nina hiding in the spare office we keep for visiting contractors. "Sorry," she says, looking caught. "Today she's on the warpath. I can't even."

"We have that meeting at two," I remind her reluctantly. If I were her, I'd keep a hiding place, too.

"Fuck. That's right." She gets up. "I may as well show my face so I look indispensable. Or worthy of a promotion."

We cackle together. It's a running joke at More than Marketing that the only way people get promoted is into other companies. With only ten full-timers, there's nowhere to move up to.

"I'm out for your job, look out," Nina sings over her shoulder as she sashays down the hall.

I almost hope she is. I've spent the week I've been back in Danborn job-hunting, looking for a position with an actual future. I got a technical promotion, sort of, last year, and that's only because HR—otherwise known as LeeAnne—took pity on me and released me from JJ's direct support team when Nina was hired. The tiny pay hike from switching to the marketing team didn't mean nearly as much as getting a sizeable chunk of my sanity back. Now Nina, as JJ's assistant, bears the brunt of her special brand of crazy. Our office is so small that JJ's effect is felt everywhere, which on a good day is merely idiosyncratic. On a bad one, people start pulling tequila out of their file drawers.

And because she owns the company, there's no end in sight.

"Good afternooooooooon!"

JJ singsongs her greeting as we all file into the conference room. Her eyes stay on her laptop. We take seats around her.

The meeting is about one of our biggest clients, who, JJ has heard, is thinking of walking. We have to make sure their next project is exquisite.

Seated next to JJ, I'm ready to take notes. Which I do perfectly well until twenty minutes in, when JJ gets to number four on the agenda.

"The trade show. Okay, team, Charlotte has a list of different displays we're to choose from. Charlotte, can you share those with us now?"

"Um, pardon?" A list? What list?

"The list of displays. I asked you to research it yesterday morning." As flighty as JJ can seem, she forgets nothing. Her details have details. Which is why I'm so shocked to hear this. I'm usually on the ball with her requests, if only to avoid her reaction to sub-par work.

I feel everyone's eyes on me, the distracted girl who can't get her act together. Is this a game, designed to force me to fail? I make as if I'm searching my laptop for this "list" but I'm really scanning my email. And of course, there it is. A message stamped 9:33 AM yesterday, from JJ, very clearly asking me for ideas on displays for the trade show.

"Right," I say. "Sorry, I'm still working on that. I'll have a complete list to distribute tomorrow morning."

"Well you must have ideeeeeaas, right? Tell us what you've discovered so far." JJ's smile is equal parts blank and expectant, but a dare is visible in its depths.

She wants me to fail, I realize, shaken. She's enjoying this. She drums her peach fingernails against her other forearm silently. I slide my glance to Nina, who apologizes with her eyes. No one can help me here. I open my mouth, then close it.

"JJ?" Tara, the receptionist, sticks her head in the room. "Sorry to interrupt, but it's Ted Jackman."

Ted's the client we're talking about. JJ steps out without explanation, the account manager on her heels. We're to reconvene in the morning.

Saved, Nina mouths to me.

I smile my agreement, but on the way back to my desk, I can't keep from asking myself, *From what?*

Aside from the extra twenty minutes tacked onto my commute, living at home is not so bad. As early as I'm up, Marina is still gone before I'm awake and she works late almost every night.

So far, it's been pretty easy to avoid her. And when she is home at night, her husband usually visits. Todd's presence makes Marina almost likable.

That's what makes him different. How he almost transforms her. As a teenager Marina was, to put it bluntly, boy crazy. It started with James, whom I was a little in love with myself—the first boy she kissed (I read it in her journal) and who loved *Star Wars* more than anything. I still have the Princess Leia doll he gave me when I was in third grade. Sometimes, when Marina had promised our parents she'd finish her algebra homework before going out or when she was late coming home from track or tennis or basketball practice, James had nothing better to do than hang out with me. We'd watch *Full House* together on TV—he had a killer Uncle Jesse impersonation that still makes me laugh to this day—or he'd ask me to tell him about what I was reading. His own older sister worked at a used bookstore, and one day he came over with the mother lode...a complete collection of Baby-Sitters Club books. I read them over and over, for years. I still have them somewhere.

While Marina kept updating us from upstairs on her status, he'd tell me about what he was reading in school, making me laugh with descriptions of boys on islands destroying each other or dramatic Shakespearean lines. He had this way of lounging around in our female-heavy household that made me like having a boy around. While Marina's physical positions were calculated by emotion and constant change, once James sat, he sat. I marveled at his ability to adjust himself in such a way that just watching him sitting on the couch or in the easy chair made me more comfortable. In his absence sometimes I'd try to emulate it, arranging my short legs just so, convinced that I could be as relaxed as James if I just worked at it enough.

He and Marina stayed together all through fourth grade—her freshman year—then for reasons that were never revealed to me, by the time she started sophomore year she was talking about other boys. I was personally offended when I had to take a phone message from a boy whose name I didn't recognize.

"Who's Derek?"

Marina's face immediately became expansive. "Why?" she demanded. "Did he call?"

I handed her the message I'd written down, then crossed my arms. "Does James know?"

Marina laughed at me as she dialed the phone—reaching her best friend Deanna, I noted with relief, not Derek of the left message. But as she dismissed me, shutting her bedroom door on me with her foot, I realized my relief was short-lived. As soon as she was done celebrating the fact that Derek had called, she began to plan the conversation for the return call with the precision of a military attack, allowing for all possibilities—if he asked her out, if he didn't ask her out, if he asked her out and she said yes, if he asked her out and she said she had to think about it, if he just wanted to ask her about homework and how to figure out if it was an excuse to talk to her or if he really had forgotten the topic for the essay assignment in English. From my seat on the floor outside her door, I heard her laughing in a throaty voice she never used with us.

I wanted to call James myself and ask him what he thought of this Derek. The next time I saw him, at the mall when my mom and I were getting me a new JanSport backpack, I smiled big and assumed ready position to run up to him and hug him. But all we got was a halfhearted wave and an apologetic smile before he disappeared into Walgreens.

Although Derek was the first post-James object of affection, he didn't last long enough to make an impression on me. Soon enough, although I didn't form James-like attachments, I learned to categorize Marina's boyfriends according to headwear. Gus always wore a Red Sox baseball cap, even when my old-fashioned Dad eyed him in admonishment. Trent, who lasted almost the whole winter and taught Marina to snowboard—and who earned my affections handily by convincing Marina to take me out with them a few times—was always in a fleece cap with earflaps. And to this day I can't see a bicycle on the side of the road without thinking of Cal, who drove a bike instead of a car (except when weather forced him to break out his dilapidated station wagon) and always had permanent rifts in his hair from his bike helmet.

I liked them all well enough, but I'd learned my lesson with James and kept a polite distance. Sometimes, while Marina was making macaroni and cheese for us on nights both of our parents had to work late, or when she stood for hours in front of the bathroom mirror just to emerge looking only slightly different than when she went in, I'd study her, unnoticed, and wonder why so many guys were drawn to her. She was pretty, but her nose was a little big and her stomach pooched out a tiny bit. She certainly wasn't jaw-droppingly gorgeous like her friend Deanna, or any one of the many girls she ran around with. But she was popular. She was always on the phone and always scrambling to get her homework done so she could meet people at the mall or at the game or at the car wash to raise money for the soccer team. I was mousy and shy and had no idea how she did it.

Dad adored Marina. He often joked with the boys she brought home, feigning a gruffness and directing a playful finger-shaking at the knock-kneed boy in question. Because I had the advantage of a backstage view, I knew that this was part of their game and that Marina's exasperation with Dad's "overprotectiveness" wasn't real. The older I got, the more different I realized my own relationship with him was, and I learned a little bit about jealousy.

Then Marina began a session of driver's ed in the fall of her senior year, and Steve came into our lives. She'd been without a boyfriend for about a month—a pretty long time for her—and I'd even heard her saying things like there were no boys worth dating and being single was the best thing she'd ever done. Then she was seated next to Steve from the first night of driving classes, his jean jacket still littered with the inked "I <3 U!" from a former girlfriend and chain wallet that disappeared into his low-slung jeans. Right away we knew he was different. It wasn't his looks—Marina's boyfriends all had their way of differentiating themselves easily from one another, as if she got tired of a type and moved on to someone directly the opposite. It was the way Marina acted, both when she was with Steve and when she waited for him to call.

This shocked me the most. Marina didn't wait for boys. She left them, sometimes after telling them to come over. Instead of avoiding every other call as had been her standard—"Gotta keep 'em guessing," she'd been known to say as she left for a night out with her girlfriends, knowing full well she'd asked the latest guy to call her that night—Marina would wait by the phone for Steve. She'd do her homework or listen to music in her room with the cordless phone in reach. Even though we had call waiting, she tried to not even talk to her friends on the off chance that he'd call just as the phone was ringing and he'd get a busy signal. I learned to hide my own phone conversations from her—short though they may have been—because I didn't like her accusatory, expectant look that was the facial version of a foot tapping whenever I began to dial.

Worse was how she started to treat my dad. First it was little things, like not going out of her way to make sure Steve came into the house when he picked her up. The first time Dad treated it like a joke: "What, no introduction?" But she muttered something about being late and closed the door behind her, and I was left with Dad's slightly embarrassed expression, which he morphed into a smiling "hmmm" before going back to his paper. I was embarrassed for him, and embarrassed that I'd had to witness it. I should have been happy that their tie was being loosened, after all the jealousy I felt, but what coursed through me instead was dread.

Then came the actual arguments. The one I remember best was not the worst one they had, but it was when I realized that their foundation had definitely cracked.

"What's on the docket for tonight, Rina?" he'd ask her, using the name she discouraged other people from using but tolerated from Dad. His face was behind his newspaper but his voice was too casual. On instinct, I put my finger in place in the Baby-Sitters Club book I was rereading for the twentieth time and readied myself for listening.

Marina was painting her nails. Blood red. She finished her pinky finger and blew on all her nails before responding. "Nothing really."

"Not going out?" he asked, and I groaned inwardly. Even I could tell he was fishing for information.

"Yeah, Steve's picking me up in a few minutes."

Dad put down the paper. I was right to have abandoned my book. "Marina," he said, taking off his glasses. She looked at him, defiant already. And he'd only said her name.

"WHAT?"

Dad reeled back, just a tiny bit, but enough to recognize that it was actually a blow—albeit emotional—that he'd just withstood.

Even Marina seemed to realize she'd taken things too far, nervously capping the nail polish bottle and walking around the kitchen, shaking her fingers. "Sorry Dad. I just—what did you want?"

He looked at her for a long moment. His expression didn't change. He didn't sigh or breathe audibly. After about ten seconds, he stood up. "Be home by eleven," he said by way of exit, going up the stairs.

"Mom said I had until 11:30," she said, mostly to herself, since he was well out of earshot. She seemed to feel me looking at her and swung her gaze toward me. "What do you want?"

I shrugged and went back to page 127. It was a long time before I turned to 128.

four

My eyes are on my laptop, but I know Kendra is preparing The Look. By the time we met in fifth grade, she had already perfected it—against bossy girls and annoying boys, even unfair teachers. I've seen the same expression on her mother, a no-nonsense woman who raised Kendra and her twin brother, Landon, alone, turning them into latchkey kids at eight. I was scared of her when we met, taking the attention she paid to me as evidence she wanted to beat me up. But it turned out she knew before I did that we were BFF material. Most of the time I appreciate her take-charge attitude, especially when it manifests itself in an ability to, against all compulsions otherwise, Keep It Real. But sometimes, like now, she's just pushy.

"You think one trip to Paco's is going to turn us into townies?" I ask her. "Make us surrender our hipster card?"

Kendra gives me a funny look, sort of a raised-eyebrow swirled with the most miniscule widening of eyes. I'm shamed. Kendra's the last thing from a hipster wanna-be. She truly does not care what other people think, and I only wish I did.

"I'm sorry," I tell her. "I'm just tired. And pissed off. And frustrated."

It's been a long couple of weeks at work. JJ is making me feel increasingly on edge. It's a merciless cycle. The more I interact with her, the more easily I'm annoyed. I'm normally a grin-and-bear it person, but lately, I'm starting to have a very real fear of walking out. And I can't afford to quit. Not only that, but rumors of layoffs that started circling a few months ago seem poised to land. We've already cut back accounting to part-time, and a plan to hire an extra receptionist was aborted without explanation. The sense of foreboding is pervasive.

Which is why I'm on Monster and Indeed, even Craigslist and the BostonJobs subreddit, applying for any job I'm remotely qualified for within reasonable driving or train distance. My plan tonight was ambitious: spend the entire evening exhausting job listings, leaving no possible employment stone unturned, with the goal of at least two follow-up calls next week.

But then Kendra called, en route to dinner with her brother and mom in Danborn, and did I want to go out after? I did, but I didn't have time to go all the way into the city. She didn't exactly agree, but came over—which is when I realized her goal was to convince me to go into the city after all. My suggestion of Paco's was met with a pretty blink. Then she lowered her hands in front of her chest. *Namaste.* "Charlie. *Charlotte.* You can't be serious." And I turned away from The Look.

Now she says, "If I knew you moving back to Danborn meant we actually had to go *out* in Danborn..."

I roll my eyes. "I didn't say we had to. I only said I don't have time to go into the city and back." She snorts. "I'm sorry, why did I invite you over again?"

"Moral support. Duh." Reluctantly accepting defeat—one can hope—she explores my bedroom, picking up random objects and inspecting them. "Wow, you really haven't changed anything in here, have you?" She tilts her head to inspect my CD titles. "How did I not know you had all this Nirvana?" she murmurs. At my photos, more murmuring. "Whatever possessed me to cut my hair that short, I will never know," and "We really liked our trucker hats, didn't we?" I'm swallowing a smile and cursing her for distracting me.

"I love this picture of you guys," Kendra says.

"The beach one?" I love it too—the image of me suspended in Dean's arms on the beach in Marshfield has long been my favorite.

But the photo Kendra's studying isn't the one I think it is. It's from my confirmation, me in my robe, my dad in a suit. My mom was never the best photographer, and she caught us in conversation, smiling at each other rather than the camera. It's jarring to look at now. Like it's from a different era. Or a different family. In the world of that photo, I can feel Dean next to me, joking with my dad in ways I couldn't, spurring the smiles I no longer knew how to coax.

Kendra doesn't speak for a long time, and I'm reminded, yet again, that while I lost my dad early, Kendra never had one to lose. Or one that she knew, anyway. So I say nothing, let her get her fill before she resumes her tour.

"So are you going to try to see him?"

Now she is talking about Dean. "I don't know." My fingers hover over the keyboard, and I say to the screen, "He looks exactly the same, K. Better, even."

"Damn."

Kendra got me the scoop a few days ago, gathered with remarkable efficiency on a single-evening Facebook sweep. (Even in high school, it was uncanny how people just told Kendra stuff. She always knew everything, almost accidentally. My take was that, with her penchant for out-of-town boys, she never cared to steal anyone's boyfriends—a personal pastime of at least half the girls in Danborn.) It seems that, indeed, Dean Carson no longer lives in Chicago. He *was* there, cohabitating with his girlfriend, but now he's parked in Danborn. Permanently. With his parents.

"That's impossible," I said when she told me.

"Yet somehow true."

I didn't doubt it. Kendra's information was always solid.

I go back to my computer, trying to refocus on my career history. "Do you think maybe I don't need to include volunteering at the Trailside Museum?" I ask, squinting at the screen.

Kendra looks over my shoulder. "Yes." She bounces on the bed behind me. "Okay, I get it. Into the city and back is not an easy drive. But think of it this way: it's not a black hole."

"I'll get out," I say, hitting PRINT. I ask her to fetch my résumé, thinking that will work as at least a mild distraction. She gets up off my bed, takes a step, and stops. "And the printer is...?"

"Downstairs in the dining room."

"And Marina is...?"

"In New Hampshire for the weekend." She departs, satisfied. I'm amused that she's just as unwilling to cross my sister's path as I am. Old habits die hard.

She's right, of course, about Danborn. We've said it before. The Black Hole of Danborn: You fall in and you can't get out. It's a completely different mindset in the suburbs. Adjustment isn't easy; proximity to the city is a hard thing to wean yourself from. Even lower-rent Somerville (depending on where you are in the gentrification scale) on the city's outskirts isn't that far from downtown. Outsiders don't realize it, but despite its cosmopolitan reputation, Boston's actually pretty small. You can walk almost anywhere you need to if you just have a little time. And if you don't, the subway—known as the T—can get you there.

And Danborn does seem to have a strange pull. Not even ten years out of high school and we're starting to see people drifting back to our hometown, to their parents' basements or to apartments that have been built in the past ten years. I've often shuddered over this with Kendra, who always seems to be just a job offer away from moving out of state.

Voices drift up the stairs. She won't be back for a while. I don't know what it is, but all my life, Kendra and my mom have adored one another. Maybe it had something to do with Kendra's mom never being home, but ever since the first day I tentatively brought her home in fifth grade and we shared a peanut-butter-and-Fluff sandwich at my kitchen island, the two of them have had a bond that I sometimes was convinced I couldn't penetrate. I was never one for fighting much with my parents, especially after the debacle that was Marina's senior year, but sometimes I think that if I had, Kendra wouldn't know whose side to take. My mom is probably making her some tea right now.

I stare at my résumé. It's vaguely alarming how little my professional life has added up to. I've started to feel something resembling panic about my career choice, or lack thereof. Like everyone else, I always thought I'd be something, or at least do something that could be quantified. Which is probably why I started out an engineering major, as my dad suggested. When that failed—or I did, I guess—I had to figure everything out all over again. I switched majors two more times. Graduating with a business administration major was more of a default than anything, and it would have put me on the five-year plan if I hadn't taken summer classes before senior year.

When you're a little kid and everyone asks you what you want to be when you grow up, your answer is never "information specialist" or "marketing assistant." But those are the jobs you end up qualified for. As long as you can work the right searchable SEO keywords into your résumé, that is. That's all we are, us twentysomethings. Just an assembly line of keywords. I wasn't anything I thought I'd be.

When did I stop wanting to become something?

Much as I hate admitting it, the kid next door hasn't helped. The fact that I didn't have an answer for Wade Hunter when he asked me what I liked to do has been sitting in the back of my mind like a dirty sock. I used to think that not having strong opinions about much made me easy to get along with, but now I suspect it just means I'm boring. Like my life's a single-lane road. The curtain's been ripped back from the inadequacy lurking backstage. I'm perfectly adequate, not great at anything. As my résumé so baldly displays, I'm one big mountain of good enough.

As if I've conjured him, headlights cross my window. A burst of music is followed by the slam of a car door. I check my phone for a text, but there's nothing.

I don't know how it happened, exactly, but Wade and I have become friends. Or, more accurately, running buddies. On a run shortly after I moved back, I rounded the corner of our street and spied a figure up ahead. My pace was a little beyond his, so I gradually caught up to him, but it wasn't until I overtook him that I recognized the solitary runner as my next-door neighbor. We grinned hellos of recognition—he seemed pretty winded—and then, somehow, fell into step. I didn't even mind that my pace slowed. Kendra and I had always run together in Somerville; it was nice to have a partner again.

Later, over DD coffee—my suggestion—Wade told me he'd just started running that week. He didn't enjoy it much.

That startled me, because I felt the same. But admitting it to him felt like giving away too much of myself. "So why do it?" I asked him instead.

He shrugged. "I feel pretty out of shape. In high school I was always playing one sport or another, and then in college I was always on my bike or playing rugby. Not much else to do now except run, unless I want to join a gym."

He said "join a gym" as if it were tantamount to losing all self-respect, and I laughed. "Fantasy Fitness isn't so bad, I've heard," I told him. "Pending living circumstances, once daylight savings hits I may end up joining. They have a good month-to-month rate."

"And I may join along with you," he said with something like resignation. He leaned forward on his elbows, nodding, a fellow conspirator. "Pending living circumstances." He didn't wink, but it felt as if he did.

I shoved the not-unpleasant thought of Wade in sweaty gym clothes into a drawer in my mind and changed the subject. I found out he's been back in Danborn since early summer. I got the sense that something happened to send him here, something significant, and probably not something good. But he didn't offer any details, and I had no intention of asking.

"Will you be living here long?" I said instead.

"Hard to say. I've got some things to take care of before I move back."

"So that's in your definite future," I concluded, "moving back to Colorado."

He took a sip of coffee and something settled in his eyes that I couldn't look away from. "It's my home."

I nodded like I understood, but these words, too, stayed in my head for days. He sounded so certain. Were we all supposed to have a place we knew without question as "home"? I didn't think I did. It was just... where I lived. I mean, I couldn't imagine living anywhere other than Boston, but was that why I stayed? Why I didn't have Kendra's primal urge to move far away? I didn't know.

Since then, the two of us I have managed to sync our schedules so that we run together more often than not. I was first impressed, then jealous, then annoyed at how quickly Wade was able to improve his pace. By now he's easily as good a runner as I am, and if past performance is any indication, I'll be the one holding him back within a day or two. We've developed a routine of texting to let the other one know when we're going out. It's weird, definitely, but in the same weird way, also comfortable. Being regular old friends with him makes it easier, somehow, to look at him as a person and not just the hotter-than-he-should-be kid next door.

I haven't heard from him yet today about whether he'll run tomorrow—Saturday—but I'm expecting to.

Kendra comes bouncing back upstairs into my room. "I can never say no to your mom's tea. It just tastes better than any other tea."

"Since you were ten," I agree.

She nods dreamily. "Lots of milk and sugar. And none of that blue skim shit."

"She drinks herbal tea now. Black."

Her eyes go round. "She does?"

"She even has a special pot from the kitchen store. She keeps the Lipton just for you. Don't tell her I told you." I hold out my hand. "My résumé?"

"What? Oh." She makes no move to actually hand it to me. Instead she begins reading it, as if this has just occurred to her. "Wow, you sound pretty good here. Lots of responsibilities. You were a manager?" She looks at me. "With people reporting to you?"

"The intern."

She nods. That counts. "You have letters of recommendation?"

I wave a sheet of paper at her. "It's nice knowing the boss's executive assistant."

"Then looks like you're ready for anything."

"Including being fired."

"You're not going to be fired."

"Laid off, same diff."

"Fired is you stole a computer or slept with the boss's daughter. You can get laid off and still be awesome at your job."

"Daughter?"

"All the more reason to fire you. She's been corrupted and now she's moved to San Francisco to 'find herself.'"

"I must have quite an effect on people." Kendra bats her eyes at me, then goes back to perusing the résumé. A sharp intake of breath gets my attention. "What?"

"Nothing."

"What?" I snatch the résumé out of her hand.

"You just have a little typo."

"Are you serious?" I scan down. Sure enough, I've misspelled "responsibilities," missing a consonant or two. "Did I not run the fucking thing through spellcheck?"

Twenty minutes later I have another version, proofread meticulously by me, Kendra, and even my mom. I turn it into a PDF for easier emailing and send it off to the last two positions on my list, figuring I can kiss the folks who've received the flawed résumé goodbye.

"Okay," I say when my outbox indicates it's empty. "Margaritas. Now."

She tries one last time. "And we have to go to Paco's?"

I just look at her. "Fine," she consents, reluctantly. "I'll see if Xanna can meet us out. That's one good thing—Danborn is a shorter drive from JP." Kendra pulls on her fleece jacket and leans towards the mirror to inspect her teeth. "God, it is so weird being in your room. I feel like I should be doing homework. Or you know, not doing it. So this probably goes without saying, but I can always put in a word for you at—Charlie."

I look up. "What?"

"Who are you expecting to hear from?"

"What? Nobody."

"It's like the fifth time you've checked your phone the past ten minutes."

"You're high."

Kendra raises her eyebrows and turns back to the mirror with an *if you say so* expression. I dig into the clothes basket on my bed—oh, to have a mom who will do my laundry again—for my running clothes and toss them in a separate pile on the bed.

"Are you running a lot lately?" Kendra asks, sort of wistfully.

"A few times a week."

She scrunches up her lips and nose, looking disappointed.

"Maybe we can meet you in Somerville sometime," I say over my shoulder as she follows me down the stairs. "On a weekend day or something, to run the Minuteman? Maybe even—"

"Who's we?"

"Um. Yeah. I mentioned this, I think? I've been running sometimes with Wade."

"The kid next door?" She hooks her thumb over her shoulder, actually pointing across the street, not next door. We step outside. The air is crisp, much colder than I've expected. Like fall snuck in when I wasn't looking. "No, Charlie, you most certainly did not mention the fact that you go running every day with Keith's little brother."

"Oh please."

"Oh please, what?"

"We do not go every day."

"Okaaaay," she says slowly. "Way to miss the point. Let me ask it differently: Do you run with him every time you run?"

"Kendra," I say. We both get in the car, and I wait until we're both seat-belted to look at her with purpose. "It's nothing. We run together. That's it."

"Every time you run."

I start the car. "Recently, yes."

"And you never talk on the phone."

"We—we text. To make *plans*."

"And his number's not programmed in your phone."

37

"It's just easier to..." I shake my head at her raised eyebrows as I back out of the driveway.

"It *has* been a while since you've had sex."

"Jesus, Kendra!"

She puts her hands up, chest height: *I'm only the messenger.* She leans forward to the radio, an indication that she's willing to drop the conversation. "I have the sudden urge to say 'methinks.' All I'm sayin'."

"Yeah, well, *m*ethinks you're high if you think I have anything going on with a nineteen-year-old."

"He's only *nineteen?* Jesus, Char. I knew he was young, but I didn't know he was *that* kind of puppy chow. I mean, that's a teenager!"

"He'll be twenty in the spring," I say, not sure how I've gone from pushing him aside to defending him.

"You know when his birthday is." This isn't a question. I start to speak but Kendra cuts me off, again with her hands. "All I'm sayin'."

Paco's is packed. I'm conscious of Kendra's dirty look when Xanna, who arrived just before us, tells us it might be a wait. But we spy a high table in the bar area that a couple with two kids is just vacating, and I'm so grateful to snag it that I don't even mind the food-strewn mess they leave behind. Bear-hugging a toddler who seems on the verge of losing his shit, the mother throws me an apologetic look as she whisks him towards the exit. Her husband scribbles on the credit card receipt with one hand and desperately tries to hang onto a whining, freedom-seeking little girl in pigtails with the other.

"Ugh," says Kendra, pushing away the food-littered high chair with her foot. "I'm never having kids."

"Me either," I say.

Xanna slides a half-eaten plate of nachos aside, piles a few other appetizer-sized plates on it, and begins wiping down the table with a left-behind napkin. "Years of waitressing," she says by way of explanation. "It's compulsive."

"We all have our compulsions," I say, grinning. My crap mood of earlier has dissipated. Danborn or not, I'm glad Kendra called Xanna. It's our first girls' night in weeks.

The waiter arrives to clean the table for real, and we order queso and a round of margaritas, Kendra muttering that of course this place doesn't even have tamales. Once we have our drinks, she looks around. "Shit, is that Karly Pfeiffer? With Janine Frasier? It's like a high-school reunion in here." She turns an accusing look in my direction.

I ignore her, my eyes still on the menu. "It might be a sopapilla night. Dessert for dinner?"

"Ooooooh, sopapillas," Xanna says. "Now you're talking."

Kendra looks delighted. "I love a girl who eats!"

"You forget I grew up in New Mexico," Xanna reminds us. "I'm sure they'll suck, but even sucky sopapillas are good, 'cause hey, they're sopapillas."

This commences a list of things that are good even when they're shitty, just because they exist. Parking spaces in the first row. Movie popcorn. Sales at Anthropologie. Boyfriends who cook.

"Mexican food in your hometown," I put in.

Kendra tries to shoot me a look, but whatever she sees beyond me stops her short. "High school boyfriends who keep all their hair," she says, deadpan.

I straighten up, dropping the chip I've been lifting to my mouth. I follow Kendra's gaze and turn, slowly and inconspicuously. He's just inside the door, deftly scanning the room. I take him in, and my breath leaves my body. Dean Carson. Tall. Spiky, mussy hair, swoony brown eyes, and, if memory serves, a birthmark on his left shoulder blade. I take a hefty swallow of my margarita.

"You asked for it," Kendra says. "Welcome back to DHS."

I wasn't imagining things in Dunkin' Donuts. Unlike so many of our other classmates defined by steady gains (weight) and losses (hair), if anything Dean Carson has gotten better looking since graduation. Devastatingly so. His hair's a little longer, perfectly tousled with product. His shoulders have broadened, his chin seems more square. He's long and lanky as always—I'm getting a crook in my neck just remembering—yet somehow fuller. Trying to reconcile this man before me with the boy I knew is like doing the backstroke in honey. He's mostly in profile, mid-conversation with Steve Linstrom and a couple other guys from high school.

"You know that guy?" Xanna asks us, leaning in.

"Charlie's first love," Kendra tells her.

"Well done," Xanna says approvingly. "How long were you together?"

"A couple of years," I say. Thirty-two months. One week. And six days.

Dean's shrugging out of his jacket now, smiling at something Steve's saying, and after he shakes his head in casual disbelief—towards the ceiling, like always—his eyes scan the room. And land on me. He raises his eyebrows and his chin simultaneously, a greeting that communicates he's seen and recognized me. Then he smiles.

"He's on to you, Charlie," Xanna says.

Our waiter has abandoned us, so Kendra leaves to get us all another round. I try to keep up my end of the conversation with Xanna, but my mind is wandering through the bar.

Dean Carson. Love of my life. It sounds so cliché. It *is* cliché. Dean Carson, cliché of my life.

Now that I'm flat-ironed and liquid-eyelined and actually look like myself, I'm ready for him. In the movie version of this scene, Dean would make his way over to our table, where we'd cheerfully and flirtatiously banter, referencing one or two private jokes meant just for us. Later scenes would see both of us stealing glances when we're supposedly deeply involved in other conversations. A Snow Patrol song would supply the soundtrack, one that threw us back into our sordid, shared past, and we'd accidentally-on-purpose bump into one another right around last call, when we'd wordlessly jump into a cab (the movie's set in New York City, obvs), and in the next scene we'd be horizontal, two silhouettes meeting in a kiss that would start the best sex either of us had seen in years—since each other, of course—all in a spacious apartment with square footage you'd never find in New York.

In reality, we're eating bad Mexican food in suburban Paco's, and the only present-day concrete association Dean has with me is a floor full of iced coffee.

"Why have I not heard of this guy?" Xanna asks.

I debate which story to tell. "If you haven't, be thankful," Kendra interjects, sliding up on the stool just ahead of a busboy with our drinks.

"He's been in Chicago for years," I tell Xanna, keeping it simple.

"Oh, he's *that* guy."

Looks are exchanged around the table and I excuse myself to the restroom. I stare in the bathroom mirror, fighting a sudden urge to splash my face with cold water. People always do that in books and movies, but they must never wear makeup. So I just stare at my intact eyeliner, leaning on my hands and gathering strength. Although my hair's gone through some changes in the past seven years, right now it's back to looking pretty close to what it was the last time Dean and I were together. Brown with blonde highlights, straightened, falling to the middle of my back, side part, no bangs. Never bangs. My hazel eyes look paler than usual, wide-open and nervous.

Objectively speaking, I look good.

This is ridiculous. I need to get a grip. Just knowing he's in the next room makes me want a cigarette, and I haven't smoked since college. I reapply my lipstick, emboldened by the cherry-red that's more striking than I ever used to wear around him, and pronounce myself ready.

The crowd has thickened. Making my way back to the table is an exercise in futility. Everyone's taller than me. "Excuse me," I tell a Patriots jacket as I jostle my way through the sea of bodies as politely as possible. "Sorry," I say to a light-green T-shirt. The green shirt turns.

"Charlie?"

Dean's eyes still have those crazy golden flecks. I'd just about convinced myself I'd imagined them.

We hug, because that's what you do. He holds me a beat longer than necessary, and I let him, hating and loving how his scent envelops me and liquefies my insides as if no time has passed at all. I feel his presence like adrenaline, all the way to my fingertips.

"Charlie Michaelsen." He gazes down at me, unsmiling. I hold his eyes with my own, saying nothing and everything. That's the thing about Dean, I remember now. He always said my name.

I was almost fifteen when my next-door neighbor, Marla, remarried and threw a homegrown afterparty in her backyard when the official one at the reception hall died down. Unlike the real thing, kids were invited. I have three vivid memories of that party: Marla's six-year-old son running around in his Superman costume, cape flying; the transparent, spherical candles floating in the pool; and Dean.

He was a friend of Marla's older son, Keith, who was my age. They played hockey or soccer or lacrosse, various sports throughout the year I'd never paid attention to. I paid plenty of attention that day, however. I decided Dean, in his khakis and sky-blue button-down, was the most gorgeous thing my fourteen-year-old eyes had ever seen. I was a sophomore at the local all-girls Catholic high school, so boy experience was in short supply. Not that it mattered to me then. Until fairly recently, most of the boys in my orbit had been gangly and funny-looking. If they weren't, they usually weren't very nice. Or they smelled. And after what Marina had already put my parents through, I couldn't see having a boyfriend as anything but a nuisance. Even once I started high school, I'd just as soon pass an afternoon in the treehouse as at the mall or in front of the mirror. I was also on the shy side—mortifyingly, I'd earned the title of "quietest" in our sixth-grade yearbook superlatives, before Kendra and I had to leave public school for St. Cecilia's. But I'd also won "nicest smile" (which I credited to nothing but my left-side dimple); I figured they canceled one another out. At any rate, I had always flown far under the radar. Which suited me just fine.

The friend of the boy next door was a welcome diversion, though. The comings and goings of the Hunter household, at one time not even worthy of registering on my consciousness, became daily knowledge. Soccer in the fall, hockey in the winter, lacrosse in the spring, baseball in the summer. I learned to mark the seasons by sports equipment and uniforms. I absorbed facts that I didn't even realize I knew, like that Dean's father, a Danborn cop, drove a white Explorer. Or his mom was partial to sunglasses even on cloudy days. Or, thanks to neighborhood block parties, that he liked to mix mustard and ketchup together on his hot dogs. Occasionally I'd actually be in the same room with him for birthday parties and other family events, though mostly I'd ogle him from across the room. This was easier than it sounds. He didn't pay me an iota of attention, preferring wrestling with Keith or playing video games to interacting with the girl next door. I figured he saw me in the same realm as he did Keith's little brother, Wade, who was still as prone to wearing a Superman cape as not: just part of the background to withstand.

That summer, fall rainstorms triggered a flood that rendered St. Cecilia's uninhabitable for at least a year. My parents offered to send me to Granger Academy, a private school a few towns away, but Kendra's mom was letting her go to Danborn High, so I wanted to, too. They gave in right away, probably having learned a thing or two with Marina and the wills of teenage girls who don't get what they want.

Four minutes into the first day of junior year, I recognized Dean in my assigned homeroom, leaning over Sherri Stillwell's desk. I was aghast. This Dean—oh my God, his desk was *right behind mine*—was more man than boy. He'd grown his hair out and had clearly spent many hours in the weight room. If crushing from a distance was nerve-wracking, close proximity absolutely did me in.

Probably realizing he couldn't exactly ignore me—friend of the family and all—Dean assumed a polite nod-and-smile attitude whenever we crossed paths, sometimes even punctuated with a "Hey, Charlie." But his mind always seemed elsewhere—the guy down the hall he was yelling at; Fallon Drake, the cheerleader he'd been dating for forever; the notebook in his hand as he crammed for the test in his next class. Then something shifted. I held my breath for weeks, but the proof was there—I wasn't imagining it. As we moved in and out of each other's academic circles he continued to nod and smile, but it seemed the nods were slower, the smiles wider, the eye contact more direct. Somewhere I heard that Fallon was now dating a senior.

I wanted him. I wanted him before I even knew what that meant. I'd dated one or two boys, but no one who stuck. In ninth grade Keith, who had stopped speaking to me once we hit middle school, took me to the homecoming semi-formal, but I'm pretty sure our moms arranged it. He barely spoke to me all night. The only boy I was even mildly serious about, Craig, never tried to do anything more than kiss me goodnight the summer I met him on Cape Cod. But all through junior year, I imagined Dean doing things to me I'd only read about, even things I'd never read or heard about but wanted to happen anyway. I watched him in the halls and in Spanish, the one class we shared, and was jealous of everything: the girls he talked to, the teachers he charmed, the clothes that shared space with his skin.

On the outside, thanks to my Catholic school blank slate, I maintained the same plain vanilla reputation I'd always had. Unlike Kendra, who was always the subject of conversation, when it came to gossip I wasn't even a thought. I wasn't a jock or a brain or a burnout or one of the popular girls. My fashion sense fell somewhere between "conservative" and "boring." The only sports I participated in were cross country and spring track, maybe a little bit of tennis. Crushing on Dean was my chief hobby. The longer it went on, the more alarmed Kendra became. "You might want to expand your horizons," she'd say to me periodically as she got ready for yet another night with yet another guy from a neighboring high school. She didn't date guys from Danborn. Ever. "Want me to ask Dave if he has a friend?" I never did.

One Tuesday night in spring of junior year I was on orders from my mom to go next door to the Hunters' with a misdelivered UPS package. I knocked on the door in sweats, grubby from track practice, baseball cap on my head and, worst of all, barefoot. I'd just taken off my sneakers when my mom sent me on the errand, and the only thing on my mind as I ran out the door was the shower I'd take upon my return.

I was all the way to the Hunters' driveway when it hit me how problematic it was to go without shoes. It was early enough in spring that my feet were still tender from months of indoor life, and that gravel *hurt*. Waiting for an answer to the doorbell, I alternated between tiptoes and shifting from foot to foot, cursing my stupidity as I balanced the bulky package in my arms.

I rang a second time and was about to turn for home in exasperation when the door swung open. Dean smiled down at me—when had he gotten so *tall*?—and I felt like crumbling onto the pavement. In lieu of a greeting I simply shoved the package out in front of me. It hung there in midair. Instead of reaching for it, Dean did an excruciating amount of nothing. He just continued to smile, me in my bare feet, sweaty, baseball-capped and disheveled, holding out a package he refused to take. From the most sexy lean I'd ever seen against any doorway in any structure, he tipped his head a few degrees to the side, a few degrees toward me, and said: "The UPS guys have gotten a lot better looking."

His voice sounded so even, so level. He was smiling, but there was no amusement in it. It was like he'd decided to finally let me know that he'd really seen me.

"You're as gorgeous as ever," Dean tells me.

I thank him and my eyes hit the floor. I'm recalibrating. Technically we're adults, but I can't look at the boy I loved for over two adolescent years and feel like one. Since when was he full of compliments? Conversations I remember were all "dude" and "hot" and slang I could never comprehend until after it already peaked. I should say something similar, how unchanged and beautiful he looks. But guys like that, they must know.

"What brings you to Danborn?" I ask instead.

He shrugs. "I wanted to see you."

I play along. "I guess it's lucky I'm here then."

"Very." His grin only widens, moving fully into his eyes. "I thought you were living in the city. With your boyfriend."

I raise my eyebrows. He knows this? "And I thought you were living in Chicago. With your girlfriend."

"I'm living with my parents."

"I'm living with my mom."

His face clouds over, perhaps picking up on what I didn't say. But a second later he's back to smiling. I try to concentrate on what he's saying, small talk that feels like anything but. About Keith, who's staying in Chicago, even though Dean tried to convince him to move home too. About the job Dean left, which was all right, all things considered, but wasn't what he wanted to do for the rest of his life. And—best of all—about his now-ex-girlfriend, who he was still friends with, but the relationship? Eh, it had run its course.

"So are you dating anyone now?" he asks me.

His directness is throwing me off. I don't know how to answer him. An honest no runs the risk of making me sound desperate, but lying would be ludicrous. I decide on "No one serious," hoping I sound appropriately captivating.

It's the right choice. From the back row of our conversation, the spectator in me is amazed that we're not talking about football games or finding a buyer or Mrs. Waterman's strange haircut in chemistry. We're just talking about life. And although that makes a boring amount of sense, it still strikes me as otherworldly, like he's speaking a different dialect I have to concentrate extra-hard to understand.

Kendra's ready to leave before ten. I don't mind. I'm mentally exhausted. We see Xanna off, then I bring her to my house to pick up her car. I'm turning onto my street when my phone, on the console between us, pings with a text. Kendra picks it up.

"Oh, girlfriend. You already gave him your number?"

She shows it to me. *were headed to the irish castle. see u there if u go.* Watching me, Kendra assumes her skeptical look. "You're not going to *go*."

"Of course I'm not," I say quickly. But because she's Kendra, she hears the *maybe* in my voice.

"Charlie." I don't answer. "Charlie, it's the *Irish Castle*."

We get out of the car and she heads to her own car. When I still don't answer, she continues, "You're not seriously considering going to the towniest of all townie bars because Dean fucking Carson might buy you a drink."

"I can buy my own drinks."

She snorts. "Fine. Just don't be stupid, Charlie. I mean, sleep with him if you want, fine. Get it out of your system. Get *him* out of your system. But don't be stupid."

"Jeez. I said I wasn't going."

"People don't change that much."

"What's that supposed to mean?" But she doesn't answer, just shakes her head, and I say, "Kendra. Jesus. Let it go. I'll talk to you tomorrow, okay?"

"Are you going to go?"

"What the fuck, Kendra? I said *no*." She's really starting to piss me off, which is probably why I come up with something nonsensical. "So what, you don't want me to go out with a nineteen-year-old *or* a twenty-six-year-old?"

"Charlie." She's puzzled. "I was joking about the kid."

"He's not a kid."

She shrugs and gets into her car. How is it that she's the one being offensive, but I'm the one embarrassed?

After the night's margaritas, a couple of glasses of Malbec from a bottle my mom left in the fridge renders my balance a little questionable up the ladder, but I make my way through the trap door without incident. By now I have some old couch pillows, my flashlight, and a tin of Altoids in my corner of the treehouse, plus a sleeping mat from the camping stash in the garage.

The moon is full; it's so bright it's practically daytime. I silence my phone and lay it beside me, replaying the evening. Replaying junior and senior year. Freshman year in college. Freeing myself to remember.

Why is that two and a half years in your teens can feel like six? If ever I thought that seeing Dean again, talking to him, wouldn't affect me, I was naive. Beyond naive. In his face are the hundreds of kisses we shared, the first feel of boy skin against mine. Those golden-flecked eyes are the same ones I stared into as the world shifted around me, when I was sure need and want and love and like were all the same thing. Just hearing the syllables of my name in his familiar voice puts me back in his secondhand Nissan, or on the phone under the covers when my parents thought I was asleep, or at my locker during the days when I'd carelessly, foolishly accepted that nothing about us would ever have to change.

I have his number now. Willingly given. I can contact him whenever I like.

I tell the sky: I won't contact him.

Kendra's convinced he's still the same. But she doesn't get it. I want him the same. I could see it in his eyes tonight as he took me in—a strange, intoxicating mix of curiosity and familiarity. He was remembering, just like I was. That's why, as I left, knowing I was in his view, I turned around one last time. He needed to really see me again.

five

Todd, Marina's husband, is coming out of the house as I get home from work. I throw my arms around him. I can't help it, I love the guy. I've known him since I was a teenager. Marina showed remarkably good judgment, choosing him. I keep waiting for the jig to be up, for him to leave her and tell her he can't put up with her shit anymore. But they've been married now for years. Maybe that's what it takes to handle Marina—an easygoing, laid-back guy who doesn't let much get to him. At any rate, Marina with Todd is much easier to handle than Marina alone.

"So how's it going, everyone together again?" he asks with a knowing grin. He's leaning against the railing on the tiny side porch, all khakis and clean fingernails—so much the opposite of Marina's typical guy taste. Historically, anyway.

I debate what, and how much, to tell him. The two of us "kids" back in our old rooms has given way to a sick sort of perpetual nostalgia. There's a weird comfort I hadn't expected, but it's tempered by restlessness, which I usually combat with trips to the treehouse. I try my best to exist on Marina's outskirts, but she fills the space she's in so completely. Even the rooms she doesn't go in feel as if she's present, just as they did years ago. Just as suffocating. I'm halfway expecting her and my mom to break out in a master screaming session, like the old days. But it hasn't happened. It's like it never did.

And yet. Yesterday I was walking into the bathroom as she was walking out, not realizing she was even home, never mind taking a shower. I'd been napping after leaving work early—I hadn't felt well all day—and was disoriented. "You're taking a shower now?" I asked, dumbly.

She just stared at me like she was waiting for me to make sense. No yelling, no dirty looks, not even a slight slam of her bedroom door as she closed it behind her. For Todd, I paste a smile on my face. "It's not that bad," I tell him, which is only half a lie.

As a nurse, my mom was the quintessential family caretaker. Even in the worst of my childhood illnesses—chickenpox, pneumonia that kept me sick through the entire Thanksgiving holiday sophomore year in high school, the one time I got the actual, body-flattening flu the summer before I left for college— my memories aren't of the sickness as much as they are of her: kind eyes, dimmed lights, and soft confidence that I was going to be just fine.

Cuts and scrapes, though, were all my dad's. He was the master of the first-aid kit. To this day I can't tell you if he assumed this role or it was delegated. All I know is at any sight of blood, Marina and I always ran to Dad.

I'm slicing tomatoes when my mom's landline rings. Since I've been home, Mom and I have settled into a pleasant routine where I cook dinner most every night. It's coming back to me, how much I love to cook. Marina frequently eats at work and gets home late, so most often it's just the two of us. It's a different sort of dynamic, one we've only just discovered. I know she appreciates both the company and the excuse to eat a whole meal as opposed to a single-person sandwich or Amy's frozen entrée. And it's nice to know there's a place we can invent together where Dad's absence isn't so obvious or where Marina isn't planted between us. I've actually come to look forward to mother-daughter dinnertime, even to the point of consulting the Internet for new ideas or Mom's weathered cookbooks for old ones I've forgotten. Today I've got the iPad propped on the counter and I'm attempting a fancy version of pasta primavera, julienned veggies and all, with a caprese salad featuring mozzarella from the Italian deli. I stick the old-school spiral-corded phone under my chin to answer it, then resume slicing tomatoes.

"Charlie Michaelsen."

Just like that, blood everywhere. I didn't even feel the knife on my skin. I turn haphazardly, looking for my dad. Barely in time, I bite back the urge to call out for him. I rush to the sink and throw the water on, sticking my finger under the flow.

"Dean?"

"Yeah," he says, pleased I've recognized his voice. His phone met an unfortunate demise in the washing machine, it turns out, so he looked my old number up in the phone book.

"How old school." I stick my finger in my mouth. Where are the goddamn Band-Aids? Is there even a first-aid kit in the house anymore?

"Lucky I knew where you lived. If the phone book didn't work out, I would have knocked on your door."

He's mercilessly flirting. Part of me is filled with a delicious, buzzing thrill. Mostly, though, I'm concentrating on trying to sound calm as I scuttle around the kitchen opening every drawer I can find. "That'll teach you to check your pockets before you do your laundry."

"It was my mom," he says, sounding slightly embarrassed. I want to laugh, but I know full well my own laundry is sitting on my bed, clean and folded. "Anyway," he goes on, "what are you doing tomorrow night?"

A-ha! The Band-Aids mercifully appear in the medicine cabinet in the first-floor bathroom. I wrap one around the tip of my finger, much tighter than my dad ever would have. It hurts even more. "I'm not sure," I say, lying. "Have something in mind?"

"Nothing special. Just a bunch of us headed to the Irish Castle. Meet me there?"

The Irish Castle. Where old townies go to die.

I don't even think about it. I say yes. Just like that.

When I get off the phone I re-wrap my finger. Thank God the bleeding has stopped. It looked much worse than it actually was. I've just returned to slicing—tomatoes, not flesh—when the door opens and I turn, wondering why my mom is home early.

But it's Marina. "Hey," she says colorlessly.

"Hey," I answer, matching her tone. "Why are you so early?"

She ignores me, her head in the fridge. She finds a San Pellegrino—the fridge is full of them, all hers—and takes a long drink, leaning back against the fridge door. "Wow, you'd never know it's fall. I hope it rains. It's so muggy."

Whenever Marina and I are in the same room, she carries on a conversation with herself. I keep wondering when she'll notice.

"Maybe Mom will want to go out for dinner tonight." She pulls out her phone. "Hi, Mom. I'm at the house. Our meeting with the judge got postponed, so I got out early. Should we do dinner tonight, do you think? Try that new place at Legacy Place that you were asking about? Oh... really?" Her eyes slide to me. "Well, she should come, of course. I don't know. Are you making dinner?" she asks me.

I just look at her. I have a knife in my hand, and vegetables are all over the cutting board.

She rolls her eyes. "Yeah, salad I think," she says back into the phone. "It can keep in the fridge."

"Sorry," she says when she hangs up. "But it's not that often I'm here for dinner. And don't you think it will be nice for Mom to go out tonight?"

She must not be satisfied with my level of comprehension, because after glaring at me, she deliberately turns away. "I just got back from the cemetery," she announces.

This isn't surprising; the cemetery is a regular destination for her whenever she's in Danborn. I don't answer, but of course she doesn't expect me to. Opening cabinets, searching for God-knows-what, she launches into the state of the gravesite's greenery. This is also standard. "I can't believe how few graves are tended to. Dad's always looks the nicest."

"I know." I hope it's enough of an answer to keep her from giving me another look. The moves are familiar and I've memorized this dance. But suddenly she looks sharply at me. "Do you really, Charlotte?"

"Charlie," I correct automatically.

She ignores this. "I figured today of all days you'd be there."

"What's today?" The words, in my bitchiest tone, aren't even out of my mouth when I realize my mistake—and she sees it on my face.

"Nice," she says, then walks out of the room.

Fuck you, I think. If I could, I'd explain to her that I don't go to the cemetery according to a calendar, not on Memorial Day or Father's Day or his birthday, and certainly not today, the day that seven years ago my roommate stood in front of me with a frozen look on her face, a catch in her voice, and told me the news that I'd expected yet never saw coming, the news that sent me into the stairwell for the next forty-five minutes until my

51

roommate found me there, on the floor, knees to my chest, dry-eyed and quiet.

Till now I've been able to claim geography as a valid excuse, but here I am, in my hometown, not doing my daughterly duty, and my sister is ready to finally let me know just how offensive I'm being. "Really, Charlie," I hear her say from the other room. "You'd think you never had a father."

I shuffle all the veggies back into their bags. Screw this. This is not what I moved home for. "I was going to go today actually," I say, hating myself for trying to placate her. "During my run."

The look she throws me as I pass her on my way to my room to change is skeptical, but I hide my face around my water bottle, exiting just as she seems to be searching for the next thing to say.

Kendra's going out with a new guy—more first-date secrecy—and I have no idea what any of my other friends are doing. For a wild moment I consider calling Dean back, suggesting we see each other tonight, but that would be a mistake. Sitting on my bed, hands on my knees, I realize that although I've told Marina I'll go to the cemetery simply to shut her up and get out of her way, I may have actually told the truth. Running in the cemetery is not unprecedented, after all. We went there all the time in high school track.

It feels weird not to run with Wade. We usually keep up a steady stream of conversation. He's pretty funny, actually—more than once I've had to stop running and catch my breath while I finished laughing at one or another of his one-liners. Maybe I should have texted him before I left. Oh well.

Heading up toward Danborn Square, I turn right off the main drag down a hill towards the cemetery. I pass through the gates, turning left, away from the pond. I note, as I remember doing in high school, how strange it is that the streets within the cemetery actually have names. Like their own subdivision. But I suppose people who don't know where they're going have to have some way to find their way around.

People like me.

It's not like I don't go to the cemetery. I do, sometimes. But usually, as Marina alluded to, I let the fact that there is a headstone with my father's name on it run underneath the current of reality. It's a dangerous choice, and I've been paying for it for years. For Marina, the cemetery is her North Star. She makes a point to visit, and talk about visiting it, often. When I go, I never mention it to anyone, and I always forget how to get there. Like now. Looking around with my hands on my hips, every view the same, the possibility that I can't find it fills me with determination. I hook a left in the general direction I know it is. After a few turns down Hemlock and Juniper Avenues I approach a grassy area that looks familiar, but when I get closer, it's not right. Everywhere I look shows me the same low hills, the same rows of gray stones, the same colorful splashes of flower arrangements. What kind of daughter am I that I can't find my own father's grave in my hometown cemetery? Maybe my sister is right after all. I stand again for a minute, closing my eyes and forcing my mind backwards. I see the limo, see myself getting out of it and walking towards the gravesite. My viewpoint of the limo during the service would have been... hmmm. I scan the area around me, reorient myself, then jog another street over. I place my line of vision where I expect it to be and move forty feet to my left, inspecting all the carved names on the stones that I pass.

There it is. I can make out the "Michaelsen" from where I stand, and "James" comes into focus as my feet somehow pull me towards it. It's well decorated, with plants and flowers and even—I move closer—an envelope. Without even seeing the "Dad" scrawled across it in her telltale, nearly illegible handwriting, I know it's from Marina.

Cemeteries are for other people. I've learned this by now. Some people need them. Talking to their lost loved ones in an organized and dedicated space gives them a sense of comfort, a place to focus on their grief. I'm glad they have that, and I envy it. Because as much as I keep trying, it doesn't work for me. Nothing I feel in a cemetery matches what I can conjure in my own head.

I sink to my knees, sweat cooling in the curves of my back, trying to find something in the stone carving that feels familiar. Nothing. I've felt his presence more in my house, where I keep expecting him to come around the corner or be sitting in his chair in the den, watching the Bruins. Or in the car he bought just before he was diagnosed, which my mom still drives... the same Honda Civic he bought every five years, pre-owned, usually with just a few thousand miles on it. I'm not sure I ever even saw my dad in a cemetery outside of mandatory funerals.

Trying to find him here now is like looking for him at a bowling alley, or in a wheat field. It's just not where he lives.

I hear my mom and Marina arrive home around nine, after I've showered and eaten some leftover chili, while I'm finding out what I can about Dean online. Dean never did Facebook—I've checked over the years—but I can see now that he has a profile. Danborn High School, Boston College. Horvath Financial, Chicago, Illinois.

I heard he moved to Chicago after college, and word is that he instantly fell into a long-term relationship with a redheaded girl named Ciara. That lasted at least a few years, or so my sources told me. When I met Cam I stopped wondering, and by the time our failure as a couple was imminent and I got curious again, my sources weren't sources anymore. Beyond "he's still in Chicago," I hadn't had a Dean update in at least three years.

Facebook reveals no mention of a relationship. His friends list is private, so I can neither prove nor deny the existence—or previous existence—of Ciara. That's about as much as I can see, not being friends with him. Even his photos are locked down. I can, however, see his various "likes." Red Sox Nation, Boston Strong. *Argo*. Makes sense with his Ben Affleck hard-on. (I'm a Matt person myself. I mean, come on.) It's so weird to know a favorite movie of his is one I haven't seen. I make a mental note to watch it. *Good Will Hunting* is listed, of course.

I shut my laptop when I hear my mom ascending the stairs. "Charlotte? Why didn't you come to dinner?"

Of course. I'm sure Marina made it seem as if she invited me along, and I petulantly refused to come. "I went running," I say, leaving it at that. My mom purses her lips. She's hurt. But what am I supposed to say? Any argument that Marina manipulated me out of dinner will just sound like sour grapes.

"I wish you'd come. That new place is really very nice."

"It's Italian, right?"

"Sort of. It's not the North End, but it's not the Olive Garden."

"I'll go with you next time."

She brightens slightly. "That would be lovely, Charlie. Let's plan it in advance, okay?"

I smile for her benefit. "Sure."

"I like having dinner with my girls. Marina was really disappointed you couldn't make it."

I smile and say good night, thinking, *Marina is a goddamn liar.*

It's like I'm twelve again, sitting in the treehouse and fuming about Marina. Clouds are obscuring the moon, and my flashlight has stopped working, so the treehouse is one big envelope of dark. The more I sit, though, the more I get used to it. I remember what it was like to be invisible, to have life going on around me in broad daylight while I stayed, hidden, in plain sight.

I bolt upright. The treehouse is moving beneath me. What the hell? Someone is *climbing up here.* I reach around to grab—nothing. There is not one thing in this treehouse I could use to protect myself. Before I can decide on a course of action, the trap opens and the back of a head appears. The head turns as Wade hoists himself up. His eyes meet mine, and he yelps. He loses his footing on the ladder, grabbing the floor to keep from tumbling to the ground.

My heart is pounding. "You scream like a girl."

He pulls himself up, closes the trap, sits, and looks back at me, still breathing heavily. I mash my lips together to keep from laughing. "You scared the shit out of me," he says.

"You're just lucky I didn't have a weapon."

"I'll take that under advisement."

I smile, and he settles himself back against the wall opposite me. "So, you come here often?" I ask him.

"Ever since I moved back. You?"

"Ever since I moved back."

"I guess I'm not the only person who prefers to hang out in the past."

"Parts of it," I agree.

"I knew someone had been here. I thought it might be you. I've been stealing your Altoids."

"I *thought* my supply was dwindling."

"I'll replace them. Or maybe you can just consider it payment for trespassing."

"Excuse me?"

"This is on my property." The half-grin he's wearing is like a door opening.

I assume an expression that suggests the law is on my side. "I will have you know that my dad and I arranged a binding legal agreement with your mom back when we built this."

His eyebrows lift. "You built this?"

"Yep. Me and my dad." I don't even hide the pride in my voice. His surprise pleases me. My memory rolls through it, this project of mine and my dad's, probably the biggest one of my childhood, during the pink days. Before Marina changed him. I pull up my knees, hugging the story.

"First," I tell Wade, "we had a swing set."

The set was flimsy from years of use; I remember how part of it broke when Marina and her friends tried to use it when they were far too heavy to do so. That one got thrown away, but we didn't replace it, and after a while I got after my parents to get a new one.

"Why can't we just go to Toys R Us and look around?" This was back when my mom still hung clothes on the line, and she was outside with a laundry basket and her bag of clothespins, the wooden ones with the metal clasps. I was following her around, handing her clothespin after clothespin. "You're eight years old," she said. "You don't want a swing set. I can't remember the last time I saw you on it."

"Because it was broken." In a way she was right. I didn't want a new one. I wanted one already there, one that I was too old for and claimed not to be attached to but that I could secretly play on anyway. I was a climber and a monkey-bar swinger and nothing in my yard was ripe for climbing up or swinging from. "There are these huge wooden ones that you can paint. I saw it in a magazine."

"We don't need a new swing set."

"You can even build it onto a tree," I said, remembering the magazine photos.

"Is that what you want? A treehouse?"

"No," I said sulkily and went off to play at Lauren's, across the street. But later on, in the middle of the third game of Connect Four, it dawned on me that yes, that was exactly what I wanted. A treehouse. A house in a tree. Why hadn't I thought of that?

I tried a different approach. One night after dinner when my father was reading the paper while the Bruins played—he was a hockey fiend—and drinking his Scotch in the easy chair, I wandered up and leaned against his chair for a few minutes, pretending I was watching the game with him.

"Are they winning?" I asked. He looked over the lenses of his reading glasses at the TV.

"Thanks to Ray Bourque," he muttered, like he was personally disappointed in the team's scoring. I watched a minute, my eyes following number 77. Bourque being the best defender since Bobby Orr was no secret in the Michaelsen household.

"Why do you look over your glasses like that?"

"What? Oh. Well." He laid his paper down and looked thoughtful. "Because I see differently close up than I do far away, I guess."

"Like Holly Drake?"

"Who's Holly Drake?"

"She's in my class. She has to always be in the front row because she wears glasses to see the chalkboard." My own glasses were still two years in the future.

"No, Charlie Brown, I'm the opposite. I'm nearsighted. Your friend Holly sounds like she's farsighted."

"She's not my friend." Just yesterday Holly had told Lauren not to play with me at recess because I had chubby cheeks. Lauren hadn't listened to her, but still.

"Your classmate, then. People get glasses for different reasons. Like your dad here, he got them because he's old." He looked up at me. "That all that's on your mind, Charlie Brown?"

"Yeah."

He patted my hand and went back to his paper. "Wait," I said. "Yes. I mean, no. I want a treehouse."

"A what?"

"I want a treehouse. Can you build it? I'll help."

All in the moment before he answered me, I could see I wasn't going to get it. He was sighing, which always came before he said no. But more than that, he threw a look toward the kitchen, where my mother was. Whenever he considered my mother when I asked for something, the answer was never what I wanted.

I tried a last-ditch effort. "Please. I'll help you build it, I promise. I just need you to show me how."

He looked at me without speaking, which I took as a good sign. He shook his head and pulled his paper back in front of him. "Your mother's going to kill me. I can't make you any promises." He dropped to a whisper, and I had to strain to hear him behind the newspaper. "But let's you and I go to the hardware store tomorrow and see what we can do."

It took us a month and a half of weekends over that spring to plan and build the treehouse. Dad held me to my promise and I did all the research in the library—what wood to use, how to fit it around a growing tree, why to use screws instead of nails. Before we actually built it, however, we needed to choose the tree. One morning was entirely dedicated to this selection. Our backyard abutted some woods, which of course had the trees. We didn't want to go far enough into the woods so it wouldn't be close to the house, yet the tree we used had to be sturdy enough to support what he wanted to build. None of the trees in our yard seemed to pass muster.

"What about this tree?" I asked, kicking the trunk of one that was more in line with the driveway than the house. To me it was perfect. Thick at the bottom, and with a collection of branches above my head that looked perfectly suited for supporting a wooden floor.

"That would work," my dad said, staring up for a long moment, walking around it. "But honey, I'm pretty sure that's on the Hunters' property."

He was right. We didn't have a fence separating our yard from the Hunters'—just some landscaped garden. For the most part we treated the two yards as one.

"Couldn't we build it there?"

"We could," he allowed. "But we'd have to get their permission. And they may not want a treehouse in their tree."

So I focused on Keith, who was in Mr. Henderson's fourth-grade class. I was in Miss Swenson's. In school Keith pretty much ignored me, but he wasn't too proud to indulge in a game of kickball or kick the can with the neighborhood kids. And although he probably wouldn't admit it to his friends, we played together at each others' houses. Back then, our families got along well and our parents often went out together, sharing a babysitter for me and him and, later on, Wade, the baby. Sometimes that babysitter was Marina, which was never as fun as it should have been. I loved the times I got to go to Keith's house. The babysitter was usually pretty caught up in the baby, so Keith and I were on our own. One time in third grade we even stayed home from school for almost a whole week together when we both had chicken pox. Nobody else could go near us, so we stuck together, watching movies and playing hide and seek in his big house while his mom worked in her home office. He was so impressed the time I hid in the hamper with all the dirty clothes. It was smelly, but so worth it. He hugged me when he found me. Sometimes I wondered if he remembered that I was fun to be around.

Just in case he didn't, I focused hard on something else: his stubbornness. If Keith didn't want a treehouse in his yard, he wouldn't have a treehouse in his yard. And if it was my idea, or if he thought it was for me, he wouldn't want it.

I decided the best way to get to him was through his mother. One afternoon I sat at his kitchen table eating grapes while his mom made dinner. He didn't know I was there, but he was home. "Yeah," I was saying, "my dad and I were looking around for a good tree to build a treehouse in. Nice family project."

"And did you find one?" Marla asked indulgently. She was peeling potatoes over a newspaper. She used a knife—one of those tiny, sharp, pointy ones—and not a potato peeler. I watched her in horror and couldn't believe she could do that without cutting herself. But she peeled potatoes with a knife even faster than my own mom did with a peeler.

I chewed a grape, then swallowed it. "Well, we did find one. Only we think it's on your property."

Marla smiled, still peeling. "Is it now?"

"If Keith wanted to, uh, help make it, then it would be like half his, wouldn't it?"

"Would you want to share your treehouse?"

"If he shares his tree it's only fair."

And right on cue, in walked Keith, his hand in a bag of potato chips before he even looked my way. "Charlie's here, Mom."

"I know that, Keith. She's keeping me company while I make dinner."

She ran her hands under the faucet and dried them. "Actually, Keith, Charlie and her father had a good idea." I looked at her hopefully. "They thought you might like to build a treehouse in that tree over there, the one directly out that window."

He looked out the window, then at me skeptically. "Really?"

"My dad wants to build one, and we'll both help you."

He found parental behavior just as mystifying as I often did, so he accepted this without explanation. "Does he have a square saw?"

"Yup." I had no idea what a square saw was. "He said he might let you use it."

"Mom, can we start this weekend?"

"Well, why don't you check with Mr. Michaelsen?"

"I'll find out," I said, getting up. I thought it best to leave before Keith started asking too many questions. I wanted to whoop with joy, but I knew better. "We'll start Saturday afternoon if we can. Saturday morning we'll go to pick up the materials."

"Make sure you bring the square saw."

"I will."

So that weekend we began framing the house. It wasn't a "house" as much as it was something that looked, from a distance anyway, like a wooden packing crate. But once inside it was roomy, with two sort-of complete rooms. On my suggestion my dad even built a pulley system (very *Silence of the Lambs*, as I discovered when I read the book a few years later) so we could haul things we needed up in a tray.

There was a lot of talk over whether we needed a ladder. Both Keith and I wanted to nail boards to the tree and thought a ladder would be kind of cheating. But in the end my dad convinced us that if we built the ladder, it would be just as authentic. We agreed, after making sure the ladder rungs started high enough that Keith's little brother wouldn't be able to access them when he began walking a lot.

Keith was busy with baseball and soccer, so he didn't help as much as he said he wanted to. I didn't care. When it was done, though, he used it a lot, much more than I did. I joined him when I could. With me being the builder, he couldn't very well snub me. I'd always much rather have climbed trees than dressed Barbies, so I made a habit of hanging out in my backyard after school and on weekends. Eventually Keith would see me and something—guilt, probably—would compel him to call me over with a halfhearted "You may as well hang out with us." But I couldn't do girl things like scream or shy away from bugs. As if. I was way more comfortable around bugs than Keith was. Snakes too. He'd act a good game, but I was the only one to notice the clear look of horror on his face while he handled one creature or another. But I never said anything, in return for being invited to be part of the team. I got a little bit more than grunting in school in return. And I used the treehouse whenever I wanted—with my friends, or by myself, reading or daydreaming or even napping.

Then we started middle school, my last year in public school. The gulf between boys and girls in sixth grade proved unnavigable. Keith's friends could not see him associating with a girl, even if she had known him his whole life. He would speak to me at family functions (which became fewer and fewer as his parents split up) when he had to, but other than that, in his eyes, for the time being I pretty much ceased to exist.

So did the treehouse. That was the year Keith started to let it go. It took me a lot longer. I'd wait around like usual, but more often than not he'd never show up, or be gone for some soccer game in another town or even out of state. I learned to like going up there alone. With the height of the walls, unless anyone saw me actually climbing the tree, no one knew I was up there, and I preferred it that way. Being invisible. Especially as things got ugly with Marina and my parents.

"What happened with her?" Wade asks me now. "Tonight?"

I don't answer him right away. I want to tell him that's another story for another time, but I hear myself say, "She was mad that I didn't go to the cemetery."

There's a question in his eyes. Then, "Your dad," he says in understanding. "First funeral I ever went to."

"Really?" I don't know why it hasn't occurred to me until now, but of course—Wade must have known him.

"I came back from Colorado for it."

"You did?" I'm stunned, both at what he said and that my eyes are suddenly brimming with tears. "That was... really nice of you."

"I wanted to. I really liked him. He taught me to mow the lawn," he says, and grins as if remembering. "And... other stuff. He seemed like a really good dad."

This makes me so happy. Hearing things you didn't know about someone who's died is like getting a sequel to a favorite book. It helps you forget the permanence of forever. For a few minutes, we both just sit. That comfortable silence again. Why does it exist so much more easily with some than with others?

"Do you miss him?" Wade asks.

"Not really." I shake away that answer with my head. "That's not what I mean. It's just... been so long." But that isn't what I mean either. The truth is I feel like I've always missed him. I was missing him before he died. The way I miss him now isn't much different.

"Would you rather not talk about it?"

"I never talk about it." Again the words just seem to whoosh from my mouth. There's a break in the clouds, and a tiny bit of moon peeks through, illuminating us for the first time. Wade's looking at me seriously, waiting for me to continue. Something shakes loose inside of me as we hold one another's gaze. I'm feeling almost woozy. I pull my eyes from his and say, "I mean, no one talks about it with me. Well, Kendra, does, a little. My best friend." I'm staring at my fingernail as I talk, which is carving into the floor.

"Not your family? Your sister?"

"No. Not my mom, and definitely not my sister." I shrug, then clarify. "Marina mentions him all the time. But we don't, like, exchange words. She just talks and talks and talks. But it's not like it means the same thing to me. He and Marina were just... different, I guess. Pretty close. Ow!"

I put my finger up to what little light there is. "Dammit. Is that a splinter?"

"Let me see." Wade takes my hand in both of his, running his index finger over the tip of mine. His hands are warm and gentle and strong, everything they shouldn't be. Everything in me tells me I should pull away. He turns on his phone's flashlight. "Can you hold this with your other hand?" From his jeans he pulls out what looks like a pocketknife. I shrink back. He looks at me curiously, then notices the Band-Aid.

"Did you have another splinter earlier?"

"Dinner prep casualty." Which I didn't even get to eat.

"Just a flesh wound," he says breezily. "Don't worry, I won't hurt you." Gently he unrolls my fingers. "Relax," he says, tapping my hand lightly. I unclench. He goes to work on my finger with the knife blade. I feel myself holding my breath. I can smell his hair, his shampoo, his guy-ness. Not fifteen seconds later he holds up the splinter between his fingers. "Got it."

"Thank you." I touch the spot where the splinter was, like he did. "That's pretty impressive."

"Splinter removal is, like, required knowledge in my family." As if that reminds him of what we'd been talking about, he asks me, "So your sister and your dad were close?"

I stare at him a moment, dazed. "Um, yeah. They were really tight."

"What about the two of you?"

I shake my head. "It wasn't the same. She was really upset when he died. Losing him almost did her in." At the wake, before anyone showed up for visiting hours, she sat in the room where he was laid out, just wailing into her hands. She kept it mostly together when people started arriving, but had to leave the room several times. I understood the etiquette of the receiving line, even as it seemed the most ridiculous thing I'd ever done, listening to everyone I'd ever known—and plenty of people I didn't—apologize to me, leaving me to the tight-lipped not-quite-smile I learned to perfect, or worse, consoling *them*. I hated every second of it and wished I could just get up and leave when I felt like it, like Marina did.

"They were, like, each other's favorite person." I want to dig in the floor again, but the memory of the splinter makes me clasp my hands instead. I think of how they felt encircled by Wade's, just moments ago.

"Charlie." I can tell he's waiting to speak until I look at him, and so I do. "He was your dad, too." His voice is soulful and generous. Again, out of nowhere, tears spring to my eyes.

"Not really," I say quickly. "I mean, yeah. Sure. I wasn't conceived by the UPS man." Oh God, Charlie, *shut up*. "But the two of us, we weren't like... how they were."

His eyes are so kind that it's disquieting. Looking into them makes something uproot and shift in the pit of my stomach.

"I know it was a while ago," he says finally, "and I was young, but I did live here. From what I could see it seemed to me the two of you got along really well."

"We got along," I concede. "But he was always... I don't know, more Marina's dad than mine. Even now," I hasten to explain when I realize how crazy that sounds out loud, "when she talks about him and pulls up the memories of her childhood, it's like she's talking about a different person. One I didn't even know." Anger pokes out, spiking my words. "She gives me shit for not feeling or acting exactly like her."

Wade lets out a breath. It seems like he's about to say something, so I wait. But he stays quiet. Thoughtful.

I look sideways at him. Is he thinking about himself? An image occurs to me, one I haven't thought of in years: a family portrait in their living room, a baby Wade grinning toothlessly from Keith's lap, his big brother's hands clasped across his waist. So strange to think they're both adults now, at least legally. Like me and my sister. "How many years are between you and Keith?"

"Seven," he says.

I'm about to ask him how they get along, when he says with a wry smile, "Just like us."

Us. Me and him. I was seven when he was born.

"Uh... so how do you get along? You and Keith?"

"Better than we used to," Wade says.

"What's changed?"

"Me." I look at him questioningly. "Now I'm trying."

I consider that. I tried for a long time with Marina, but along the way I must have stopped. It's hard to put effort into improving the relationship when just being in the room with her makes it hard to breathe.

"I was jealous of him for a long time," he says. "Because he was older, because he got to do what he wanted. It wasn't until recently that it dawned on me that he was jealous of *me*."

"Really? Why?"

"Because of our dad," he says, and I think, *It's all the same everywhere.* "We're a lot alike, and we're pretty close. He wasn't happy when I moved." He smiles. "But what Keith doesn't realize is because Dad and I are so much alike, we fight way more than the two of them do."

"Where do you live, again?" I ask him. "In Colorado?"

"Fort Collins. It's where I go to school, too. My dad grew up there."

I try to conjure Wade and Keith's dad, to see what my memory can extract. Nice guy. Big smile. Brown hair. Blue pickup. "You look like him," I say suddenly.

He leans back on his palms. "So people say."

I scrutinize him. "But you have your mom's smile."

And there it is, the mirror of his mother, conjured from my words. "So people say. And she's still the potato-peeling master."

That makes me laugh. I ask, "So why are you back now?"

He shrugs. "Take your pick. Things to do. Unfinished business. Mending fences."

"You have fences to mend?"

"A few."

"And you have to mend them here?"

"I broke them here. Plus I miss my mom." He grins again, and for a minute, I can't help returning it. Warmth spreads through my veins, like how a blush would feel extending to my extremities.

The sky gets brighter as the clouds move away. For a while we don't speak, our gazes wandering as we take in our respective views of the trees laid like black lace over the sky. I can hear his breath rising and falling, this boy who knew my dad.

I concentrate very hard on not looking at him. "I was supposed to go to the cemetery because today's the anniversary." What an awful word to mark the date of someone's death. It should be banned for any occasion that can't involve a cake.

"The anniversary," he says, getting it. "I'm sorry."

"It's okay," I answer automatically. Because that's what you say.

six

In some ways, returning to your suburban hometown after an absence is like being a C-list celebrity. You don't know anyone, not anymore anyway. But everyone knows you. You're the novelty. You get curious looks of recognition, and not from people you necessarily want to see (if you did, you never would have lost touch with them in the first place). But you have to play the game. Be polite. Find common ground. Especially when you're living with your mom, who's not going anywhere.

Walking in to the Irish Castle is this brand of surreal. Almost every face turning my way is filed away in my brain, though the last decade has absorbed most of their names. It's unnerving. I planned to walk right up to Dean, but he's surrounded, boxed in by these faces, the same people he was friends with before we dated. And during and after, actually; I was the odd one out. Consumed by awkwardness, I stand stiffly and check my phone for nonexistent texts.

I wasn't even going to come. Kendra didn't want to join me, but she got out of admitting that by legitimately having to work late. Asking Xanna or our mutual friend, Marc, would be asking for trouble; if the Irish Castle wasn't Kendra's scene, it was even less theirs. The only one left was Kelly, who's also from Danborn. But she's way in the suburbs and planning her wedding and always seems to have family obligations besides, so I hardly see her. For close friends, that's it. Sometimes I wonder if I should be concerned about that.

So I decided to stay in. But then, about nine, Dean texted me. *r u coming?*

Not sure I can, I hedged.

hope u can. ill be here.

Call Dean clueless, or forgetful, but I've never known him to be deliberately mean or rude. He's like a politician, always concerned with being liked. So I took a chance that Kendra was right and he hadn't changed and I Ubered, crossing my fingers that I'd find a ride home.

Dean spots me and beckons to come over. I start towards him but want to sink into the floor when he announces, "Hey everyone, it's Charlie!"

Sherri Stillwell, who hasn't gained an ounce since high school and by my estimate seems to have bigger boobs, chirps, "I heard you moved back to town! You look great!"

This is another thing I'm getting used to. We all look so *great*. It's what everyone says when they see people from the past—even if some of us look decidedly worse. From Sherri, it's just as saccharine as anything she said to me in high school, but I decide to give her the benefit of the doubt, if only because I may end up spending actual time with her tonight. Or in the future. I trade niceties with her and another old classmate, Felicia Knoll, whom I genuinely liked back in the day.

"So you're living in Danborn?" The precision of Sherri's eye makeup fascinates me. It makes me want to examine it for longer than I should.

"For a little bit," I say.

"How fun. We'll have to get together, okay? You should find me on Facebook. Or Snapchat! Or Instagram!"

I'm handed a drink. Then another. I relax. Settle into myself. I don't even mind talking to Sherri and Felicia and Steve Linstrom and Justine Cantor and all the people who would give me the time of day, but not much more, in high school. I actually have a decent time, even a good one. Felicia, in particular, seems genuine and warm, and my friendliness toward her isn't a struggle or an act.

After a while—and my third drink—Dean guides us off to the side, where we find an unoccupied two-top. We sit down as a whoop erupts from the group we just left. "You sure you don't want to be over there?" I ask him.

"Right now this is good," he says.

It genuinely is. Close up I can see Dean has the faintest promise of laugh lines around his eyes. It's not hard to see how he'll look in five years. He's friendly and respectful and not anywhere near as full of himself as I remember, or at least as hindsight told me he was. He updates me on his family, his brother's marriage, his dad's retirement from the force, his parents' vacation home in Florida. For now he lives in a pseudo apartment, remodeled originally for his brother, in his parents' basement. We exchange a look at the word *basement*, and although everything inside of me is screaming to look away, I don't. From the faux-leather couch to the Matisse paintings his mom favored (but his dad didn't, hence the basement placement) to the clock that chimed with birdcalls, I knew that basement well. I shift in my chair at the memory of carpet on my back, the undercurrent of panic that at any moment his mother could suddenly descend the stairs, bathing us in light.

I have to change the subject. "So what about Keith? He's really staying in Chicago?"

"He really is."

Dean without Keith is hard to imagine. They've been inseparable for as long as I've known both of them. No one was surprised when they went to Boston College together, nor when they both picked Chicago as their post-college home. "He'll probably visit more now, though, now that I'm here," Dean says, with a charming smile. "Plus his brother's here too."

His brother. The phone in my jacket pocket buzzed earlier with a text: *Let's take the streets by storm tomorrow. 10? 11? You make the call.* I responded to Wade under the table while Dean tried to track down waitstaff. Since our night in the treehouse, thoughts of Wade have been perpetually sneaking into my mind. Like the way his hands felt that night. How he took care of me. Or how he makes me smile just reading his properly punctuated text.

But that's a stupid crush. An unreal fantasy. Tonight, across this tiny table, *this* is what's real. And tangible. And germane to my life. Dean and I keep our conversation surface-level, but eventually it's clear we're carrying on another one, unspoken. I vacillate between wishing the crowd would disappear and being grateful for everyone's presence. Every once in a while the group erupts into laughter, sometimes spiked with a girly scream. People are calling over to Dean, including him in conversations he's not participating in. I feel myself nodding invisibly. I remember this. Dean, everyone's buddy, the guy everyone wants to be next to. Or sleep with.

I haven't had sex since May. Almost five months ago. Which may not sound like a lot, but considering that for three of those months I was living with my boyfriend, that's not a great track record. And it's been even longer than that since I've had anything that can qualify as good sex. God, no wonder I've been having inappropriate thoughts about Wade. A girl has needs, after all.

I swallow the last of my fourth drink and the crowd migrates in our direction. People move tables and take seats all around us. The alcohol warms my blood. I'm comfortable, not just with Dean or Felicia but with everyone, even Sherri. I cheer on the jukebox music choices with everyone else, complain about traffic on 128 with everyone else, and greet latecomers with everyone else. By the time Dean waves goodbye and holds the door open for me to walk out into the night, I want to call Kendra just to tell her how wrong she was. It's possible to have a good time in Danborn, even at the Irish Castle with remnants of Danborn High. I'm warm and giggly and totally down with whatever Dean's suggesting, which happens to be heading back to his place, the same place I knew so well in high school, except now there's an actual bed and a door that locks. And yes, maybe I do feel a little slutty as I sink onto his bed, his familiar hands already sliding over the skin he probably doesn't remember as well as he should. But tonight, I have an advantage. I've been here before. I'm old enough to find the way out.

Kendra bites carefully into her Saltine spread with marshmallow Fluff. "Look at that!" She shows me the perfect arc of her bite mark.

"You are amazing," I tell her.

"I know, right?" She finishes off the cracker. "So what are we going to do today?"

I shrug, twisting the knife to scrape the inside of the blue and white jar. "Eat Fluff. Pick up Xanna."

"Besides that."

"Should we consult Netflix?" We've been making our way through '80s sitcoms and have almost finished *Family Ties*.

"I could be down with that." She glances outside. "Though we should probably take advantage."

It's a gorgeous, cloudless fall day. "We probably should," I agree.

She bites another cracker. "Yeah."

"Maybe later," I reply, licking my finger.

"My gosh, girls," my mom says, walking into the kitchen. I instantly recognize her on-my-way-out mode. "I can't believe you still eat that. How can you stand all that sugar?"

"It's a skill," Kendra says. "We were just saying that maybe later we'll get off our butts and do something constructive."

"You could come with me," she says. We look at her blankly.

"Manwell Park," she says as if we should be able to figure out why.

And there it is, right on the calendar. "Ah." I turn to Kendra. "Danborn Day. How could we forget?"

"Good luck with the cow shit," Kendra tells her. My mom makes a face, then combines it with a smile as she takes her keys from the hook by the door. I shake my head. I could never get away with talking to my mom like that.

Danborn Day is a long-standing autumn tradition. It started about twenty years ago as a fundraiser for the town—a carnival with kiddie rides, a band or two, food stands, and the highlight of the day: cow patty bingo. Grass in the athletic field is sectioned off in squares, which are then sold like raffle tickets. A cow is released onto the grass and if she poops on your square, you're the lucky winner.

It's exactly as fun as it sounds.

I've been there only a handful of times since I graduated high school, but my mom goes every October like clockwork.

"Marina won once," I tell Kendra.

"Cow patty bingo?" she asks me, surprised. "No kidding?"

"Well, third place." My dad and Marina, their relationship still tentative, got adjoining squares, and even though it was clearly her square, Marina made a big deal of the fact that the winnings could easily belong to either of them. My square was across the field from theirs, in a corner the cow didn't even look at.

"Bitch," Kendra adds, loyally.

We both sit there for another minute, sticky and silent. "So has Dean called you?"

"Yup." My answer is as abrupt as Kendra's question. "I saw him Friday. Don't judge," I add quickly, seeing her start to speak.

"Did you sleep with him?"

"Seriously? That's the first thing you ask?"

"I'll take that as a yes." Seeing me roll my eyes, she says, "Charlie, seriously, you slept with him? How could you not tell me?"

"I just told you."

"When I *asked*. Were you even going to mention it to me?" She waits a beat, then says, "How am I supposed to stay all up in your bidness?"

I spread another cracker. We both continue eating. Finally she asks, "So was it like before?"

I could pretend I don't know what she means. But I do. Of course I do. "Yes... and no." How can I even explain it? The edges were harder, the moves more deliberate. Less exploratory than methodical. Yet... it was still Dean. More than that, it was still Dean and me. I could tell by the way he touched me, even started laughing here and there, that he was pulling from inside of him, jogging his memory unexpectedly. And him—he was bigger, certainly. (Well not that. Just everywhere else.) And hairier. Kissing him and having him inside me felt familiar, but in a way I couldn't quite wrap my head around. Like live theater compared to a movie, the slightest alteration from what I remember. Rehearsals, complete with mistakes, instead of the actual performance.

It was nice.

"Are you going to see him again?"

I shrug. "I don't know."

"But you want to?"

I shrug again. "Probably. We actually had a really nice time."

"At the Irish Castle."

A pebble of anger rattles around inside of me. "Kendra, I'm having fun."

"You're a totally different person now, Charlie."

"You said that before."

"So we don't think he's an asshole anymore?"

"*I* don't. I mean, all he did was break up with me. Happens every day, all over the world."

"He *didn't* break up with you," she snaps. It feels like this slipped out, but Kendra assumes an air of defiance, as if now that it's out, she's going to stand behind it. "Charlie, you have to remember—"

"Kendra. I remember. Let it go. I'm a big girl."

"I know you are." She looks at me for a long moment, and I brace myself for what she's preparing to say. But she doesn't say anything. Instead, she jumps down from the stool. "Okay, let's go."

"Now?" My mouth is full of crumbs and Fluff.

"Now. We're going to pick up Xanna, and then we're going to Danborn Day."

Danborn Day is a strange combination of the town spirit of a football game and the long-distance recognition of a high school reunion, complete with parents and every kid you never wanted to see again. Xanna, Kendra, and I walk around chewing gum Xanna has handed out and stare at people from behind our sunglasses.

"I feel like the Pink Ladies," I say.

"And we're gonna *rule* the *school*," says Kendra.

Xanna, new to the whole thing, gawks. "This is so weird. Everyone is having, like, the time of their lives."

"I know," I say. "And you know what, I think they really are."

When we first arrived, the excitement for bingo was just building to its fever pitch. "I got another square!" a girl who looks about eight yells as she runs by us, presumably to her parents. The competition is supposed to start any minute.

"We have to buy one," Xanna says, decisively.

"A square?"

"Oh my God, *yes*," Kendra says. "I'm buying all of us one." We look around for a ticket booth and the three of us wait on line.

"So it's true, Charlie girl? You and the big guy?" Xanna asks me. I eye Kendra. That was fast. "First love reignited and all that?"

"I wouldn't go that far."

Xanna blows a bubble, then smiles at a girl walking by, whom I recognize from the graduating class two years behind me—and who is most definitely not gay. But the girl smiles back, even looking over her shoulder as she passes us. I look at Xanna, grasping how a stranger might see her, hair in bleach-blond (for now) spikes, her heels adding another two inches to her already-substantial five-eight, rock-climbing-solid frame. For some reason, *svelte* is the word that has always come to mind since I met Xanna.

"Xanna," I say, shaking my head. "You're unbelievable."

"I know," she answers, switching her smile to me. "Do you know her? She's cute."

"She's straight."

"Minor detail."

"She's also, or so rumor had it in high school, a little slutty."

"But boy-slutty, I'm sure you mean, yes?" She goes on: "Those are the best kind. Adventurous." She looks back over her shoulder. "I'll have to find her later. But back to you: you, Charlie girl, are every bit as unbelievable as I am, and if this Dean person doesn't think so and act like it, I'm gonna get all Xanna on him, 'kay?"

"Okay," I sigh, but grateful nonetheless for her loyalty.

"Still," she says. "High school boyfriend. Shit, I don't know how I would handle it if Shira showed up."

"As I recall, she did show up, over and over."

"Yeah, it took us like three months to break up. But after all this time? I would definitely be weirded out."

"Do you think you'd get back together?"

"No. Definitely not."

"Not even for one night?"

"Oh, we'd have *sex*. We just wouldn't get back together."

The way she says it, so deadpan, strikes me as hilarious. I'm laughing like I just learned how, and she joins in, and I get worse. Pretty soon neither of us can catch our breath. Kendra returns to us and demands to know what's funny—"Please share the joke with me or I will be very angry at a certain shitty cow"—which makes me laugh even harder. The three of us sound like thirteen-year-olds and I couldn't care less. Tension from avoiding Marina is flowing out of me; I feel like it's been so long since I laughed like this.

Over Kendra's shoulder, a familiar profile turns toward us, the shrieking girls. Wade and I simultaneously recognize each other. He offers me an almost imperceptible chin-lift while seemingly listening to an impossibly beautiful girl in red Uggs and a miniskirt, which I return with a private smile in the middle of girlish laughter. He turns and walks away, one of a crowd, and I watch him go. I gradually stop laughing, but the smile stays on my face.

And then Xanna goes ahead and wins bingo.

When I get home Monday evening Marina and my mom are sitting at the kitchen table. They're clearly waiting for me. Bowls of spaghetti, salad, and sauce with meatballs sit in the center of the table, untouched.

"Charlotte," my mom says.

"Yes?" I'm suspicious as I hoist my books up on the counter. I stopped at the Danborn Public Library after work. HR has told me I have mandatory vacation days coming up that won't carry over into next year. I protested, insisting I'd saved vacation days to roll over in the past, but all I got was something about a new policy. So now I'm facing six days of vacation that I have to use up before the end of the month. Which would be great if I actually had money to go anywhere. So my only escape, sometime in the next three weeks, will be literary.

It's only six; Marina's never around this early. Washing my hands at the sink, I joke, "Is this an intervention?"

"It's not funny, Charlie," Marina says, and it's so obvious that's she's making an effort not to sound condescending. Her voice is tinny and fake, but her face is serious. She doesn't do authentic well. I honestly can't help laughing.

"Then what's the deal?" I say, willingly sitting down. Marina seems annoyed that I'm in such a good mood. My weekend with Kendra and Xanna—not to mention Friday night with Dean—has done me a world of good. Even facing Marina doesn't feel as daunting anymore. I start to fill a plate with pasta and sauce, determined not to let the team they've clearly become get to me. Whatever they want, how bad could it be?

"Charlotte"—my mom looks from me to Marina—"Marina had a suggestion, and I think it's something we ought to give some thought to." Marina starts to speak, but my mom is already continuing. "We're thinking about having group therapy sessions."

My brow furrows. "Like... grief counseling?" It's been a while, but hey, if my mom thinks she needs it, I'm in favor.

"No... for the family. Family counseling."

It slowly registers what she's saying. I reach for a napkin and spread it in my lap. Evenly, I say, "No."

"Charlotte—"

"No. We are not that family."

Marina sits back, triumphant, with a *See what I told you?* expression on her face. I give her a dirty look. "Mom, I'm sorry. But it's too late for that. Marina and I are both adults. We're fine."

"Oh, Charlotte, you're not fine. The two of you barely speak. I want us to be a family."

"We are a family. Just not the one you want."

My mom sits back like she's been slapped. My insides deflate. But what am I supposed to say? In an ideal world, Marina and I would have been real siblings. She would be the protective, loving big sister worthy of my adoration. And as long as we're making things up, my dad would still be here, and I'd have enough family memories to fill a scrapbook. Happy ones that I was part of without trying.

Even though intellectually I know I haven't done anything but tell the truth, I can't face the guilt of looking at my mom. Even at a distance Marina and I at least agree on her—we'd do anything for her. She's a widow, for God's sake. She deserves whatever breaks we can give her. All she'd ever done to me was let me get lost in Marina's shadow, and that wasn't her fault. And I'm over it. I'm twenty-six. I'm fine.

But even as I'm squaring my shoulders, proving how fine I am, I feel my throat start to swell. Is it me, after all? Maybe Marina is trying. Maybe she's ready to apologize, to admit, to explain. I turn to her and take a deep breath. I'm choosing my words when my mom says:

"Can't we become that family again?"

And it's that word. *Again.* "You don't get it, Mom. We never were that family. Not for me. And there's your problem," I say, lifting my chin at Marina, my voice shaking not at all. "You want things to change, change her." And I pick up my fork and start to eat.

As the fighting between Marina and my parents got really bad, I took more and more to the treehouse. For weeks, it seemed like, all my mom and Marina did was scream at each other, but with a book and my headphones I was, quite literally, above the fray.

Then it got quiet. Two weeks after her eighteenth birthday in the spring of her senior year, Marina left home. Ran away, really, with Steve. No one knew where she was. My parents were frantic but because she was eighteen, there was nothing they could do. For two months they didn't hear a word from her, but eventually we found out she'd gotten an apartment with Steve in a bigger town thirty minutes away. It took about a year, but after a come-to-Jesus with her and my mom in a coffee shop near where Marina and Steve lived, the two of them slowly began to rebuild their relationship.

My dad, though, was stricken. Irrevocably damaged, it seemed. He refused to speak to Marina when she finally visited home. For months he'd leave the room whenever she walked in. She was finally in college, Steve long gone, but still Dad acted as if she wasn't there. One day I discovered her with her head on her arms in the kitchen table. She was quiet, but when she lifted her face it was obvious she'd spent a lot of time sobbing. "I've done everything," she said. "What else can I do?"

I didn't answer. She didn't expect me to, never had expected me to. I was fifteen by then, with my own sullen teenage moods, much of which were based, I would realize later, in a black hatred for Marina and what she'd done to our family. To my family.

I didn't go to the treehouse anymore. I can't quite say when I stopped, but I do know that by the time I was entrenched in honors biology and getting my hair just right every morning the treehouse had somehow been bequeathed to Wade, Keith's little brother. I hadn't even noticed. One summer evening while making phone arrangements to meet Kelly at the movies, I caught sight of Wade being chased up the tree by one of his neighborhood friends. He'll kill himself, I thought. Is he old enough to climb that? Someone thought he was, apparently. Once Wade and his friend both disappeared through the trap door, a flag appeared at the top, where it would remain, presumably, until the war was over.

Seeing this, I felt an odd mix of pride, happiness, and jealousy. On the one hand it made me strangely happy to know the treehouse had been passed on. On the other, I didn't like to think about this little kid and his grungy friends hanging out in my space. But that's what we'd been, after all, back then. Little. Grungy. Full of imagination. In the end all I could do was smile at the immovable flag as I pulled on my jacket and turned on the outside and hallway light. I hated to come home to the dark, but lately I was the only one who remembered to put the lights on. When Marina was first gone the lights were always on at night. I could still hear my dad saying: "Claire, make sure the porch light is on," as if my sister could be guided home by light bulb alone. But after they found out she was living with Steve, I think they gave up. They were willing to live in the dark.

seven

Our run tonight is later than usual. It's been getting colder, so our pace is pretty fast. I don't know if it's my anger, the cold, the impending darkness, or Wade's improving speed that's propelling me, but it feels good.

Marina's at home, cooking again. Ever since the spaghetti incident, she's pretty much taken over the kitchen. Marina, of course, sees this from Marina World; she's making an effort, not pushing me out. Like the counseling thing is also her making an effort. That night at dinner, in a last-ditch, award-winning performance, she even started to cry. In the end I gave in: I would go to one therapy session. Satisfied, she wiped her eyes (and collected her Emmy) and called for the appointment.

Suffocated. It's a word I find myself using often regarding Marina. Even thinking about her makes my breath thin. Now that she's around in the evenings, I'm doing everything I can to avoid going home. *Home*, I think with each step. *Home home home.* The word starts to sound strange to me the more I hear it in my mind. I can't spend the next few weeks not wanting to go home.

It's late and dinner's likely ready, but I take a right onto Peter Street instead of staying straight on Pine, which will lead us back to Shasta Street and Wade's and my neighborhood. "You got a destination in mind?" Wade asks, catching up to me.

I just smile and run faster, daring him to follow. We pass the soccer field and then the baseball diamond at Peters Park, and then I slow down and turn into the playground. I haven't been here in years, and they've updated it since. It's barely recognizable, but I know what I'm looking for. Every playground has them. I find them in the middle of a structure that features a curly slide at one end and a couple of balancing bridges on the other.

Wade stops in front of me, hands on his hips and panting. "You're proving a point, aren't you?"

"Who, me?" I pull myself up, once, twice on the monkey bars. Can't make it the third time, and I drop to the ground. "Your turn."

I sit to catch my breath on the bottom of one of the slides. "Or you can do the *girly* hanging thing. Like I have to do the *girly* pushups."

Wade sighs in answer, then hoists himself up effortlessly and does two pull-ups.

"Go ahead, do more," I encourage him.

He drops to the ground. "Nah, I'm good with two."

"No, no." I wave my hand at him. "Go on, show off. You're supposed to."

Wade just laughs and sits next to me on the slide. It's one of the smaller, little-kid ones, wide enough for two.

"Is my feminism lesson over?" he asks.

"It's never over."

Even though I'm looking at straight ahead, I can hear him grinning.

"So when do you leave?" I ask. Wade has plans to drive to Colorado to deliver his friend's car. He told me about it a few weeks ago, that he'd be driving out "sometime in October," as soon as the car was fixed. Dante Lawson—his Colorado friend, known mostly as D-Law, or simply D—left it behind when it broke down during a visit last summer. Or something like that. I've forgotten the details. But I've seen the unfamiliar car in his driveway for a few days now, so I figure the trip is imminent.

"For Colorado? Couple days. Thursday morning, I think."

"Yeah? How long will the drive take?"

"Depends. Two days minimum. More if I stop."

"You can't drive all the way to Colorado without stopping."

"We've done it before."

"For serious?"

He nods and leans back on his hands. "This past summer. We switched off drivers, made it in a day and a half."

"Let me guess. It was in this car, the one you now have had to fix?"

I swear, Wade does at least half of his communication in smiles. He's got a different one for each subtly different expression. "But the whole transmission's been replaced. It'll be fine."

We sit that way for a while, our voices giving way to other sounds—the soccer game on the other end of the field, the wind in the trees, cars bringing people home to dinner in the neighborhood. I'm as at ease with Wade as I am any of my friends. Such a mundane thought, but it surprises me: We're genuinely friends. I've forgotten that my being in high school while he was learning to read is supposed to bother me. By now, nothing about Wade bothers me.

The sun's going down. It's gotten chilly suddenly, the way it does in the fall when winter's inching forward. My sweat is starting to turn cold, which I hate. I know we have to stand up and run home soon, but I like being here with Wade on the slide, the sounds of lives being lived around us. It's certainly better than the alternative.

"What?"

I must have sighed without realizing it. "Nothing," I answer. "Just my freaking sister." I half-laugh. "I'm staying out late on purpose to avoid going home."

He checks his phone, and it occurs to me I'm dragging him along on my own whim. "I'm sorry. We should get going. Do you need to be somewhere?"

"Nah. I mean, I do, but not yet. I still have a few."

"Thanks for hanging," I say, feeling selfish. "What do you have going on tonight?"

"Just meeting someone."

I smile. "A girl? Do you have a girlfriend I haven't heard about?"

"Not really." He shrugs. "Do you know Lindsay Linstrom?"

I shake my head. "Related to Steve?"

"Yeah, she graduated a couple years ahead of me."

"Is that the girl you were with at Danborn Day?" I don't know what makes me say this. I remember her—blonde and sinewy. Fucking *luminous*.

He looks at me again. "Yeah. I saw you there, too, with your friends."

"Why didn't you say hi?"

"You were otherwise engaged," he deadpans. "Why didn't *you* say hi?"

"*You* were otherwise engaged."

"Steve's friends with Keith," it occurs to me to remind him. And then I hear myself say: "And... Dean."

"Dean Carson?"

"Yeah. We... used to go out."

"I remember."

It's funny, I've gone on ad nauseam to him about my dad and Marina—topics I barely broach with Kendra—and yet Dean, who has been filling my mind incessantly, has been absent from our conversation. I don't know why I haven't mentioned him, and it's this very realization and the fact that I can't explain it that makes the words fall out of my mouth.

"I've been sort of seeing him." If sleeping with him constitutes seeing.

"Yeah?"

I nod. I lean forward, pushing the wood chips on the ground around with my fingers.

"What's that like?" He clarifies: "Getting back together with an ex."

"We're not back together. But it's... familiar." We've had one other evening together, after the last time Wade and I ran. We'd run unexpectedly hard, and at one point Wade stopped to remove his long-sleeved T-shirt, tying it around his waist and leaving only a tank top. He removed his baseball cap to shake out his hair, then stuffed as much as he could back under it. "What?"

Which is how I knew I was staring.

I texted Dean when I got home. Later on, at his house, we happened across *Good Will Hunting*—just before the Harvard bar scene—and by the time Chuckie was chastising Will by the pickup for wasting his talent, we were back in Dean's bedroom replaying scenes from our misspent youth.

"Yet different," I add. "It's like I'm getting to know him all over again." Some things, like the under-the-eyelashes look that still fires straight into me, are right out of senior year. And the feel of his hands, the way he runs them up my back and over my shoulders with a special kind of thumb pressure, is like a fingerprint on my soul. But two sexual encounters with him have also made it clear that he's forgotten a few key things.

"Did things end well when you broke up?"

I shrug. "Do any relationships end well?"

He gives me a look that says *touché*.

"And you and Lindsay?"

"Me and Lindsay?"

80

"Is she your girlfriend?" *And why I haven't I heard about her?* I regret the question instantly, but he answers gamely enough.

"Nah. We're just hanging out."

"Such a guy thing to say," I tease. But I'm thrown, too. Is that what Dean and I are doing? 'Hanging out'?

"Why? She's hanging out, too. It works for both of us."

"You don't do relationships?"

"Me?" He looks at me. "I do relationships."

I don't know if it's his words, his tone, or the look with which he delivers both, but I can't hold his gaze. I feel thigh-deep in none-of-my-business territory. Partly to cover my awkwardness, I turn towards the wind and plunge forward. "Dean was my relationship." I think of Cam, of others, of forgettable sex and forgettable faces. "He mattered."

He nods. "I've got one of those. I don't think she was my 'person,' as you girls like to say"—he smiles to let me know he's joking—"or at least I don't anymore. But it mattered."

"And did it end... badly?"

He nods. I wait for him to go on. He doesn't.

"Our breakup came out of nowhere," I continue. "I was kind of blindsided. But I always felt..." I try to figure out what I'm even thinking, how to put the images and feelings into language that doesn't try too hard to be what I want. "I just always had... faith, I guess. That we weren't done. Like we were just... interrupted."

Sitting on a slide in the middle of Peters Park, it hits me. That's why I'm here, in Danborn. Why Dean's here. And why it never worked out with anyone else. I've been waiting for Dean to come back. The story—our story—stopped in the middle.

"He still lives at home," I go on. "With his parents. I mean, not still. Again." On the *Good Will Hunting* night, hearing his parents—whom I have yet to greet, even though I knew them quite well back in the day—moving around upstairs was unsettling. I even started to ask Dean about his plans to live somewhere that wasn't under his parents' roof, but he thought I was talking about my own plans and it seemed too complicated to correct.

Dean's going to Chicago this weekend. When he told me I half-hoped he'd invite me to come along, even as I wasn't sure if I wanted to go. I certainly didn't have the money. I suspect that what I really wanted was simply to get out of my house.

I laugh in spite of myself. "I'm sorry. Here I am, killing time, forcing teenage boys to stay out late with me because I can't bear to go home and there's nowhere else to go."

"Teenage boys," Wade scoffs.

We're silent, dark falling around us. The games next to us have ended, and it's just me, Wade, and the wind.

I'm about to stand and suggest heading home when Wade suddenly says, as if confirming, "So you don't really want to be home right now."

"Not really."

"So don't be."

"Dude. I can't, like, check into a hotel."

"*Dude.*" He smiles. "I mean, come with me. I could use the company."

At first I have no idea what he's talking about. Then I get it. "To Colorado?"

"You have to take vacation, right? How were you planning to spend that time?"

I shrug. "Camped out in the library, reading? Watching *The Bachelor*?" I grab his eyes with mine. "Just kidding. I don't watch *The Bachelor*."

"Liar."

"I don't," I say, lying. "No, what I'm actually going to do is avoid my sister and hang with Kendra and Xanna and encourage Dean to get his own place so I don't end up meeting his parents for the first time in however-many years while doing the walk of shame. And go running. Except not with you," I add, suddenly realizing this is true. "Because you'll be gone."

Wow. He's told me he's eventually moving back to Colorado. It hits me that when he does, I'm going to miss him. More than I would have realized.

"So come with me."

I start, thinking maybe I spoke out loud. But no, I didn't, because he goes on. "Come on, take a ride. You ever been cross country?" He shakes his head at my skeptical look. "You have no idea what's out there, holed up in New England."

He's talking like he's forty and I'm a wide-eyed child. "And I suppose you do," I say, my tone clipped. He shrugs. More defensively than I'd like, I say, "I've traveled."

"Where besides Florida and spring break in Mexico?" He answers my glare by bumping my shoulder with his. "So come on. It'll do you good."

"But what would—" *What would people say?* I want to ask. But that would be implying that whatever we're doing is worth talking about. Which it isn't. Even though a shoulder-bump from him doesn't feel like a shoulder-bump from anyone else.

"What would... I do all day?"

"Same as me. Watch the scenery. Listen to music. Podcasts. Audiobooks. Have engaging conversations."

"You'd be talking if I weren't there?"

"Maybe. You never know. That's why you have to come. Prove I'm not one of those people."

"And to keep you company."

He shrugs. "And because you need it."

"I need it." I'm just repeating him, not agreeing. "And what is 'it,' exactly, that I need?"

"Something that doesn't remind you of anything."

eight

"Just do it!"

"Arrgggh!"

"Trust me!"

I touch my tongue to the roof of my mouth, and miraculously, the freeze in my throat is lessened.

"Wow," I say when I can speak. "That really works."

Wade takes a sip of his own Slurpee. "I know it does. That's why I told you to do it."

Oh, the arrogance. I make a face at him, and he sticks out his chemically blue tongue at me. Mine is similarly artificially colored—cherry red.

Seven hours into our drive to Colorado, and I'm still a little surprised I'm here, sharing the close quarters of a well-used Volkswagen Cabriolet for the next two days. From the get-go, I didn't intend to come. Wade didn't ask me again after the park, on the slide, when I told him "Thanks, but no thanks" before we ran home. Which I appreciated. But it also made me wonder about it all the more.

Over the next couple of days, I thought it through. Why couldn't I go? What was the real deal? Was I embarrassed? Was I worried about what he would think? Was I worried about what I would do? He had never implied anything that wasn't respectful of our friendship, and I believed firmly that he deserved the same from me.

But still. We were still a guy and a girl, and when the guy and the girl go on a road trip together... I mean, we've all seen *When Harry Met Sally...* on AMC.

And—I have to give voice to this thought—it's possible I was flattering myself unnecessarily. It was entirely probable that he was not interested in me in that way, *would* never be interested in me in that way.

After hemming and hawing and turning every possible permutation of the situation over in my head, I landed on the issue that bothered me the most. I was acting as if I needed some sort of permission—from whom or what I did not know— to be friends with him.

I argued with myself over the next two days. As I unloaded the dishwasher after dinner, drying the plastic cups that infuriatingly never seemed to dry on their own, I objectively considered the simple appearance of my taking such a trip. If one of my friends had embarked on a cross-country road trip with a guy seven years younger than her, what would I think? Would I think she had a problem? Would I think she was delusional?

Would I envy her?

Times like this, faced with a decision I couldn't get past, I'd call Kendra. But ever since Dean and I got together I've been, well, not avoiding her necessarily, but not exactly seeking her out either. If I asked her advice, she'd probably just tell me to go to steer me off the Dean trajectory—which would annoy me enough to stay home.

Had Wade asked me more than once, I would have said an easy no. But he didn't. I was forced to be alone with my own thoughts. Which meant facing this: I didn't want to ask Kendra about it because I didn't want to end up not going because of it.

Which meant, unfortunately, that I wanted to go.

Still, it wasn't as simple as just saying yes. I also would have to let people know where I was going. My family I could fudge with, but there was no way I could skip telling Kendra. And then we were back to me dismissing the whole idea.

So it was decided. I wasn't going.

Then, Wednesday afternoon, Kendra texted me: *Last-minute Cape long weekend with my brother. Leaving tomorrow after work! You have time off, right? Come with?*

I took so long thinking of a reply she texted again:

Bueller? If you don't go I'll have to ask Xanna and spend the weekend in P-town.

Wish I could, I texted back. *Got some stuff to do this week. Kiss a girl for me!*

We pulled out of Wade's driveway in the dark at 4:30 in the morning. He assured me that if nothing went wrong, we'd make Iowa sometime tonight. Google Maps told me that meant sixteen hours of driving. He'd have to drive like a crazy person.

But I'd signed up for this maniacal journey, hadn't I? I settled back, wondering how my sudden absence had been taken. *Gone to the Cape with Kendra*, read the note I'd stuck on the fridge for my mom and Marina to wake up to. *Back Monday.*

Part of me hated that I had to account for my absence—I was twenty-six years old, for God's sake—but that part was canceled out by the fact that I was lying. To my mom, to my sister (well, not that that bothered me), to Kendra. And, of course, to Dean, whom I didn't tell at all.

We're on the very edge of western Pennsylvania—a state we seem to have been in for days—when, between sips of my Slurpee, I realize that absolutely no one knows that I've left the state, or that I'm about to leave the time zone. I share this with Wade.

"You didn't tell anyone?"

"I told my mom I was going down the Cape with Kendra for the weekend."

"You lied? Why?"

I shrug. "People get ideas. I don't want to the be the subject of anyone's speculation."

Thankfully, he lets that go. I sit back and marvel, yet again, at the beauty of western Pennsylvania. The rich foliage flies by on either side of the interstate. We're not all that far from Massachusetts. I've always thought of Pennsylvania as a coastal state, which is of course illogical. How did I never know it was so vast, so pretty?

I roll down the window to get a sense of the temperature outside, but roll it back up quickly when my hair wraps around my face. I didn't feel like wrestling with the straightener this morning, so my hair's a little haywire, random waves in full force. I smooth it down best I can under a baseball cap.

"Finally," I say as we flash by a sign indicating the Ohio state line is just ahead. "This state is gigantic."

"I told you. It's a whole big world out there."

He's baiting me, but I don't rise. I've learned patience with Wade, and payback's a bitch.

Just since dawn, I've learned a few new things about him. Car rides will do that. Like, he's a quoter. I'd seen bits and pieces of this while running or in the treehouse, but the confines of the Cabriolet reveal just how far gone he is. He's like a walking Trivial Pursuit game. Movies, TV, books. Obscure songs I've never heard of.

"They're not that obscure," he counters when I say as much to him.

"Well, I've never heard of any of them."

"Charlie, don't take this the wrong way"—I stare at him, prepared to take whatever he says exactly the way I like—"but it's not like your music tastes are that wide."

"There's more to life than music," I say mock-haughtily. Wade just grins. As far as he's concerned, for every scene in life there is a song lyric equal to the occasion.

Although I'll never admit it to him, I secretly sort of like it. I've pretty much relied on the radio for the soundtrack of my life. Sometimes, when a lyric Wade quotes that I don't recognize remains stuck in my head, I Google it in the privacy of my room. I don't always come up with anything substantial, but often I do. Sometimes I even like it enough to download the song from iTunes, adding it to a growing playlist I've called *Hunter*.

The most unfair part of his savant-like references is that he doesn't stick to one genre or time period. Even straight-up pop culture is ripe for sampling. He tells me again that he's a pop culture junkie. I find that odd. It seems to go against who he is. Or who he says he is.

He dismisses the notion with a shrug. "I like pop culture."

"You hate pop culture."

"Not true. I don't particularly engage in pop culture, nor do I seek it out, but I enjoy it."

"You enjoy ridiculing it."

He considers that. "Noooooooooo... it's more like, it's the fabric of who the society is, isn't it? And I like knowing where I fit in that, even if it's off to the side."

"Left of center?"

He starts singing a song about how if I want him, I can find him. I roll my eyes.

Away from familiar eyes and unasked questions, I'm looser. I feel myself unwinding, relaxing into my body in a way that's new to me. I'm barefoot—and thankful my last pedicure isn't too far in the past—sitting Indian-style on the passenger seat for much of the ride. As the miles of Ohio and Illinois slip by and we exchange stories of teacher crushes and embarrassing cafeteria moments, one thought washes over me, clear as the western skyline we're chasing: I could be having these conversations with anyone. Absolutely anyone. But I'm glad that it's him.

Wade fills me in on his Colorado family. His Dad has lived there since he and Marla, his mom, split up when he was two. Wade moved when he was twelve, the summer after sixth grade.

"Was it hard, starting a new school in a new state?" I've lived in Massachusetts my whole life; two of my best friends are from elementary school. The time zone change alone would screw me up.

"It wasn't great," he allows. "But I learned to love it. I can't imagine living anywhere else."

His dad was born and raised there. After the divorce from Wade's mom, he moved back and married his high-school sweetheart, Jess. They have a daughter, Fiona, who's nine.

"Your dad's married to his high-school girlfriend?"

"Now he is."

I'm amazed I don't know this. "Is that where we're staying?"

"Yep. With my dad and Jess and Fiona."

"Your sister."

"Yep."

Till now, I admit, I haven't paid much attention to the details of the trip. All I knew was that Wade assured me everything was "covered"—even my return flight home, which he dismissed with a wave of his hand and something about his dad's airline points. It's so crazy to think of Wade having a whole other family half a country away. A father, a stepmother, a little sister. Even a dog. American standard.

"How does... do your mom and dad get along?"

"Now they do. It took a long time." He smiles ruefully. "I think I was the result of a last-ditch effort."

I remember this. Or at least, Wade being a baby, and their dad being there in the beginning—and then not. I never thought to ask questions back then, I guess. What was was what was.

"But it sucked for a while," Wade goes on, "especially after I moved. My mom was not happy."

"Why not?"

He shrugs. "She didn't want me to go."

"You moved across the country against your mom's wishes?" I couldn't imagine—can't imagine—openly defying my mom like that. Or my dad, back then. I'm sort of impressed, awed really, that Wade made a permanent decision like that at such an early age, especially knowing the potential repercussions.

He shrugs. "I was an angsty twelve-year-old. I didn't like my stepdad telling me what to do. Figured it had to be better with my real dad."

"Was it?"

"Yes and no. I mean, it was, but not for the reasons I thought. Plus I wanted to see Fiona grow up, have her have a big brother. It wasn't the best at first, but I learned to live with it. In the end, it was the right thing to do."

We both fall silent. I steal a look at his profile, his right hand on the wheel, his left tapping his thigh in time with the music, low, on the radio. He's unfolding himself before me, willingly, unselfconsciously. I want to speak, but none of my thoughts are things I can say. The words I finally choose, after a while, are neutral and lame: "I can't believe I didn't know any of this about you."

"I'm like an onion," he says mock-poetically, adjusting his rearview.

"Oh yes," I say, all innocence and sarcasm—and relief. "Layers of mystery."

Wade was right about his mad driving skills. At half-past midnight we make it over the Iowa border to the hotel we reserved that afternoon. He drove *hard*. And we stopped only when necessary—gas, meals, bathroom, usually all at the same time. Wade promised he wouldn't drive any longer than he knew he could stay awake, chugging iced coffee during the last few hours (and adding in a few extra side-of-the-road bathroom breaks in the process, which were... awkward). I've already fallen asleep twice. By the time we check into the hotel, I'm dozing on my feet, overnight bag in hand, as I hear Wade through a fog correcting the clerk, no, we requested a room with two queen beds, not one king.

"I'm sorry, we have a king on the reservation."

"Well, can we switch?"

A bland smile. "I'm sorry, sir, that's all that's left."

Wade and I exchange a look. Okay, it's awkward. But king beds are ginormous.

Our room is on the third floor. I immediately disappear into the bathroom to brush my teeth, throw my hair up in a ponytail, and change into sleepwear (yoga pants and a T-shirt). "Okay for me to come out?" I ask through the door.

"Just a sec," he says. "Okay, all good."

He's pulling on a Colorado State University T-shirt when I come out. "Go Rams," I say. He taught me many CSU football cheers on the ride.

We gingerly step around each other in the small space. "Want to just pick a side?" he suggests.

"Sure." I throw the comforter on the floor (have you *seen* those hidden-camera shows about how gross hotel room beds are?), get into bed on the far left side, and pull the sheets up. You could fit three other people between me and the opposite edge of the bed. Five minutes later, when Wade comes out of the bathroom, I'm pretending to be asleep.

All through my extra-long shower the next morning, I funnel all my mental effort into shaving. Summer's end means I've been lax in the hair removal, so I decide to correct that. Down and up the left leg. Down, then up. Why the hell don't I wax? Down, then up, gingerly navigating the ankle bones I used to slice as a novice pre-teen. *Don't think,* I recite to myself. *Don't think. Don't think. Don't think don't think don't think—*

I'm nineteen.

I've accepted that Wade's nothing like whom I've taken him for, but really, whom have I taken him for? I'm not sure I've even thought about him in seven or eight years, except perhaps as an extension of Keith, and then only in passing. The last time I saw him—not that I remember it, and I certainly have no recollection of him being at my dad's funeral—he couldn't have been older than eleven or twelve. What grade was that? Sixth, probably, before the summer he moved. Hardly a person at all, more just the too-old-to-be-cute next-door neighbor who made the standard amount of adolescent boy noise. He existed; that was it.

He was your dad, too.

Next, armpits. A light touch. I know I should be at least slightly uncomfortable around him, and the fact that I'm not is disquieting. He was in high school less than two years ago; I'm staring down my ten-year reunion. When he was born, I was already riding my bike and learning to multiply.

I broke them here.

Bikini line. I don't wax here because I'm not a masochist. I should use a hair remover, but I never remember when the hair is long enough. I only remember after I shave.

Something that doesn't remind you of anything.

Why the hell is there hair on my stomach? I swear that's never been there before. A month ago, I might not have been able to pick Wade out of a lineup. Now there's hardly anything about him that I can't recall in razor-sharp (heh) detail. This disturbs me, as does my reluctant acceptance that he seems to read my mind. Not even just that; he knows my thoughts before I do. Too fucking often. That's disquieting too.

I slam the shower off. I fixate on drying my body, my feet, my back, my legs. I bend over to towel-dry my hair upside-down, a habit formed long ago in the bedroom I sleep in now in Danborn. My mind is blank, I'm willing it to be so, but then I flip my head up and catch my reflection in the mirror, and I can't get away. There it is, right in front of me.

His hipbones.

When we've taken to the streets of Danborn together I've managed to ignore him in his running clothes, mainly by not looking at him or by keeping my glances brief and sweeping. But last night, leaving the bathroom, just before I made my stupid Rams comment, my eyes caught the slice of flesh under the bottom of his shirt. In the longest nanosecond ever I took it all in: the lightly tanned smooth skin. His navel and the sliver of hair below it. The sleek muscling of his torso. And, just above the waistband of low-slung shorts, on either side of that taut stomach, his hipbones. The glorious jut of his hipbones.

Then the shirt fell.

And then, lying awake next to him, far enough that my longest reach couldn't touch him. Hearing him breathe. Knowing those hipbones were there.

Not quite dry, I shove myself into my clothes. This will not do at *all.*

91

nine

I spot the familiar sign in North Platte, Nebraska. "Starbucks!" I thump Wade on the shoulder from the back seat, where, until five minutes ago, I've been sleeping.

"You don't drink Starbucks," Wade reminds me.

"I do in Nebraska," I decide. "It's like being in the desert and seeing water. Desperation breeds tolerance."

"I'm sure the Nebraskans would love to hear that."

"Remind me what state is next?" I ask Wade as we cross the parking lot, already savoring the aroma.

"Colorado," he says, yawning. "Actually, Wyoming, because we have to drive through Cheyenne."

My eyebrows shoot up. "Colorado borders Wyoming?"

He shakes his head. "Such a coastal mentality."

"Such a coastal mentality," I mimic. "I'm learning, okay? Leave me to my revelations. They won't get in your way, I swear."

I get a caramel macchiato and Wade gets plain old coffee. "You have to do it up in Starbucks," I stage-whisper. "Your order has to have at least seven syllables."

He grins, handing a ten to the barista. We're switching off paying for refreshments. He tells me he needs to use the restroom and I deliberately turn away as he exits.

I'm a little punchy. It's been a tense day. My post-shower admission opened even more floodgates to what is clearly my very dirty mind, putting my imagination into overdrive. As a diversion I've been reading, listening to my music through earbuds, and thinking fervently about Dean. I'm both thankful the tension exists only in my head and comforted yet again by the certainty that despite all evidence otherwise, Wade truly cannot read my mind. But knowing he's dammed off from my lascivious thoughts doesn't do anything to stem their tide. I should clarify: It's not like the fantasies are perverted. In the grand scheme, they'd barely qualify as PG-13. *I want to kiss him. His hair is probably soft. How would his leg muscles feel against mine?* But the fact that they involve a nineteen-year-old—that alone makes them feel illicit.

On my own visit to the restroom, I do the math. Nine-thirty PM in Boston, which means eight-thirty in Chicago. Dean should be there by now.

How goes it? I text.

I use the restroom and then wait, but he doesn't text back. *Talk later,* I type, hating myself a little bit.

I find Wade leaning against the hood of his car, checking his phone. "How much longer do we have?" I lean on the car next to him, just far enough not to touch.

"Three hours till Cheyenne, then less than an hour after that to Fort Collins."

"So four hours." I take a dramatic breath. "We're fortified with caffeine. Let's do this."

It's pitch black when we pull into a driveway later that night. Wade stops, peering through the windshield at whatever is in front of us. "You gotta be kidding me," he mutters. "Have they not heard of lights?"

He leads me through the blackness to a side door—"Watch your step, it goes up here"—into what feels like a kitchen. We both instinctively feel for a light switch on the wall. Our hands get in each other's way, and I snatch my fingers back as light floods the room.

His face, suddenly illuminated, is just inches away. Whatever he sees on mine makes him whisper, "What?"

Hearing someone whisper for the first time is like hearing the first time they sing. Or a first kiss.

In a movie, we *would* kiss now. He'd reach for my cheek, gazes would drop to our slightly parted lips, and we'd tentatively meet in the middle, exploratory and shy at first, then bolder as our mouths relaxed against each other and our tongues got involved. That would be the cliché, audience-pleasing thing to do. But it's not a movie, and he's nineteen and

I'm twenty-six and I know better, and he probably does too, and he's not my person anyway. So I step further into the kitchen and embrace the awkward, asking him where I'm sleeping. He shows me and points out the bathroom. I thank him and don't even say good night before I'm gone, shutting the door on whatever it is between us.

I wake with a fully-formed thought in my head. *I'm in Colorado.* The name feels exotic, as if it's not simply a state in the union, but another state of mind.

I find my glasses and slide them on. The half-light of Saturday morning reveals a dusty hardwood floor full of cardboard boxes, sports equipment, stacked and empty beer bottles, and, inexplicably, a birdcage. The only piece of furniture is the bed I'm sleeping on, presumably Wade's. This is his room, the one he was supposed to be living in this semester, before whatever happened that made him head back to Danborn.

At home it's ten, but here it's eight. I am wide awake. My phone is dead; I forgot to charge it overnight. I dig in my bag for my charger, but my attention snags on my running clothes and sneakers, untouched since Boston.

I have no idea where I'm going. I'm tempted to just run wherever the wind takes me, but with my phone sitting on the charger back in the house, I shouldn't risk getting lost. If I try to keep my route reasonably circular I should find my way back. I take a right out of the driveway, making a note to memorize the street name at the first intersection.

The morning is frosty, but the sun has a promising edge of warmth to it. Perfectly October. It feels good to run. I take another right, onto a wider, two-lane street that has a much narrower lane painted down each side—like the width of a walkway. Is it a walking lane? No, there's also a sidewalk. Maybe that's where I'm supposed to run. I keep to the lane.

The elevation is noticeable right off. Barely half a mile and I'm winded. I take a left onto a less busy street lined with trees and houses with basketball hoops in the driveway and recycling containers on the sidewalk. The Colorado air may be thin, but it's still glorious.

It occurs to me that I feel fantastic.

I've been thinking about it. Taking this trip with Wade is the most spontaneous thing I've done in a long time. Maybe ever. I

94

like it. I feel brave and daring and not like myself. All through my adult life I've been mired by security, by an addiction to the familiar—familiar negatives as well as positives. Case in point: my relationship with Cam. I was restless, but I just plodded on with my life, because it wasn't in me to shake things up.

But maybe spontaneity suits me. I should take advantage of it more often. Beyond the physical high, I feel emotionally empty—the good kind of empty. I am ready for life in a way I've always balked at. Kendra says I've changed since high school, and if I'm honest, I've never fully believed her. Maybe I have.

I take another left, and every thought slithers out of me except what's straight ahead. The trees have dropped off, the scenery has suddenly opened up, and there, in front of me, against a backdrop of impossible blue, are the mountains.

I slow to a walk, hardly aware of it. The mountains stretch as far as I can see from left to right, across the immense cloudless glass expanse of the sky. It was so dark when we drove in, I didn't see anything beyond traffic lights and gas stations. Now the craggy peaks are so close I feel like they could be part of me if only I could reach them. I begin running again, my pace faster and faster, towards the west.

An hour later I'm back at the house with coffee from a shop I found a couple streets over. I find Wade in the kitchen, looking as if he just woke up, barefoot under the frayed cuffs of his jeans. *His feet. Even his feet are cute.*

"I've already gone for a run," I tell him, handing him one of the coffees. His thanks is so grateful and surprised, I look away. "And, um, hello? Why didn't you tell me?"

His look is quizzical as I gesture to the window. "Mountains!"

"Oh yeah." He smiles sleepily and sips his coffee. "You're in Colorado."

"In the mountains! They're right there! Out the front door!"

"What's out the front door?" a dark-haired guy asks, coming in behind me.

I spin around. "Mountains!" I say accusingly. He looks a little frightened.

"This is Seth," Wade tells me. "Charlie, Seth."

Seth looks at Wade, who shrugs and says, "She likes the mountains."

The living room picture window frames the western landscape perfectly. I stand in front of it and marvel. "This is insane."

"Those are just the foothills," Seth says between sips of orange juice from the carton.

"They get bigger?" I say. "Jesus. And you live here. You can see this *every day*. From your *house*."

I'm still looking out the window, but gather that Seth is in need of an explanation, because Wade offers one. "Charlie's my neighbor," he says. "She drove with me out here, because she needed to get out of the house."

"Clearly," Seth says, eyeing me.

Seth's hair is the biggest thing about him. It's black and bushy and while I watch, he tames it back into a ponytail. The rest of him is slight and skinny. The jeans he's wearing are definitely smaller than any I own.

I hear thumping on the stairs and another guy appears in the kitchen, freshly showered and not nearly as disheveled as Seth. His hair is wet, but it looks red, and he has hardly any of it. "My man," he says to Wade, knuckle-bumping him. "I forgot you were bringing back the beater."

This is Dante, I realize. Otherwise known as D-Law, Wade's first roommate at CSU.

"You around for a while, man?" D asks Wade.

"Flying back Sunday."

"Staying with your dad?"

"Yeah."

"Cool, I'll catch you there." He's got his bike helmet in his hand, and I have a flash of Cal, Marina's bike-riding boyfriend. "Where's Jacko?" D asks Seth, turning back.

Seth, fiddling with his phone, rolls his eyes. "Don't even."

"Shit. He up there again?"

"Up where?" Wade asks.

"Don't *even*," Seth says, eyes still on his phone.

"D?"

D indicates the window with a tilt of his head.

"He's in the backyard?"

Seth leaves the room, shaking his head.

Jacko—the fourth guy on the lease, I learn—is indeed in the backyard. "He's in the tree," D explains.

We all peer out the window. Sure enough, across the backyard, about forty feet up, there does certainly seem to be a person. I see legs in jeans and green Chucks.

96

"Christ, how long has he been there?" Wade asks.

"Well, he came down to sleep. I hoped that was the end of it."

"This isn't about Kayla, is it?" Wade asks.

The look on D's face says it is, indeed, all about Kayla. "She ended it maybe Thursday? He's been up there ever since."

"Does he eat?" I ask, still processing. The guy lives in the *tree*?

"Not really," D tells me. "But he does drink."

College houses. I remember now. Somehow my standards have changed without my noticing. This bathroom doesn't seem to have a close relationship with Clorox wipes, though I do find some under the sink. I wipe down the shower before stepping in, grateful we'll be spending tonight in a real, grown-up residence.

I'm coming downstairs, shouldering my overnight bag, when I hear voices from outside. I stay in the kitchen, not sure if I should interrupt.

"Come over for dinner tonight," Wade is saying. "Dad and Jess'll love it. I'd invite Jacko, too, but..." I imagine them both looking up at the tree.

"Fucking Kayla," D says.

I'm about to step outside when D goes on. "Oh shit, man, that reminds me. Jordan came by. Couple days ago."

I don't hear Wade's response, but D answers, "She left something for you. It's in my room." Another unintelligible response. "Well, it's there if you want it."

I start to back away.

"So what's the deal with her? You guys together?"

Wade must have stepped closer to the door, because his voice is so loud I'm startled. "Nah. We're friends. She lives next door to my mom."

I assumed they were still talking about Jordan. But *her*, it seems, is *me*.

"She's seeing someone anyway."

I don't hear D's reply, just Wade saying "Shut up" with a smile wrapped around it.

"All right man, I'm heading out. Just gotta get the master his breakfast." I disappear up the stairs, then reenter. Wade and I watch together as D crosses the yard and deposits a bottle of beer in what I now identify as a Tupperware-like container attached to a rope. The container starts to rise, and thirty seconds later Jacko retrieves the beer, takes a swig, and leans back against the tree.

I guess he's got his own bottle opener.

"Jacko's a weird guy," Wade tells me on the way to his dad's. "But weird in a good way, you know? I like him a lot. He's from Tennessee, and he's brilliant, scientifically anyways. Total free ride at CSU. He and I get along really well. He's the kind of guy you feel like you've always known."

"He's also the kind of guy who lives in a tree."

"True. But he's pretty sensitive. He was really into Kayla."

"So he moves into a tree?"

Wade shrugs. "That's Jacko. And knowing him, once he comes down, he'll be fine, and we won't hear about it again."

"It's just... I mean, you have to admit that's weird."

"I don't know," Wade says, turning on his left blinker. "Whatever works, you know?"

Something about the way he says it makes me search my mind for something familiar. Of course. Wasn't I the same? Didn't I turn to the treehouse when things got rough?

"Tree therapy," I say, hoping Wade will get it without my having to explain.

The way he smiles to himself says he does.

ten

Wade's dad's house is on the north (and more established, I'm told) side of town, at the end of what I would call a dead end but here is called a cul-de-sac. Before we're even stopped at the end of the long driveway, a skinny, bespectacled girl is running out of the house.

"WADE!" she screams, barely waiting till Wade's out of the car before throwing herself against him. He takes her attack like he's used to it. "Take it easy, Fee," he says and kisses her on the top of the head.

Fiona is followed by a big furry thing that throws itself against Wade with even more enthusiasm than Fiona, which I didn't think was possible. "Hey Burton," Wade says, bending down and hugging the dog's neck.

"How you been, buddy? You miss me?" Burton's entire body is quivering with excitement. Wade hasn't lowered his voice, but this still feels private, like I'm intruding just by witnessing it.

"Who are you?" Fiona is looking at me with undisguised suspicion. Good grief. She's *taller* than me. She turns to Wade. "Where's Jordan?"

My face flames. Wade looks at me apologetically. "Fiona, this is Charlie. Charlie, Fiona."

She shakes my hand primly. "That's a boy's name."

"Well." I swallow. "Maybe you should call me Charlotte."

"No, I like Charlie. Mom's going to make enchiladas," she tells Wade, apparently done with me. "And I'm doing the guacamole. I bought eight limes."

99

"Sounds perfect," Wade tells her. "D-Law's coming to dinner, too. Do you know where your mom set us up to stay?"

"No clue," she says, running ahead to the house. "Mom, Wade's here! He says D's coming to dinner. And he brought a girl and it's not Jordan!"

We stand watching her for a minute. "I'm sorry," Wade says, absently scratching the dog's neck next to him. "I didn't even consider that."

"The relationship that mattered?" I say, and for a moment he looks taken aback.

"Yeah," he answers, holding my gaze for so long I want to look away. "That one."

We didn't want him to drive." Jess, Wade's stepmom, hands me a dripping knife to dry. "He's a maniac when it comes to making good time. Comes by it honestly," she adds, sounding resigned.

"It *was* a little scary," I admit.

There's already a load of dishes in the dishwasher; we're washing the overflow and the larger pots and pans, and the knives that need to be hand-washed. Dinner was a full Mexican smorgasbord—the best I've ever had.

"But I'm glad you made it." Jess smiles at me. "So do you remember Wade from way back?"

Over dinner we established I was Wade's neighbor—his *just-friends* neighbor, Fiona stressed no fewer than four times—and that I had known his family my whole life. Damon, his dad, was delighted I'd come along and told the table he remembered me when I was "this high," which wasn't embarrassing at all. I spent the whole dinner trying not to stare at him. It's true I had known him before, but none of the details had stuck. He was bigger than Wade, slightly stockier and more weathered, and he had a beard. But other than that, he and Wade could be twins. Damon has Wade's way of half-grinning, his bluer-than-blue eyes, his unruly sandy hair. I felt like I knew him well instantly, recognizing Wade in his laugh, his voice, even the lines around his eyes, as yet invisible on Wade's face. Watching them from behind as they walked across the yard together after dinner, flanked by Burton running circles around them, was eerie.

"Sort of," I say to Jess. "I'm—I'm a few years older than him, so I remember him more as a kid."

"That's right," she says, as if suddenly making the connection. "You're closer to Keith's age, aren't you?"

"Yeah. Keith and I went to school together."

Keith, I have learned, doesn't come out to visit nearly as much as his dad wished he did. "He's a city boy," Jess tells me. "We keep inviting him, but he's pretty busy."

"I'm sorry," I say, meaning it.

"So am I," Jess answers in the same tone. "But he's a different kid than Wade. Or was. He had a different experience, you know? He was ten when his dad moved out. He was angry. And although Damon and I didn't get together—well, we didn't get back together—until he moved back here, he didn't handle our relationship well, or our marriage." She sighs. "Divorce is tough. On everyone."

"Wade said you were together in high school."

"We were," she says, like *Can you believe that?* "It wasn't your typical situation, though." Her features turn thoughtful, like she's remembering.

Which makes me wonder what *is* your typical situation. When she doesn't elaborate, instead of asking for details they way I want to—I can only be so nosy—I say, "That's incredible. But why did Keith have such a hard time with you? I mean, his mom remarried too."

"She did," Jess says. "But our wedding was first. I'm sure it felt fast to him. And we had our history, which probably didn't look good."

"Still," I say. "People grow up."

"Yeah. They do." She looks down at me—she's got to be at least five-ten; it's clear where Fiona gets her height—and smiles.

I pick up a dripping knife and carefully run the washcloth over it. "My ex was Keith's best friend, so I spent a lot of time with him. In high school."

"Dean, you mean? We've met him a few times. Really nice guy. Very polite."

She laughs, and I join her. "He's still nice," I say. "He moved back home, actually. We're sort of... revisiting things." Why am I telling her all this?

"Oooooh," she says girlishly. "There's nothing quite like that high school boy, is there?" She looks out the window, where Wade and Damon are leaning over a car's open hood, Damon's hand on Wade's shoulder, Burton sitting patiently next to them.

No, I think. *There isn't.*

At Jess's suggestion, after dinner we all squeeze into Damon's Expedition. "You have to show Charlie Old Town or she's going to think Fort Collins doesn't have any life to it." Old Town is the city's downtown—nothing like Boston but way bigger than, say, Danborn Square.

"Main Street in Disneyland is based on Old Town," Fiona announces. She's next to Wade—this will be her theme for the rest of the night—in the backseat. On her other side is D, and I'm next to him, squeezed against the back passenger window.

"Really?" I ask.

Fiona ignores me, but Jess turns around to answer. "Isn't that cool? Fiona found that out when she did a report on the town's history."

"I also found out it's haunted. Dad, can we—"

"Not at night," Damon cuts her off in a way that indicates he's answered this question a lot. "Why don't we go play pinball?"

Fiona's screech nearly blows out the windows of the Expedition. "I am so going to beat Wade."

Old Town Square, a block east of the main drag on College Avenue, is a pedestrian-only, newly-remodeled street studded with statues, pianos (pianos?), and a music stage. Both sides are lined with stores and restaurants. We descend the stairs into a basement filled with pinball machines and arcade games.

Damon produces a roll of quarters and hands out coins. Fiona drags Wade to a machine towards the back while D and Damon jointly marvel over a new addition to the game collection that they haven't seen yet. I hang back with Jess. "This is a pretty cool place," I offer.

"Yeah, the kids love it."

A beat later I realize that "the kids" includes Wade. Jess is smiling quietly to herself, leaning against a machine, her arms crossed... probably, for a moment, forgetting I'm there. She's watching her family, and even though I don't know her, I can't imagine her looking happier than this.

"Ready to face off?" In the semi-dark, Wade's eyes are shining as he holds out two quarters between his thumb and forefinger.

I glance at Jess, who nods in a "go get 'em" way. "You're on."

Later we get ice cream and samples of fudge at Kilwin's. "You guys are right, this is really cute," I say to Wade and D. The three of us are on the bench in front of the shop, people-watching on College Avenue. Fiona's still inside, choosing her ice cream flavor, which is the only reason we're alone.

"It grows on you," D says agreeably.

"You'll have to see it in the winter sometime, around the holidays," Wade adds. "They really do it up."

His wording stirs my stomach. But, I remind myself, he's just being logical. It's likely the two of us do have a future. We're friends. There's no reason we can't continue that, seven-year age gap or not.

"Brothaaaaa!"

A burly guy is in front of me, along with five or six other people, including some squealing girls. Wade and D rise to catch up with their friends. It's clear they're thrilled to see Wade. As I'm digging in my purse for something I'm sure I need, the word "Jordan" registers from one of the girls' voices, and I look up to two of them turning in my direction—a kaleidoscope of beanies, streaked hair, short skirts, and tall boots, the quintessential college students. Jordan's friends? Jordan herself? My face is burning, and I wish I'd worn my contacts.

Fiona bursts out with her ice cream, announcing that she got cherry, just like Dad gets for Mom. Realizing Wade isn't there to hear her, she inspects the crowd, then launches herself into the arms of one of the girls. The girl hugs Fiona, her nose ring glinting as she glances at me over Fiona's shoulder. I pull out my phone and begin scrolling through my texts, trying not to notice how close the nose-ring girl is standing to Wade.

The conversation resumes and Fiona, bored, wanders back. She plants herself on the bench and gives me a stony look. "So why do you have a boy's name, anyway?"

Here, sweetie." Jess hands me a sweatshirt. CSU Rams. I pull it on and adjust my glasses, which have gone askew.

"You look like a local," Wade tells me. He's placing pieces of wood strategically into the fire pit, from which several small flames are rising. His smile takes on a hint of mystery in the dark, by this light. I feel the difference in my stomach and fix my attention elsewhere. But I return the smile first, shoving my hands in either side of the pouch pocket of his stepmother's sweatshirt, gripping my forearms.

Chairs are arranged. Burton wanders around, periodically sitting or lying down next to Wade. Someone produces a guitar, and D starts playing. After a few false starts he begins to sing, surprisingly decently. His voice makes up for what seems to be his limited playing skills. He strums carefully, concentrating. It's miles better than anything I could think of doing. Sunk into my camping chair I steal looks at Damon and Jess in a double chair under a blanket. From a distance they could be in their twenties. Their skin is glowing, the fire making suns on Jess's cheeks as she sings quietly along with D.

Fiona has settled herself into Wade's lap, even though she's clearly too big. With a nine-year-old's authority she directs him exactly how to roast her marshmallow. "Take it easy, Fee," I hear him say through the song. He seems to say this a lot to her. "You know I am the king of this."

"But you haven't been *home*." The last word is a whine. I sneak a look at my phone. It's got to be her bedtime soon.

D starts another song, again one everyone seems to know but me, even Fiona. He scratches out the words, closer to saying than singing them, which is not as unappealing as it sounds; the song is easy to get lost in. As D sings, everyone else's voice is a quieter echo of his.

"I love that song," Fiona says when it's over, sighing back against Wade. I find myself agreeing with her, though I don't say so. There's something so beautiful and magical about it.

"Bright Eyes," Wade says to me, as if answering my unasked question. I'm embarrassed. Was it that obvious I didn't know the song?

"Who sings it?"

Everyone laughs, and I can feel my face flush even more. But Wade smiles at me, standing up and easing Fiona off his lap. "The song is 'First Day of My Life.' Bright Eyes is the band. AKA Conor Oberst. D-Law's hero."

"Omaha gotta represent," D says. "At least I don't listen to country-fried."

"Hey now." Damon's deep voice is magnetic, and his face is Wade's, sly grin and all. "Don't make me make you a Waylon playlist."

Playful begging ensues among the boys, and Jess, following Wade's lead, gets up and holds her hand out. "Come on, Fee Fee. Time for bed."

Of course she whines. "One more! Please!"

Damon motions for D to hand him the guitar. "I'll play you to bed, Fee."

It's clear from the moment Damon starts to strum that he's much better at the guitar than D. Fee dances her way to the house, Burton following, and I almost want to get up and dance with her. Damon's singing what sounds like nonsense words mixed up with real ones. If I had to choose a way to describe the song it would simply be happy. The song makes me happy.

Wade's voice is suddenly in my ear, and I jump. "Woody Guthrie," he says. "Reimagined by Jeff Tweedy."

Either he moved his chair directly next to mine, or there was an empty chair there that he took and I didn't notice it. I'm not sure if he's expecting a response. I say, "I really like it."

"So does Fee. My dad used to sing that to her every night." ("Bye everyone!" Fiona calls from the house. "Bye Charlie the girl!")

"She wouldn't go to bed without it," Wade goes on, looking amused at Fiona singling me out, "even when he wasn't home."

"And then did you do the honors?"

"Once or twice. No one wants to hear me sing."

Wade leans down to a cooler and produces a beer, offering it to me. I leave it midair, glancing at Damon, and at Jess, back from her walk to the house.

"It's okay," Wade says to me. "We're just here."

I don't know what that means. Jess catches my expression immediately, though. "Who's driving?" she asks, and D raises his hand like he's in school. "Yes, Charlie, we're too lax around here, it's true. As long as the boys behave themselves."

"Thanks Jess," Wade says, raising the beer. "Love you."

It's nothing, really. Four words, a simple exchange between stepmother and stepson. Nothing that should make me want to cry. Wordlessly I take the beer Wade's still offering and raise it to my lips. He's already opened the bottle, and this simple gesture of thoughtfulness pushes me further into my head, tightening the ache in my throat.

I'm having the opposite of a déjà vu moment. Like I've never felt like this before. I'm missing someone I haven't met, or craving a touch I've never felt. I'm positive anyone can read my face, but everything is still going on around me as usual—Damon leaning forward, beginning another song, his hands moving across the guitar like a musical surgeon's, Jess next to him with the blanket wrapped around her, Wade and D sitting back quietly. And me in the middle of it all, feeling neon, like there's a spotlight pointing out how much I don't belong. I finish off my beer, and then another. Damon goes through song after song—the Grateful Dead, an old Marty Robbins song (I'm told, something about El Paso), some song I recognize from the '80s by the Georgia Satellites, "Keep Your Hands to Yourself." By the second verse even I'm singing along to the chorus. D gets up suddenly and dances around the fire, serenading us all. But it's not just us anymore in the audience. I turn behind me and follow D's gaze. A figure is coming up the driveway.

"Jacko!"

Jacko from the tree. No one mentions the tree, or the fact that he's been living in one. Wade gets up for the fist-to-back man-hug. Jess gives Jacko a real hug and tousles his hair, which is black and curly and front-heavy. He steps back and levels his gaze at me.

"I'm Jack."

"Charlie," I say. "I—" I met you yesterday, was what I was going to say. I catch myself and say instead: "—live next door to Wade in Massachusetts."

He nods at me, slowly. "Glad to meet you."

Someone pulls a chair up for Jacko, and the guitar is handed to him without discussion. "*Now* it's a party," D says.

Jacko lights a cigarette and balances the guitar on his knee. "Who has a beer?" He takes a long swallow from the bottle Wade hands him, then strums a couple times. He looks up in to the air pointedly, as if his repertoire of songs resides there.

"Play anything," D says. "Just don't get all Elliott Smith, aight?"

Jacko looks from Wade to D, who are sharing the same expression.

"Fuck all y'all," Jacko says around the cigarette, his eyes on his guitar. "Sorry," he adds to Jess, who smiles blandly at him and lifts a hand, acceptance of an unnecessary apology. I get the feeling that Jacko is well liked—everyone's favorite. Everyone except Kayla's, I guess.

Then he starts to play, and I see why he the guitar was surrendered to him. D has a decent voice and passable guitar skills; Damon's crazy-talented on the guitar and his voice is marginally better than D's. But Jacko? He can play. Jacko can sing. I seriously feel like I'm at a concert that I paid money for.

I lean over to Wade, touching his shoulder with mine. "Wow," I whisper.

"Yup." I turn to him, planning to go on, but Wade's done the same thing, because there's his face. The words die in my throat. Teenager or no, Wade + dark + firelight = dangerous combination.

Jacko may not want to talk about Kayla, but he'll sure as heck sing about her. Not overtly, but song after song comes out about breakups and anger and sadness and resignation. I recognize one or two—like "Somebody that I Used to Know"—but most I've never heard. All absorb me completely. The campfire smell, still pungent with nutty burnt marshmallow, transports me. I'm both ten years older and ten years younger all at once. D's leaning back, ankles crossed, quietly singing backup; Wade stays quiet, his knee moving up and down to the beat of the music, sipping his beer.

Jacko doesn't talk between songs, just takes a drag on the current glowing cigarette and another long swallow of beer and moves right into the next. Every once in a while he slides his eyes in my direction. I find myself on guard, sitting up straighter.

Shortly before midnight, Jess and Damon say good night and head to the house. It's just the four of us, me and three college students. Three college boys. D pulls out a joint. Huh. Well, this is Colorado, after all. Wade takes a hit after Jacko, but when he offers it to me I shake my head. Speaking of dangerous combinations, Charlie + alcohol + weed is something I never need to experience again.

After the last notes of a song called "Happiness" die away—apparently a one-song violation of the Elliott Smith ban—Jacko's glance lands on me. He lights another cigarette and exhales, guitar hands at the ready. "What'll it be?" he asks me.

"What?"

"I know what these bozos like. What do you want to hear?"

"I—I like what you've been playing."

"No requests?" He looks at Wade questioningly, who turns to me.

"He can play anything," Wade tells me.

Great. It's now public knowledge that I'm musically illiterate. What song could I possibly suggest that would fit into this playlist? I'm self-conscious, and starting to feel defensive. Never a good sign. I'm not quite thinking when I burst out: "Does it have to be a breakup song?"

Jacko just looks at me, his eyes narrowed, cigarette in mid-air. Oh, shit. I open my mouth to apologize for my utter lack of tact, and he smiles. "I do know a lot of those. But no, whatever you want."

Wade starts to speak, but someone speaks over him, drowning him out. I realize it's me.

"There is this song..." I close my eyes, trying to replay when I've heard it. I've caught it in public a couple times—in Xanna's car, once in a store in Harvard Square—but the first time was on TV. Somehow, I'm sure Jacko knows it, and can play it. "I don't know who sings it, but it was on an episode of *Friday Night Lights* years ago." I half-sing what I remember, and D smiles like I've passed a test. "The Avetts. Good choice. I'm surprised they haven't come up yet." Just before he starts, he gives Wade a look that I can't decipher, and Wade gets up and goes into the house. A bathroom break, I suspect. I'm starting to really have to pee myself.

The song, I'm reminded as it plays, is "If It's the Beaches." Duh, I think as D sings those words in the middle of the song. I knew that. Wade returns just as the song is ending. "Sorry man," I hear D say, but by the time I look in his direction I can't tell if he was speaking to Jacko or Wade.

I guess my request was the finale. Jacko's standing, handing the guitar to Wade. "Tell your dad he's gonna need at least one new string."

"Sure you don't want a ride?" D asks. This is apparently an old joke; Jacko just looks over his shoulder and waves as he disappears the way he came in, down the driveway into the dark. I hear him call back: "Nice meeting you, Charlie!"

"He biked here," D tells me, and now that I know what I'm seeing, there's the reflector, shakily fading in the distance. "Dude does not own a car. Probably never will. See you tomorrow?" he says to Wade. The two of them drift down the driveway to D's truck. The fire's low, and I can feel cold creeping up my back. We have a fireplace at home. A long time ago it was wood-burning, but my parents switched it to gas: now all you do is flick a switch, turning the fire on and off like a light. One time when I was about eleven I got up out of bed to get a drink of water and found Marina on the floor of the den, in front of the fireplace, with her boyfriend at the time. He had all his clothes on, but she was completely naked. It was winter, and I remember wondering, before she spied me and threw a blanket around herself to escort me upstairs, why she'd want to risk being so *cold*.

"Ready to go in?" Wade's back, holding a milk gallon container filled with water.

"Just about done." I raise what's left of my third beer, and I finish it while Wade douses the fire. The sudden smoke stings my eyes. I swivel backward. When my vision is functional again, the first thing I see is a hand. Wade's. Offered to me. There are eleventeen reasons I know I shouldn't, but I can't think of a good way to avoid accepting his hand. So I do. And I'm momentarily glad; those camping chairs are tough to get out of, especially after three beers.

He turns to walk back to the house, and I follow. Two thoughts race to the forefront of my mind, slamming their brakes in a perfect photo-finish tie.

He's still holding my hand.

I have to pee like nobody's business.

It shouldn't matter. He's just leading me, like a little sister—like Fiona—or Burton. We're both drunk-ish, and he's stoned besides. I'm in an unfamiliar area. He's being polite and helpful, showing me the way back, making sure I make it all right. But even as I'm thinking this, a plane pulls a message through the sky of the scene of Wade holding my hand: *He doesn't know.* He can't know. If he knew what touching him did to me, he wouldn't do it.

Or maybe he would.

I'm buzzing. Low wattage creeps all through me and all I can focus on is our points of contact. My index and second finger, part of my palm, the heel of my hand. I have to focus there, because the heat inside me is doing some concentrating of its own in places I don't dare think about, not with him. Not now. Not ever.

Wade, infuriatingly oblivious, just continues walking. I trail him with a slackening in my hand, inviting him to let go if he wants to. But he doesn't. He steps up to the porch. If he turns around, I decide recklessly, I'll kiss him. I will. Even though I'm about to pee my pants. I'm part shocked, part impressed by this display of invisible boldness. Kendra would be proud.

It's probably the alcohol, but I don't care. Because it's also this boy—this man—who likes me in glasses and whom my dad taught to mow the lawn. My neighbor. My friend.

We cross the back porch to the door, still linked. The porch lights are off and we're in the last slice of darkness. Any second now, he'll turn around and—

He pushes the door open, steps in, and drops my hand all at once. "Do you need to fill a water bottle for the night?" I shake my head. He downs a glass almost completely in three swallows. "Do you remember where you're staying?" He starts down the hallway toward the room Jess showed me to earlier. I follow, studying the back pockets of his jeans. Another reckless decision threatens. He pushes the door open and flicks the light on, then turns back to me. My eyes spring from his waist to his face. I feel caught.

"Wade, is that you? Could you help me for a sec?"

He turns toward Jess's voice, then looks back at me. An apology is wrapped in one of those half-smiles, and he presses lightly on my shoulder as he moves past me. "Night, Charlie."

It's a good thing our flight isn't until late afternoon, because by the time I stumble into the kitchen the next morning, it's past eleven and Wade is nowhere to be found. It's raining heavily outside, giving the yard a misty, gray Sunday-morning feeling. I spy a half-full coffeepot on the counter and help myself to a cup.

I'm hesitantly hunting in the fridge for something to doctor my coffee with when Jess appears, carrying a laundry basket. "Charlie, my word! I thought I was going to have to wake you up!" She produces half-and-half and a sugar bowl for me, saying, "Good, you found some coffee."

"Thanks," I say. "I guess the trip finally caught up to me."

"Well, when people sleep extra it's usually for a reason, I say. Except teenagers," she amends with a laugh. "Wade often needed to be dragged out of bed. Fiona still gets up before me, but she's only nine. All in good time, right?"

She places something in front of me on a plate. It's the biggest cinnamon roll I've ever seen. "Feel free to warm it up. We made them this morning."

"You and Damon?"

"All of us, really. But it was Wade's kitchen."

"Wade made these?" The first bite is heavenly. The next one, even better.

"Wade is the cinnamon roll *master*."

I was becoming weary of all these Wade discoveries. Was there nothing the boy could not do? Sing, I guess, remembering last night.

110

"If you're wondering where he is, he's out doing the rounds. Visiting, as we Kansans say. Should be home any minute, I would think," she adds, glancing at the clock.

I'll bet you five dollars his visitor itinerary is spelled J-O-R-D-A-N. The image of him hugging her goodbye outside Kilwin's is burned into my brain like a tattoo. Which I'm sure she has several of, symbolic sayings in different languages, nothing trite or cliché.

Jealous? Me?

I take my coffee and what's left of the roll, wrapped in a napkin, to the front porch. I saw a porch swing yesterday. I have a thing for porch swings. We've never had a front porch—just some steps—so I've felt mildly deprived my whole life. My ideal house is a pseudo farmhouse with a wraparound porch, like my grandmother used to have before she moved to assisted living. This house's porch isn't wraparound, but it'll do.

I love coffee in the rain.

I know I have no right to be jealous. Nor is there any logic in such feelings. It's not like we have a thing. Or even *can* have a thing. But it sure is something, the way natural emotions just reveal themselves, 2000 miles from initial denial.

The colors of a Colorado fall aren't like they are in New England—nothing is—but they're pretty. The house is set back far enough and the trees, even multicolored and dying, are still so lush that if you squint, you can pretend the neighboring houses aren't there. I sip my coffee and rock absently. The rain thins to a drip as I watch, and I absorb the wet quiet.

Damon's pickup crunches into the driveway. He waves at me and exits the truck, Burton in tow. Burton shakes himself, spattering me with wet. "He's not the most polite dog," Damon says. I give him an *It's okay* look and scootch to make room for him next to me. "I can spend way too much time on this swing myself," he says.

"I love porch swings. My first house will definitely have one."

He smiles. "That's a noble goal."

Damon squints, looking so much like his son it's startling. Wade does have Marla's smile, but the rest of him, from his broad body to his eyes, has been chiseled straight from his dad. "As I recall, your house has the front steps with the wrought-iron railing, is that right?"

Whoa. Why do I keep forgetting Damon was my neighbor? It's so odd how the happenings of my childhood just happened, but I never considered the hows or whys of anything.

"I remember when your dad put that in," he says.

"You knew my dad." I've known this, factually, but only now does the whole truth of it hit me.

His face is kind. "We were neighbors." Of course they were. Keith and I, running around his house while our parents spent time together. Our families' lives were stitched together at one time. I feel like I'm falling down a hole.

"He was a good man," Damon goes on. "I looked up to him quite a bit. I was really sorry to hear of his passing, Charlie."

"Thanks," I say as the swing glides slowly.

"I'm glad you and Wade became friends. And I'm glad he brought you. He seems more himself than he has in a while."

I have no idea what this means, but any question I'd ask would betray my colossal ignorance. For all Wade is willing to share with me, there seems to be far more he keeps under wraps. "He's the happiest person I know."

"Like I said," he replies, smiling down at me as if I'd just proven his point. The door creaks open and Jess hands Damon a cup of coffee. Her hand lingers on his shoulder. "Do you need any more, Charlie? I just made a new pot."

"Not yet," I say. "But thank you." Next to us, Burton's tail thumps on the wooden floor.

Jess goes back in, and Damon catches me off guard with what he says next. "You're good friends with Keith, aren't you?"

"Not... not really. I mean, a long time ago we were. And my boyfriend—Dean—was his best friend. *Is* his best friend. We're not together anymore." I sigh, exasperated with my feeble language skills. I apologize and clarify: "When I was with my ex, years ago, I spent a lot of time with Keith. Since we broke up, I haven't."

"I see. Dean Carson, was it?"

"Yes."

"Can't separate those two. Well, we'd love for him to visit more. Fiona misses him."

"And you do, too, I bet."

He looks at me, like he's pleased to concede this. "Yeah. I do too." I make a mental note to mention this to Keith. I know I'll see him at the wedding, at least.

"But Fiona loves having at least one big brother around. She's been lost with Wade gone."

I smile to myself. I can see that.

"Having him go to school was one thing, because it was close by at least. Him being in Massachusetts has been hard on her.

If he hadn't come out here now I'm not sure she could have waited till December."

"Is Wade coming for Christmas?"

"I'm not sure." He chuckles. "I'm just the dad, I don't know anything. All I've heard as the target date is New Year's. Whether that includes Christmas is anybody's guess."

It's not until twenty minutes later when I see Wade pulling into the driveway after Damon has left me alone on the porch swing, chewing my cinnamon roll, that I decipher what he's said.

Wade's moving back to Colorado in December.

This thought lodged in my brain, I watch Wade without him knowing it. There's something about the way he pushes himself out of the car and pauses, as if giving himself permission to switch gears from whatever's occupying his mind, then swings the car door shut with a sort of finality, that unlocks something for me.

It's my home.

He spies me on the porch and changes course, the slow saunter and smile I've long since memorized getting closer. I make room for him, just as I did for his dad, as Burton runs to greet him. Yes, he'll move from Massachusetts, and yes, I'll miss him. But, watching him, I know one thing for sure: Wade Hunter belongs in Colorado. He's as natural here as the aspens.

eleven

I'm only fifteen minutes late for work on Monday, but my luck, JJ's already there. "My office, please," she sings as she walks by my cubby. I exchange a look with Nina. Fuck. The five hours of sleep I hoped to get after we got home from the airport last night turned into three, and I stifle a yawn.

"Charlotte," JJ says, squinting down at her laptop. "I don't have to tell you again that we take punctuality very seriously, do I?"

"No, JJ. I'm sorry." I don't offer excuses. I've made that mistake before.

"Did you enjoy your vacation?"

This is an odd segue. "Yes, very much so," I say carefully.

"Good. I wanted to give you something."

And she hands me my résumé.

My face burns. It's the oldest mistake ever, leaving a résumé on the copy machine.

"I hope you didn't need it on vacation." This is the first time she's looking right at me.

"No, I didn't." I swallow. "Um, is there anything else?"

"There is not," she says, back to smiling. "See you at our two o'clock!"

For the rest of the day JJ asks me to perform asinine duties that are clearly below my level. It's pretty clear I'm being punished, but I do them without complaint. I even spend my lunch (a bag of Doritos and an oversized Cadbury bar) doing research at my desk. Nina sends me looks of sympathy all day. I grit my teeth, and my anger builds.

By the time I'm waiting outside a Newton office building that evening, five minutes late to meet my mom and Marina for counseling, my mood is sour. By the time they show up *twenty minutes* after that, I'm fermented.

"It's 5:40!" I say as soon as they're in earshot, walking from the parking lot in the back. "We're ten minutes late!" This was Marina's idea after all, and she insisted on being 15 minutes early so we could "regroup." What we had to regroup from when we hadn't even grouped, I didn't ask.

"The traffic on 128 was maddening, even going north," my mom says.

"It's maddening whenever you drive these days," Marina adds. "But Charlie, our appointment's not until 5:45."

"No, you told me 5:30."

"It's always been 5:45."

It's the way she says it without even looking at me, as if I'm not worth the time to even argue with. It's on the tip of my tongue to tell her to fuck off, but at the last second I resume my teeth gritting and sigh. *Make an effort, Charlie.*

The extra 15 minutes does mean I'll likely be late to go running, so I text Wade. Then I have to shut off my phone, doctor's request. Our therapy session, or whatever it is, is with Dr. Estelle Kenton. She shows us into her office, where we all sit around a round table. She's got long brown hair and big hoop earrings, looking like a transplant from the Brady Bunch, and not in a good way.

I don't know what to do with my hands. I try folding them in front of me on the table, but that feels forced, like I'm posing for a kindergarten picture. I'm repositioning them for the third time when I notice Marina watching me curiously. She of the lawyer suit and impeccable posture, hands resting lightly in her lap, where they should be.

"So," Dr. Kenyon says, looking around at each of us, "with that said, who would like to start?"

I'm alarmed. I must have missed something. To my relief— and no one's surprise—Marina steps up.

"I would just like to get to the point where we can all talk to one another," she says.

"All right. Claire, what about you? Is what you hope to get out of this different than Marina's goal?"

"No, that's good," my mom says. "I want the family to enjoy one another, and yes, that comes with communication."

"Good," Dr. Kenyon says, then turns to me. "Charlotte?"

Deducing that we've been asked to share our goals for the session, I shrug. "Those sound good. It was not my idea to come, so I don't necessarily have any goals, not for me anyway." Then I add, in a smaller voice: "I do want my mom to be happy."

My mom takes my hand under the table. Marina smiles thinly and says, "We should probably talk about ourselves, I think."

"I am talking about myself," I snap.

Perhaps sensing this isn't going anywhere good, Dr. Kenyon says quickly, "Okay! Marina, you want to talk to Charlotte. What would you like to talk to her about?"

"I don't know, anything really. Just things to help me get to know her. I feel like I don't know her at all."

Dr. Kenyon pauses. "Tell her that."

Well, that was quick. We have already reached our first Awkward Moment. Seeing Marina screw her head around to look in my direction is almost painful to watch. Her voice is wooden when she says, "Charlotte, I feel like I don't know you at all."

Having Marina speak to me while looking directly at my face is jarring. Which probably proves her point. We're both so uncomfortable we're probably pleasing the heck out of the therapist.

"Okay," I play along. "What would you like to ask?"

"Anything!" she says again. She turns back to the doctor. "I just want to know how she's doing, what's going on with her. I'm not even sure what she does for a living," she adds, almost accusingly. "I don't even know what or how her current job is."

Marina is conveniently leaving out that until a month ago, she didn't see me enough to even wonder what I was doing, but okay. Whatever. I'll play.

"Tell her," the doctor says again. "Ask Charlotte what you want to know."

Marina turns back to me and swallows. "How's your job going?"

"It's fine," I say, trying not to sound as suspicious as I feel.

"It's a marketing company, isn't it, Charlie?" my mom asks, clarifying for Marina's sake.

"Yeah, it is. But it's not... " All three of them are looking at me expectantly. "Well, it's *not* fine, to be honest."

So that's how I end up, crazily, telling them about JJ's impossible standards and insanity and my horrible mistake leaving the résumé on the photocopier. It's otherworldly. My mom and Marina strategize together, and somehow my résumé is being passed around, and Marina's making suggestions, and we figure out that she has a friend whose sister owns a marketing firm in the city, and she'll ask them about what's available.

And the next thing I know, our 50 minutes is up and we're all back down on the sidewalk.

"Let's get dinner!" Marina suggests. "There's a great place near Newton Corner I read about in the *Globe*."

I almost want to. I'm not too proud or arrogant to admit that I'm actually regretting that I can't. But I already texted Wade and made him wait. Never mind that after today, if I don't run I just might hit something. Or someone. So I beg off.

"I'm sorry, I have plans."

"Can't you postpone?" Marina says, unable to resist her pushy side. "We had such a good session."

"I can't," I say. "I'm meeting... Dean."

I don't know why I said that.

"Dean Carson? Really?" My mom's eyebrows shoot up.

"From high school?" Marina asks, equally curious.

"Charlie, that's wonderful," Mom says, all hopes of me joining them for dinner forgotten. "He was such a nice boy. Your father and I really liked him," she tells Marina, who doesn't answer, still staring at me.

"We've been hanging out a bit," I say, which, at least, isn't a lie. But it does the trick. The two of them part like the Red Sea, and I'm on my way.

The sound of a car's engine drifts up to my room, but a trip to the window tells me it's not Wade. Dammit.

After rushing home from therapy, I finally turned my phone back on and realized that Wade texted me back, saying he was glad I was late because he was running behind, too. Now I'm antsy. It's getting darker earlier and earlier. I've already texted him asking for an ETA, but I haven't heard back.

It's not often that I feel this way—the utter need to run. My routine has always been to grit my teeth through the first twenty minutes, until it starts to feel good. But running with Wade, I don't even notice my reluctance anymore. There's no need to overcome anything. And now, today, I'm straining at the bit inside my skin. I have to *move*.

Of course, I can go running by myself. But I know I won't enjoy it as much without him. I need his challenging pace propelling me. And, if I'm honest, being alone with my own thoughts is what I've been trying to avoid. Despite what I told my mom and Marina, I actually haven't heard from Dean since before I left for Colorado. My text sent from Nebraska went unanswered. And then, of course, there's my job. JJ and the CFO are going to be in an all-day meeting tomorrow, which may well be a harbinger. I've gotten a couple bites from résumés, and the vague promise of an interview or two, but nothing substantial so far. I can't believe I'm even thinking this, but after what happened in the therapy session, I'm actually seriously hoping Marina can help me out.

If I'm out of a job, I won't even be able to move in with Xanna. I could end up stuck here *forever*.

In the copy room today, I confessed to Nina about the résumé-photocopier snafu. She stopped sorting copies and stared at me. "Oh girl."

"That's bad, isn't it?"

"Well," she said, and I could tell she was looking for any way to put a positive spin on it, "I wouldn't ever question that woman's capacity for revenge."

Maybe Wade is driving. And he can't text and drive, can he? I decide to break protocol and do something I've never done before: I call. After several rings, I'm about to hang up when he finally answers.

It's always weird to hear someone's voice on the phone for the first time. It takes me a moment before I can plunge in. Caught off guard, my words come out all in a rush. "Hey-Wade-it's-Charlie-any-idea-when-you'll-be-home?"

It's a few moments before he responds. "Sorry. Five minutes?"

"Sure, that's—"

"Hey, can I call you back? I'm dropping someone off."

What an idiot I am. I should just leave on my own and wallow in my own mortification and job anxiety.

My phone rings and I snap it up. But it's Xanna. "Hey lady," she says. "I have some great news."

"Good, I could use some."

WORST-KEPT SECRET

She seems to hesitate. "The thing is, it's good for me, but it's not so good for you." And she goes on to tell me that thanks to the chunk of change she won at Danborn Day, she was able to make a down payment on the condo she's been eyeing.

"So you're moving?" I ask, confused.

"I ... I actually already moved. I'm sorry!" she bursts out. "It happened super-fast. I'm not even closing until next month, but we worked it out so I could get in now. Charlie? Charlie? Are you there?"

"You moved."

"Yeah. So I had to give up our lease..."

"So when Liz moves out..."

"They... they already have new tenants. Oh, Charlie, I'm *sorry*. I didn't think this through. This sucks for you."

I won't do it. I'm not going to be pathetic and make Xanna feel guilty for buying a place to live. For succeeding. "It's fine," I say, and I almost mean it. "I'm happy for you. Really. Is it that converted school?"

"Yes. Oh Charlie, you have to see it. Next Saturday!"

"Which is what?"

"My housewarming! It's the twenty-ninth, costumes optional. If you have plans, break them, okay? You're the guest of honor."

"Me? Why?"

"Because you're the whole reason I have the money! You and your amazing Danborn Day!"

Right. Great. I get screwed by my hometown. Again.

I listen to Xanna go on for a bit, then beg off the phone with some lie about dinner. I hang up promising to see her next Saturday. She tells me to bring Dean. I say I will.

I have no intention of doing either of those things. Because right now, I hate Xanna.

I know. I am a terrible person. And, fuck. I *really* need to run.

Wade's car finally pulls in. When we leave I follow slightly behind, content to let him chart the course. We circle Edenburg Estate, a mansion that doubles as a town park with its fifteen-acre yard. Wade turns into the estate's driveway and throws a questioning look my way. I smile my assent, and we find a bench to rest on just inside the fence.

"That was hardcore," I say, breathless.

119

"Yeah, I kinda needed hardcore today."

"So did I."

It's getting so I enjoy the breaks from running as much as I do the actual exercise. Talking to Wade, or even just sitting while the evening happens around us, is just as laden with endorphins as running is.

Maybe it's the endorphins that make me say it. "I have a confession. I never used to enjoy running either. I just did it because—" I pause, thinking, running my hand along the wooden seat. Why *have* I always done it? "It was the easiest thing to be good at, I guess. Well, not *easy*. But I discovered I do have endurance. The skills are pretty simple: just keep going. And I'm hopeless at other sports." I lift a shoulder, drop it. "But I'm surprised at how much I enjoy running with you. I actually look forward to it." Wade's watching me, but before he can say anything, I laugh suddenly. "I kissed Jay Werner on this bench."

Wade laughs, too, because he knows exactly what I mean. Edenburg was well known as an after-school destination for middle-school couples. "My first kiss, and the only one from him," I continue. "Pretty sure he only did it on a dare."

"I doubt that."

I roll my eyes.

"Charlie, trust me. No one would ever have to be dared to kiss you."

My mouth falls open until I remember to shut it. I shift just the tiniest hairsbreadth away from him. "So anyway," I say, looking out over the estate's grassy hills, "I may have fucked up my job. And now I have nowhere to live." I brief him on the résumé mistake, the layoff fear, and getting the apartment rug pulled out from under me.

He's pensive, then shrugs in a *what can you do* way. "So, what now? Onto plan B?"

"I think we're up to plan F. But isn't life what happens to you while you're busy making other plans?" I gloat when Wade nods his grudging approval. I can't help it. I might not know much about music, but I do know John Lennon.

Wade reads an incoming text, then puts his phone away without saying anything.

"Don't tell me you have bad news too."

"No." At first that seems like that's all he's going to say, but then he bursts out: "Seriously, what is it with you?"

I raise my eyebrows at him and lean back a bit, away from him.

"Sorry. I don't mean *you* you. I mean females. It's just, Jesus. You would think I wasn't speaking English. Or she wasn't."

I take a guess. "Is this Lindsay?"

"I mean, we're not even together. If she wants me around, she should say something, right?" He looks at me, and when I nod, he sits back triumphantly. "Right. She should. I'm not a fucking mind reader."

"Should I apologize on behalf of all women?"

This makes him smile. "I'm sorry, really," he says, rubbing his eye. "This has nothing to do with you. It's probably just her. I couldn't begin to tell you what I did to offend her."

"In the wise words of my friend Marc," I say, my tone serious, "relationship problems between men and women can be boiled down to two truths: men are idiots, and women are vague."

The look on Wade's face when he tries to keep himself from smiling? Especially at something I said? It's a glorious thing. It's even more glorious when he really loses it, doubled over and laughing harder than I've ever seen him.

"Marc *is* wise," he says finally. "That's fucking brilliant. It's going on my list." Leaning forward, resting his elbows on his knees, he turns back to me. "Why can't all girls be like you?"

There it is again. Like a rocket diving into my stomach, hot with burning fuel. "Because then the world would implode from awesomeness," I say with more confidence than I feel.

"It would," he agrees. I've been loosening my hair from the bun I've stuffed it into and running my fingers through the tangles, preparing to redo it, when I notice Wade watching me intently. "You have really beautiful hair, Charlie."

"It's more of a pain in the ass than anything," I joke reflexively, conscious of the blood rushing to my face. He doesn't smile, just keeps his eyes on me until I finish. I don't know if I'm more freaked out about the compliment itself, or about Wade's ease in giving them.

He stretches. "Oh well, I'll deal, I'm sure. I'll invite her over tonight and apologize for something I didn't do, and everything will be fine. Right?"

"Right. And I'll go to work tomorrow and get fired and be forced to live in my mom's house forever. It's okay, though. Apparently living at home is the new black."

"You'll be fine. And seriously, Charlie." He puts his hand on my thigh, absently. "Thanks for letting me vent."

"Always happy to be the voice of reason." And then I have to get up, because the top of my leg is like a live coal and I don't know how to remove his hand without making contact with his skin. "Come on, you have a girl to call."

We start toward home, racing the dark.

It turns out I actually didn't lie to my mom and Marina. When I get out of the shower, there's a text from Dean. Inviting me over. He greets me at the door by sliding his arms around me, much more enthusiastic than I expected. "I missed you a *lot* when I was in Chicago."

Something about the way he says that makes me cock my head and ask, "And you didn't expect to?"

He gives me a long look from under his eyelashes, then kisses me. Despite having sex twice—well, twice since our relationship ended—this is our first, bona fide, standing-up kiss where that's all we're doing: kissing. I feel his jeans change shape against me, and I smile to myself. I feel like I've wanted this for days.

"That was nice," I say.

I guess he never got the text I sent him while he was in Chicago. He says he didn't, anyway. I decide to believe him.

I'm in the mood to go out—I'm sort of over the basement— but Dean suggests we order in and watch TV. I acquiesce, but only because I'm starving. We get Chinese food and eat off the coffee table in front of the TV, where a rinkful of hockey players can't seem to keep themselves from beating the shit out of each other (my suggestion of a *Sex and the City* rerun was voted down). I yawn. It's not even the Bruins.

Dean offers me a beer, but to me, Chinese food screams for water. He starts to get up, saying there are water bottles in the fridge upstairs. "I think my mom even has those flavored waters, if that's your thing." He pauses. "Actually, you're welcome to go yourself and pick one. Don't worry, no one's home."

Upstairs I select a raspberry vitamin water from the fridge. Then I can't help it—I open the freezer. I count at least four cartons of Phish Food. Yep, Dean lives here. I take a sip of water and linger in the kitchen.

Every house has a smell. While it's true that not every house smell is pleasant, I've always loved Dean's. I felt very much at home here back in high school. I don't know if it's potpourri or essential oils or air freshener, but I swear his mom still infuses the house with the same scent from back then. Is that possible? I wonder if I could be imagining it. I close my eyes, try to smell without thinking. Nope. Definitely the same.

I wander to the living room, which is also unchanged from my memories. And all at once I'm not twenty-six, standing in the doorway drinking vitamin water. I'm sixteen. Dean's parents are away and he's supposed to be at Keith's and I'm supposed to be at Kendra's and we both will be, later, but for now we're on the blanket on his living room floor. Or maybe it's a tablecloth. It's red-checked, just like an old-fashioned picnic, which I told him one time I loved. And he remembered. Dave Matthews is playing and we're drinking white wine from the bottle and it's not as bitter as I expected and I'm tasting him between sips. There's cheese, too, and chocolate-covered gummi bears because they're my favorite. And ice cream, Phish Food straight from the carton. And first we're sitting and laughing and eating but then I'm naked on the floor looking up at him and I make him turn most of the lights off, except the kitchen one because the dimness makes him beautiful. My hands circle his neck and I think about that part of him where my fingers are resting, how I look at him when he doesn't know it, when we're going somewhere together and he's leading me, marveling at the way his hair meets his skin, how that makes me melt. I'm melting now, and he's melting into me, all the way in, and why was I so scared it would hurt? It doesn't hurt at all, and I was so foolish to worry like I did because it's more than just the lack of pain, it's the presence of him, the total sum of his body concentrated into mine, flowing everywhere. It's nothing like I feared it would be and it's perfect, and in this moment I'm sure of nothing but the fact that I will love Dean Carson for the rest of my life.

"Charlie? Did you find what you needed?"

"Yeah. Sorry." I gesture to the room. "I was just... remembering."

He reaches for my hand and pulls it to his lips. "Yeah," he says. "I know."

Like running, somehow the treehouse has become something that Wade and I just do. We don't talk about it or plan it. I'll be up there, reading, and within ten minutes, he's pushing the trap door. Or if I pull in after dark and see a small glow in the vicinity, I'll grab a couple of Luna bars and my phone and join him.

It's not the pinnacle of maturity, a treehouse. And being with Wade is probably not the wisest way to spend my time. But he doesn't care—has never cared. And sometime in the past few weeks, I've decided not to, either. The Colorado trip knocked something loose for me. Not just about spending time with him, but my behavior when I do. Lately I've even been flirting with him. Sometimes outrageously. It doesn't bother him at all. At most, he seems mildly amused. And being with him makes every day feel like the weekend. I can't not be happy when I'm with him. And it's not like I'm the only beneficiary. According to his dad, I bring out something in him that's been missing. I can live with that.

At the end of the day, we both know nothing will come of anything. Wade is leaving soon, and in the meantime, he has Lindsay. Rightly. And I... well, there's Dean. Whom I don't *have* exactly, but we're getting there. At least we better be.

The treehouse is like a geographical version of the Truth game. We haven't explicitly said that no one can refuse a question, but it feels like an unspoken rule. "So you and Lindsay," I say boldly one night. "You're 'hanging out.' And that's it? There's no boyfriend-girlfriend thing going on?"

He shrugs. "Nah. It's good like this."

"Good for you? Or for both of you?"

He shrugs again. "She seems fine with it."

"What if she wants more?"

"She won't."

"You know this."

"I do. Your move, chica."

We're playing Scrabble. On our phones. Within three feet of each other. Which has become another thing we do. I'm a little bit competitive, but come to find out, Wade's worse. Much worse.

I try to put together a word from too many vowels and wonder what Dean would think if I asked him to classify our relationship. "Tell me this. Why do you think Dean wouldn't want his parents to know we're seeing each other again?"

"Is that true?"

"The other night, we were in his basement, and I went upstairs to get a water. But he said 'Don't worry, my parents aren't home.' I didn't think anything of it at the time, but... what the hell?" If we were back together, I couldn't imagine not telling my mom. Just thinking about how happy she'd be makes me smile. Which is why I definitely won't say anything unless it's official. No sense getting her hopes up. His parents really liked me back in the day. I have no reason to believe they wouldn't be pleased, too.

"Sounds like he thinks he has something to hide," Wade says, his concentration on his phone. Then he laughs, evilly. "Oh girl, you are going to *hate* this move."

I also manage to extract bits and pieces of the Jordan story. He's cagey, but willing to answer fact-based questions. She's two years older than him, a senior at CSU. Yes, he did go see her that Sunday morning in Colorado. No, they didn't get back together. It was more the finalization of their breakup than anything. "We're moving on," he tells me with a sort of finality.

"But would you still 'hang out'?"

It's not often I catch Wade off guard. For the first time, his face looks vulnerable. Confused. I have a wild desire to take his hand. I shove my fingers under my thighs so I won't.

He recovers reasonably quickly, but his tone suggests he knows what I saw—and that he's okay with it. "That," he says, then lifts his eyes to mine, "is a very good question."

He holds my gaze. The subject is over. I fish in my jacket pocket for my second Luna bar. "Have you eaten dinner? I've got extra. Lemon Zest."

Another big reason I'm spending so much time with Wade is Kendra. We've barely spoken in the past couple of weeks. Which is sort of a relief, to be honest, to not have her judgment interfering with anything I'm doing. Or not doing. But the lack of communication has nothing to do with me, or with Dean, or even with Wade.

Kendra's in love.

His name is Patrick. She met him when I was in Colorado, when Xanna's inability to join her on the Cape left her to fend for herself. While fending, she found Patrick. So far none of her friends—including me—has gotten more than the most cryptic of details. Like that he's twenty-eight, and a scientist, and from California. In a way this is to be expected, as Kendra's secrecy surrounding new "prospectives" (as she calls them) is well documented. But we also know that she's more smitten than any of us have ever witnessed, so we're all a little antsy for the story, not to mention to meet him in the flesh. Apparently she's bringing him to Xanna's housewarming.

Yeah, I'm going. Of course I am.

"So have you thought about Saturday?"

"Saturday?"

"Xanna's housewarming party. In JP."

"Oh right," Dean says, cracking his second beer. He leans back against the couch, then turns my way with that under-the-eyelashes look. "Do I have to?"

"Well, no, you don't *have* to," I say, determined to never be *that* girlfriend. (Not that I'm his girlfriend.) "I'd just like you to. We haven't hung out with my friends yet."

"Xanna's the gay one, right?"

"She's actually... yes. I was with her that night at Paco's. You met her."

"Right. Oh. Saturday, you said? Yeah, I already made plans to hang out with the guys."

"So bring them. It's a party. Who is it, Steve? Jeff?"

"Jeff?" Dean looks confused. "Oh, Moorhead?" I will never understand guys' arbitrary rules about who gets called by their last name. "Charlie, you don't want to hang out with them, believe me." His attention is back on the TV. I didn't even try to suggest going out tonight. It's Thursday Night Football, and the Patriots are playing. That happens, like, once a season.

As far as he's concerned, the matter is settled. I try not to act as irritated as I feel. I remember this now, Dean's tendency to make decisions for me, to anticipate how I'll respond to something and act accordingly. Back then it hadn't occurred to me to mind. It felt considerate, actually, as if he was taking care of me. But we're not kids anymore. He hasn't spent significant time with me in years. How does he know what I want?

He cuts his eyes at me, and I realize I've actually asked the question aloud. He pauses the TV and sighs. "Okay, *I* don't want to hang out with them, with you. But why don't you come back here late-night?"

Late-night? Were we in college? "Dean." I climb up on his lap and face him, sliding my arms around his neck. Reflexively he pushes himself into me. "Come to Xanna's. Please. You already know Kendra. We've been out with your friends. I want you to meet mine."

"I have." I give him a look. "I will." He kisses me lightly. "Just not that night. I already told the guys."

I slide back on his thighs toward his knees. "Dean, what are we doing?"

"Oh, come on, Charlie." He pulls me back. "Don't do that."

"I'm not doing anything," I say, making sure my voice is calm and even. I climb off him and stand up. "Do you eat dinner with your parents?"

He eyes me cautiously. "Sometimes."

"So invite me over. Have them 'meet' me properly again. We can do the same with mine. I mean my mom. Aren't we too old to be sneaking around?"

"We're not sneaking around. This is just the best place to be alone."

"Then why haven't you introduced me—or re-introduced me—to your parents?" Wade's words come back to me, and I steady my voice. "Don't you think that's weird, that we've been seeing each other for weeks now, and I'm still being hidden in the basement?"

"You're not being *hidden*." I give him another look and he exhales a resigned breath, as if I've pushed him to resort to this. "You want to go up and see them now?"

"They're not home," I snap. I always know whether his parents are home, because I always check for cars in the driveway and the garage. And then I listen for them like a sound engineer the whole time I'm here. "You know they're not home."

"Charlie, you're overreacting."

"You make me park in front of the neighbors'." It's true. I hadn't thought anything of it, because Dean explained that there were always a lot of cars coming and going, so it was just easier that way. But there were, in fact, never any cars coming and going.

Suddenly I feel way too small. I scan the floor for my shoes. "Forget it. I should just go."

Dean sets down the remote on the coffee table. "Is this going to be a thing?" he asks, sounding bored.

"What? Going to Xanna's or meeting your parents?"

He shrugs. "Both. Either."

"Not if you don't want it to be," I say, exactly like *that* girlfriend.

"So what, if I don't do what you want, you leave?"

"I already told you, I won't *make* you do anything."

127

"But if I don't you'll be pissed at me."

We're in rhythm, back and forth. A routine we know. Our bodies are rigid, our shared glare well-honed and set with stubbornness. We perfected the performance long ago. His face is impassive, probably as much as mine is as we share a ten-year-old stare.

Oh my God. What am I doing? What are *we* doing? Dean notices my face soften, and his voice drops. "Charlie. I'm sorry. I want to be with you. I just have to... figure some stuff out."

"What stuff?"

"Just stuff. Can you be patient? Just a little longer?"

He's never asked me for this before. I search his face. He seems sincere. I lower myself next to him, taking his hands in mine. He's definitely not the same; Kendra was wrong. There was a time when I was able to read his thoughts before he had them. Now he's like a puzzle.

I know one thing: I don't want to fight. We're older now, beyond teenage drama. We have to learn to interact as the people we are now, not the people we were. However much work it takes. I take a deep breath. "Of course I can. And I'm sorry, too. I just want us to... move forward."

It's the closest I've ever come to asking him to categorize us, to name this thing that we're doing. I let him pull me back onto his lap. He reaches up, smooths my hair back, away from my face. It's an old trick that my body remembers and responds to. "Charlie, the housewarming thing... it's just not my scene."

The thing is, I know this. Try as I might to picture Dean—never mind his friends—in Xanna's living room, finding common ground with Xanna and her artsy co-workers, or even Marc and Kendra, the image won't materialize. So why am I acting like it's so important?

"But," he goes on, sliding his hands up my back, between my skin and the tank top that's under my hoodie, "if you really want me to go, I will."

I shake my head. It was foolish to expect him to go. I tell him it's okay, and I lean in and kiss him. He tastes like beer and Doritos. I revel in the feel of his mouth and all the places it sends me. We start off slow, exploratory, but almost immediately we're pushing further in unison, this tandem dance we've performed a thousand times. Isn't that the thing with first loves? Even if we don't think we remember, we do. Our bodies do. Our blood pumps with memories that urge us on like a nostalgic movie director.

"It's halftime," I say, rising with a throw blanket under my arm. "And they're up by two touchdowns." At the bottom of the stairs, I turn back. "How long till your parents are home?"

He smiles and follows me up the stairs to the living room, and I spread the blanket out. We sink to the floor, my hoodie and tank top tossed to the side. Somehow my bra's already off; I didn't even notice him undoing it. I wrap my legs around him, squeezing him and pulling him close. I stare at the dark, thick look on his face and lift my hips to offer better access to my jeans.

"How long?" I repeat. I give him a slow smile, dragging my nails down his bare chest, just short of enough to leave a mark.

"Hours." He bends to kiss me down my body, stopping at my inner thigh. "Hours and hours," he whispers, switching to my other thigh.

And then, right there in his living room during Thursday Night Football, Dean and I have our first make-up sex of our adulthood. At one point he suggests moving back downstairs—probably to keep one eye on the game—but I hold fast. Nostalgic or not, staying here feels illicit. Everything is heightened. Plus, I have a hunch. I'm bolder than I've ever been with Dean, calling every shot without saying a word. He makes a tiny, halfhearted attempt at resistance, but it's just for show. I think he likes me taking over.

My hunch pays off. It takes a little extra concentration and maneuvering on my part, along with more encouragement than I've ever had to give him. But today, in the same place my teenage world divided into before and after, Dean finally makes me come.

Next to Xanna's killer hummus she never shares the recipe for, the best part about her party is that I get to see Marc. We met in college on the heels of the Dean breakup, when we were paired up on a statistics project. Right after college we were a foursome—Kendra, Xanna, Marc, and me—sharing a house together in Watertown. We partied together, learned to cook together (well, Xanna and I taught the others) and Kendra and Marc even worked at the same law firm—when their short-lived, ill-advised fling brought out the worst in both of them. Then Marc went to law school at Villanova, I moved in with Cam, Kendra struck out on her own, and Xanna was called to

JP. Marc returned to Boston last year, to the South End, but for all I see him he may as well still be in Philadelphia.

When I find him we share a long hug and trade accusations about who never calls who. I fight the good fight, but it's a ruse. It's common knowledge that out of all of us, I'm the worst about keeping in touch. I tend to only text to solidify plans. I've fallen out of the email habit, and I usually think of calling late at night or during the work day—all inopportune moments. Facebook annoys me, although I'm on it, for convenience's sake more than anything. But I mostly lurk, and I don't check it every day.

"You know who does call..." Marc begins.

Of course I do. If I'm the worst about being in touch, it's equally well known that Kendra's the best. Xanna even started calling her *superglue* for the way she keeps us together. It was no accident that she pulled Xanna in for our impromptu girls' night at Paco's.

But as I mentioned, lately she's been falling down on the job.

"Do you know any more than I do?" I ask Marc.

He raises his eyebrow at me. "I don't know—what do you know?"

I roll my eyes. "She's not here yet, is she?" I ask, even though it's not that big a place. If she were here, I'd know it.

Marc pours me a glass of red wine from the liquor table. Xanna's getting fancy. "To new relationships," he says, raising his own glass. "Or old ones?"

I return his questioning look with a blank one of my own.

"Aren't we sleeping with our old boyfriend?"

"Ah. Kendra *has* been talking to you."

"Not about her personal life, of course. Just yours."

"Of course."

"So what's the deal?"

"With Dean? We're... hanging out." Oh my God. Did I really say that? "'Sleeping with' makes me sound like a hussy."

"Oooh, I like that word. Charlie the Hussy."

"Maybe that's what I should have dressed as." I eye the rest of the partygoers. Halloween is just a couple days away, but Marc and I have both opted out of costumes. The rest of the crowd is pretty creative. I spot Tippi Hedren across the room, surrounded by birds, and there's a Miley-Cyrus-circa-twerking-with-Robin-Thicke to my left.

Marc elbows me slightly. "Speaking of hussiness, let's talk about the crush you have on your teenaged next-door neighbor."

"Seriously?" I'm dumbfounded. "Why am I not getting the sordid details on *your* life?"

"I'm a workaholic. Nothing to tell." He smiles into his wine. "So it's true?"

"It's not." This, I am more comfortable denying. The best part about Kendra meeting Patrick while I was in Colorado was that I never had to explain my trip to her. Which meant that no one else found out, either. "We run together. That's it. And anyway, he's moving."

"Which shouldn't matter to you if there's nothing going on."

"Right." I smile prettily. "It doesn't."

A woman wearing several scarves jostles me with her elbow as she moves by, and I squeeze closer to Marc. The party's getting loud, and Marc directs his next words into my ear.

"So the Dean thing isn't serious?"

I shrug. "I asked him to come tonight. He thought it wasn't his scene."

Marc looks around as if to assess this. The party crowd is a testament to colliding worlds. Xanna's Jamaica Plain friends are a blend of Boston hippies and foodies. Her work friends are artistic, too, as would be expected of an architectural firm. Then there's us—Marc, Kendra, and me—her non-work, pre-coming-out crowd.

"Is it?" Marc asks.

"Probably not. But opposites attract, right?"

"Like the kid next door?"

Marc means to be clever, I know. And I do smile. But neither of us expects the blush that accompanies it. He commands me with his eyes through to the tiny kitchen, where he slides his personal stash of Xanna's hummus over to me. We sit at the counter under her most recent wall decor—a framed sepia-toned photo of her with Bridey, the cow from Danborn Day.

I scowl. "I hate that fucking cow."

"She did sort of screw your life up," Marc agrees. "But you love Xanna."

I sigh. "But I love Xanna."

"I love you too, girlfriend!" Xanna bounces into the kitchen and hugs me. "I'm so glad you made it. Is she here yet?" She looks around, as if it were possible to miss Kendra in the tiny kitchen. As it is the three of us form a crowd. "I can't wait. Kendra in love. What a trip."

"So seriously," Marc says, leaning in after Xanna gets called away again by the JP contingent. "Aside from men. What's really new?"

"The really real news is I may lose my job, actually. If I don't quit first. My boss is cray-cray."

"Still?"

"Worse."

"Every office is a cray-cray on some level."

"And she doesn't like me."

Marc dismisses this. "Oh, you think everyone doesn't like you."

I hide my surprise in a bite of Triscuit and hummus. I'd almost forgotten Marc's way of looking straight into you and not being afraid to share what he sees, or to face any hurt feelings as a result. Compared to him, Kendra holds back. It's unnerving. I'm out of practice handling it.

I decide to stick to the facts. "Well, I'm job-hunting mightily. I had my first interview yesterday. And I've got to start apartment-hunting for real. I'm done with the home life." I've been seriously crunching the numbers. With what I've managed to save since moving home, as long as I keep my job or get a better one, and I'm willing to live with other people, I can probably swing first and last month for a lease beginning the first of January. I even coughed up for a gym membership at Fantasy Fitness. Wade did too. Now that daylight savings is kicking in, their month-to-month holiday special fit both of our short-term lives perfectly.

But we don't go to the gym together. Somehow we've agreed to this without acknowledging it.

My phone pings with a text. *having fun?* Dean asks.

More than should be legal, I type.

come over later?

My fingers hover over the screen. It's not the worst idea, meeting up with Dean later ("late night"). Granted we probably both know what we'll end up doing, but at least by now that's getting better. For a while I was too caught up in simply being with him—and, at least the first time, too drunk—to be discerning. But on the living room floor, I felt like I found what was missing. I felt better about him, and about us, than I had in a while. We turned a corner, and we were ready to get to know the people we were now.

Just then a screech comes from the living room, unmistakably Xanna's. Marc and I battle the crowd as politely as possible. For Xanna to make that sort of noise would mean only one thing: Kendra's here, and she brought Patrick.

Oh God, she's glowing. She stands there beaming up at him, red-cheeked with her curly hair in an artfully disheveled updo. He's got her coloring, with blonde hair a shade or two lighter than hers and smiling eyes directed towards her face. He's wearing glasses.

I lean against Marc, hugging my wine glass to my chest. "Look at that."

"Uncharted territory," he agrees. "I wonder if they'll get married," he adds in the same musing tone.

I shake the thought away. "Bite your tongue. Kendra's not getting married anytime soon. They just met."

"How old is he again?" Marc asks, squinting. "Twenty-eight, right?"

"They'll get married," a voice next to us pipes in. It's the woman from earlier with the scarves. Very pretty, with a classic line of bright red lips, and way older than us, maybe mid-thirties. I glare at her with barely concealed irritation. What business is it of hers?

"That's Kendra, right? I work with Xanna," she says, as if that's all the explanation we need. "Her boyfriend there is of the age."

"What does *that* mean?" I sound snappier than I mean to, and Marc shoots me a look.

But Scarves just laughs. "The marrying age. You'll see. It will happen to your friends. It's actually interesting to watch."

Scarves' friend, a tall, thin woman with spiky orange hair and small, square, cobalt-blue glasses—it makes a surprisingly striking combination—leans in, overhearing us. "When men hit a certain age—late twenties, usually—it's as if it occurs to them suddenly: 'I need to get married.' And they look around, see who's next to them, and they say: 'You. You're the one.'" She even points at an imaginary girlfriend with her finger, and she and Scarves both laugh. "It doesn't matter if their relationship is three years old or three *days* old. When they're ready, they're ready, and it doesn't matter who."

"Not that these two aren't really in love," Scarves puts in quickly, smoothing things over. "They well could be."

"Then they'd be the lucky ones," her friend adds. So obnoxious. I move slightly away, disgusted. My phone pings with another text, reminding me that I haven't responded to Dean yet. But this message isn't from him. *Tomorrow morning, 10:30?*

A burst of laughter makes me look up, and Kendra catches my eye. She smiles bigger—*look!*—while still politely following the conversation Patrick is having with Xanna. I slowly nod at her, and she nods back with measured excitement. This guy with his arm on the small of her back... he's it. I haven't exchanged a word with him yet, and Kendra's all but notorious for her lack of attention span for any guy who calls her more than twice. But I can tell, in a way I didn't even know I could. There's no question. He's the guy.

Before I left tonight, I saw a little blue car in Wade's driveway. Something told me it was Lindsay Linstrom's. I check the time. 9:43. Why is he texting me? Although a secret part of me hopes she's left already, another part wisely tells me to shut up.

I'll be there, I text back—to the right guy.

Spin classes always make me feel like I'm going to puke. But I like how I feel after them more than I hate participating in them. So Tuesdays and Thursdays at six that's where I am. Trina, the Amazonian instructor, tells me that pukey feeling means I'm doing it right. Whatever. As long as it burns the eight hundred calories it's supposed to, I can put up with anything for fifty minutes. I've definitely been eating too much at my mom's, and now that it's too dark to run on weeknights, it's the gym or nothing. I'm up at least five pounds since summer and a new wardrobe is not in the budget.

I'm late today, and I hate being late to spin. The sucky part is that I was actually supposed to be early. JJ was out of the office in meetings all day, which meant work was almost pleasant. With Nina on vacation (a forced one, like mine was), all I had to do was catch up on the tasks I put aside preparing JJ for her meetings in Nina's stead. I'd already changed into my workout clothes when JJ walked in.

"Charlotte, would you be a dear?"

For the next hour I fetched documents, updated her laptop and her phone, and scheduled more meetings. In the midst of it all I caught an email on my phone from a company I interviewed with last week. I ducked behind a cubicle to read it, but the singsongy voice called to me again, and I closed my email, promising myself I'd go back to it as soon as humanly possible.

But I must have hit the wrong button. When I finally got in my car, I couldn't find the email. It was gone. Vanished. Telling myself not to panic, I drove to Danborn, parked at the gym, and tried again. Nothing.

Which is why I'm fighting tears now as I rush across the parking lot in the dark November evening, two minutes past the start of class. If you don't arrive five minutes before class, you miss out on the good bikes. And there are barely enough bikes to go around, so if you don't arrive on time, you may miss out, period.

I'm pushing the gym door open, head down, trying to isolate my membership fob on my keys to run through the scanner when I bump into someone, hard.

"I'm so sorry," I say automatically.

"Whoa," Wade replies, hands up: *I surrender.* His hair is wet from the shower, and he smells like spring.

I instinctively back up, quashing the jolt coursing through me. "Oh. Wade. I'm so sorry," I say again. "I just... I just..." I look up at him, watching and listening to me politely, and I mumble something about a shitty day. I have to get out of here. I know this feeling. One millimeter to the left on the emotional scale and I'm a goner.

Wade studies me. "Are you okay?"

"Yeah, I'm fine," I say, beginning to step around him. "Sorry again."

"Wait a sec," he says, still looking carefully at me. He takes my arm. "Charlie. What's wrong?"

And that's all it takes. One question. One gentle squeeze of his fingers. I cover my face with my hands and begin to sob. I'm mortified but I can't stop. Somehow I manage to hiccup out enough intelligible words that Wade is able to comprehend the situation—JJ, the email, my phone, no spin bike. "And now I won't get to do the one thing that will make me feel better," I whine. I huff up a big glob of snot and wipe my eyes with my sleeve. So attractive. "I'm sorry. I'm fine."

Wade holds his hand out. "May I?"

He wants my phone. I hand it over, and he fiddles with it for a bit. Then he smiles to himself and hands it back to me. "Is that it?"

On the screen is the email from Crawford Tech, the company whose corporate offices I sat in last week. My eyes scan down it. "You found my email," I say to myself, verifying.

"I did."

I keep reading. "They want me to come back in. For a second interview. Tomorrow."

"Good for you!" Wade says, sounding genuinely happy.

I shake my head in wonder, murmuring, "I would have never even known to show up." When I lift my eyes to Wade's half-smile, the words just fall out of my mouth. "You know what, Wade? You're amazing. I don't care that you're seven years younger than me, or that you're barely old enough to vote. We're friends." He gets a funny look on his face, like I'm telling a joke, but in Russian. I shake my head, dismissing his confusion. "Forget it. It doesn't matter. You're a good friend." He's amused, still trying to figure me out. "I'm sorry, I'm babbling. What I mean is," I say deliberately, "thank you, Wade." And I hug him, for the first time since I re-met him seven weeks ago. "Thank you so, so much."

"You're welcome," he says, squeezing me back.

Even now, looking back, when I rewind my mind and play the next scene back at half-speed, I still can't figure out what happens next. It's as if I'm drunk or stoned, not quite in control of my faculties. But we're in the stark, neutral gym lobby. I'm in workout clothes, my hair stuffed into a bun and tamed by a headband after a long day in the office. Nothing's in my system but coffee and water. Following my thoughts and my motions cell by cell, there's no definitive line from A to B.

What actually happens, in quick succession, is four things:

One, I stop hugging Wade. Two, I step back. Three, I step forward. And four, I kiss him. Quickly, on his mouth, almost as part of an exhale, as if I've done it a million times before.

It takes me a moment to even realize my gaffe. My smile fades at the same rate Wade's face, all cheekbones and blue eyes, comes into sharp focus. His expression, halfway between surprise and amusement, startles me. Wait a minute. What just happened?

Half a second later the instant replay hits. Abruptly I let go of him and step backwards. My hands find their way to my cheeks. Holy shit, *I* am what just happened.

Fire burns through me. My mouth opens, then shuts. "I'm—"

As Wade advances I step back instinctively. I have the vague idea that there is a wall behind me, and eventually I will hit it.

But he's caught up to me now, and he's shoving me. That's really the only word for it. If it's possible to shove someone gently, that's what he does: gently, quickly he shoves me out of sight of passersby, into the wall behind the stairs. Just when I expect my head to smack against the concrete, it doesn't, and he's protecting it with his hand, while his other hand finds my lower back, and for a moment I am distracted by the heat of his hand through my shirt. His face is so close to mine I can feel his spicy coffee breath more than smell it. My eyes are fastened to his. His hand travels from the back of my head around to my cheek. So slightly that I'll never be sure if I've really seen it, he lifts the corner of his mouth in what might be his half-smile.

I know exactly what is happening for the one long second before his mouth is on mine. I know what I should do. With my elbows bent, my forearms against his chest, my hands in loose fists, I could easily, handily, push him away. But I don't. Even though I know what's coming, and even though I'm pretty sure what's coming is a bad idea.

My gym bag slips from my shoulder. I think of Scarlett O'Hara. Remember Rhett's "You need to be kissed, and often, and by someone who knows how"? I've always mildly scoffed at the sentence, thinking it meant something akin to force—or at least, kissing someone you really don't want to kiss. But as Wade kisses me, the long-forgotten phrase surfaces as if I've known and believed it all along. I've been waiting to be kissed like this. A kiss that lasts for a millisecond and a year at the same time. In the January of the kiss I am limp with shock, but by March, involuntarily, like there is nothing else my body is capable of putting energy into, I'm kissing him back. In June my hands find his hair. By September I am pressing my limbs against his.

Through layers and layers of awareness I know that this is wrong. Ultimately it's not going to go over well, possibly even with me. But my body doesn't care. The mere thought of pulling away pushes me further into him. *You have to stop*, I tell myself weakly. *Stop stop stop.* But I'm not refereeing between my body and brain, I'm not doing anything except kissing him back and wondering where the hell a nineteen-year-old learned to kiss this way.

All of this goes on, all this unavoidable kissing, in the space of about sixty seconds. One minute. One minute to run through more emotions than I've felt in the past year. Maybe ever. Somewhere past that, it's as if both of us accept that the sea change is complete. Our long uninterrupted kiss becomes an ellipsis of kissing. I take one shaky breath, then another. He pulls away and rests his forehead against mine, eyes closed. Our breathing matches, slows. Then he cradles my face in his palms, watching me with soft eyes and no words.

There is only one thing I can do. I reach up and gently remove his hands from my face. I clasp and lower them and hold his gaze for a moment, a bride and groom facing one another for their wedding vows. Then I let his hands go, bend down for my bag, and dash into the gym.

twelve

What the hell have I done?

Sienna Cash

PART 2:
during

t h i r t e e n

Today's spin nausea has nothing to do with athletic prowess. It's because today's lunch consisted of a bag of Cheetos. And, oh yeah, I just made out with a kid. Not that the actual making out made me want to puke. I could have kissed him for hours. Days, even. WHAT IS WRONG WITH ME?

Elsie in accounting at work, in her forties, jokes about her crush on Ross Lynch, some rock-star kid on a syndicated Disney show her daughter watches. We all tease her. She calls herself a cougar. Jokingly. Is that what I am? A cougar? He's only seven years younger than me. But still—seven years. He's not even twenty.

I'm embarrassed and confused and jacked up all at once. It takes all my concentration to keep the bike's flywheel pedals from catapulting me through the air every time I accidentally slow down when I forget where I am. Which I do. Often. Because periodically, I'm not in the exercise room on a spin bike. I'm back in the foyer with Wade's palms against my back, tasting him.

Oh my God, his mouth. His beautiful, expressive mouth. So alive and inviting. Sweet-tasting. Soft. Electric. Sinewy. While I may have admitted being attracted to him, at least to his sigh-inducing body and devastating smile, until now I have never given serious thought to his mouth. Or his tongue. Now I'm so distracted simply imagining everything that mouth and tongue are capable of that I'm becoming a danger to myself.

Trina whoops and hollers from her bike in the center of the room, our own insane cheerleader. I pedal and pedal. If I get off the bike now, Trina will make a spectacle of me. Her reputation precedes her. Sweat pours down my temples. It drips into my eyes from my forehead. Dammit, my towel is still sitting in my bag.

I get into a pedaling rhythm, trying to rely on muscle memory while I force my brain into rational logic. Okay. Let's dissect this. So I had a moment of severe weakness. It's not like I *like* Wade. I mean, I'm attracted to him. That much is clear and undeniable. But, at the risk of sounding like a character on the Ross Lynch show, I don't *like* him like him. Not like Dean. There's a difference.

"Take it up!"

I stand up on the pedals, giving Trina a mental middle finger. In cosmic response she rides one-handed to point at me and then give me a thumbs-up. Showoff. I'm pedaling and huffing and puffing. Even squeezing my eyes shut can't banish the feel of Wade's lips, of his breath, of the way his eyes fixed heavily on mine for that eternal moment.

Already the whole experience feels otherworldly. Only seventeen minutes in the past and seventy-five feet down the hall, yet it's as if we spied a rip in the space and time continuum and flew right through it.

"Still climbing!" I pedal harder. Back to rational thought. So Wade kissed me. No, not true. I kissed him first. Briefly. Even if I wouldn't necessarily classify it as a "kiss" kiss, semantics should not stand in the way of accuracy. The truth stands: I did kiss him.

But then. He took the opportunity to kiss me in return. Fiercely. Ferociously. A waterfall of kissing. Which, to be fair, I did not fight. Nay, I kissed him back, gave as good as I got.

"Now up... and down!" I rise and fall with the others on my "ride," pretending to be climbing a mountain or racing alongside the ocean or whatever it is I'm supposed to be doing with fifteen of my closest friends, and face the most important question: the why. Not why it happened; the body wants what the body wants. What I need to know is: why now? Why not that night in the hotel with the hipbones? Why not the next night, in the kitchen? Or on his porch? Why here, tonight, in the gym, when the future I've been waiting for is on the cusp of really beginning?

In the hotel or the kitchen or on the porch in Fort Collins, a kiss would have been a mistake. I would have kissed Wade, and he would have let me, and we would have willfully ignored our own best interests as we stumbled to the first horizontal surface and had forty-five minutes of sex that I would regret immediately. And then our friendship would end, because who needs that shit.

I search my brain for an excuse, trying to put myself back in the moment to trace its origins. The first brief kiss felt reflexive, as if it was something I'd been doing all along. A habit. Like kissing a longtime boyfriend. Any boyfriend. Cam. Dean. I was comfortable enough with Wade that following a hug with a casual kiss actually made sense.

But he had to go and screw it all up by kissing me back.

If he hadn't, that could have been it. I would have apologized, he would have laughed. I'd have been mortified, sure, but at least it would be over. But he kissed me for real, and as wrong as I knew it was, I let him.

But even that doesn't sit right. Because of Wade's face, and his cheekbones, and the heat of his skin through fabric. Because of the flames that coursed through me, my every nerve ending rising to meet the prospect of his body up against my own. All of it. Naked. Horizontally. Vertically. On the lobby floor. Against the wall. Whatever.

Absolutely nothing about that felt wrong. Everything about him felt a hundred kinds of right.

The man in the pink tie sticks out his hand, and I shake it, I hope firmly. "Thanks for coming in, Charlotte. We'll be in touch."

On my way back to the parking garage, I exhale for what feels like the first time all day. Everything since I woke up has felt surreal, a black-and-white scene waiting on the Technicolor. I zombie-walked through my hours at the office, thankful Nina wasn't there to read everything on my face. I left at five on the dot for my interview, where it took everything I could muster to present myself as the competent, professional person I know I am in Crawford Tech's conference room. In reality, I felt like everyone but myself.

I almost hit Kendra's speed-dial half a dozen times. In times of strife, that's always what I do for levity: call my best friend. But assuming I even got ahold of her—she's on a special-occasion date with Patrick tonight, and I'm not itching to interrupt that—I don't know what I'd say. She can't talk me down from the ledge, because she doesn't know I'm up here. Which means I'd have to start with the backstory, and there'd be so much I-told-you-so-ing and I-can't-believe-you-lied-to-me (I didn't actually lie about going to Colorado, but we both know which way she'll see it) that we'd likely never get down to the real question, which is what in the name of God do I do *now*?

The longer I don't call, the more another thought settles in, floating in from the horizon and landing dead-center in my mind, where I can't miss it: I don't want her reaction to affect how I feel. I want to acknowledge and own every sensation and be enveloped in this cloud, so I know who and what and where and why I am. I feel alive and prickly.

So I dial a different number, then take the Mass Pike west to Waltham, back near the office.

"Please tell me your interview sucked and there's no way you're leaving me alone with JJ," Nina says when she opens the door to her apartment.

"I wish I could."

"No you don't."

"You're right. I don't."

If Nina's surprised to hear from me, she doesn't say so. She's leaving tomorrow to visit a childhood friend in Tucson. I sit in her living room while she packs. "I gotta thank JJ," Nina says grudgingly. "I don't think I would have ever found the excuse to take off like this without a mandatory vacation."

"Strong words."

"I know." Nina methodically consults her phone, where her packing list resides, as she packs and repacks with an efficiency that boggles me.

"That's pretty impressive," I say.

"I'm going to be the only person ever to go for a week's vacation with just a carry-on," she boasts. Watching her, I don't doubt it. I could take a lesson (or twelve) from her. That makes me think of Wade, and the whole reason I'm here.

"Charlie, that was a joke. You laugh at jokes."

"Sorry. I... uh. Well. Something happened yesterday."

"Ah-ha!" She fist-pumps the air. "You got with your neighbor, didn't you?"

I gape at her. "How the hell did you guess that?"

She shakes her head at me, slowly and deliberately. "Girl, hello? I see you every day, all day."

"But if I talk about any guy at all, it's Dean!"

Another shake. She sits next to me on the couch. "You *talk* about him, yeah. All these what-ifs and maybes that don't mean jack. Are you even having good sex with him? Because you sure don't talk like you do. The Dean guy is a side man. You actually live your life with—what's his name?"

"A side man?"

She shakes her head.

"His name's Wade," I say.

"Wade. You live your life with Wade. And I bet you didn't do anything more than kiss him."

My mouth drops open. "You're officially scaring me."

Nina's smile is small but triumphant. "Charlie, you should see yourself. Day after day. You text him, you mention him in passing, you talk about your silly little runs. I swear it was weeks before I realized he *wasn't* your boyfriend."

I can't believe this.

"Frankly, sometimes you make me want to puke. It's just too damn cute."

I'm speechless. "You mean this," I say, needing confirmation.

"Are you really surprised?" Disbelief colors her face, then she shrug-sighs with an *If you say so* look and bends to rearrange a couple pairs of shoes. "Girl, it's been obvious since day one. You're in some serious like."

I cover my face with my hands.

"Why is this a bad thing?" she asks me. "Because he's young?"

"He's not just young, he's a teenager."

"Who cares? He's legal. You like him, he likes you."

"It's not that simple."

She snorts. "People like you think everything has to be simple. Life is complicated. All of it. We're all just stabbing in the dark, figuring shit out."

Nina may be right, but I can't just go along with her suggestion. (Which is, ultimately, to sneak into Wade's house in the middle of the night, generously offering him full use of my body. I'm not joking.) Plus, she's making a big leap, assuming he likes me. The kiss came out of the blue for both of us.

And Dean. He's not a side man. Last weekend, after Xanna's party, was a—dare I say it—real, honest-to-God turning point for us. We agreed to go to Kelly and Dave's wedding together. Our public debut as a couple.

Long after spin class last night, I lingered in the gym's locker room. In my reflection over the sinks, with my eyes half-shut I could see hints of the high school girl I had been. I wiped the day's eyeliner from beneath each eyelid with my index finger, making my face as naked as possible. I pulled my hair out of the ponytail holder, letting it frame my face and fall down my back. I tried to see myself as a stranger would, as an ex-boyfriend would, as a long-ago next-door neighbor would, as my dad would. I couldn't tell whether they were the same or not.

One thing is certain. Nina never should have been able to conclude what she did about my feelings for Wade. If this is truly what I'm projecting, I absolutely have to stop this thing— whatever it is—before it gets any worse.

The bar in the den has been locked since I was old enough to notice it, but not anymore. I mix myself a strong Jack and Coke from a bottle in the back. Half of it I down right away, then bring the rest to my room. Pillows propped, I lie on my made bed the way I used to in high school, when Dean had only been a wish and a hope. Or when he and I argued over the phone, minor, piddly fights that we forgot the next day. I lie there the way I did when I'd listen to Marina and my mother screaming at each other, my dad deafeningly silent, before I gave up and brought my headphones to the treehouse.

I should call him. On the home screen of my phone is a photo of last year's fall colors, taken in Vermont, but my vision is obscured by bubbling-up thoughts of Wade that I keep having to pound down, a perpetual Whack-a-Mole game. Like his eyes. Those magnetic, impossibly blue eyes that turn down at the corners. As if they've already seen too much.

Whack.

There's so much about him that is beautiful.

Whack.

I love to watch him walk away.

Whack.

His car is in the driveway. He's been home since ten after six. I could knock on his door. I could text him to plan a run. I could act as if nothing happened.

But I have to be responsible. *He's nineteen.* These two words have become my mantra of caution. *He's nineteen, and Dean is your person.*

What was it they said about young people's brains? My mom went on about it when I was a teenager myself after she read some magazine article or watched a Dr. Phil show. I recall vivid examples that she held onto, like the time I wanted to hitch a ride home from the Cape with a guy I met in line at McDonald's. Teen brains, she told me over and over ad nauseam, aren't fully developed to the point where they can see the consequences of their decisions. They can't see around corners. Thus they fuck up a lot of their lives. Wade is likely right in the thick of this. He might think we have something between us, but unlike me, he can't see the fuckup potential. It's not his fault; it's just the way it is. And it's up to me to explain it.

The kiss, I'll tell him when I'm finally ready to face my penance, was a one-off thing that won't happen again. Hopefully, that will be it.

At a quarter to eight, Wade pulls out of his driveway. On his way to Lindsay. Maybe. I'm only guessing.

His taillights have barely disappeared when I'm on my laptop, searching Facebook. I don't find much but a few duck-face photos. I try Instagram. Bingo. LinzeeBoston's Instagram feed is filled with selfies. Jesus, she's stunning. Shoulder-length blonde hair, luminous eyes, boobs out to here. Judging from the number of photos in which it's prominent, she seems to be quite a fan of her own ass. She's the kind of girl I would have looked away from self-consciously in high school, unreal and ethereal and not quite belonging in my world.

I go through the motions of a self-indulgent night. I watch two syndicated, cuss-free episodes of *Sex and the City*. I read four chapters of the last novel from my vacation library haul. I re-organize the photos on my computer and write a few emails to friends I don't see as often as I should. I get into my preferred pajamas—ancient velour yoga pants and a raggedy Cake T-shirt that used to belong to Marina. At the improbably early time of 9:50, I brush my teeth and get into bed.

I'm still awake at 11:23 when a car pulls in. I watch Wade go inside alone. I tell myself I'll wait fifteen minutes, but after twelve I can't take it.

Can I see you?

His response is immediate: *Of course.*

Ten minutes, I text back, knowing he'll know where.

I show up in fifteen. It takes me that long to change out of my pajamas into regular clothes, then back into them when I decide I don't want him thinking I've gotten dressed for him, then back *out* of them when I realize he doesn't know I've changed into them in the first place. And then I have to brush my hair, because all those clothes have electrified it. I shove on a beanie to keep it tamed. The backyard lawn hides my footsteps, but as much as I don't want to announce my arrival, there's no way I can sneak up the tree. I clomp like King Kong, so I'm not surprised to see his hand extended when I poke through the opening. Still, I hesitate; this entire night could benefit from limiting physical contact. But I can't figure out how to refuse his help politely, and I don't want to offend him any more than I expect I already will.

Mistake. New rule: No touching at all. Ever.

I sink into my corner, knees to chest, and try to figure out where to begin. Across from me, he leans against the wall, chewing a toothpick. He seems comfortable. He's looking at me, but not expectantly, neither smiling nor frowning. His eyes are hypnotizing glints. I tear my eyes from his and take a breath to speak.

"We have to talk," he says, being me. His voice is calm, betraying no sense of heightened emotion. "This shouldn't have happened. It was a 'moment,'" he says, and you can hear the air quotes in his voice.

I have no answer, but I mentally shrug. That's pretty much what I've been planning to say. If he wants to let me out of it, all the better.

"Did I get it right?"

"Sort of."

He laughs. "So how does it feel?"

He sounds like he's teasing, but I bite anyway. "How does what feel?"

"Kissing a teenager."

I swear to God I meant to brush it off. I pledged to keep my responses to myself and stick with the rehearsed speech. But instead of saying, as I know I should, "It felt wrong," to my horror I let out a shaky little sigh, which I turn into a choky little cough. "Wrong," I say, supposedly with conviction, but it comes out meek. I steady my voice. "It was wrong," I repeat.

"Absolutely wrong," he says agreeably.

"You're too young for me."

"Way too young."

"I'm too old for you."

"Way too old."

He's playing with me. Magnetically my eyes are pulled back to his. The moonlight makes his face bright. He says nothing, and I wait to see how long I can go. Ten seconds. Twenty. Thirty.

Oh, fuck it. "Wade, you can *kiss*."

He laughs softly. "Charlie, I could say the same thing. I've never been kissed like that before."

I don't know which part of that to argue with. I settle for the obvious. "*You* kissed *me*!"

"Technically, you kissed me first. Okay, fine," he says, heading my protest off, "I know what you're saying. But then you sure did kiss me back."

"I was only reacting."

"I could say the same thing."

I shake my head. "Wade, I don't want to hurt your feelings."

"You think you will?"

"I don't know. I hope not."

"I'll take my chances."

"It's not going to happen again," I say as firmly as I can.

"Because it shouldn't or because you don't want it to?"

I know a trick question when I hear it. "Don't make me say it. I have to do the right thing."

"And the right thing is?"

"I'm seven years older than you."

"I can count."

"I changed your *diapers*."

He cocks his head, flips his hand like *Oh well*. "So we both saw each other naked."

"*What?*"

He shrugs mischievously. "You were pretty hot in high school."

150

I want to laugh and slap his face, equally. Keeping my composure, I say carefully, "Please tell me how it happened that you saw me naked."

"From here."

"Here?" I swing my gaze over to my house. We're level with my bedroom window. The light's off now, but it's obvious that with light and no curtains, it could easily be the Charlie Show.

"Huh." I pause. "Well, you couldn't have seen me *naked*."

"No, just topless."

He laughs at the look I give him. "I was ten. Not nearly old enough to appreciate it."

I think of exactly what *appreciate* might mean, and I close my eyes. "Gross."

"Don't worry, Keith never saw you. I kept the secret view to myself."

Why is he even mentioning Keith? But before I can ask him anything, his voice turns serious. "Charlie. About last night—"

"There you go, quoting movies again."

He smiles his *Touché* smile, begins to speak, then laughs again. I'm puffing up with pride—he's usually the one making me laugh. When he's composed, he says, "Just tell me this: did it feel wrong?"

I've gone this far, I might as well be honest. "No."

"So it made sense on some level."

I think for a minute. "Maybe."

"Definitely maybe?"

"*Maybe* maybe. And on the *wrong* level." I sigh. "Wade, you need to understand. The whole thing was just the result of some stupid crazy emotions of mine. I was so grateful about finding the email, and I just went haywire. I'm used to having a boyfriend, and I'm comfortable with you. I just didn't think."

"You treated me like a boyfriend?" he asks. I raise my eyes skyward. There's a sly glint in his eye, and he leans toward me, removing the toothpick from his mouth. "Did you leave anybody behind?"

"What?"

He smiles. "Do you have a boyfriend?"

I shake my head, skeptically.

"You want one?"

It's impossible not to return his grin. I feel like there's a joke I'm not getting, but I don't care. I don't think he'll ever not be able to make me smile against my will.

With a sense of satisfaction, he resumes his leaning-back position and returns the toothpick to his mouth. I try to apologize again and he waves me off. "Stop saying sorry, Charlie girl."

"But I am. It was an accident."

"Like a car crash?"

Yes. *Crash into me. Call me Charlie girl again. Whack.* I poke his foot with mine. "Accidental."

He pokes me back. "I'll be your accidental man."

I know him well enough to know he did not make this up. "Yes, I stole that from a song," he tells me, poking me again.

"Of course you did."

"This conversation has been full of references you're not getting."

We both fall silent. I poke his foot again, more lightly, feeling like a footsie-playing third grader. "So can we agree? That what happened was a... mistake?" His exaggerated wince tells me the word rings as false to him as it does to me. But, perhaps as concession, he nods.

"I'll act like it didn't happen if that's really what you want. But do me a favor," he says, without bitterness. "Stop being sorry and looking sorry. I'm a big boy. I'll be fine."

I rise and step down through the trap door as he adjusts the nest of bedding behind him, making a spot to settle himself into more deeply. Is he—oh. He's lying down, jeans pulled taut against his leg muscles. *Keep going, Charlie*, I tell myself. *Whack.*

"Charlie?" I turn back to him, only my head poking out of the floor. Wade's resting his head back on his arms, the length of him running from one end of the treehouse to the other. "One thing. I'll never say it was a mistake. I make my share of dumbass mistakes, but kissing you? It's the most right thing I've done in a long time."

I have no words to respond to that. None that would be wise to voice, anyway. "I better go."

And I leave him there, talking to the sky.

I think over his words in bed that night. "I'll be your accidental man," he said. Hell, I'm not sleeping anyway. I fire up my laptop. Googling tells me there's a song with that title, "Accidental Man" by the Damnwells. Is that the song he was referring to? Neither piece of information sounds familiar. I download it and lay in bed, listening.

"I'll be your accidental man," the guy sings in the chorus. "I'll be your circumstantial lover." I start to smile. I hate that word, LOVER, but I like how this guy is using it. "I'm gonna take you by the hand." I think of him pulling me into the treehouse. "I'm gonna steal you from your mother."

I sit back, still smiling, enjoying the music. Wade's music. "You'll be my worst-kept secret."

Secrets. I'm not good at them. Nina showed me that. It's no use even trying to pretend I don't feel exactly the way she—and Wade—said I did.

And Wade isn't going to pretend at all.

He's right, of course. Our kiss wasn't a mistake. I'm surprised it hasn't happened earlier. Stripped away of numbers and labels, the simple, bald truth is that we work. The two of us, together. I love to hear him talk. The sentences that come out of his mouth are so often the end of half-formed thoughts in my own head. And physically, it's like nothing I've ever felt. I can't even touch his hand without everything inside of me combusting.

Perhaps worst of all, the idea of him with that skinny blonde skank...I can't even.

Would there really be any harm in a tryst? A one-time thing that he can take back to Colorado?

The song ends and I put it on repeat. Thinking of the glow of his skin, the taste of his mouth, the feel of his hand over mine tonight as he helped me into the treehouse, creates a dull ache in my stomach. The more I try to ignore it, the bigger it becomes. I draw my hands across my abdomen slowly, singing the chorus. I roll off my back with force, slapping the pillow. I watch the old-fashioned clock radio turn. Five minutes. Ten. Sleep. Just go to sleep.

But he's still in the air. My curtains and shade are open; he could, right now, be looking toward my dark window. When I close my eyes, I can still see him, leaning down to me, kissing me like that's what the world expects him to do.

Whack, whack, WHACK.

It was a good move to get out of the treehouse when I did. I know for a fact that if he showed up in my room right now, I wouldn't have the strength to do the right thing. I would do exactly the wrong thing. Several times.

I try to think of Dean. I picture him seeing me in Paco's, that knowing nod. And above me in his living room, recreating the beginning. Does he recognize *us* when he looks at me? Or does he look past me to what's next?

I want him to look at me like Wade does.

God. This is not helping at *all*.

I turn to my back again and slip my hand under the waistband of my yoga pants. If this is the only way I'm going to get to sleep tonight, so be it.

fourteen

Marina lets the shower stream run over her hand. "Wow, this is pretty good." She steps out of the bathroom, drying her hand on her jeans, and sees me staring at her. "What?"

"Nothing," I say. "It's just that I do that too."

Most people think I'm crazy, but water pressure is a serious deal. You know what kind of people care about water pressure? People who have lived with bad water pressure. Like Marina and me, who dealt with the same horrific shower in the upstairs bathroom of our house until it was finally fixed when I was sixteen.

"I swear that's why I refuse to take baths," she says. "I took so many goddamn baths in high school."

"I just thought you really, really liked baths."

We stare at each other for a minute. Then we both burst out laughing.

When's the last time Marina and I laughed at the same thing, at the same time, together? I honestly couldn't say.

The landlord leads us into the bedroom and out the back hallway to the laundry facilities. If you had told me two months ago that Marina would be accompanying me to Somerville to check out potential apartments, I would checked your person for reality-altering substances. But here we were, just outside Davis Square—my old 'hood—traipsing through a couple of apartments owned by Carl, one of my creepy former landlords. I wasn't crazy about signing a lease with him again, but on a lark I'd called him, and he had properties available.

At the end of today's therapy session—another exercise in patience and pretense—my mom and sister again wanted to go to dinner, and again I had to beg off. The way they exchanged a glance made it clear they think I have an issue with them, but I really did have plans.

"I have an appointment to look at a couple of apartments," I said. "I'm sorry, I would join you if I could."

"Well then," Marina said, looking at my mom, "we'll go with you."

Go with me? Because I had no way of saying no, I said nothing, which was the same as saying yes.

And then my mom upped the awkward with some far-fetched lie about something she forgot she needed to do at home. But Marina could still go with me, she urged. She'd just meet us both at home; she'd heat up some leftovers or get take-out; she'd be fine. And she was gone, as pleased with herself as if she'd just set up a successful blind date. I couldn't think of what else to do besides let Marina follow me to my car.

The drive was tense at first, but I gradually realized the tension was coming entirely from me. Marina actually seemed pretty relaxed. "I think therapy's going well, don't you?" she said as we drove east on Route 2. "I know Mom's hoping for a miracle, but it's not as bad as it could have been."

Was that a compliment? I glanced out of the corner of my eye to see if I was being set up. But Marina was calmly looking ahead, as if we had this kind of conversation every day.

"Of course," she went on, "we still have a ways to go." I wondered what she meant, and then I decided I didn't want to know.

Carl walks up to us. "I gutta get this one filled by the fifteenth," he says. "The udda one, I can give ya till the first."

I sigh. The first apartment we looked at will definitely require a roommate—which I don't have yet—and this one is a little out of my price range. Even a roommate wouldn't work, since it's a one-bedroom.

Marina motions me into the kitchen. "So this one is nicer," she says, correctly. It's also in a slightly better location and has off-street parking, which is huge in Somerville. "But it's more expensive."

"Yup, probably too expensive," I say, looking around. "I probably shouldn't have even looked at this one."

"Do you have anyone in mind for a roommate?" she asks. I shake my head. I've been wracking my brain to come up with someone I know who needs a place to live that I wouldn't mind living with.

I'm peering in the freezer to see how it defrosts when Marina says, "So I don't mean to pry, but are you and Dean back together?"

My head smacks on the ceiling of the freezer.

"I just wondered why you were looking at this apartment. It's not big enough for two, but it's big enough for a couple." She shrugs, like this is the most logical conclusion to draw.

Of course it is. I can feel myself blushing, like I've been caught in a lie. Carl told me the square footage, mentioned the people who moved out were a couple. I had, indeed, pictured Dean and me here.

"We haven't really qualified anything," I say. "But it's... getting there."

She gives me a look I can't quite read. "How long were you together before?"

"Almost three years."

She whistles, low. "Young love. Intense."

"You lived with Steve when you were really young," I say, boldly. "How did that go?"

I thought she might hesitate, considering this none of my business, but she answers right away, as if I asked this sort of question every day. "It was fantastic for about a week. Then, you know, you realize it's just life, like everything else. He's just the guy who forgets to put the cap back on the toothpaste or who can't quite come up with his share of the rent." She seems lost in thought, then smiles. "God, I have to say I have no idea where Steve is or what he's doing. And I'm pretty sure I don't care."

"You're not friends with him on Facebook?" She gives me a look, and I have to smile to myself as I open the door to the back porch. I may not know Marina well, but I do know she will likely be the last Facebook holdout.

"Charlie," she says, and I turn back, my hand on the doorknob. *She called me Charlie.* "Why did you and he break up anyway? I don't think I ever knew."

"We just grew apart," I say finally, which is at least one truth.

Her smile, after a minute, is small and slight, the realest I've seen on her face in years. "I remember how much he loved you two as a couple." She means Dad. She walks out to the living room, and I follow, my throat tight, because I know she's right.

157

Steve Linstrom is drunk. I'd know this even if I didn't personally witness him consuming multiple Bud Lights and at least three shots of Jaegermeister. Clue number one: he's taking his shirt off onstage while attempting to channel Billie Joe Armstrong. No one seems to have told him that if you haven't played football or lacrosse in ten years, your body's not worth showing off.

"This is not good," Felicia says to me, her eyes glued anxiously to the stage.

"Does he do this often?"

"Well." She puts her water glass down. "I don't know, exactly. I didn't think so, but it's starting to look like a pattern."

Onstage, Steve finishes his unwelcome duet with Reggie Forester, a guy who graduated a couple years ahead of us in high school, and the whole reason I was able to convince Dean to come out tonight. I knew Reggie would probably just be playing a bunch of covers, but anything was better than another night in front of the TV. The pattern we'd developed—TV in his basement, beer, sex—was so old it was in syndication.

"To the bartender!" Steve raises his glass skyward and steps offstage, only slightly nudged by the patient Reggie.

Clue number two on how drunk Steve is: He is toasting everything.

He turns back towards the stage. "To Reggie!" Amazingly, people actually chant back: "To Reggie!" I guess when you're Steve Linstrom, anointed the hottest guy in eighth grade and who never relinquished the title, anything can become cool.

Felicia leaves to pee, and Dean appears behind my stool. I haven't seen much of him since we arrived. He's mostly been on the other side of the bar, with the guys. I'm trying not to wonder whether he's punishing me. It was surprisingly difficult to get him to come out.

"It'll be fun," I'd said, punching his arm playfully. We were on the couch. As usual. "I hear Reggie's fantastic."

"I don't know, babe. I'm pretty tired." He stretched. My heart turned over at the *babe*, and I scrunched myself under his arm as it came down, sand to the incoming tide.

Ever since the accidental kiss with Wade, I've been spending more time with Dean. I started taking the initiative in plans, not simply waiting for him to text me. It helps that pre-winter weather has set in. It's way too cold for the treehouse. Now that we both go to the gym—separately—I've hardly seen Wade at all. His absence has helped clarify a few things. I felt closer than ever to Dean, and to our inevitable, official "reunion."

Still, I was restless tonight. He couldn't be *that* tired on a weeknight. Shortly after I arrived, after venting about work, I asked him what he'd done all day. He couldn't remember. I pursed my lips, not judging. It was none of my business how he spent his days. Or how many bags of Cheetos he ate. Or whether he got any sunlight.

"So what kind of job are you looking for?" I asked instead.

This was a bit of a reach, as he hadn't actually told me anything about a job search. "I'm not sure yet," he answered. "Still figuring that out."

I clasped his hand absently with both of mine, running my fingers over his knuckles. "Something like what you had in Chicago?"

He shrugged noncommittally. "I dunno, maybe. It's not like I have to pay rent right now."

"Want me to take a look at your résumé? I have, unfortunately, become quite the expert in job-hunting."

He shrugged again, but told me sure, if I wanted to. I could find it on LinkedIn.

Now, behind my stool, his hands press on my shoulders. He runs his thumbs on the back of my neck, under my hair, making me involuntarily shiver. "Let's get outta here."

His voice has the come-hither sound. I'm glad for how public he's willing to be about us being together-ish, but I plant myself more solidly on my stool. "You know I'm not staying over tonight."

The last time I stayed over—a Sunday night—I was so late I had to go to work on Monday *without showering.* I'm lucky I had time to even change out of the holey jeans and Boston Strong T-shirt I'd been wearing. Not to mention that tomorrow JJ and I have a mandatory nine o'clock, and there's no way I'm going in anything less than completely prepared and professional. She's been looking at me differently lately, like she's just waiting for me to fuck up. It's not in my head. Nina's noticed the same thing. And although I've made it to the third-interview stage with Crawford Tech—I'm going there again next week—and I've been emailing with another company about coming in to meet them, no one's offered me a job.

"I'll make sure you get home by midnight, Cinderella," Dean says directly into my ear. "I promise. I want to thank you properly for working on my résumé for me."

"I haven't done it yet."

"But you will. You're responsible like that."

I see Felicia coming back from the bathroom, but then Steve steps in front of her and she's lost from my view. She'll probably take him home. They're not dating, but they've been close for so many years they may as well be. She takes the big-sister role with him, but I wouldn't be surprised if they were friends with benefits.

"Whattaya say?" Dean is saying, still in my ear.

Friends with benefits. Is that what we are? I sigh. It's already 11:30. It's not like the night is going to get any better. "Half an hour. No more."

The tiniest bit of light is making its way through the window when I wake. I roll over, and something keeps me from moving as far as I want. An arm. A male arm. Dean's arm.

I bolt upright. It's *morning*?

I jump up out of Dean's bed, tripping on my shoes. "Dean. Dean!"

He sits up, groggy and confused, morning erection poking through the slit in his boxers like a middle finger. "What's up?"

"I'm late!" Oh God, it's five after eight. I'm supposed to already be in the office! And JJ and I have a nine o'clock. A *mandatory* nine o'clock. *Where the fuck are my clothes?*

Dean drops back onto the pillow. "Help me!" I hiss.

"Just call in sick."

"I'm not sick! I'm late!"

He gets up, but not without heaving a sigh that makes me want to slug him.

How did this happen? I didn't mean to fall asleep, and I definitely didn't mean to spend the night. But just as I was about to leave, halfway through *Game of Thrones*, which Dean somehow convinced me to watch with him, a particularly gruesome sex scene that I didn't find the least bit scintillating had the opposite effect on him. And once Dean's hands, mouth, and other pertinent body parts found their destinations I had, apparently, stopped thinking.

Oh, God. It's coming back to me. My protests over moving to the bed, Dean's soothing promise: *I'll make sure you get up early.*

"Where's my purse?" I whirl around to find Dean back in bed, face-down. Seriously? I throw a pillow on him. "Dean!

Help me! I need my phone." He's not moving. I find my purse hanging on the bathroom doorknob, my phone between couch cushions. I rush out the side door that serves as a semi-private entrance to the basement as silently as I can.

I'm next to my car digging in my purse for my keys when the garage door opens and a silver Outback slides slowly out. I keep my head down as the Outback starts coming my way, finally locating my keys in the outside compartment.

The Outback passes me. Stops. Backs up. A window rolls down.

"Charlie? Charlie Michaelsen? Is that you?"

Curtained by my hair, I swipe under each eyelash before looking up. "Hi, Mrs. Carson," I reply, trying to smile.

"Well, it is you! Do you need help, hon?"

"Just looking for my keys," I say, holding them up and trying to sound breezy.

She seems to hesitate, like she's about to say something. But I'm already getting in my car.

"Well, it's really nice to see you," she says. "Tell your mother I said hello, will you?"

I notice the fuel-warning light on as I pull onto my street. Fuck. Maybe I can take my mom's car to work. But when I get home the driveway is empty. Refueling will only take ten minutes, but my margin for error is so razor-thin ten minutes could make a difference. I know it's childish, but when I get out of the car, I can't help it. I kick the tire. "Fuck fuck *fuck*!"

"I don't think that will help."

I whip my head around to see Wade on his way to his backyard, towing the recycling bin behind him.

"I have no gas!" I scream. He just stands there, blinking. "I'm sorry! I can't talk! I have to get in the shower."

When I emerge from my house sixteen minutes later—a new record—he's still there, sitting on my steps. He stands and hands me something. My keys. "Car's full."

"Wade, I really have to—what?"

"I filled it up while you were inside."

The last time Wade saved my ass, I went down the wrong road. My head is whirling, but one thought takes the lead: *Do not touch him.* "You're awesome," I say, my feet rooted to the ground. "And I seriously promise to pay you back."

I get to work at five till nine. JJ is there already. I barely have my computer booted up when she calls me into her office. I'm guessing whatever JJ has to say to me before the nine o'clock is going to make or break my work day, so I square my shoulders and prepare to pay serious attention.

And I do. Pay attention. The whole time she's letting me go.

Go back and talk to her. You can explain."

"Dean, I don't think you heard me. I was *fired*."

"That doesn't make any sense. You were, what? Twenty minutes late?"

"You don't know my boss."

"It sounds like you don't want to work there anyway. Aren't you looking for a new job?"

"But I don't have one yet!" Either Dean can't understand the utter importance of how he just severely fucked up my life, or he won't.

"Charlie, just come back over here. No one's home. You'll forget all about it."

Right, because sex will solve everything. I roll my eyes. "Your mom's still out?"

"She's at work," he says, then backtracks. "You saw my mom?"

"She was *awfully* surprised to see me."

When Dean finally speaks, it's with flat distance. "What's up, Charlie?"

"I told you I did not want to see her for the first time during the walk of shame."

To my fury, he actually laughs. "So you're ashamed of me?" He's trying to tease his way out of it. I grip my phone so tightly I wouldn't be surprised if I broke it.

"Dean." Jesus Christ, this is my *life*. How can he be so casual? "Please. I got *fired* today."

"You will get another job, Charlie. Stop worrying. Look at me. Do you see me worried about not working right now?"

"You're living at home!"

It takes two seconds of his silence for me to catch up. "I'm not here by choice," I snap, even though I am.

"Neither am I," he snaps back.

"What? Of course you are."

I hear him take a deep breath. "Just come back over," he cajoles. "Is there really anything else you can do? Right now?"

As a matter of fact, yes. There is. I can pay someone back.

If it has to be my day for meeting boys' mothers, at least Wade's sees me with makeup on, sans bedhead.

"Charlie!" A smile of genuine delight spreads across Marla's face when she opens the door.

"Hi Marla." Hugging her, I'm momentarily jarred that I haven't talked to her since I moved home. Living next door to someone used to mean something, but proximity doesn't matter like it used to.

"I see your mother here and there, but you have been a stranger," Marla says with good-natured reproach, ushering me between several suitcases stacked on the floor. "Sorry, sweetie, William and I are headed to the airport and everything's in your way." I think of Nina's minimalism as I count at least seven bags. Marla pushes two of them further off to the side and looks down at me again, hands on her hips. "My goodness, how old are you now?"

"Twenty-six."

She shakes her head. "And just as gorgeous as ever. I swear I don't know where the time goes. Wade tells me you've moved home for a while?"

"Yeah, it's a financial thing. Just temporary," I add. "Is he here? I... have something for him."

"He's in the basement." She steps to the basement door and calls his name. "Well, it's nice to see you around anyway, Charlie. Especially since you seem to have turned Wade into a runner." She looks impressed.

"That's all him," I reply, not even trying to hide my jealousy. "It's amazing. He went from wheezing behind me to blowing me away. Totally not fair."

That makes her smile again. I think of the T-shirt I couldn't help buying last week. "Your Pace or Mine," it said. It's in my closet now; I bought it in Wade's size.

Marla's been inspecting her luggage. She stands back, apparently satisfied, and glances at the still-vacant basement door. "It's nice to see you two as friends, Charlie. I think you've been really good for him."

Luckily Wade spares me from responding. Despite all my convictions I return his smile. I'm not sure anyone has ever greeted me the way Wade does. Just looking at his face makes me glad that I exist.

"Hey," I say to him. My voice is subdued by both shyness and embarrassment. "I came to... um..."

To my horror, Marla looks between the two of us and seems to conclude we'd rather be alone. "Let me know if William arrives, okay, hon?" She disappears, and Wade and I share an Awkward Moment.

"They're going to Turks and Caicos," he explains. "I'm driving them to the airport in a few."

"Oh."

He ushers me outside. Once we're on his porch, he faces me, hands in the pockets of his jeans. "You were saying?"

I dig in my own pocket. "I came to pay you back," I say. He accepts the folded bills without taking his eyes off me, the warmest of blue ice. Our fingers don't touch. "Thanks for the gas. You saved me."

"Glad to help." He frowns suddenly, no doubt realizing that if I made it to work, I should still be there. "You got to work, right?"

"Yes, I did. And I got fired."

His eyes grow wide. "Seriously?"

"Seriously." I press my lips together and sit down on the steps. He joins me.

"Do you want to talk about it?"

"No." The last thing I want to broadcast to him is my anger at Dean. I don't even want to *be* angry at Dean, not in Wade's presence, anyway. I force a smile. "I'll talk about something else, though. So you're going to the airport during rush hour?"

"I am indeed. It's okay though, I'll be going against traffic."

"Until the way home."

"True. Hopefully it'll be late enough."

"Hopefully." Why am I so nervous? I used to be able to relax around Wade. It was what I loved about being with him. Now I'm tense as a guitar string.

"You seeing Dean tonight?"

"I... I don't think so. And you?"

"Am I seeing Dean?"

I shoulder-bump him.

"Yeah, Lindsay's supposed to call sometime today."

"Oh?" I say primly. "Please tell her I said hello."

"I will."

He doesn't go on, and I wait as long as I can until I can't take it. "I thought you weren't dating her."

"I'm not."

"So you're just..."

"Hanging out," he says with something like satisfaction. It's all I can do to not give him a dirty look; the bastard is *smiling*.

"Of course," he goes on, deadpan and with emphasis, "I'd rather *hang out* with you."

And I can't help it. Maybe it's the nervousness, or the jealousy I can't seem to get away from, or the panic that hasn't quite set in about not having a job, but I lose it. One minute I'm sitting next to him, strategically not touching him to the point where I'm regretting a simple shoulder-bump, doing everything in my power to maintain an even keel, and the next my emotions have collided and exploded into uncontrollable, hysterical laughter. I lower my forehead to my knees, my entire body convulsing with silent giggles.

"Charlie? Are you okay?"

Wade's worried. I can't even breathe, and I'm sure it looks like I'm crying. The more I think about reassuring him, though, the harder I laugh. All the while he's asking over and over, "What's the matter? Charlie? Are you okay?"

Finally I manage to raise my head and meet Wade's anxious eyes. "Oh," he says, understanding spreading over his features. "Yeah, this is pretty much hilarious, isn't it?"

I try to speak, but it comes out in a wheeze.

"This is obliterating my self-esteem. You know that, right? Tell a girl you want to sleep with her, and she can't stop laughing?"

"I'm... so ... I'm ...." My voice is useless.

Wade assumes a deeper voice and speaks to an invisible audience. "No, it's fine, it's fine, everyone, she'll be okay. It's me, actually—I'm just getting crushed by a girl. She's heartlessly trouncing my ego. No problem, you can go. Move along. Nothing to see here."

That night, Wade doesn't go out with Lindsay. She comes over. At eight-thirty she pulls into his driveway in her little blue car. He meets her at the door, and they disappear inside. I know this because I see it all from the window of my bedroom, where I'm hiding.

Once they're out of sight I slide to the floor, contemplating the lowly wormness I have sunk to. Spying on the boy next door and his date for the night? I don't even recognize myself. I blame my bedroom and the Linkin Park poster. This is complete high-school behavior.

His mom and stepdad are gone. For ten days. Which means he and Lindsay are the only two in the whole house, and likely will be for days and days. They're probably having sex on his parents' bed right now. Or in his bedroom, on a twin bed, the way college students do. Or on the living room couch. Or all of the above.

He said he wants to sleep with me. That he'd rather be with me.

I fall onto my own bed, pulling the pillow over my head to kill the unwelcome images of him and this girl, jealousy stabbing me from all sides.

I let the pillow fall and stare at the ceiling. God. Being jealous *sucks*. Especially when it makes no sense. He's doing exactly what he should be doing. He's nineteen. A guy like him *should* be having sex with someone his own age. Lots of it. Especially with impossibly beautiful girls like Lindsay. And the last person that should matter to is the perverted, cougar-like next-door neighbor.

Lindsay's not gone at 11. She's not gone at 11:30. After that I wait, chin on my arms in the windowsill, until I see her get into her little blue car, alone, at 11:53. I watch her disappear down the street before texting him. I know how this will look, the utter obviousness that I've been watching, waiting until the moment she left.

I don't care.

How did it go? I type.

As expected.

Oh?

The phone rings in my hand. He's never called me before.

"Charlie."

"Hi."

"I can see you in your window."

"I know." I wave.

"Are you going to do this every time I have a girl over?"

"It depends. How many girls would that be?"

He laughs softly.

"I don't know," I say. "Maybe."

"So I'll just look for you, then."

I smile in spite of myself, hugging the phone to my cheek. "I'm sorry. I know this is silly of me."

He sighs. "Considering we just watched a movie, and she's probably pissed at me for not paying enough attention to her, and I'm not allowed to *hang out* with you, yeah, I'd say so."

I echo his sigh, again turning away from the mental image that *hang out* conjures. *Whack.* I stare at him in the window, willing him to see more in my face than I can say across the yard. "Good night, Wade Hunter."

"'Night, Charlie. Sleep well."

I sit soundlessly for a minute. Then I throw the phone across the room.

fifteen

Since I got fired, Dean has texted me twice and called once. All ignored. But by Sunday, three days later, a sneaky thought begins to take root. I shove it down, but it floats to the surface again and again until I have to face it.

My getting fired wasn't his fault.

Certainly he played a part in it. And he wasn't very mature about the actual firing. But it's not like I had no agency in my decisions that night. If I wasn't so antsy to go out instead of staying in, for example, I wouldn't have been out so late. I could have stayed firm and gone home, or even stuck around the Castle with Felicia, but I chose to go back to his place. And certainly no one forced me to have sex with him.

His texts have been apologetic. When I finally listen to his voice mail early Sunday afternoon driving home from Xanna's, I'm surprised—and touched—to hear him inviting me to dinner with his parents tomorrow night.

I am not a nice person.

It's the Wade thing. It must be. He's got me feeling stabby, being all next door and alone and entertaining teen girls. (Fine, she's twenty-one. *Whatever.*) But it's time to get back on track, towards a definite future. With Dean. Dinner tomorrow will be the start of it all.

First, though, I want to make it up to him. So I do what I said I would. I download his résumé from LinkedIn and spend the afternoon perfecting it. I rearrange bullet points, improve phrasing using tips gleaned from both my job-hunting research and time spent on the other side of the hiring desk. I switch the font to a career-friendly sans serif. I insert keywords. I make him searchable and findable.

When the résumé is freshly printed I slide it into a manila envelope and call him. Voice mail. No matter. I'll drive to his house and deliver it personally. Just drop the envelope at his door and wait to hear from him.

He must have just missed my call, because his car is parked at his house. Résumé in hand, I knock lightly on his entrance door, which isn't fully closed. Hearing nothing, I push it open. "Dean?"

He's in the shower. I can hear the water running. For a wild second I wonder if I should join him. Wouldn't *that* surprise him. I place the résumé on the coffee table and pick up the remote. The TV is frozen on *Project Runway.* I unpause the show, laughing to myself. The things you learn.

"Dean?" A girl's voice, from the left. From the bathroom. "Is that you?"

Bit by bit I take in the scenery I should have noticed immediately. A purse on the coffee table, a phone in a turquoise case spilling out of it. Black wedge sandals on the carpet. And, near the door to the bathroom, a haphazard pile of clothes.

White.

Denim.

Pink.

I drive home calmly, repeating the same thing to myself. *Such a dumbass. Such. A. Dumbass!*

Dean Carson can die in a fire. Meanwhile, I'm a gullible, stubborn, complete and utter fool. Of *course* he didn't want us to be out too much in public. Of *course* his mom was surprised to see me. She had no idea we'd been dating. He's been playing me, pretending, lying the whole time. The *whole time.*

And getting laid all the while.

I want to hate him, but I know better. Just like me getting fired wasn't his fault. He never told me we were serious. Even when I asked, when I poked and prodded and hinted, he wouldn't cop to anything that had the faintest whiff of commitment. I conveniently assumed he felt the same way I did but just wasn't ready to say so, figuring it would all work itself out in time. Much as I want to be furious with him, I can't shift blame again. This is all me.

It's after nine that night when I remember I left the résumé behind on Dean's coffee table. My phone is in my car where I left it, dead. Sure enough, when I charge it, Dean's already texted me, and I have two missed calls.

were u here this afternoon

I delete the message. Fuck him and his bad grammar.

There's also a text from Wade, suggesting a run this afternoon. The timestamp is 3:02 PM. I look out the window into the darkness. The little blue car is in his driveway. But as I watch, Lindsay—blonde and beautiful—emerges from his house and gets into the car, tossing her hair expertly over her shoulder, already on her phone. She backs out and turns back down Shasta Street, the way she came.

I won't text him. He'll think I was spying again. I won't text him. I won't. Just as I'm chanting that in my head, my phone vibrates in my hand.

So you never told me why you got fired, Wade has typed.

You never told me Lindsay was coming over again.

Am I supposed to?

Am I supposed to tell you why I got fired?

A pause. Then, *Lindsay's an unhappy girl.*

Oh? Why is that?

I can't seem to be anything close to what she wants.

Funny, I type. *That's pretty much why I got fired.*

At 11:23, the light in Wade's bedroom goes off. At 11:30, I'm dressed. I descend the steps on the side porch of my house. It's not like he's underage. It's not like it will mean anything. And he's leaving next month.

I stop. Turn around. Go back in.

I can't. I won't. I undress again and get back in bed.

Screw Nina and her dangerous ideas.

sixteen

At 12:35, I sit up again. Something has pulled me awake. He's alone. In that great big house. I don't have anywhere to be tomorrow. Thanks to Dean, the cheater. And it's not like having a little fun will mean anything. To us or anyone else.

My moral code stands in the doorway, hands on hips. The full moon betrays the darkness, lifting the room into light. The same moonlight that is probably in his room. "Don't do it," I tell myself out loud, in front of God and everyone. The code nods.

But even as I'm saying the words I'm getting up. I'm out the kitchen door into the night. I don't even change or put on shoes. The motion sensor light in the Hunters' front yard snaps on. I freeze. Nothing happens. The key is where I remember it, under the fake rock in the side garden. Years of familiarity wash over me as I tiptoe up the stairs and down the hall, where I stand outside the door, digging my bare toes into the hallway carpet.

I've never been in this room, the last one on the right, with the window that has been teasing me for months. The door is slightly ajar, and for a moment I simply stand, soundless, wondering what I'll dare. I make sure that I'm aware of the most important thing: I can still turn around and go home. Opening the door means tilting my world, and his. Permanently. I'll never be able to rewind our lives. Any fallout will be mine to own.

I wait, wondering if I'll want to leave. My skin prickles. The depth of my lucidity, my absolute awareness of what I'm doing,

171

is vaguely alarming. I steady myself. Take a breath. Accept certainty. I don't want to leave. I want to be in his room, in his bed, with him. Physical proof of this throbs and drips between my thighs.

Slowly I push the door open. Straight ahead, under a window, a white comforter rises and falls with breath. The bed is queen-sized, much larger than the twin I've been picturing. The sparse furnishings resemble a guest room more than a kid's bedroom, reminding me again of Wade's transience, his visitor status. I know I should give myself one last chance to change my mind. But even as I'm telling myself that, I'm lifting the comforter and sliding in behind him, my body all parallel lines to his.

His breathing changes. He knows I'm here. Mentally I give him props for not jumping out of his skin. Oh my God, his *skin*. He's bare from the waist up, his back miles long, taut, smooth. Radiant heat pulls me in. I reach cautiously around his waist and he meets me, laying his arm over mine, pressing, inviting me closer. I dare to kiss him, lightly, between his shoulder blades, and he squeezes my arm again.

He turns around, his face two inches from mine. Sleepy. Sexier than I even realized.

"Hey you," he says in a low, throaty voice that dives straight inside me.

"Hi."

"You know about the fake rock?"

"I know about the fake rock."

We shift and I'm in his arms. It's as close as we've ever been, and I can feel my heart reacting, its thrum a vibration I'm convinced Wade can feel. "You wouldn't be doing this out of jealousy, would you?" he asks me.

"Maybe." I've never lied to Wade, and I'm not going to start now. "It also could be that I found out I've been having an imaginary relationship."

"What's an imaginary relationship?"

"The kind that doesn't exist except in my head." Watching him ponder that, I ask him, "How much does that matter?"

"Right now?" He smiles ruefully, pushing his hips toward mine. "Not a whole lot."

"Then you should know there's another reason, too." I trace down his bare chest, skimming across his abdomen to the hipbones I've been wanting to touch for weeks. His stomach pulls in, tightening under my fingertips.

"Yeah?" he whispers. "What's that?"

"I might have a crush on you."

He's mock-horrified. "On a teenager?"

"You'll be twenty in April," I say, drawing circles over his pectoral muscles. "And we're just hanging out, right?"

"Heck yeah," he says, and I stifle a laugh at the expression— or the way he says it, I don't know which.

I wait for a deliberate moment, so he knows I mean it. Then I kiss him. Or maybe he kisses me. It doesn't matter. It's like it was in the gym lobby, times a thousand. No conflicting feelings are invading telling me I'm doing something wrong. I'm just kissing Wade, absorbing his sweet, spicy taste, relaxing my tongue onto his, for as long as I want. I don't even care where we're going from here, literally or figuratively. I'm sinking into him, enjoying the simple act of kissing—of making out—more than I have since I was sixteen.

He breaks to reveal the tiniest of grins, and with one deft move I'm on top of him, the architecture of his body a foundation for my own. I'm intoxicated by the musk of his skin, the taste of his tongue, the way the length of his body feels against mine, the sensation of his hands down my back. I wander from his mouth, putting my lips to his cheekbones, his forehead, his eyelids, his chest. He waits patiently, his every breath another beat of permission to explore him. This body that, for the moment anyway, is all mine. I run my fingertips over every crest and fold. I kiss his hipbones, each of them, and I feel devilish when he shudders. I make my way back up to his mouth. I kiss him like it's not a means to an end. I kiss him and kiss him and kiss him and kiss him.

Time stops. It could be minutes or hours later when, after sitting up to remove my shirt, I try to lie back down. But Wade keeps me there, trapped in the moonlight. His hands move from my cheeks to my neck down my ribcage to my hips. Then he reaches up again and releases my hair from the loose ponytail it's been in, slipping the band onto my wrist where he knows I like to keep it.

"I don't think you have any idea how beautiful you are."

"How very One Direction of you." I wish compliments didn't make me so uncomfortable. I swallow a self-deprecating remark and tell myself to believe him. I obediently stay where I am, but then I can't help slanting a look at him. "Is it like the view from the treehouse?"

He smiles and pulls me down beside him, maneuvers his mouth to my ear. "Better."

I've spent two months pushing everything into the ground, ignoring twinges, denying sensations. But Wade's body against mine strips me of my entire defensive cheat sheet. Every iota of resistance crumbles. I'm uncorked, a deluge of raw want flooding every pore.

Each kiss from him is a tease. Deep, tongue-tangling teases I get lost in. Slight, barely-there teases that keep luring me back. I can't get close enough. I rid myself of my underwear and his fingers sense me so expertly I can't help but be impressed.

"What's so funny?" he says into my ear.

"What?"

"You were smiling."

I guess I was. I bury my face in his neck, breathing him in. "Your mad skills are surprising me."

"Good." He pulls me back, ever so slightly, and looks into my eyes. "But it's not just me."

"Oh?"

"You're forgetting the Treehouse Girl factor."

I grin widely. He kisses my dimple.

I'm opening myself to him in every way. He gamely accepts each moan, every sigh into his own mouth. He's right. Our chemistry is elemental, flowing between us and fusing into a compound. Bodies communicating in a rhythm so predestined I feel like a passenger. It's all I can do to simply follow.

I've had my share of promiscuous times. A month or so in college, trying to drown my Dean-inflicted heartbreak in kegs and fraternity parties. And my slutty summer, just before I met Cam. But even then, I was never sleeping with more than one person at once (nor was I sleeping with one person more than once, come to that).

And now, three days. That's all it's been since I had sex with another person. Thirty minutes earlier or later to Dean's basement today and it could easily be his ass under my hands. But it's Wade's, and I'm struck by how different it feels. How different everything feels. The stability of his body. The rhythm of his breathing. Even the things I'm compelled to do have a different tinge. With Dean I ultimately find myself taking control, guiding him to our best interests. But control is the one thing I don't have with Wade. I have no say in how my body responds to him. My palms are buzzing, my hips drawn to his, the back of my neck prickling in ways I've only read about. I don't have to concentrate, hoping against hope that he'll go where I desperately need him to be. He's already there. Waiting for me. He keeps bringing me to the point where my mouth goes slack against his, somewhere between just in time and too late. I pull him in over and over until I'm wound up like a spool of thread, no longer relaxed, unable to keep quiet as I trade one dimension for another.

He makes room for me to slide beneath him, closing his body around me like a curtain. I map his body, marveling inwardly at the cut of his chest, the messy waves of his hair, his jawline. My hands skate back down over his stomach and inside the waistband of his boxer briefs. My smile is private as I push them off and examine him in the dark. Again, the divergence. How different he feels compared to Dean, to Cam, to the drink-buying men I never got to know. Not worse. Not better, necessarily. Actually, yes, better. The perfect size for me, thick and silky. I reach over to the nightstand for what I dropped there when I arrived. He smiles when he realizes what I'm handing him, shaking his head in an *I can't believe you* way. He lifts away from me slightly, holding himself up in a plank. "You're sure?"

I can't stand to not be touching him. "Definitely," I say, sliding his sweat-matted hair out of his eyes. Then I pull him back down and guide him. It's such an unnecessary question, but I love that he asked it. He moves slowly, like I knew he would, until he doesn't. It's like a delicious book I can't put down, the graceful way he fits into me, again and again, the most exquisite of assaults. I thought I knew a thing or two about sex. I knew nothing. This. This is the way the world ends, with a bang *and* a whimper, and then it begins anew.

Did you know cell phone chargers are the most common left-behind item in hotel rooms?" Nina says, stabbing her salad with her fork.

"I did not."

"I had to go out and buy her another one. She swears she didn't leave it behind, but, well." She takes a violent sip of her water. "I should have gotten a real drink."

Nina's crabby. Today is her first day back to work after vacation. We're meeting for a very late lunch after she spent the morning preparing JJ for another trip. She'd just seen our illustrious boss—my former illustrious boss—into a cab to the

175

airport when I emerged from the cluster of benches across the street, where I'd been waiting for her.

"You're not even eating," she accuses with scowl. "You're too skinny as it is." I roll my eyes, but she is at least half right. My pasta is untouched. I've forgotten how to be hungry. An aura's following me like Pigpen's dust cloud. Except my cloud is benign. Like pixie dust, or fairy dust. I smile at the thought.

"What's with you today?" Nina's looking at me sharply. "I was prepared to have to cheer you up for a couple of hours, which I am not in the mood for at all. But I was going to rally for your sake, because getting fired sucks. Yet here you are, not needing any cheering. What gives?"

I exchange the smile for my most innocent stare. "Nothing."

"No," she says, as if I'd asked her a question. "Incorrect." She puts down her fork and sits back, waving away the waitress approaching to refill our water glasses. "It's chat time."

"Well, *you're* a little pushy."

"It's what you love about me," she says, deadpan, and I smile again because she's sort of right. She's the only one in the office who can get away with saying no to JJ and not getting penalized for it.

She doesn't smile back. "I'm fine," I say. "Look, I'll take a bite."

My voice sounds odd even to me, like I'm hearing myself through a seashell. I slept till noon, and feel like it. By the time Wade walked me home this morning—he *walked me home*—it was just after five, the barest sliver of sunlight slanting through the woods behind our houses.

"Oh, you're more than fine, I can tell that much."

I stir my pasta with my fork. Who can I tell, if not Nina? It's only a matter of time before she figures it out anyway. On the one hand I want to protect the experience with Wade, keep it to myself. But another part of me is compelled to hold it up to the light.

"I had a pretty good night last night."

"You slept with the kid!"

I smile again.

"You did!" She leans over and finds my hand, to squeeze it. "Look at that. You actually cheered me up. Did you do it the way I said?"

"Sneaking into his house?" I nod, and she screeches.

"Girl, I am impressed. Way to go after what you want."

I poke at a piece of penne. "It wasn't quite like that." I explain the Dean situation, realizing as I do that I haven't thought beyond today. "What do I do now? I'm supposed to go to the wedding with him."

"Do you want to go with him?"

"It would be easier. And it's not like Wade and I are a couple. Or are going to be. He's moving to Colorado next month."

"But do you want to go with him?"

I put my fork down. "It's going to be with all of our friends. To be honest, I can't see *not* going with him. But maybe he'd rather go with the chick from the bathroom," I add bitterly.

Nina stirs her Diet Coke with her straw. "How does the kid fit into this?"

"Wade."

She laughs at me. "You always make sure I remember his name. So how was it? Last night?"

All I can do is give her a look that I hope conveys everything that went though my head for several hours last night. She sits back. It may be the first time I've rendered Nina speechless. "Jeez," she whistles. "That good?"

"I didn't know it was even possible. For guys to be like that. Never mind at nineteen."

Nina nods knowingly. "Old soul."

This gets my attention. I've thought that often about Wade, myself. "But aren't old souls disinterested in sex?"

"Maybe about having it every second of every day. But when they do, they know what the hell they're doing. It's all about the learning for them."

"Well then he's learned a *lot*. He made me feel like a fucking amateur." I think a minute. "No, that's not true. I felt that way, but he didn't make me feel that way. If that makes sense."

"You liiiiiiike him." I roll my eyes. "So where do you go from here with this?"

I shrug. "Nowhere. I mean, he's moving."

"But you like him."

"I love hanging out with him. We're good friends."

"So you'll just have some fun until he goes? And he's down with that?" She shrugs. "That sounds like a win-win to me."

It does to me, too. With his expiration date in Danborn, Wade's certainly not looking for anything serious. I mean, look at how he's been with Lindsay. And with Dean pissing all over my expectations, I guess neither am I. I'm attracted to Wade—and clearly have been since the Colorado trip, or even before—

and maybe there's nothing wrong with that. I was also attracted to my Brit Lit professor in college (probably gay, now that I think about it) and the guy who used to fix our copiers at work. That didn't mean I was going to pursue anything with them. It was fun just to *like*.

And maybe *like* is okay. Something light and fun, no strings. It may well be exactly what Wade and I both need. He knows me well; I can talk to him like I do Kendra. It's the best of both worlds: all the fun and excitement of hanging out without the worry of a relationship.

Maybe this is what I should have been doing all along, rather than waiting for Dean, hinging my future on a promise that was never going to come.

Going to the treehouse without a plan to meet Wade there feels a little strange. At the same time, I love it. The night is warm for November, and I don't need an escape, I want to be alone with my thoughts. Solitude is a luxury, not a last resort.

But as I'm climbing the ladder, I realize he's had the same idea. The floor creaks above me, and my pulse quickens. I push the trap door open with a flourish. "I swear I didn't know you were here!"

But when I step up all the way through, the face I'm smiling at is Marina's.

My smile fades. "Oh, hey."

She looks embarrassed. "Sorry. I just wanted to see what it was like." She holds out her hand. "Do you need help?"

"No, I'm good." Leaving would be rude, so I sit in the corner, pulling my knees up as I usually do, but this time they feel like a shield. Being in the car with her recently was strange enough. Any space becomes ten times tighter with her in it.

But Marina, for her part, looks perfectly relaxed. I suppose the mental-health professionals, the ones who want it to work, would have called our therapy session earlier today a breakthrough. The session was wonky to start because my mom had a doctor's appointment, so Marina came alone. Without our mom to run interference, the fifty minutes were heavy on sister interaction. It was unnerving, but Marina seemed pretty pleased by it, actually. I talked in fits and starts about my job search, the friends she knew, and those she didn't—she actually worked with a cousin of Marc's, it turned out—and she told stories about the case that had her in Danborn. She also

178

confessed she and Todd were thinking about having kids. For a long time they'd both been against it, but they were starting to change their minds. I knew Todd would make a fantastic dad; until now I'd assumed Marina was the force behind their no-kids policy, although I had no proof.

It seemed odd that the only way we could have a conversation was by paying someone to be a go-between, but if that was how it had to be, I was willing to roll with it. Everything went well enough until about forty minutes in. I was looking at my locked, silenced phone and reminding myself there were only ten minutes left when Marina tossed out a breezy comment with the therapist:

"It's hard to share the everyday things when you're not really speaking."

Dr. Kenyon seized on that: "Is there a specific reason you think you and your sister don't speak often, Marina?" She'd asked this question before, more or less, using different phrasings. But this was the first time she'd been quite so direct.

Marina didn't answer for a moment, and she wouldn't look at me at all. But I could tell she was trying to craft her answer.

"Well, I left. When she was pretty young. And it caused a lot of trouble. That must have been hard for her."

"Was it hard for you, Charlotte?"

That's another thing about therapy. Marina, who hardly ever calls me Charlie, set it up, so Dr. Kenyon now always calls me Charlotte. It's jarring, but correcting her now would just seem petty.

"Her being gone?" I shrugged. "Not really."

Now Marina did look at me. I couldn't decipher her expression. Somewhere between hurt and contrition. "What was worse," I went on, looking at the denim on my knees, "was before she left."

"When?" It was like Marina forgot she wasn't supposed to look at me. Her face, so like my mother's with her wide-set eyes and widow's peak, a smattering of pale freckles on her nose, was familiar and foreign all at once.

"The year or so before you left. All the fighting. That was the worst." I'd been eleven and then twelve, unnoticed in the wings of the action, holding my breath. "Well," I said after a beat, "no, that wasn't the worst. It was equally as bad after you were gone, in a different way."

Marina looked confused, and Dr. Kenyon, damn her, didn't say anything. I waited for her to intervene, to ask Marina a question, to save me.

"Why?" Marina finally asked, in a voice so slight I only heard it because the room was silent. "What made it different?"

Didn't she know? How it was? But I guess she didn't. She wasn't there anymore. That was the point, really. She was gone, unaware of the continent of silence we were left to inhabit. She was looking at me so imploringly, almost desperate. I kept my fingers splayed on my knees to prevent them from closing into fists.

I wouldn't look at her. I wouldn't look at Dr. Kenyon. I reached for my phone, pulled it in and out of its Otterbox case. Because of Wade, I now knew the company was based in Fort Collins, that there was a real spiral slide for the employees to freely use in place of a stairwell. *Whack.* They both were waiting, and I knew they'd keep at it until I gave in.

"He stopped talking to me."

Why did they make me say it? It was so obvious. If only my mother were here she'd know it, she could tell them both how it was. "You fought, and he forgot about me. And then you left, and he ignored me. And then he *died.*"

Dr. Kenyon sliced through the silence, her voice gentle. "Well, we're out of time for today."

This time, when I said goodbye to Marina on the sidewalk, she didn't invite me to dinner.

Here now, in the treehouse, Marina doesn't seem like she feels the need to talk. Is she thinking about what I said today? Was it really that much of a surprise to her? She had to know how things changed. The way they got quiet. And Dad... so mute and mad. The only thing that disappeared along with Marina was the noise. The smiles and laughter and backyard cookouts were still gone. She was gone. And in a sense, he was, too.

"It was about my curfew," Marina says.

"What?"

"There was a concert coming up, I don't even remember who. Some metal band Steve liked, Korn or Staind or something. And I tried to do the right thing, asking Mom and Dad beforehand so they'd have time to think about it. There was no way I'd make it home from Worcester even an hour after curfew. I mean, I could have lied. I could have said I was spending the night with Deanna. But I told the truth. I figured, I was a senior. I was going away to college in the fall. What did it matter? But Dad wouldn't even listen to me. And Mom was deferring to him in everything—I was so mad at her for not standing up for me. She had become so passive." She's looking off into the woods at the bare trees. "I guess I was mad at him for that too. And then I got to thinking about how I shouldn't have to ask them to extend my curfew. I was going to college the next year, blah blah blah. You know how your mind gets when you see freedom so close and you just feel smothered? So much you have to scream?"

She looks at me as if expecting me to agree.

"No. I never felt like that."

I've derailed her. This is classic Marina, so sure everyone else shares every feeling she has. She looks at me like she finds me confusing. Then she continues.

"Well, that was the only thing I felt at the time. I couldn't believe I couldn't negotiate, in advance, something as simple as a curfew. So I left."

"For the concert?"

"For good."

"That was when you ran away?"

"Yup."

"All because of one night of curfew?"

She shrugs. "I wouldn't have done it again, and I don't recommend it. But at that time it seemed like the easy way out."

I shake my head. How can going out on your own, trading college, security, and parental support for rent and bills be the easy way out? You're just exchanging one small problem for several big ones.

"You were pretty selfish," I say. She looks at me sharply, like she's poised to argue. Then she looks away.

"You're right," she says quietly. "And I'm sorry. I never should have done it."

"So why did you? What made you decide to? That night?"

She lifts her shoulders, drops them. "Sometimes the easiest way to solve a problem is to make it irrelevant." She takes a deep breath, then looks up. "Hey, did you know you can see straight into your bedroom from here?"

It's the wettest fall I can remember. Rain has become normal. All that week, my first full week of unemployment, even the days it doesn't rain are lethargic and gray.

I steel myself and return Dean's call. Or calls, I guess. There have been six. I tell him we should take a break. It's all so predictable and cliché, right down to his protests. "Just because I got you fired?" he asks, incredulousness clear in his voice.

"No, that wasn't your fault," I reply, honestly. "I just think we need some space for now."

How very Ross and Rachel of me. I've surprised him, because his defensiveness dissipates. "Charlie. I'm sorry. If I ever thought you'd get fired... God. I really am sorry."

"It's okay," I say. "Really." I am not used to Dean being contrite. It's maddeningly appealing.

"My mom said you looked upset that day, when you left," he says, like he's trying to guess the answer on a test. "And then you came by my house to drop off the résumé."

"Right," is all I say.

"Thanks for doing that, by the way."

"You're welcome," I reply formally.

He takes a long breath. "Listen, Charlie, there's something—"

I talk over him. The last thing I want is for him to go explaining those clothes on his floor, the voice from his shower, telling me how *it's complicated* and *it just happened* and that he won't let it happen again. He should be happy. I'm releasing him, not expecting him to stitch together whatever gash is still open in my life. "Dean, it's nothing personal. I just need to step back. It will be good for both of us. I'll see you this weekend after the bachelor party, okay?"

I don't want Dean's excuses or the explanations he'll invent. When you hear the words you've been waiting for but they no longer mean anything, it's just white noise. Like the rain.

seventeen

Driving home, close to sunset, the sky pulls back and the sun blooms for the first time all day, in the west. Like it's doing it just for me, and the news I carry.

Wade's empty house taunts me. The whole structure feels different, outlined like a glow stick visible only to me. He and I haven't crossed paths—intentionally or not—since he left me on my doorstep last week. Every day I'm perpetually conscious of his car in the driveway or its conspicuous absence. The three days until his mom and stepdad are expected home feels like a countdown. I don't know if I've been waiting for him to contact me or waiting for myself to screw up the guts to go see him. It's like we're both playing chicken, waiting to see when the other will break.

I haven't seen the little blue car at all. Not once.

Certainty. I'm going there. He'll be pleased to hear my news. Why shouldn't he, when he's the person I want to tell the most?

The storm door bangs shut. Framed by foggy outside lights, Wade looks exactly as he's been appearing in my head, ethereal with slightly fuzzy edges.

"Your family likes porch swings," I say, rocking slightly.

He holds my gaze a minute, as if he's trying to decide how to respond. "I guess we do," he says finally. For the first time since I met him in my driveway, I don't break eye contact.

Wade sits. The sky is clear, but the specter of moisture hangs over everything. The woods that line the backyards of all the

183

houses on our street shine with wetness. I had no idea the swing was here, on Wade's back patio. It's not visible from my house. But the weather made the treehouse problematic, and knocking on his front door felt too direct. When I happened across the swing, I knew that's where I had to meet him.

I sip from the glass of wine I've brought. There are at least two, possibly three, inches between us, but my skin knows he's here.

"So," he begins with exaggerated casualness, "are you going to tell me what a mistake you made the other night?"

I smile towards my feet, appearing and disappearing under the chair. "I am not." I shift so his face is in full frame. I find the scar just inside his right eyebrow, a tiny bald patch that isn't noticeable unless you're kissing his eyelids. His blue eyes look a little different than usual, and I'm becoming aware of a certain flavor in the air. Slightly off, but familiar. Sweet. Smoky.

"Are you stoned?" I ask him. He says nothing, just half-smiles. "You are!"

He shrugs and his smile widens, an admission. Digging his booted heels into the ground, he pushes us back and leaves us suspended slightly, in air. "It's legal in Colorado."

"You're not in Colorado."

Another shrug. He lets us go, and we swing, controlled, but only just, by his feet.

"So I'm here for a reason," I tell him. "I got a job."

"From the other day?"

"Third interview was today." I hold up my phone. "And here's the offer, fresh off email."

"Charlie. Congratulations." Sweet Jesus, I love his face. I love it all the time, but especially like this, when unabashed joy for someone else turns his features into artwork.

In normal circumstances, this would be a hugging moment. Neither of us moves. I feel electrified.

"Thanks to you," I say, hoping my sincerity is palpable. "In more ways than one."

"I didn't do anything anyone else wouldn't have done."

But that's not true. I know this now. I've spent the past two months relaxing into this knowledge. "Just let me say thank you."

His glassy, lazy-lidded eyes stay with mine. "You're welcome," he says.

I honestly don't know if, when I texted him to meet me here, I intended to kiss him. Maybe. Partly, I think, it was a test. To see if the voltage between us was real, or if a simple half-smile would still compel me to picture a dozen ways I wanted to touch him. My eyes are drawn to his mouth, his perfectly shaped lips. I feel him studying my face in turn. He lifts his hand. His knuckles only barely graze my cheek, but there it is. That current. This is why we call people we're attracted to *hot*. All I can think of when he's near is heat, embers glowing on the underside of everything. When we make contact, it's scorching steel.

We're still far enough apart that I have to stretch toward him. Wine meets weed in a cocktail of smoky sweetness. We're barely touching, yet in the history of the world there has never been a kiss so slowly sensual, building from nothing to everything. The taste of him fills every nerve ending, making my breath hitch. My hands go to his face. Even when we separate, hours or minutes later, opening my eyes is a chore. Like I'm the one who's stoned.

His breath is on my face. "I'm getting a beer. You want one?" I shake my head.

When he returns he takes my hand in his, dewy and cool from the bottle. Then we just rock. And talk. About everything. Marina. Dean. The company I'll be working for—which, admittedly, I have only a cursory understanding of, through online research. Kendra and Patrick. He shares the discernible differences between Colorado and Massachusetts, how he misses New England autumns more than anything else, but he wouldn't trade it for the mountains. We both chuckle at stories about his dad, whose childhood seems to have been rife with mischief and good-natured lawlessness. The rain continues to fall steadily as the night cools. I lean into him, unconsciously seeking warmth.

Night has well and truly fallen. Moisture is still in the air, on the very edge of my skin. We relocate to the basement family room. He flicks the light switch that ignites the gas fireplace, just like ours next door. On the couch he lifts his arm for me to rest next to his heartbeat. He has removed his hoodie, and on his T-shirt I recognize the Colorado flag that was everywhere in Fort Collins. "I don't even know what the Massachusetts flag looks like," I muse, tracing the sun-like design on his chest with my finger.

"There's a lot of state pride in Colorado."

"Like Texas?"

He smiles. "Not *quite* like that."

My hand slips under his shirt to find his pectoral muscles. "My ex-boyfriend's brother lives in Texas. It's like a whole different world."

"I thought you'd never been to Texas?"

I give him a look. "I spent time with his wife." Partridge was her name. Her real name. They called her—I swear I'm not kidding—"Parti" for short. She was from Big Money in Texas and I spent one excruciating week skiing in Vermont trying to find common ground with her. We ended up drinking wine and watching The Bachelor.

"Is that the relationship that just ended?"

Distracted thinking about Parti, it takes me a second to hear what Wade asked. "In August, technically. But it was probably over six months after it started."

His face is a question, so I sigh and explain, as briefly as I can, about Cam and Katherine and my unintentional matchmaking role. "I'm glad it happened, ultimately," I say, shrugging. "He's really happy now. He deserved that."

"You didn't love him?"

"No. I thought I did... at first. But I didn't. At least not the way I was supposed to."

"The way you loved Dean." I tense slightly, searching his face. "No, I get it," he says.

I shake my head. "You're something else."

"Compared to what?"

"What do you mean?"

"Well, if I'm something else, what's something? What am I an alternative to?"

He's always doing this, I realize. Calling me on seemingly innocuous statements, making me think far too much about the words I choose. But fair enough. It *is* kind of a weird expression. "To the norm. The cliché. The stereotype of a guy."

"The stereotype of a teenager?" he says archly.

He's baiting me, but I just smile. "No. Of any guy." I yawn and check my phone. Twelve-fifteen.

Wade lifts a shoulder, drops it. "We're all stereotypes."

"Most of us are," I say agreeably. "But you're not."

I realize I mean this. I'd stereotyped him all over the place at first, hadn't I? Lazy, immature, impulsive. All derivatives of "young." All false. What a waste of time. Who cares how old he is? He's hot, and he turns me on, and we laugh together. We're not doing anything we can't step away from.

I wake alone, in Wade's room, but knowing exactly where I am. I find him in the kitchen at the stove, spatula in hand, his back to me. I vaguely recall falling asleep on the couch, him leading me to his room, the steady hum of music from his phone lulling me back to sleep. Leaning against the wall, I absent-mindedly grasp the silver cross around my neck as I take him in. Barefoot, wearing only jeans. I'm reminded of him in the kitchen of the rented house in Colorado, similarly barefoot. I wanted him then, even if I wouldn't let myself see it. Just like I want him now.

I come from behind. He lays a hand over both of mine clasped on his stomach. "Good morning," he says, most of his concentration on the pan in front of him. He's made us both eggs. And bacon. And toast. "I don't have hazelnut, but it's good coffee," he says, gesturing to a cup he's already poured.

"I'll be expecting this every day," I warn, smiling around my sip. "Seriously, Wade. Thank you. You don't have to do this."

"Oh, don't worry," he says with a sly smile. "I'll be asking for something in return."

Something turns out to be what I'd planned to give anyway. After we eat we return to the bedroom with coffee. He undresses me slowly, generous with pauses, as if taking me in bit by bit. I feel a surprising absence of self-consciousness as I hand my body over to him. Daytime sex always has a different feel than in the dark. More honest. Less phantomlike. I forget about the extra fifteen pounds I can never manage to shed while Wade reveres every part of me, tasting, licking, stroking. By the time he's finally inside me, I'm closing in on my third orgasm.

I stayed on the pill post-Cam—routine habit or wishful thinking, take your pick—but even so, I've been using condoms regularly with Dean. This time, with Wade, we ditch the condom. Feeling him without a barrier is suddenly my most ardent wish, and I choose to believe him when he assures me he is clean. The risk is worth it. It's the closest sensation to zero gravity I've ever known.

"I could do this every day," I say-sigh when I can speak again.

"We have two more," Wade reminds me, lying next to me on his back. I love to hear his gradual transformation from breathlessness, how his inhales and exhales slowly lengthen.

"But the bachelorette party is tomorrow," I say reluctantly.

"And I'm going mountain biking," Wade adds, like he's just remembering.

I face him on my elbow. "And isn't Keith going to be around for the bachelor party?"

"He is, but the guys are all renting a place near B.C. for the weekend."

The rain has stopped again, leaving the day cool and crisp. We decide to go for a run together, the first time in weeks. I go home to change, and when I return I hand Wade the shirt I bought him.

He holds it out in front of him. "You bought me this?" he asks, and I suddenly feel shy.

"I know, it's sort of stupid." I can't meet his eyes. "You don't have to wear it."

"Charlie." He drops his hands and pulls me in to kiss the side of my head. "Thank you."

After we run I shower at home, then join Wade back in his basement. He's going to introduce me to *Seinfeld*, he says.

"I've seen *Seinfeld*. Many times." With Dean most recently, though I do not say this aloud. And Kendra's always been a *Seinfeld* addict.

"Not the way we watch it." This, it becomes clear, is true. "We" means Wade and his dad, and they aren't just fans, they're superfans. It is actually is kind of fun watching with someone who can point out every last bit of ludicrousness—the guest stars, the origins of certain one-liners, the names of all of Elaine's boyfriends *and* Jerry's girlfriends. I do the math and determine Wade wasn't even born until *Seinfeld* was well into its run.

We interrupt the marathon once so I can show him how to make popcorn on the stovetop, once he reveals he doesn't know how. "That microwave shit is full of chemicals," I admonish, pouring melted butter carefully over a bowl spilling with popped kernels.

"But the other stuff smells good."

He slides his arms around me, and I swivel towards him. I reach into the bowl and feed him a few pieces, reminded yet again how tall he's not, maybe five-nine to Dean's six-two. But he feels bigger. More robust. More there.

"This is better." I kiss him, tasting butter.

Marc may have an apartment for me.

I've ignored my phone all day, but when I check it I discover that Kendra and Marc both have called while I've been hanging with Wade. Marc left a voice mail. My eyes widen as I listen to him explain how it dawned on him that his aunt had a newly-vacant apartment in her house in Medford, since his older cousin recently moved to D.C. Medford's not Somerville, but the apartment may as well be, just over the town line. And Aunt Anita would be delighted to rent out the apartment for a very reasonable rent to her nephew's good friend. If I like it, it's mine after Thanksgiving.

I can't believe it. I could be out of my house within a week. Three days before I start my new job. The timing couldn't be more perfect.

I call Marc back and promise him I'll contact his aunt ASAP. I'm bursting to tell Wade, but I find him distracted, clearly thinking about something other than George and Jerry. He pauses the TV when I sit. "I have to ask you something," he says. "What's the deal with Dean?"

He doesn't sound accusatory, or demanding. He's just waiting patiently for me to answer. "I... I don't know," I say. It's lame, but it's honest. "Do I have to know?"

He half-smiles at that. "I guess not. But he is my brother's best friend." He looks pointedly at me as if I need emphasis on this particular aspect of familial relation.

The truth is, I do need that emphasis. Putting the super-hot, super-young guy that I'm fooling around with together with Keith in the same family is like assembling a puzzle I don't have all the pieces for.

"That really bothers you," I say.

"Actually, not really. But it *will* bother him."

"But what are we even—" I stop. I was going to say "what are we even doing?" but we are nowhere near needing to have the *what are we doing?* talk. Hell, we haven't even had the *what have we done?* talk. And time being what it is, it's likely we never will.

"Are you okay with what we're doing?" I ask Wade instead.

"Hanging out?"

"Sure," I indulge him, through a gritted-teeth smile. "Just like you and Lindsay were doing."

He makes a point of catching my eye and holding it. "You know it's not like that. Not even close."

"I know." The two words are like a sequel I'm afraid to read. Hadn't he just told me this morning, after we were back in bed, that Lindsay was no longer an issue? And hadn't been since the night I snuck into his house? Thinking this, I realized that somehow, along the way, I'd made the same decision about Dean.

I drop my head against Wade, inhaling the half-sweet, half-woodsy smell I've come to associate with him. I take a breath, trying to figure out how to articulate something I'm not sure I've explained to myself. "Wade, all I know is, what Dean and I have isn't serious. Was never serious." For the first time, I'm thankful this is actually true. "And even though that's what I wanted for a long time, right now, I want this more." I give him a squeeze at *this* and I look up at him. "That's all I know."

He hands me the popcorn bowl. "Good enough for me."

"Great." I grin, putting my hand over his so he can't start the TV again. "Would you like to come look at an apartment?"

eighteen

S tanding in the white kitchen of Aunt Anita's apartment, I know it. This place is it. It's not my old neighborhood, but that also means it doesn't have Davis Square's prices. One bedroom—not even a studio—with a dining room *and* a living room. I run my hand along the counter in the tiny kitchen and turn back to Wade.

"I'm seriously going to clean Marc's entire apartment for this," I tell him.

Aunt Anita, whom I've just met, walks around the corner to us in the kitchen. "So whattaya think?" she asks me, old-school Boston Italian, friendly as can be. "Is it fa you?"

"It's fa me, Aunt Anita," I say. "I'll take it."

She eyes Wade. "Marcus said it was just you?"

"What? Oh!" I gesture to Wade, who smiles politely. "No, we're not... together. He just came with me to check out the apartment."

"Okay." She hands me a prefab lease to sign. "You move in next weekend, ah? Afta da holiday."

When Wade and I come out of the house, Marc is on the sidewalk. He's on his phone, his back to us. I instantly drop Wade's hand, which I didn't even realize I was holding, just before Marc swings his glance in our direction.

Charlie! he mouths. I give him a careful hello hug while he wraps up his call.

"Hey stranger! Checking out the new digs?"

"Yes," I say. "Thank you. It's perfect."

"I know, right?"

I feel a flush creep over my cheeks as he takes in the two of us. I'm no Lady Gaga; I never have and never will have a poker face.

"This is Wade," I say. "My next-door neighbor. Wade, this is Marc, my best boy." I see a flash of recognition in Marc's eyes, but nothing more. I'm grateful. The two of them shake hands and trade niceties. "So I didn't know you'd be here tonight," I say to Marc.

"I didn't either, to be honest. Family thing. Boring. You have the bachelorette dealio tomorrow, right? You and Kendra hanging out tonight? She said she'd be calling you."

"Um. I must have missed her."

"Oh. Right."

I can't decipher his look. The situation is not awkward, yet, but the awkwardness potential is looming large. "Let's all do brunch Sunday, though, okay?" I say, my words rushed. "Or dinner. Debrief you on the bachelorette debauchery."

"Yeah," he says, in a tone that implies he couldn't be less excited to hear about it. "Call me."

We all laugh and say our goodbyes, and Marc disappears inside his aunt's house.

"I'm sorry," I say.

"For what?" Wade replies with that half-smile of his, taking my hand back. "I think that went well."

"I'm buying," I tell Wade firmly. "This is a celebration."

Jimmy B's is a Somerville music venue that's also a restaurant, but we're early enough that they haven't yet started collecting tickets for tonight's entertainment, some blues guitarist. Which also means, I'm relieved to note, we don't have to show ID just to have dinner.

But it's Friday night, after all, so the place is still crowded. The only immediate seating we can get is at the bar.

"I like that you'll eat at the bar," Wade tells me, accepting two menus from the bartender and handing one to me.

"Other girls won't?" I ask.

"Some. Not many."

I shake my head, knowing better than to wonder where he has acquired this knowledge. Perusing the menu, I sigh audibly in pure pleasure. "No more Marina, no more sharing a bathroom, no more Linkin Park poster."

"You could take that down."

I wave him off. "Missing the point. I am so ready to have my own space again. There is nothing good about living on Shasta Street." As soon as the words are out of my mouth, I realize what I've said. "Except you. Not living next door to you will be a definite negative."

Wade smiles, his eyes on the menu. "Doesn't matter. We're not together."

"Right. We're not." I, too, stare straight ahead. "Think you might come visit?"

"Only if there's a sleepover involved."

I smile and curl my fingers around his knee under the bar, running my hand backwards up his thigh. Sleepovers. I think of blanket forts and cinnamon-sugar popcorn like Kendra and I used to make. Our later sleepovers, well into college, often involved showings of *About Last Night...*, a sexy '80s Rob Lowe/Demi Moore movie based on a David Mamet play that the two of us discovered late one night sophomore year. We'd always loved it, especially after we learned the original play was titled "Sexual Perversity in Chicago."

I suspect that a sleepover with Wade would be more like the actual movie than watching it.

The sign for the Danborn exit has just come into view when my phone rings. I debate answering it, but it's Kendra. Whose call I ignored earlier. I fumble for my Bluetooth. "Girl, where have you been? I miss you!"

"I miss you too!" I tell her. "How's Patrick?"

"Stop. Yes, he's awesome, and things are great, yadda yadda yadda. But don't try to steer the conversation away from the fact that we haven't seen each other in weeks."

"We'll see each other tomorrow."

"Yes we will, but we'll be among the masses. Listen, I—are you driving?"

"Yeah."

"Did you work this late?"

God. She doesn't even know I got fired.

"Let's see if Xanna's free," she speeds on. "Go crash all over your mom's place and annoy Marina. Unless she's in New Hampshire. God, I hope she's in New Hampshire."

"What's Patrick doing?"

"He's got other stuff going on tonight. Whatever, doesn't matter, please do not talk as if I am that girl. My boyfriend will not get in the way of my besties."

I smile, because he already has, but that's okay.

"So, what? Say, like, an hour? I'll bring tequila, we'll make margs."

"Um..." I put my blinker on, trying to maneuver off the exit. I shift my gaze over to Wade. "I can't do tonight."

"Why not?"

Because I want nothing more than to take this beautiful male specimen back home while we still have a house to ourselves. So much so that I don't want to see my friends. So much so that I'm afraid to even touch him while I'm driving.

I'm such a bad liar. Everyone knows this, including me. I take a big breath through my nose and don't dare look at Wade. "I'm not feeling the greatest, to be honest. I think I need to take it easy so it doesn't get worse for tomorrow."

Kendra, as usual, pulls no punches. "Charlie, is something up?"

"No, not at all. I'm fine. Everything's fine." Good grief. *Shut up, Charlie.*

She's silent for a beat longer than necessary. "Okay, I'll talk to you tomorrow then," she says, her voice almost icy. She knows I'm lying.

I feel terrible. But what can I do? The bottom line is, whatever I'm going to tell Kendra, she'll need to get the whole story. And she'll need to hear it in person. While sitting down. Likely with a shot of tequila in front of her.

"Sorry," I mumble to Wade when the phone goes silent.

"Why did you lie to her?"

Of course he would ask me that, point blank. Feeling a flush creeping up my cheeks, all I can do is give him a look.

"Oh." He turns back to face the road in front of us, and I feel his hand on my thigh. "Yeah. That's what I'd rather do, too."

We make one stop on the way back to Wade's house. I'm so excited with what I find. "Brewed in Fort Collins!" I announce triumphantly, holding up the six-pack for him to see.

His full-on smile transforms his face. I love that I can make him look that happy. "Fat Tire tastes like home," he says, reaching for me. "Thank you."

It's a long few minutes before I start the car, and by then, we're thinking less about the beer than being alone again. I grab the six-pack and we shut the doors to my car as quietly as possible, then run over to his house in the dark hand in hand, giggling at our silly stealth. He's kissing me before the door's even shut, and pins me against it while we both shed our jackets and he keeps missing the light switch in the dark. "Fuck it," he says, giving up and sliding his hands up the bare skin of my back, pulling my shirt off in one jerky movement while I switch the six-pack from hand to hand. We feel our way towards the couch in the next room, giggling again like little kids as we almost trip over one another in the darkness.

A waterfall of pure lust floods through me. No wonder Nina noticed long ago. Who was I kidding? I've wanted Wade Hunter ever since I watched him walk into my basement carrying my alarm clock. It's almost animalistic, the way I crave him. Unprecedented. I may just fuck him on his parents' living-room floor. I need his mouth, his skin, his hands on me. Now, and all at once. All of him melting into all of me.

His shirt is off and I step out of and onto my skater skirt, still trying to find somewhere to put the beer. We smile into each other's mouths as I reach down with my free hand to his button fly. Our fingers tangle; he's already there, helping me.

Light floods the room.

"Jesus!" Keith says, as the Fat Tire crashes to the floor.

n i n e t e e n

I'm not ready to open my eyes. I slide my phone out from under my pillow and check the time. 7:45. Why am I up so early on a Saturday?

I roll over, and that's when I see Kendra sitting in my desk chair, fully dressed and made-up, facing me.

"So I thought," she says, as if continuing a conversation we've already started, "that something was a little off last night on the phone. But you've been acting distant for weeks, so, you know, I figured I had a little something to do with it, what with the Patrick newness and Dean... whateverness."

She pauses. Strategically.

"But," she goes on, "when Marc texted me that I should talk to you, I got a little worried. So I call him, and of course he's not willing to tell me anything he knows, just tells me to talk to you."

Another pause.

"And then, when I call your house this morning, knowing your mom will be awake, because for some reason I actually feel a little awkward about contacting you directly"—she raises her eyebrows, either daring me to defy this or underscoring its truth, I'm not sure which—"she tells me she hopes we've had fun the past few days, you know, at my place."

She lets that sink in before she goes on.

"Okay, I think. Now, Charlie wouldn't lie to me, would she? Where on earth would she have been for two days that I don't know about? And what in the hell does Marc know that I don't?"

She gestures. "Oh, parentheses?" Like that. "I didn't rat you out to your mother. Not that it's not completely ridiculous that a twenty-six-year-old has to hide her overnight shenanigans from her mother, but I know this is an off-the-grid situation, so we let it slide. Anyway..."

She lets the last word hang in the air like a question mark. It must be time for me to speak.

"Can I at least make some coffee first?"

Like a magician she produces a Dunkin' Donuts cup from its spot on my desk. "Bless you," I say, taking a glorious sip. It has been out in the elements just long enough to cool to a perfect temperature. When that's followed by a Boston Kreme donut, I proclaim, "You're the best friend ever."

"I know. And I'm waiting."

"Okay." I sit up. "I'm sorry. I may have left a note indicating I was hanging out with you."

"But you were..."

Where to even start? "I... I slept with him."

"I know. You've *been* sleeping with him."

And I remember she doesn't know any of it—not the Colorado trip, not the kiss at the gym, not my getting fired or Dean's part in it. Nothing. "No, not Dean," I say softly. "Wade."

"Wade?"

I nod.

"The kid from next door?" she repeats, pointing across the street again.

"That's actually—yes. From next door."

A slow smile spreads across her face. "Charlie! I am so fucking proud of you!"

I let her high-five me. "Why's that, exactly?"

"You need to do this! Expand your horizons! Sample the goods! Sow the oats! There is way more than Dean out there."

"It's not what you think."

Her face turns quizzical, like I've presented her with an algebra problem. "Did you not have sex with an extremely hot brand of puppy chow?"

I give her a weak smile. "That's not what I mean." But I can't go on. I don't know how to.

"What you mean is ..." Kendra prompts.

"What I mean is ..."

"Charlie." She sits down on the side of the bed. "What the hell is going on?"

I take another sip and play with my coffee cup.

"Wait a minute." Her eyes bulge. "Charlie, do you *like* him?"

I wrestle with the tab on the coffee lid, opening and closing it.

"Charlie!"

I shrug.

"Oh my God. Charlie, he's *nineteen*."

I glare at her. "You're the one congratulating me for hooking up with him!"

"For a night! To get Dean out of your head!" Kendra gets up. Is she actually *pacing*? "Listen, Charlie, I know things have been weird with us. I know I have not been in your corner as far as Dean is concerned, and I'm sorry about that. But going after a nineteen-year-old—the little brother of his best friend, lest we forget—just to make him jealous is not a wise move."

"I'm not trying to make him jealous."

She looks at me with—is it pity?—then goes on as if I haven't spoken. "Patrick has this friend. Topher. I wasn't going to suggest anything now because I figured you were too wrapped up in the Dean idea. And he's a scientist, too, but not the geeky kind. I really, really think the two of you would hit it off. He's very cute, and very unattached at the moment. Let's set something up, huh? Dinner at that new Turkish place? I know we've been wanting to try that. Or something more low-key? Brunch at Jimmy B's, like old times?"

I turn away from her wide, expectant eyes and hopeful smile. Something has shifted. Being set up with another guy isn't going to change anything. I don't want to meet anyone new. What I want—*who* I want, I correct, the thought washing over the ceiling of my mind like the white text of the *Star Wars* intro Marina's first boyfriend James made me watch over and over—is one house away, probably busy keeping a wide berth from the guy who thinks his little brother is messing around with his best friend's girlfriend.

Yeah. Apparently, Dean's been telling people I'm his girlfriend. News to me. And, no doubt, to the girl in his shower.

"—best thing for you right now," Kendra is saying.

I blink. "What?"

She's dialing her cell phone. "Let me see if Patrick knows Topher's plans this weekend."

"Kendra, hang up."

She holds her finger up at me. "Wait just a sec. Hey honey. I know, it's early, I'm sorry. I love you too. Listen, your friend Topher? Remember how I—yeah. Well, no time like the

present. Any idea what he's doing this weekend? I have the
bachelorette party till late. Maybe tomorrow, for brunch? Marc
was saying something about—"

"Kendra."

A slight shake of the finger. "Okay, just give me a call back
when—"

"KENDRA."

She lifts her eyes to me in surprise.

"*Hang up the fucking phone.*"

"Let me call you back," she tells Patrick, staring at me.

"Kendra." I take a deep breath. "You're my best friend. Be
happy for me."

"I am happy for you," she says automatically.

"No, Kendra. Be happy for me."

And, like a sunshower, her face clouds and brightens at the
same time. "Oh shit. Are you in love with him?"

I lay back down on the pillow. "I didn't say that."

"You are!" Then she smiles, and her voice changes. "I've
missed so much."

"Are you ready now?"

"For what?"

"To be a best friend."

In seconds she's beside me on her stomach, hands clasped in
front of her. "Tell me everything."

"Blue," Kelly says. "It's your color."

I stare down at my toes. I've never been a blue-toenail girl.
Red, maybe, if I was feeling fancy. Gold once, for that Nefertiti
Halloween costume. But usually a peachy-pink—never blue.
Certainly not sparkly blue.

Kendra wobbles over on bare heels. We're still five days from
Thanksgiving, but each of her toenails has a Christmas design
on it—holiday lights, candy cane stripes, even a mini Rudolph
on her big toe. "My Festivus pedicure," she calls it, which
makes me think of Wade. She inspects my feet. "Oooooo, that's
a nice one. Electric-like. You down with blue, Charlie?"

I wiggle my toes. "I guess so."

Pedicures in late November in Massachusetts aren't the
easiest thing to pull off—we've all packed our flip flops in
addition to our real shoes—but a spa day is what Kelly wanted
for her bachelorette party, so that's what her bridesmaids have
arranged. First was saunas (where I couldn't breathe), then

facials (which felt like elegant waterboarding), now mani-pedis (which I love), and next massages (the best part).

I slip on my flip-flops, readying myself for the transfer to the massage wing of the spa. There are at least a dozen of us: Kelly's got a big family, and all of them seem to be her bridesmaids. Then there's Kendra and me, plus Holly and Taryn, who knew Kelly in college. We're supposed to eat sushi after spa-ing it up, then meet back up with the "boys" at a bar. Kendra made a face when she found out the plans, probably because there weren't any penis-shaped cupcakes or X-rated dares on the itinerary. (As I recall, her seventeenth birthday party involved both.) I, the boring one, have been looking forward to a day of pampering on someone else's dime. Now I'm spending the day trying to think of excuses to bag on the bar outing. It's definitely not a good time to see Dean.

"You guys!" Kelly hugs both me and Kendra together, at least the third time she's done it today. "I am so happy you're here. Are you still having fun?" It's just like Kelly, concerned that we're enjoying ourselves at *her* bachelorette party.

I adore Kelly. It's impossible not to. She and Dave secretly crushed on each other in high school, but didn't get together for real until they were both out of college. She's as low-key and sweet as Kendra is direct and brash. (She's also super-Catholic and made Dave wait *forever* to have sex, which we teased her about mercilessly.)

We drifted in recent years, for no reason other than life. She relocated for a job in Hopkinton, and last year Dave moved in with her—scandal!—after he got a teaching position in a neighboring town. Hopkinton isn't far from Boston. It is, in fact, exactly twenty-six miles away; that's where the Boston Marathon starting line is. But it's still suburbia, and I never manage to get out there. The wedding is a welcome, legitimate excuse to see her.

"So much fun," Kendra says to her, meaning it. She loves Kelly too—more protective of her than of me, even, or at least she was until Dave. "Don't you worry about us."

"You," Kelly tells her, pointing, "have the best toes here. Photo?"

Kendra models her foot for a shot on its way to being Facebooked, Tweeted, or Instagrammed. Kelly's swallowed up again by the bridesmaids, and Kendra follows, blowing a kiss over her shoulder. "Don't forget, tables next to each other," she reminds me, phone poised in her hand, probably to call Patrick.

I hang back with Holly and Taryn. They've mostly kept to themselves today. Probably like Kendra and I have, I remind myself sheepishly.

"Do you guys get to see Kelly often?" I ask. One of them was her roommate—Taryn, I think.

Holly shakes her head. "Hardly ever. I'm so glad we're getting to see her now." Yup. Kelly makes everyone feel like her best friend, in a way that it never occurs to us to be jealous. I think about the people like that in my life. The ones I can count on even if they're not there. Be real with. Fall in step with no matter how much time has passed. Marc. Kendra. Xanna. Kelly.

And yes. Wade. Whom I pretty much just met, but feel like I've known forever.

I check my phone for the eleventh time. No texts. It's strange that I haven't heard from him since he left for Vermont. But at least he and Keith are no longer in the same physical space. After he scared the wits out of us last night, Keith simply left the room, leaving us speechless, breathless, and thanking God we still had some clothes on. (Wade was much luckier than I.) Wade was all apologies as he squired me home, but I didn't blame him at all. I didn't want him to go back, but he felt he should explain to Keith. But Keith was having none of it, just kept throwing out accusations about messing around with—he swears he said this—his best friend's girlfriend. If I was Dean's girlfriend, that was news to me.

Neither of us was sure if Keith was more angry at him—or at me. I couldn't suss out why Keith was taking this so hard. Even if he thought Dean and I were seriously involved, why was it his business? Was it the betrayal of Dean that bothered him, the prospect of his little brother getting it on, or the prospect of his little brother getting it on with *me*? Keith's and my friendship, if you could even call it that, was spotty and fragmented enough that I couldn't begin to take an educated guess.

Right now, though, there's only one thing I need to know about Keith: whether he's going to tell Dean. It would be *really* shitty of him to do it on a day they're supposed to be celebrating someone else. Although personally I question whether Dean will even be bothered, I still want him to hear it from me first. Thankfully, so far, the only rumors about today's activity is that the boys are knee-deep in paintball.

We're ushered into the locker room to change for massages. Our robes are white, super-soft, and emblazoned with the setting-sun logo of Serenity Spa. "How's Patrick?" I ask Kendra as we slide them on. "Damn, these are comfortable."

"He's perfect," Kendra replies, matter of fact. "As usual. How's Wade?" Unlike my question, hers takes on a serious tone. Now that she's fully in the loop, she's as worried as I am about the ramifications of last night.

"He's fine. At least as of eight this morning."

"Will he be back tonight?"

I nod. "Pretty late though."

The room we're led into has just the two tables we've requested, dimmed lighting and a very romantic air.

"They think we're a couple," she mouths to me. She gives me a seductive look as the therapist adjusts the blanket over her, and I catch a glimpse of her hip unmarred by even the tiniest string of undies.

"Kendra!"

"So? They said we could wear underwear or not."

Of course they did. And of course, Kendra took advantage. The obligatory new-age music fills the room and our massage therapists get to work.

"Do you think you'll go public?" Kendra whispers, facing me.

I sigh. I don't want to think about that. I hate that the ticking time bomb Keith has turned us into may mean we have to. "I'd rather not," I answer. She reaches out to clasp my left hand in her right one and squeezes. Not for the first time today, I'm so thankful she barged into my house this morning. I count on her like I count on my own breath, and I've missed her.

The massage therapist hits a particularly stubborn muscle in my upper back—painful in a good way. I breathe deep into the pain and force myself to relax, shifting my hips slightly on the table. Ever since I timidly stepped into the low-lit room where I got my first massage—at Kendra's behest, of course—three years ago, I've longed for the budget that would allow them monthly. I'm very good at shutting my mind off from everything during massages. Some people meditate; I pay people to rub oil into my body. It's the closest I get to feeling like I do in the treehouse. Today, as the minutes tick by and the new-age music loops, I get lost pretending the therapist's hands are Wade's, oiled and soft, carving soft valleys along my muscles, stopping just short of pain. A slow burn travels through my body.

I'll hear from him soon. Everything will be okay. It has to.

Because somehow no one actually thought to make reservations at the sushi restaurant, showing up at 6:45 on a Saturday night means a two-hour wait in the bar. By the time we get our table, I'm famished—and more than a little drunk. Eating sobers me up a bit, but with sobriety comes exhaustion. We don't pay the check until almost eleven, way beyond when we said we'd meet the boys out. My only saving grace is that maybe now, bailing on the night won't seem so strange.

"New plan," Kelly tells the table brightly, putting down her phone. "Since it's so late, we're all just going to hang at Keith's house. They got a keg."

I snap to attention, and Kendra and I exchange looks. I can't very well say I don't have it in me to stay out when "out" is next door. But—new, better thought—maybe I'll get to see Wade that much sooner.

I still haven't heard from him. I'm not angry, or at least trying not to be—he can do what he wants, including ignoring my texts—but I am concerned. The last couple times my calls went right to voice mail, which means, I'm guessing, his phone is dead and he can't charge it.

On the way back to Danborn I decide that I'll just make an appearance. Say hello to Dean. Somehow manage to find Wade, who will hopefully be home by then. Then we'll figure out what to do.

Keith can't have said anything yet. Even he's not selfish enough for that.

The street is packed with cars when we arrive, but Wade's isn't one of them. I do a ten-minute walk-through of the premises to be sure. I don't see Dean either, so I opt to sit alone by the covered-for-the-winter pool, despite the cold. Like a middle school dance, genders are keeping to themselves, boys gathered around the fire pit, girls warming up inside. I'm trying to think of a good enough reason to stay.

But just as I'm preparing to leave, here Dean is, entering the gate to the pool.

"Hey stranger. Have a good time today?"

"The best," I reply. He sits on the chair next to me. "What about you?"

"Eh, I got hit a little too often at close range." I look at him quizzically until I remember the paintball. Dean runs a hand over his thigh and winces exaggeratedly.

"Sorry," I say. Studying him, it seems safe to deduce that Keith hasn't told him anything. Yet. I quietly accept how good he looks, ruggedly disheveled from the day's activity, appealing in that lanky way. He's as striking to me as he always was. I suppose there's no way that goes away, especially with someone who seems to get better looking with age.

Dean looks as if he's getting ready to say something else, and I cut in. Screw it. If Wade isn't here, I'll do this myself.

"Dean, there's something I have to—"

"Charlie, I think we should—"

We both stop. I don't want him to go on, but I don't want to be rude. Over Dean's shoulder at the fire pit, I catch a look on Keith's face that I'd never describe as friendly. Dean follows my gaze and raises his beer, which Keith returns with no alter in his expression before he turns away. "What's with him?" Dean asks, mostly to himself.

I have a pretty good idea. All I say is: "He looks pretty wasted."

"Not surprising," Dean says, and takes a sip of his beer. "Business as usual." He shrugs. "You know how in college, when you get drunk, no matter how drunk you get, it's still fun?"

"Sort of. I was never a big drinker in college, really."

"You weren't, huh?" He nods with purpose, like he's filing this fact away. "Anyway, Keith's not fun anymore."

I'll say.

Dean reaches out, takes my hand. "Charlie…"

I'm sure of it now. Keith hasn't said anything to him. I pull my hand away and place it on his chest lightly. "Really, Dean. You don't have to. I'm fine," I insist. "I did see her, but I'm okay. Really. I'm not even mad anymore."

He leans back a millimeter, like I've presented him with a puzzle. "What? Who did you see?"

I shake my head. "We don't have to talk about it. In fact, there's something—"

"Wait. What don't we have to talk about? I told you I was sorry you got fired."

"I know, and I told you it was okay."

Dean lets his breath out through his teeth and says, "Listen, I could use a beer. Can I get you one?"

He walks away, and I take a deep breath and check my phone again. If Wade doesn't show up, I can handle this.

"What the hell are you doing?"

It's not until I awkwardly stand to make sense of the approaching shadow that I realize the menacing voice belongs to Keith. He steps toward me. I instinctively back up. "Do not mess with him, Charlie."

"Mess with who?"

He laughs without mirth, like we share a bitter joke. "Yeah, you would ask that. You don't even know whose life you're going to screw up more, and it doesn't even matter to you. Well, it does to me. This is my best friend you're fucking around. And my little brother you're just... fucking."

"Keith," I say quietly. Holy shit, he's *really* wasted. "Please calm down."

He takes another swig of beer, drains it. He shakes his head, sneering. "You think you're just the innocent girl next door. But I know better. I've known better for a long time." He fixes me with a glare. "He broke up with his girlfriend for you!"

What the hell is he talking about? Whose girlfriend? Dean's? The girl from the shower?

"You're a dicktease," he goes on. "You always have been. Dean's lucky he has me to stop him."

"Stop him from what?"

He just looks at me for a moment, then says evenly, "Wasting his life with you again."

I'm frozen. No one has ever talked this way to me in my life.

"What the hell, man?" Dean's standing there, holding two bottles of water.

"Deano." With one last, hard look at me, Keith abruptly turns to Dean. "Let's get out of here, bro."

Dean appears to size up the situation—my pleading look, Keith's set jaw and obvious intoxication, which appears way worse than either of us has realized. "Sounds good. How about in a few? I was going to hang with Charlie for a bit."

Keith shakes his head. "No way, man. Don't do it."

Dean approaches Keith, lowers his voice. "Dude. What the hell? I want to talk to her."

Keith just keeps shaking his head, still looking in my direction. His voice gets louder. "You don't know how much she's fucking you over."

My face is flaming. "Keith," Dean says again, clearly getting angry. "Watch it."

Keith spins around to him. "She's totally playing you," he yells. "Fucking SLUT!"

The whole place drops into silence as Bob Marley gives way to Foo Fighters. Every face in the yard is turned my way. I take a step backwards, chanting inwardly *Do not cry, do not cry.* I have no idea what to do. Dean stares straight at Keith, who glares back. No one speaks.

Then, someone does.

"What the fuck did you say?"

I feel a hand in mine, fingers intertwining. Still holding my hand, Wade takes another step towards Keith. Keith is about two inches taller than his younger brother, but Wade is broader, and somehow just as menacing.

Dean's looking at me, his expression a question. "Charlie?" He glances at Wade, then at our still-locked hands. Realization mixed with disbelief spreads across his face.

"I told you, man," Keith slurs. "She's a slut."

Wade squeezes my hand, turns to face me. "Are you all right?"

I nod, still frozen. "Okay," he says. "Go somewhere else, please."

I shake my head. There's no way I'm leaving him alone with Keith.

"Go, Charlie."

"I'll take her," Dean says, and to my surprise Wade nods, his eyes never leaving Keith. I'm too stunned to do anything but let Dean lead me diagonally across the yard to my door.

Voices are rising behind us as we walk, but then, just as I reach the last step, they go abruptly silent. "Dean, go help them. He's crazy."

"He's drunk," he corrects me. "Don't worry, I'm going back." He hands me both waters, as an afterthought. "They were out of beer."

Thirty minutes later, I get a text. *Are you awake?*

Yes, I type. *Please come.*

We act out of habit, despite the cold. I get there first, so I spread out the blanket I've brought and wait until I can hear him stepping below me. When his head pops up, I want to cry with relief. Then I get a good look at him.

"Oh my God!" There's blood on his face.

To my annoyance, he laughs. He moves himself in behind me and wraps us up in the blanket. "Charlie, I'm fine." He kisses my cheekbone. "Keith was too drunk to fight."

"Then why are you bleeding?" I touch the tip of my finger to his face. It's dried blood, I realize, with the only source seeming to be his nose.

"We did have to 'escort' him away, and I think someone's elbow caught me. No big deal."

He's right. The blood makes it look far worse than it actually is. "Thank you. And I'm sorry."

"No big deal," he says again.

I frown, and the trees, leafless and swaying with a sudden wind, seem to agree. "But it is, actually. This never should have happened. Not like this."

He doesn't answer, just squeezes me. It *shouldn't* have happened, I say to myself again. How did this become such a mess so quickly?

"I'm sorry I didn't talk to you today," he says. "Left my phone in Ken's car, and it died. He has a Droid, so no charger."

"It's okay. I was just worried." It was the right thing to not get upset about not being able to contact him. Once upon a time, I would have. Apparently I'm maturing. How ironic. The most mature relationship I have is with a guy who I almost wouldn't date because he's too young.

Wait a minute. We're not in a relationship.

Are we?

I shake the thought off and fling it far away. I steer towards something I've been wondering since it happened. "Why did you let me leave with Dean?"

He shrugs. "Because I knew you'd be safe." It really was that simple to him. What confidence he had. Not arrogance—not the kind that puffed up his chest or made him compensatingly insecure. Just pure quiet confidence. He was sure of me, and adult about it. That irony again. I wonder about me and Dean. Are our interactions forever doomed to be operated on a seventeen-year-old level? Towards the end of our relationship, I was the neediest I'd ever been, and needier than I've been since. At one time I was glad to put that girl behind. I don't want her to show up again.

"So I guess we're out of the closet," I say.

"And apparently we're sleeping together."

"Ah, yes. Has it been good for you?"

His mouth is directly in my ear, a whisper. "Can't wait for next time." A shivery jolt winds its way through my bloodstream. Right now my back is against his chest, my legs tangled in his, his arms around me, our fingers enmeshed, and I still can't get close enough to him. I feel him react to my presence, and I press myself back against him.

"We could stay here all night," I say thoughtfully.

"We could. Might get cold though."

"It is cold."

"Might get colder."

"Wade?"

"Charlie?"

I hesitate a second. "Why... why did you stick up for me tonight?"

"What do you mean?"

"Well, he's your brother."

"And he's an asshole when he drinks."

"But you could have done irrevocable damage, you know? I mean, he's going to be your brother forever."

"Yeah," he agrees. "But he also might be a drunk asshole forever." He shrugs. "I'd do it again."

"Are you that much of a white knight?"

He leans away, gets me to look at him. "Is that what you think, for real? I wanted to be a hero?"

"Nooooooo... not exactly." I can't really put my finger on what I mean. I close my eyes, try to picture the colors of my thoughts, this situation I can't articulate. "I mean, it's impressive that you don't want girls talked to that way—"

"You, Charlie. Not 'girls.' Do you know what it was like for me, to hear him saying that? To know he was my brother?" He pauses. "Did it bother you that I outed us?"

"No," I say. "Maybe a little. But you didn't, anyway. He did."

"Well, I wasn't exactly thinking clearly. I just heard him as I was coming home—you kind of get to know your brother's danger tone. I had no idea he was talking to you until I was right there."

"And then you had to stop him."

I can feel Wade shake his head. "I wasn't thinking about him, okay? I was thinking about you. Charlie." He doesn't speak for a moment, and I realize he's said my name as a command; he's waiting for me to look at him. I twist my neck to meet his gaze, and he locks me in.

"I will always have your back."

I don't realize I've been holding my breath until I exhale. For about five seconds, we stay that way, eyes glued to each other. *Thank you*, I think. I shift to face forward. He kisses the top of my head, and I pull his arms even tighter around me as the branches rustle above us.

The following Tuesday, before Thanksgiving, I walk into my house after spin class. My mom's cooking dinner. Next to her, dumping what looks like a pile of peeled potatoes into a pot on the stove, is Dean.

"Look who came by, Charlie!"

"Your mom promised me some bread," he says with a wink. He dips his head toward the counter, where two loaves of her specialty rosemary-walnut bread cool on the stacked wire rack I bought her from Pampered Chef.

"Always your favorite," I reply stiffly.

"Dean's promising his famous mashed potatoes," my mother tells me. I raise my eyebrows at him, and my mom opens the oven to check whatever's in there.

"Pioneer Woman's famous mashed potatoes," he clarifies. "They used to go over pretty well in my apartment."

Seeing Dean cook is like seeing him run for president. Or lasso a steer. This is my high-school boyfriend. Who used to eat on paper plates to avoid doing the dishes. I've never seen him cook more than a hot dog.

What the hell is he doing in my kitchen?

"I'll be right back," I say. I had been planning to shower, but screw it. He's uninvited; let him smell my exercise stink.

My mom nudges Dean in my direction. "Oh, the potatoes won't be done for a good thirty minutes. Go on up with her," she says, hands clasped in front of her as if they're part of her smile. "The two of you don't need to worry about me."

Well *that's* a far cry from the keep-your-bedroom-door-open rule of my high-school years. So trusting.

It feels otherworldly to have Dean in my bedroom. He used to know this space so well. I grab some clothes and head to the bathroom. When I get back, Dean looks spookily enthralled, as if he's seen a friendly ghost.

"This really looks the same, doesn't it?" he says, his voice practically a whisper.

"Yeah. So what brings you here?"

209

Getting that I'm not exactly in the mood to reminisce, he sits down on the bed and motions for me to do the same. He turns slightly, facing me. His face stretches into something that's equal parts smile and cringe. "So I can't believe I'm saying this, but what exactly is going on with you and Keith's brother?"

Ah. That's what this is. I have no idea how to explain that even to myself, let alone Dean, but I'm not going to give him the satisfaction of trying. "It's nothing. We're friends." He regards my answer skeptically. "What? It's not serious. We're hanging out. Just like you and I were."

It isn't until after I've said this that I realize how brilliant it is. If he says it looks more serious than we were, then he's admitting what I've known—and tried to get him to admit—all along. But if he agrees, he has no choice but to stand down.

I've stumped him. I feel triumphant.

"So he's the reason you wanted us to take a break?" he asks me finally.

"No," I say, hoping he can tell it's the truth. "We needed that. Neither of us was happy."

"What do you mean? I was happy."

"Fine. *I* wasn't."

He cracks his knuckles, which I know he only does when he's uncomfortable. His gaze wanders across my room again. "This really sends me back." A sly look crosses his face, and suddenly he's at the other end of the bed, looking behind the headboard. "Christ, Charlie. It's still here." He shows me the small hole in the plaster, hidden by the bed. "Remember?"

I wouldn't have believed it, but I actually had forgotten. The last week of summer, just before senior year, my parents both at work. To the drumming of a summer storm's pouring rain that canceled work for both of us, we holed up in my bedroom, devouring each other for hours as only sneaky seventeen-year-olds could. Somehow we knocked a piece of the bed frame loose, piercing the wall in the process. As I recall, we raided my dad's wood scraps to repair the bed, succeeding mere minutes before they arrived home.

I hug the salvaged memory to me like a teddy bear. "I'm surprised you remember."

"Are you serious?" He looks away, as if the thought distresses him, then turns back to me. "Charlie, you were the best part of high school for me."

He says that to me *now*?

"I *liked* that we were back together," he goes on.

I shake my head. "Dean. We weren't. We were just sleeping together."

"Aw." He pauses long enough to deliberately tilt his head down towards me. "You know it's more than that."

"More than a booty call?"

"Come on, Charlie. Give me some credit."

"Jesus Christ, Dean. I *saw* her."

"What? Who?"

"At your house. In your shower. The day I brought your résumé."

"In my shower?" He's walking towards me, a question still on his face. His confusion is crazymaking.

"In the basement. *Your* basement. I heard her, the day I brought your résumé. She had a turquoise phone case!"

He stares at me for a moment. Then light dawns. "You mean Daria?"

Daria? Something shakes loose in my memory and tumbles to the forefront of my brain. I do know his cousin Daria, but she's only in middle school—

Oh.

"She's eighteen. And bratty as hell," he says with a grim smile. "Did you think...?"

My head swims. Daria. The girl we took for ice cream at Bubbling Brook and Friendly's. We babysat her while her parents were at a holiday party. I got her a tween makeup kit that Christmas, which her mom did not appreciate. I paid thirty-five dollars to watch her fucking dance competition.

Dean sits back down next to me. "That's what you were talking about, then, at the pool, wasn't it? I get it now. You thought I was cheating on you."

I squeeze my eyes shut. He's right but he's wrong. "You couldn't be *cheating* on me. We weren't together."

He ignores me and continues musing aloud. "So that's why you're messing around with little Wade."

"Wade has nothing to do with you."

"Or Keith?"

"Why would he have anything to do with Keith?"

He shrugs. "He *is* his brother."

"Keith hasn't even liked me since we were kids." Dean gives me a funny look. I study him. "Wait. You're saying Wade has a thing for me because of Keith?"

"Or because of me," he says, lifting a shoulder. "I *am* Keith's best friend."

"I see." I stand. It's getting too crowded in here, what with me, Dean, and his ego. "You know, I bet the potatoes are done by now."

The rest of the evening, shockingly, goes extremely well. I look on like a spectator as Dean maintains an impressive level on the charm meter. I'm reminded again how he won over my parents so easily back when we first got together. Beyond his mashed potatoes (which include cream cheese and are, I hate to admit, fantastic), his praise of my mom's bread makes her happier than I've seen her in a while. A long while.

After dinner, walking him out to his car, I'm in a good enough mood to joke. "And this is the proper way to say goodbye to a guest," I say, gesturing to myself walking. He's parked across the street, which is why I didn't see him when I came in. It makes me wonder if he planned it that way, to catch me off guard.

"Fine, you got me." He makes no move to get into his car, just turns and faces me, like he's assessing. He stares down at me a minute. "I took you for granted, didn't I?"

I shrug. "Really, Dean, it doesn't matter anymore."

I'm standing a respectable distance away, but Dean reaches for my hand anyway. "Are we still going to the wedding together?" I open my mouth to tell him I don't think so, but he stops me. "Charlie, these are our friends. Mine and yours."

Dave was part of Dean's jocky crowd in high school, and Kelly's one of my best friends. He does have a point. I squeeze his hand and pull away with, I hope, a sort of finality. "I just think it's better if I go alone. Kendra said she'd take me. But I'll see you there, okay?"

His eyes have that liquid look, the same one that has melted my insides more times than I can count. He sighs, like I'm making the wrong decision but he'll indulge me. "Save a dance for me?"

Inside I help my mom load the dishwasher. "Feels like just yesterday he was here all the time, doesn't it?" she says. "It must be nice to reconnect with him."

She turns her smile in my direction, so I know she expects a response. "Yeah," I say, positioning some silverware in the drainer. "It is." It's true at least, even if it's not the way she thinks.

twenty

Winter shows up along with Thanksgiving. It's way too early to be as cold as it is, but that's New England for you.

Wade goes to Rhode Island with his mom and stepdad, and I spend the holiday at Marina's and Todd's house, only because I'm unable to think of a plausible alternative. Surprisingly, it turns out fine. Marina is more laid-back than I've ever seen her. She's invited a few of her friends whose families aren't local—including one tall drink of water whom I would have definitely looked twice at any other time, including finding out if he was single—and we all have a perfectly ordinary Thanksgiving dinner with no snide looks or implied accusations. Even more surprising than the lack of drama is the news Marina shares that night, after the non-family guests leave: She's pregnant.

"You just told me you were thinking about it!" I burst out, excited in spite of myself.

"The thinking's been going on for a while," Marina says, sharing a look with Todd. "It just hadn't been resulting in anything quite yet."

My mom cries, of course. And we all get quiet after she says, "He would have made such a good grandfather," because he would have.

I'm getting up to leave the table—there is no way I'm letting them see me cry—when my mom presses my arm gently. I sit back down. "Wait a minute. I just want you both to know how happy my heart is seeing the two of you together. It's all I want.

Please don't forget us when you leave again." I turn to her in support, but she's looking right at me.

Friday is moving day for me. Snow is in the forecast, so I wake up raring to go to beat any bad weather. Thanksgiving Friday also means Kendra's annual board-game soiree, a tradition we started back in high school when we needed to unwind after Black Friday shopping. It's usually a girls' night, but Kendra's routines have changed a lot in the wake of her relationship with Patrick. Me being with Wade confirms it: this year, we're going couples.

A few hours in my mom's basement with Wade means my stuff is not only properly packed and taped up in boxes, but it's also all labeled, even down to the destination room. I never thought I could be so excited about a box labeled KITCHEN: POTS AND PANS.

I consider confessing Dean's visit to Wade, but I don't want it to seem like it was more than it was. If anything, it made me more sure than ever that distancing myself from him was the right thing to do. Mentioning it would only give it credence it doesn't deserve.

For the furniture moving, Wade has recruited one of his mountain-biking friends, Walt from Brighton, who won't take anything but a six-pack for his troubles.

"This guy's me mate," he says as if that's all the explanation I need, knocking Wade on the shoulder as he passes him with a box. The guy's at least forty, but neither will say how they met when I ask. From Wade I get a shrug and a smile, from Walt the more colorful "I'd tell ya, but I'd hev'ta kill ya."

"That attitude doesn't sound very Australian," I tell Wade when Walt goes back outside for another box of books.

"That's probably because he's from New Zealand."

When it comes time for the two of them to move the huge, unwieldy mattress in to the bedroom, Wade asks Walt to wait a minute. Walt emits an exaggerated sigh, feigning extreme difficulty balancing the mattress on its side by himself. In the bedroom, Wade strategically moves everything out of the way so the mattress can lie directly on the floor.

Walt smiles approvingly at Wade's effort. "He's a clevah one," he tells me. "Must be why you like 'im."

"Okay, smartass," Wade says. "Back to it."

Everything's in by four. Wade leaves to drop Walt at home and return the moving van, and I follow him in my car to bring him back.

"My own place," I say, almost to myself as we ascend the steps—just four of them!—a final time into the apartment. I turn around and lock the door with finality. Standing inside and surveying the collection of neatly organized, labeled, and located boxes, I almost want to cry. "Unpacking is going to be so easy," I say, leaning against Wade. "Thank you."

"You're welcome."

I take out my phone and start towards the kitchen. "Pizza? I'm stahvin'. Like, ravenous."

"Me too," Wade says. But he takes my hand, leading me towards the bedroom. We both stop at the foot of the mattress.

"Ah," I say, getting it. "But we'd need sheets."

In response, Wade points downward, where his right boot rests on a box labeled BEDROOM: SHEETS.

I look up at him. "You? Are my favorite mover ever."

The door opens, and Kendra's there with mistletoe. "Merry Christmas season!"

"It's not even December," I remind her, kissing her cheek.

She shakes her head. "It's past Thanksgiving, thus I've decorated. Costco has had Christmas decorations up since August. It's even supposed to snow tonight, did you see?"

Xanna's already in the living room, her previous white-blond hair dyed red—fire-red, not ginger-red. She's with Tavie, a friend I recognize from her housewarming, small and thin with stick-straight black hair that falls just to her shoulders, red-framed eyeglasses the exact shade of Xanna's hair, and puffy eyes.

Tavie stands and holds out her hand. In the other is a tissue. "Nice to meet you," she says.

"Tavie brought the best games," Kendra says.

"Tavie's also drunk," Xanna says, squeezing her friend's shoulder. "But that's okay."

"Tavie's going through a breakup," Tavie says with a tearful laugh.

Kendra pours from a pitcher into two margarita glasses. "You guys need to catch up, and quick. Did I not say seven?"

Wade and I exchange an embarrassed look. By the time we emerged from my new bedroom this afternoon, we had seven

215

minutes to shower, dress, and eat if we wanted to make it over to Kendra's on time. From the looks of it everyone was fine starting without us. Kendra alone has probably killed a pitcher—or shared one with Tavie.

Wade and I take our places on floor pillows and accept the drinks. The night hangs before me like a glass ornament, delicate and subject to sudden and spectacular breakage. It's our first public outing, Lesson 101 on what it's like to have Wade moving within my orbit. Would we be a star, shining brightly but burning out, or a planet, solid and permanent?

I'm ridiculously excited for him to meet Patrick, someone with no preconceived notions about him. I know this because I checked. "Does Patrick know about Wade?" I asked Kendra this morning, on the phone.

"That you're together?" She sounded confused. "Oh, that he's practically in high school. Yes, I know you're rolling your eyes. It's fun for me, get used to it. But you know, to answer your question, I honestly don't think so. I wasn't privy to the early days of your courtship. By the time I knew he was a thing, I was more into the fact that you *had* a thing."

That sounded good enough to me.

The collection of board games is piled in the corner of the room. We start off with Pictionary, Kendra's personal nostalgic favorite, dividing into off-couple teams—Wade and Kendra, Xanna and Patrick, and me and Tavie. Tavie proves to be a surprisingly gifted artist. "Oh, God, she's an architect," Xanna says, getting it. "Duh!"

Tavie shrugs. "I'm a frustrated artist."

We run out of margaritas and open a bottle of wine. I watch Wade draw a drawbridge for Kendra, hesitating and erasing to make it perfect. "Stop with the caution!" Kendra yells at him. I just sit, a cloudy smile on my face. When I colored with crayons as a child, I'd always outline everything first, filling in later on with the same color, just lighter. The effect of the fully colored page, to me anyway, was that everything glowed. Tonight, that's how I feel about everyone in the room: outlined in color—the same, only brighter. Kendra throwing her arms over her head in victory. Xanna sitting back with a self-satisfied smile, her eyebrows lifting toward her minuscule bangs. Patrick pulling off his glasses, rubbing his eyes, and laughing at himself. Snow beginning to fall outside the window. Tavie giving me a look like "we've got this" before nodding to Kendra to set the timer. Wade's eyes, blue as the Colorado sky, on me in a way I can feel, not just see. There are so many bright reds and blues, some greens, and lots of gold. The gold glints off Wade's cheekbones, settles in Kendra's eyes as she smiles like a crazy person, and glimmers in the slosh of wine glasses.

The world feels different. Every once in a while, with Wade in my line of vision, the air thins slightly and I'm back in my bedroom, this afternoon. Truly alone with him finally, not just a bed or a temporarily empty house but an apartment all to ourselves, no one to furtively watch for, no unconscious worries about interruption. I'd anticipated the opportunity with exhilaration, but once it was here, what I felt was more of an overwhelming sense of calm. We took our time. Even under the sunlight pouring in from the bare windows, Wade had a way of making every ounce of my self-consciousness evaporate. He pulled the top sheet over us and smiled at me, looking as if he were about to kiss me, then disappeared, making my body hiccup as he embarked on a mission with his tongue. Automatically my legs opened to him, my fingers snarling through his hair. With others oral sex—at least when I was the recipient—had always been something we worked up to. Never was it the appetizer. Hell, at the moment it was the glass of wine before the appetizer. But like with so many other things with Wade, everything took on a different tinge.

"How in the hell do you know how to do this?" I asked, rhetorically, at one point. He just smiled. At least I think he did. And it wasn't just that he did it, but that he did it so well. He did *everything* well. It was unnerving. Despite the one-night stands of my Slutty Summer, the longevity of my relationships had the unfortunate effect of more or less stunting my own sexual exploration and curiosity, so I probably seemed like an amateur to him. I tried not to think about it.

We stayed that way, tangled and not working towards any particular destination, for as long as we could. Lying on Wade's chest, tracing his skin with my fingertip, I thought of how Xanna had once described lesbian sex as being circular, with no beginning or ending, just being. It was presented as a selling point, to better explain the draw of sex with women, and why she loved it. And today, in an unfurnished bedroom at Aunt Anita's in Medford, Massachusetts, I had an idea of what she meant. Wade and I had so much to learn about each other's bodies, this new sexual home to move into. We were going to savor every second we had.

We move on to Cards Against Humanity, making us all laugh so hard I almost pee. Patrick, it turns out, is rocket-scientist smart, one of those guys who knows a little bit about everything. Somehow, this actually helps in the game.

"MIT," Kendra says proudly when I point this out to her. We're in the kitchen, scrounging for food. "I told you he's a biochemist."

"And I said, 'yeah, uh huh.'" I'm slicing cheese, and I take a big piece for myself. "Like I know from biochemistry. But seriously, Kendra, I love him. And I love the two of you together." All night I've been noticing their interaction. When they're not on opposite teams he's forever touching her—a palm on her knee, his fingers on her shoulder blade when she's sitting on the floor. He always makes sure she's got everything she needs, before she can even think of it herself. I heard something once: with certain people, your husband's always got to be a little bit more in love with you than you are with him. Patrick was smitten, and it was exactly what Kendra needed.

"I could tell he was the one pretty much right away," I tell her.

"How?"

"Because you never talk about him."

Kendra opens her mouth as if to argue, then her face collapses into a smile. "That's paradoxically accurate."

"You and Wade, too," she says. "You are having yourself a time."

I won't argue with that, I think. We reenter the living room, and Kendra arranges the plate of cheese, a bag of salt-and-vinegar chips, and two packages of Pop Tarts. "Who's hungry?"

It's one-thirty by the time Wade and I stumble back to my apartment. It's a good three-quarters of a mile from Kendra's, and we could have Ubered—we walked there to begin with, since we knew we didn't want to drive home—but there's an inch of snow on the ground and it's still falling. We amble down the street hand in hand, singing Christmas carols. Waiting for the light to change at Powder House Square, Wade takes my face in his hands and kisses me, a long, deep drunken kiss that lasts until the beeping of the walk signal makes us both laugh.

Everything is silent and beautiful. We walk along, part of the winter decor. There's something I'm trying to figure out how to say. Something the night brought. I keep looking at Wade. He's waiting. I can tell. He's different, I remind myself. He lets me be silent and figure out where I'm going without talking over me.

We've just turned onto my street when I find my voice. "I started thinking tonight. About us. Whatever 'us' is." A car comes down the street, cautiously. We wait on the sidewalk as it passes, then step back into the street and the car's tracks in the snow.

"So did you come up with anything?" Wade asks finally.

I blurt it out. "Am I like Lindsay?"

"Am I like Dean?"

Sometimes the way he answers a question with a question is charming. This is not one of those times. "That's different. Dean was a serious, long-term relationship from years ago."

"Who you've been hanging out with pretty recently."

"But I'm not anymore," I say. "Because I don't want to. So no, to answer your question. You're nothing like him."

"And I told you before. You're not like Lindsay. Not even close."

We're under a streetlight. I let go of Wade and take a few steps away, out of the orb.

"Charlie."

I turn around. I speak across the falling snow. "I just like *being* with you."

"Charlie." He holds his palms out. "You got a boyfriend?"

I shake my head.

"You want one?" he asks.

I take a mental photo. This scene would go with the script, him standing under artificial light, glowing in the snow in the middle of my brand-new street. He walks slowly over to me, stopping just short of easy reach. The light behind him surrounds him in a wintry halo.

I hook my index fingers through the belt loops on his jeans, closing the last inches between us. "I think I do."

"You got one."

He takes my hand and begins to walk the last few hundred feet towards my house, but stops when he realizes I'm not moving. He looks back at me questioningly.

"That's from a movie," I say accusingly. "You used it before."

He smiles in a way that shows I'm right, then turns away again, tugging me along.

"Which one?" I demand, trailing behind him.

"If you don't know, I'm not saying."

At my door I try one last time. "Tell me. Which one?"

Again, that smile that suggests he has no intention of answering. But he sings: *"Take it easy."* He leans in to kiss me, and even though I'm annoyed, I can't not kiss him back. He pulls me to him. "You don't need to know," he says, his voice like a secret in my ear. "That's seriously the only good line."

twenty-one

I have nothing to wear. Nothing.

The wedding is tomorrow. Wade and I have plans tonight—to do what, we have no idea—but I call him to cancel. "I'm sorry. I figured something in my closet would work, but unless I can lose ten pounds by tomorrow, I have absolutely nothing to wear to the wedding. I can't see you tonight. I have to go shopping."

I chide myself for putting myself in this position. I really should have been on top of this this past week, but since starting my new job on Monday, I haven't thought of it. The job is going swimmingly, in a boring, non-JJ sort of way. There are sixteen people in my department alone. I've already promised Nina I'd check on any other open positions.

"So I'll go with you," Wade says breezily.

I snort. "Dress shopping? I don't think so."

"I can help."

"Wade, I mean this in the nicest way, but no. You really can't."

"I mean it. Don't you want an outsider's opinion on how you look?"

"Not yours!"

"What does that mean?"

"Wade, the women's dressing room is one of the ten circles of hell. Even I turn into a raging lunatic in there."

"Oooo, I didn't even think about the dressing room. Naked Charlie. Yeah!" I laugh, if only because, lately, he's been getting his fill of naked Charlie.

"Trust me, you'll be bored out of your skull."

"I think I can risk it."

I sigh. "Wade, for real. You don't want to shop with me. You'll see a whole side of me you don't like." *The fat side*, I think.

"I'll be fine. We can get coffee after. Some cheesecake at that place all the girls like."

"I hate cheesecake."

But he's relentless. And because I'm always going to opt for a night with Wade versus a night without Wade, somehow I give in. In the end, we agree to meet at the mall, where he'll follow me into whatever stores strike my fancy. And he's not allowed to talk unless I ask him a direct question. "You're going to have to be willing to do my bidding," I warn.

"And then we'll go back to your place, where you'll have to do *my* bidding?"

I hug the phone to my cheek. *This is what he does to me*, I think, my skin sparkling. *This.*

He's waiting for me on the bench outside Nordstrom, revealed bit by bit as I come up the escalator. "Seven minutes late, as always," he says, standing.

It's so freeing to allow myself to fully feel my feelings. *This is my boyfriend.* I spend a moment just taking him in, absorbing whatever flows through me as his presence registers in all corners of my body. Long, lean legs in faded jeans. Scuffed boots. Ice-blue eyes that change to slits when he smiles. Cheekbones from here to Alaska. Tangled hair that borders on unruly, resting just above his collar. I'm sure I've never seen a more beautiful man in my life.

He catches me looking and half-smiles. "What?"

"You're... very easy on the eyes."

He laughs and takes me by the hand. He leans down and says: "You're the easy one." He cuts off my sputtering with a kiss. "Let's go find something to put on that sexy body of yours."

"You sure you're up for this?"

"Lead the way."

Okay, ready?"

I exit the dressing room and twirl around stiffly. In the fourth store, starting the third hour of shopping, I'm not feeling very twirly. The closest I've come was a gorgeous sage-green dress that made me sigh, but I made the mistake of bringing it into the dressing room without looking at the price tag.

When I first went into the dressing room with an armful of dresses I stayed hidden, examining my choices in private, expecting Wade to simply wait me out. But as I struggled through the straps of my third dress, I heard his voice.

"Charlie, are you coming out?"

"I'm only on the third dress."

"Why didn't you show me the first two?"

Why didn't I show him? Was he high?

"Seriously, have you been toking today?" I marched out of the single dressing room to where I'd left him waiting outside. He'd dragged a chair—where had he found a chair?—over to the outside of the dressing room and was looking at me expectantly. "I'm not going to show you each dress!" Why would he want to see me parading around in dresses I didn't know I was going to buy?

But he insisted he was here for a reason and that if I wanted to drag him all the way to the mall (I rolled my eyes at this, and he grinned) the least I could do was give him a job to do. "I have an eye for this," he said. "Trust me."

He looked so sincere that I couldn't think of a reason to say no. I still wasn't hot to let a guy—let alone a hot guy I was really into—see me wearing my rejected clothes (which most of them would be), but in the end we struck an agreement where if I knew it was a definite no, he didn't have to look, but if I was on the fence at all I would venture out and get his opinion.

"I don't know," he says about my latest choice. "What do you think?"

"It's not really my color," I muse. "And these sleeves." I bat at them with my hands, little cap sleeves that looked so much better on the hanger. "They'd drive me crazy."

"I think we can do better."

I look a moment longer. He's right. The thing is, after four stores, I'm inclined to agree with him on almost every opinion he offers. I'm not the twiggy type, and it's hard to find clothes that flatter me or don't accentuate the fact that the thigh gap is never gonna happen. I've grudgingly concluded that he does have a knack for knowing what looks good on me.

After another fitful exchange of clothes, I stand in front of him in a black minidress, flared at the bottom and gathered through the torso. "How about this?"

"Turn around." He reaches out and smooths the small of my back. Will I ever stop reacting to his touch? "It looks good everywhere but here. See how it bunches up?"

"Yes," I agree forlornly. Who am I kidding? I'm not going to find anything. I look at him in resignation. "I think we should call it a night."

"But we haven't even"—he's whispering now—"you know." He throws a glance into the dressing room.

"Oh, gross. That's strictly a guy fantasy."

"Is that so?"

"Those mirrors are hideous."

And there it is—another thing I love about Wade. He laughs. All the time. With me, even at me, but never mean-spirited. I think I've laughed with him more than I have with anyone in the past year. More than that, he thinks *I'm* funny, which is a first.

"Seriously now," he says, "you wanna quit without buying anything?"

"Have you seen anything worth buying?" I throw the words over my shoulder as I head back into the dressing room. Isn't that always the way? I come to the mall on a mission, ready to buy, credit card at the ready, and can't find a single thing. I'm going to have to get up early tomorrow and interrupt Kendra and Patrick's morning sex to raid her closet.

"I guess that's it," I say, walking over to Wade's chair. I put my hand on his shoulder with finality. "Let's go get something to eat. Actual dinner, not just cheesecake."

"Let's do that," he tells me, looking up at me and snaking his arms around my hips. "But let's go to one other store first, okay?"

I shake my head and ruffle his hair. "I really cannot handle another store. Thanks anyway."

"Just come with me." He takes my hand—he knows what that does to me, I can tell in his smile, and the way he squeezes—and winds his way through the winter coats and the lingerie. As I willingly let him lead me I have a sudden thought: Dress or no dress, I am exactly where I want to be. He could take me to CVS pharmacy or the Disney Store or even the Rainforest Café with its schmaltzy gift shop and overpriced appetizers. I wouldn't care.

"I think," I hear him saying, "we should go back and get the green dress."

"What green dress?"

"At Anthropologie."

I sigh. The sage green dress again. I hadn't put anything that beautiful on my body in a long time. On the hanger it resembled a handkerchief; I'd glided right past it after stopping to marvel at the lovely color. But Wade noticed my interest and checked it out after I'd moved on. "How about his one?" he said, holding it up.

I glanced over from two racks away, and shook my head. "Not for me."

He put it over his arm; it was as good as added to the pile. "Humor me."

So I brought it in with three other dresses, none of which worked. One was too long, one was too tight, and one, which I was sure would be perfect, bunched up under my armpits in a way that made me wonder exactly what kind of toothpick-limbed waif they expected would be able to wear it. "Honestly," I muttered, yanking on the green dress with resentment that it was starting to feel impossible to conceal. All I wanted to was to find one damn dress that looked decent. Just one. I pushed my arms through the sleeves and shoved my hair down violently, trying in vain to control the static electricity that defined Boston winters indoors, particularly in dressing rooms—all that flying fabric.

The full-length mirror had never done me any favors, it was true. And at first I was skeptical. I even went so far as to begin to take the dress off; surely it didn't look as good as all that. But then I stopped. I turned slowly around, craning my neck. I got outside of the smaller dressing room into the three-way mirror in the main area. I was dumbfounded. How could that dress—that shapeless nothing of a dress—do this to my body? It was tight in all the right places, loose everywhere it needed room. I examined it top to bottom, side to side. Wraparound to a V-neck, fitted down to a flouncy skirt with an uneven hemline, just above the knee on one side, just below the knee on the other. Such a deep beautiful light green, the color of sage, a color that I knew from experience brought out the hidden green in my hazel eyes. Hadn't Dean always liked me in green? Hadn't Cam?

"Jesus." I leaned forward and double-checked in the mirror. Yup, I even had cleavage. Classy cleavage.

Unfortunately, when Wade first handed the dress to me I forgot the crucial step of looking at the price tag. I finally thought to check only after I exited the dressing room and he and I both were admiring what clearly had been made to be Charlie's Dress.

"It looked amazing on you," Wade reminds me now.

"Yeah, $300 worth of amazing." I shake my head to obliterate the image, like an Etch-A-Sketch. "Please don't make me feel bad. I'm already about to cry that I can't have it."

He's quiet a minute. "What were you planning on spending?"

"Oh, I dunno. Under a hundred if I was lucky or hit a good sale. One-fifty at the most."

"So." He seems like he's trying to figure out how to word something. I wait in barely concealed amusement. What is he going to do, suggest we steal it?

"What if I gave you the difference? Just pretend it was on sale."

Not what I was expecting. "You're not serious."

"I'm serious."

"You cannot buy me a dress."

"Technically I'm only buying half a dress."

"Wade. Seriously." I make my way through the makeup counters to the exit into the mall. "Let's just get something to eat. How about Johnny Rocket's?"

"That dress belongs on you."

I snort. "Wade, I'm not going to take your money!"

"I'm offering it."

"I can't."

"Seriously, it would make me happy."

"No way."

"Please. I'll take it personally."

No question he's being sweet, and half of me wants to hug him simply for the gesture. But there are logistics to consider. Obvious logistics. "But aren't you"—I can't think of a nice way to say it—"broke?"

His brows knit. "What gave you that idea?"

"Well, you dropped out of college and ..." I realize there is no way to tactfully finish that sentence. "I don't want to contribute to your problems," I finish lamely.

He laughs and throws an arm over my shoulder. "It's true, Charlie, I have problems, more than a few," he admits. "But trust me. Lack of money isn't one of them."

I'm going to pay you back," I vow, swirling a French fry in ketchup. "As soon as I get my first paycheck." I think a minute. "Maybe my second."

"I already told you. It's a gift."

"You're not even going to see it on me!"

He elevates his eyebrows lasciviously. "But if I'm lucky, I'll get to take it off."

I shoulder-bump him. "If you're going to spend so much time at my place, you should probably tell your parents about us," I muse, stirring my root beer with a straw.

He shrugs. "I already told my dad."

"What!"

"And Jess."

"Wade!"

"Oh, come on. What do you think their reaction was?"

I shake my head. "They don't even know me."

"They *love* you. And that was before you sent them a thank-you card. Now I think they want to adopt you."

I shrug, smiling. "They were really nice to me in Fort Collins." His dad and step-mom's approval makes me happy, but the Colorado-based reaction to our relationship that I'm most curious about is probably the one I'll never know.

"When did you tell them?"

"Two weeks ago, maybe? Right after my mom and William left."

"But I wasn't your girlfriend then!"

"Yeah, but you were gonna be."

This guy.

"You're only my third boyfriend," I say thoughtfully. "It's only fair that you know I'm not that experienced in relationships."

He's incredulous. "Didn't you have two long-term relationships?"

"Well, in years, maybe. Not variety."

"You think variety matters more than longevity." I'm not sure I've ever seen better eyes than his. He stares all the way into me. It's like a vibration.

"Sort of. Maybe. I dunno." I wrinkle my nose. "Just don't be surprised if I get boring."

For some reason, this gets his dander up. "So what if you do? Why is that bad? Real life is the boring parts. It's easy to be

227

with someone when it's new and exciting. Keeping it going when the novelty wears off, that's when it gets hard."

"Personally," I say, "I think that's when it gets better."

"Damn straight."

"Wade, don't take this the wrong way, but sometimes you sound like you're forty."

He smiles, a little ruefully. "I get that a lot. I dunno. I guess I'm like my dad. He's taught me a lot."

"About relationships?"

"About everything. But yeah, relationships too. Getting Jess back was not an easy thing for him."

"I'd love to hear that story."

"You will someday."

The thought of that makes me smile. It also makes me daring. "Wade? Do you mind if I ask? What happened with Jordan?"

"You mean why did we break up?" He's playing with his fries, not really eating them.

I try to read his face, but it's impassive. "I'm sorry," I say quickly. "It's none of my business."

He pushes his plate away and leans on his arms on the table. "No, it's fine. I mean, it's not much of a story. Infidelity is pretty cliché, right?"

"She cheated on you?" I'm stunned. Okay, maybe I'm biased—of course I'm biased—but I cannot fathom how a girl would even *think* to cheat on him.

He shrugs. "It's more complicated than that, I guess. He-said she-said. I thought we were exclusive, she didn't, and somehow that discrepancy was my fault."

"Is that why you came back?"

"Here? Not exactly. I mean, no. It's when I came back, but not why."

Girl to girl, I'm pretty sure that even though she's not the reason he left when he did, it must have felt that way to her. I wonder how she's going to feel when she finds out he's not coming back.

twenty-two

I wake later that night to Wade sliding into me. He does it so easily I must have been dreaming, already slick and ready. Heavy with sleep, I grip his glutes, pulling him, holding him, commanding stillness. He is taut and electric. I run my hands up and down his back, and I don't even realize when my fingertips give way to my nails. His teeth graze my shoulder. He cries out, maybe from pain, maybe not. We both dig in deeper.

Kendra's picking me up in two hours. I should be in the shower, but for the moment I'm opting to marvel at Wade's sleeping profile. His perfect nose, the smattering of stubble on his chin and jaw, his kissable lips, his untamed hair. He needs a haircut probably, but the sexy-sloppy way it spills out everywhere makes me hope he doesn't find his way to a stylist anytime soon. My fingers are in it before I even think about what I'm doing. He stirs.

"I could get used to waking up with you," he says, half asleep, turning to me and running his hands down my ribcage to my hips. "As long as you always sleep naked."

With the feel and memory of him in the middle of the night still front and center, I'm bold. "Maybe you should."

"Should what?"

He moves slightly onto his back and I rest on his chest, chin on my forearms. "Move in here."

Wade looks at me for a long moment.

"I know," I say. "It's crazy."

"But you told Aunt Anita," he says in a mock-warning.

"Maybe she'd make an exception. Just think about it. We can both think about it."

He rises on an elbow, really awake now. "Charlie," he says lightly, "much as I'd love to have morning sex with you every day, I'd have a bitch of a time getting to class."

"I'd make sure you got there."

"From two time zones away?" He's smiling, like we're sharing a joke.

"What do you mean?"

He volleys the same question with a look. I sit up, like that will let me think straighter.

"Wade. I thought—you're staying, right?"

He looks confused. "Staying where?"

"Here. In Massachusetts."

"Just until Christmas. I told you that."

"Well, you did. But I thought things... changed."

His expression doesn't alter. And then it does. And I realize I'm looking at him from the other side.

His face is an apology. "Charlie..."

Oh my God. This isn't happening.

Oh my *God*. Not only is this happening, I'm *naked*. I grab the sheet, suddenly very conscious of being laid bare. I scan the room for my clothes, any clothes. Screw it. I get up and head to my partially-unpacked boxes. I should have done laundry this past week. God only knows where I can find clean underwear.

"Charlie." Wade's behind me, reaching for me.

I stay facing away from him, rummaging through clothes.

"Charlie. Talk to me."

I find a tank top and yank it on.

He gently but firmly forces me to turn around. "Charlie. Please don't ignore me. I hate that."

I know he does. I collect my feelings and raise my head and wait for him to talk.

"Charlie, you're right. A lot of things changed with you and me. Good changes. But I can't stay here. I was never going to stay, no matter what happened. My reason for being here in the first place is done. And I have to finish school."

"Couldn't you finish here?"

He shakes his head, never losing my gaze. "I have to go home."

"So, us, this"—I gesture around the all-but-empty apartment, meaning to encompass so much that isn't visible—"doesn't mean anything at all?"

"Of course it does. Charlie—"

"Then why are you—"

"—come with me."

I rewind my brain to hear what he said. "Come with—to Colorado?"

"Yes."

"But my life is here." He looks at me, like he's waiting. Oh, right. Shit. "Wade, I just signed a lease."

"I know. For a year. And I know how much you wanted this place."

"And I just got a job."

"I know." He sighs. "Charlie, I know all that. So stay here. Live here. We can wait it out. We can visit each other. Do the long-distance thing, see how that works. For the spring semester. Then we—"

"No."

"What?"

"No! Just—no! I am not going to do the long-distance thing!" I wrest myself from his hold. When I reach the doorway, where I have room for my feelings to spread out, I turn around. "I can't do long-distance," I say, more quietly. "I did it once."

His face darkens. "I'm not Dean."

"I know. But I'm still me."

The longer we stand there, the bigger the words get in my head, flashing by. Holy shit. This is it. Is this really how I lose him? So quickly? Like this?

"We're at an impasse," he says, unnecessarily.

"Ya think?"

I'm never this rude to him. He looks at me for a long, sad moment, then sits on the side of the mattress, collecting his clothes.

It takes all the effort I can muster to steady my voice. "You can't stay for a little while? Go back in... the summer? Fall semester?"

"I'm registered for classes, Charlie."

"So postpone it! Just a few months!"

"And I *really* miss my dog." His pulls his jeans on and stands, facing me. "Charlie, you want me to uproot my life completely, but you won't even entertain the idea of doing the same. How is that fair?"

231

If I said what I'm thinking, it would be this: *You're only nineteen. What the hell do you know about being uprooted?*

"It's not that I won't," I say. "I can't."

"Can't's just another word for won't." He sighs, rubs his eye. "But I'll bite. Why can't you?"

"You know why. I just got a job. I just signed a lease."

He waits.

"And Marina's pregnant," I remind him. "I want to be there for that."

His face hardens in a way I've never seen, and I want to bite the words back. Of everyone I could have said this to, there are some who would have believed it. Wade isn't one of them.

When he finally speaks, he sounds defeated. "Then you should be."

The wedding's in Danborn, and my mom wants to see us all dressed up, so Kendra's bringing us there first. When I get in Patrick's car Kendra's on the phone, so she doesn't fully see me until I step out at my house.

"Jesus, Charlie. How fucking good do you look?" She pulls out her phone, indicates I should pose.

"Thanks." I smile stiffly.

"For real. That dress was made for you."

"I know. Wade picked it out." *And didn't even get to see me in it.* His car, I can't help noticing, is absent from his driveway.

Kendra's face registers surprise, then she nods. She takes my arm. "I thought I needed to help you find the right guy, but I'm going to bow out. You know what you're doing, girl. We *like* you with him. Oh! That reminds me. I saw Cam yesterday at Patrick's company Christmas party!"

"Cam?"

"Cam. Apparently Katherine works in Patrick's lab. Or something. Don't worry, I briefed him on your blissful coupledom. Made it sound even better than his." She winks, then shrugs. "Actually, I didn't even have to exaggerate. I just told it like it is."

I escape to my room to touch up my makeup. I didn't have time to do it properly at my apartment. I'm just finishing when there's a knock at the door, and I call to Kendra to come in.

But the door opens and it's Dean, looking like he could be in a magazine ad.

"You're wearing a *tux*?"

"Go big or go home." His smile is brilliant but feels practiced. He holds out his hand. "Ms. Michaelsen, will you do me the honor of being my date to the Dodson-Farnham wedding?"

So corny. I shake my head. Isn't it just like Dean, to ignore me and do what he wants anyway. "Dean, I told you..." I start to protest. But then I just can't. I don't have it in me. Not today.

He doesn't seem to even hear me. His eyes are traveling up and down, and he takes a step back, as if he needs more room to see. "Charlie," he says. "Wow. You look... just, *wow*."

"Thanks," I answer with a nervous laugh. I'm not used to him being at a loss for words, and I have to admit, it feels nice.

"Charlotte," my mom says when I come into the kitchen, Dean in tow. "Dean. Don't the two of you look gorgeous."

She insists on taking photos outside, with her flower garden as a background. God, even Marina's around. With Todd. So embarrassing. I stand stiffly on Dean's arm, posing in a bizarre replay of prom night. Dean charms everyone as usual, sparkling in his tux. He's remarkably at ease, like he knows he belongs.

"Look at the two of you together," my mom says again. Then, to my horror, she bursts into tears. My mother, who stood stone-faced through her husband's funeral, who always advocated stiff-upper-lipping every hardship, is crying in my driveway.

I rush to her side, almost tripping on my heels. She waves me off. "Oh Charlie, I'm fine. I just can't tell you how nice it is to see the two of you together again." She walks with purpose over to Dean, pulls him down to her level and gives him a strident kiss on the cheek. "Take care of my girl."

"Mom, *they're* not getting married," Marina says, laughing.

"Oh I know. I'm sorry, I'm embarrassing you." She gives me a hug. "You kids have a good time, okay? Give my love to Kelly."

I steal a glance at Kendra, who's looking at me helplessly. She doesn't know the half of it.

"Ready?" Dean asks me. I look back at my mom, tears still visible in her smiling eyes. When did she get so old? And when did I start feeling like such a disappointment to her?

"Yeah," I say. Then, louder, "I'm ready."

The church is the fanciest, most ornate church in this part of the state. It's an absolutely gorgeous ceremony, very traditional. I'm surprised to see it's not a full Catholic mass. Kelly must have fought hard for that. Her face exudes utter joy as she floats—I swear she does—to the front of the church on her dad's arm. Some of my more feminist friends balk at this custom (usually the ones who swear they're never taking someone else's name when they get married), equating it to the father handing over ownership of his daughter to another man. But I've always thought of it as more like... caretaking. *I've taken care of her till now, son. Now it's your turn. Don't fuck it up.*

Judging from the look on her dad's face, that may well be what he's thinking.

Later, in the receiving line, I hug Kelly tight. "Congratulations, Mrs. Farnham!"

"Oh, it's Mrs. Dodson," Kelly tells me, brushing aside of the notion of changing her name with a *pshaw* gesture. "I've been Kelly Dodson my whole life, becoming someone else would just confuse me!"

She's joking, but if I know Kelly, a lot of thought went into this decision. "You look beautiful," I tell her, meaning it.

"So do you," she says, as if she's been thinking it and just waiting for the chance to tell me. "That dress is killer." She glances at Dean, still shaking Dave's hand next to her, and says into my ear: "You need to update me! Kendra says there's a new guy?"

Open bar at receptions can either be very good or very bad. An hour in, ordering my third Jack and Coke, I decide that in my case, it might be very bad. My phone buzzes with a text as I sip. *I'm sorry.* I wonder exactly what Wade's sorry for, but decide I don't want to know. I text him the picture Kendra took of me in my dress.

I manage to avoid Keith all day, which isn't as hard as it sounds, because I think he's doing the same. And Dean sticks close to him, so we don't end up spending much time together either, even though we're technically at the same table. Which is just as well. I'm a mess.

Earlier on the way into the church, Kendra yanked me aside. "Did he just show up at your house? Without telling you?"

"Yup." I wanted to tell her about this morning, too, but I didn't. I couldn't.

I do see Lindsay, flawless in a black strapless cocktail dress. I remember now, she and Steve grew up in the same neighborhood as Dave. Their families must be friends. During Dave's brother's best-man speech, I catch her giving me the dirtiest of looks. Great. Now I have an enemy. Wade probably broke things off with her, and he probably told her the truth because he's Wade, and now she's pissed. Maybe I did make the right decision this morning. I mean, even if I decided to try to handle long-distance—which I'm not—this is what a relationship with Wade would mean? Dealing with the wrath of hometown bitches?

The longer the day goes on the more I desperately want to confide in Kendra, who would no doubt have some spot-on insight, or at least tell me to get a grip, shake it off, whatever I need to hear. I'm too emotional to dare. Having stolen the show at the bachelor party, I'm determined to lay low today. My petty problems are not Kelly's circus, not her monkeys.

Kendra brings us Key lime pie from the dessert buffet (which is open the whole reception; what an utterly perfect idea). Usually Key lime pie is one of my favorites—it beats the hell out of cheesecake, anyway—but after one bite, I slide it aside and turn to Patrick. I'm now on drink number five and can feel myself beginning to wallow. There may as well be a "danger" police bubble flashing on my forehead.

"So where are you from, Patrick? I don't think Kendra told me."

"Just outside San Francisco. I traded one coast for another."

"Have you been back a lot?"

"For one job, once. I occasionally get offers there. I could end up moving back someday."

"And have a long-distance relationship?" Kendra interjects.

"You'd miss me too much," he teases. "But if I had to I could handle one with you." Kendra takes this as the compliment it's intended as and kisses him.

"Look at Wade and Charlie," Patrick tells her. "They're going to be fine."

"I'm sorry, what?" She turns to me. "Who's leaving?"

Patrick goes on, oblivious, emptying sugar into his coffee—he's the designated driver—not realizing Kendra's not speaking to him. "Wade's going back to Colorado at the end of the month. I told him I was jealous. I'd move there in a second." He smiles at me, raises his glass. "If anyone can make it, it's the two of you." His smile fades as he takes in both of our faces. "What?"

It's the alcohol. My defenses are not just lowered, they're nonexistent. So much for laying low. But I'm not going to cry in front of everyone, so I stand. "Excuse me."

Kendra bursts into the hotel bathroom after me. "Charlie?" It takes her a while to find me, back in the corner sitting area. She sinks next to me, gives me a hug. "I'm so sorry. So is Patrick. He didn't know. I guess the two boys got to talking at game night."

"I didn't know until *this morning*."

She sits quietly next to me, then says the only thing that matters. "He won't consider staying?"

"No."

She pauses. "Could you move with him?"

"I can't. There are so many—I just can't, Kendra. I can't."

She seems to accept this, or at least doesn't say anything to refute it. Embarrassed, I assure Kendra I'll be okay and send her back to Patrick, asking her to please apologize to him. For now I have to be alone. I slide my phone on and read Wade's last text, his response to the picture of me in my dress. *Beautiful doesn't begin to cover it.* I can't call him. There's no way a conversation with him wouldn't end in an ugly-cry.

I've composed myself enough to chance leaving the bathroom when the door opens, just as I'm passing the mirrors. Lindsay. And a friend. "Slut," Lindsay says, plain as day, as she pulls out her lipstick.

I'm not cut out for this. In a movie I'd have the perfect one-two punch of a one-liner that would both put her in her place and leave her speechless. The reality is not nearly so glamorous. The best I can do, after I pass her, is to turn around, my hand on the door. "Oh," I say, like I'm just remembering. "I almost forgot. Wade says hi."

I'm hyperventilating. I beeline to the bar and contemplate another Jack and Coke while surveying the room. Kendra's not at our table, so I make awkward circles scanning the dance floor. I need Kendra. She'll be able to assess how drunk I am, whether I should leave. I kind of think I should. Maybe I just will. By myself. Uber to my mom's. I should at least tell her I'm leaving.

The terrace. Maybe she's outside. I make an abrupt left and hit an elbow.

I look up. All the way up. It's Dean, and he wants to dance. We move into one another's arms. The song has just changed, something ancient and slow by U2. How many times have I danced with Dean in my lifetime? All the proms and homecoming dances, at least two family weddings. We both know just how to hold our arms, exactly the angle at which to tilt our heads to speak.

"Sorry I haven't seen you all day," Dean says. "Keith," he adds, and shrugs, as if that's all the explanation needed. "For what it's worth, he feels pretty bad."

I'm wondering exactly what he feels bad about—I really want to know—but Dean looks down at me then and steps slightly back for a moment, just like he did earlier. His eyes come to rest on my cleavage. "You look so unbelievably hot." The compliments again. Clearly he's been imbibing, too.

"Thanks. Dave and Kelly look really happy."

"Yeah, they do." He lifts his head and looks at me from under his eyelids. "So are you planning your wedding still, based on what you see here?"

I smile. "Yes, as a matter of fact."

"Still partial to eggplant?"

He looks pleased with himself at my surprise. Honestly, I'm touched. It was always my plan to have all of my bridesmaids wear eggplant-colored dresses. I thought it was the most beautiful shade of purple.

"Actually, no."

"No? What's changed?"

"I don't know... I think I might just have everyone wear what makes them feel the prettiest."

He seems to consider that. "I like that idea."

Bono's voice flows on. Temples. Higher laws. I get the feeling Dean wants to say something else. But the longer I stay in his arms, the more I know I need to leave. The alcohol, the tears, everything's got me in a corkscrew. I can feel him looking down at me. "I have something to tell you," he says, low, in a voice for just me. "I wanted to tell you for a while now. I got the call from the police academy. I start in January."

"The police academy?"

"I didn't want to say anything unless it was sure." He grins. "I'm going to be a Danborn cop."

Like his dad. "Dean." I stop dancing and hug him. "That's wonderful."

"There's something else," he says, when we're back at arm's length. He clears his throat. "My parents decided to retire permanently to Florida. They're going to rent the house to me. The whole thing."

The song changes. It's a stupid line dance, the Cha Cha Slide. Dean guides me away from everyone piling onto the dance floor and steers us toward the terrace, warm with outdoor heaters. He looks at me for a minute, as if trying to decide how to begin. "Charlie," he says. "Um..." He looks away and laughs, almost nervously, as if he can't believe what he has to say. "So Wade's not, like, an issue, is he?"

I don't know how to answer that. Last week, last night, even this morning, it would have been easy.

"Are you together?" he asks. That amusement again. Of course he's amused; he knows what's possible.

So does Wade. He made that clear this morning: We weren't possible.

"No," I hear myself say. "We're not together at all."

Dean looks at me squarely. "Well, I'm not seeing anyone else. I just needed some time to think. And I was... depressed, I guess. I didn't tell you this, but..." He cracks his knuckles, unable to meet my gaze. "I got laid off. Six months ago. I only came home because I ran out of money." He looks back at me now, puts his hands on my shoulders. "But now everything is happening the right way. It makes sense. I came home, and here you were. Here you *are*."

Here I am.

I feel his thumb on my cheek, see the golden flecks in his eyes.

Dean, a cop. In Danborn. Living in his parents' house. I think of my mom earlier, the rare tears on her cheeks. The last time I was really happy with him, everything was intact. *I* was intact.

"Charlie, I'm ready. I know what I need."

The love of my life is standing in front of me saying all the right things. Everything I've wanted and waited for for the past seven years.

"Dean. I... I don't know what you want me to say."

"Just tell me you'll think about it."

Think about what? About the future? With him? Marrying Dean, living in Danborn forever? As a cop's wife?

"I'll think about it," I tell him.

It's the right thing to say. Even Kendra would think so. Where is Kendra? Why is it so cold out here?

I try to clear my head. I woke up this morning in love with someone else. How can things change so much in eight hours? But the writing's on the wall. In less than three weeks, Wade's leaving. Permanently. I wasn't enough to keep him here. *I'm not enough.* Nothing I said could convince him to stay. The ride is over.

It's almost a relief to know I've been right all along. I knew it in high school, I knew it after we dissolved. Someday, Dean was going to come back, and we were going to get it right. Even my mom knew it. The two of us are pre-programmed. It's like a dance I learned in sixth-grade gym or the way I turn toward my mom's voice. My synapses will always go to this place.

"Excuse me." An older, heavyset woman is trying to get by, and Dean moves us aside to make room. As he does so, I catch movement behind him, in the doorway back to the reception hall. A black dress. Watching and within earshot, a small, devious smile on her face. Lindsay.

Sometimes the easiest way to solve a problem is to make it irrelevant.

Fine, bitch. We both lose. You want to look? I'll give you something to see. And I reach up to the back of Dean's neck and pull him down to kiss me.

twenty-three

On the Fourth of July, you watch the fireworks, and you're always waiting for the finale. You think you see it, then you realize that's not it. Then you think you see it again. By the time the real finale begins, it's so overwhelmingly beyond everything you've seen so far, so very obviously the finale, that you wonder how you thought anything else even remotely qualified.

That's what breaking up with Wade is like. There was the fight at my apartment, which was awful. Then I drunkenly, purposely kissed Dean with Lindsay watching. I told myself it was over. But I didn't know just how over until he and I were in his car in the snow.

After the wedding, he doesn't contact me at all. No texts, no calls. I have to say, I am impressed with Lindsay's quick work. On Monday night after work, I camp out at my mom's. He pulls in a little past eight, and before I can think about it too much, I go over to his house and knock.

Judging from his face, he knew it was me before he opened the door. He steps out of the house and closes the door behind him.

"Can we go talk?" I say.

"Where?"

Reflexively I start to look toward the backyard, and towards the sky to judge the weather, but he stops me, shaking his head. He plants his feet. "Here's fine."

We're standing on his front steps under the lights of his porch. I cross my arms against the chill of the December night. "Wade. I'll go wherever you want, but here is not fine."

"I'll drive."

We get coffee and sit in the parking lot in his car. He won't look at me. We've been told to expect snow since this morning, and now, as we sit, it begins to snow for real, flakes melting into oblivion on the windshield.

Wade's not saying anything, just sitting and stonily drinking his coffee. I remember how, right after we first kissed, he assumed my perspective, leading the conversation for me. Part of me wishes he'd do that now. It's a lot easier when you don't have to talk.

Hmm...

"You humiliated me," I say.

He turns an incredulous look my way.

I go on. "You just told me you wanted me to move in with you, what, six hours before, and you kiss someone else? What the fuck is that about?"

He turns back toward the windshield. I keep going. "I don't deserve that, not then and not now."

"Stop it. You're no good at that," he says. I start to smile, but stop when I see there's no humor in his face.

"Wade," I say. "I am really sorry. It was a dick move on my part. And believe me, I know how this is going to sound. But it's not you. You're amazing. You're the best thing to happen to me in a long time." I take a breath. "But me and Dean—I don't know. It's like... we're just supposed to be together. Everyone thinks so—"

"Like Kendra?" he cuts in.

"Well, not—"

"What about your other friends?"

"They're warming to it," I explain, frowning. "They just need time because our breakup was pretty bad. But that was my fault. I don't think I ever told you this, Wade, but I was super-needy back then, and I pushed him away. I'm not proud of it. But don't you see? That's how I'd be with you. That's why I can't do long-distance." I shake my head, sadly. "We wouldn't survive."

He's silent for a long time. I sip my coffee and wait, wondering if I should turn on the radio. But his face tells me he's processing, so I keep waiting.

Finally he says, "Charlie, you don't know *shit*."

His voice is icier than I've ever heard it. When it's clear that's all he's going to say, I answer quietly, "No, Wade, you don't know *me*."

He studies my face. "Didn't you guys break up right after you lost your dad?" When I nod, he says, "That's not neediness, Charlie. That's grief."

"No." The force behind my voice surprises us both. "He was there for me, but I needed more than he was able to give. I pushed him away. I'd do the same to you, I know it."

"You don't know it. It takes two to make a relationship, good or bad." He shakes his head, back and forth, methodically. "You're doing the convenient thing," he says, almost to himself, like he can't believe it.

"I'm not."

"You are. What would you have done if I'd agreed to move in with you?"

"What would I have done if—what?"

"Don't stall, just answer. What if I'd said, yes, I'll drop everything of my life in Colorado and start over completely fresh with you here in Boston. What would you have done?"

"But you didn't."

"But if I had?"

"Wade, you don't want it."

"Right. That's why I was Googling transfer requirements to UMass while you were at the wedding." It's the closest I've ever seen him to looking disgusted, and the fact that his disgust is directed at me makes me sick to my stomach. "Don't worry, I came to my senses. I mean, you made sure of that." He sits back, even laughs a little. "It's brilliant, actually. You gave me an out. You get what you want—your apartment, your high-school sweetheart. And you handed me a reason to give it to you on a silver fucking platter."

"You're making me sound so manipulative." Tears have filled my eyes. It takes everything I can to keep them out of my voice.

"It *was* manipulative. You hooked up with Dean, six hours after we were in bed together, in pretty much a public place, in front of *Lindsay*. That doesn't sound like an accident. It sounds pretty fucking orchestrated, in fact. I mean, whatever, I don't even give a fuck that you kissed him. Not in this context. You were drunk, or so I'm led to believe. It was a weird day. We all do stupid shit. But the reasons behind it... " He trails off, shakes his head. "You thought you could force my hand."

He exhales loudly, then turns to look at me. It's obvious he doesn't really want to. For the first time, the ice in his eyes is not warm. "I thought—you *said*—you weren't into him. I asked. I *checked*. Remember?"

"I know. And I meant it, then."

"And you changed your mind. Since then. Since *yesterday morning*."

"I... didn't realize."

He shakes his head. "That is so fucked up." He takes a deep breath. Then another one. "What I really don't get is, why do something so shitty, Charlie? Why not just break up with me?"

"I don't know," I say in a small voice.

"You do, though. You do know."

I try speaking three times before I get the sentence out. "I could... never break up with you."

"Why not?"

"Because I—" *Because I love you*, I want to say. But I know that doesn't matter now, perhaps never did. "Wade, please. You don't understand."

"Fuck that. You think I don't understand anything. I'm too fucking young to understand the sophisticated intricacies of relationships. I'll tell you something: what you did at the wedding? That's what high-school girls do."

I look away.

"And I'll tell you something else: You're a coward. You wanted to hide me, just like Dean wanted to hide you. It was easier to keep me a secret rather than admit what was really going on."

"Wade." Is this really what he thinks? Is this really what I've done? "I meant what I said. You're the best thing—"

"Shut up." His hands are over his face. "Just stop saying that. Jesus Christ, I'm not a *thing* that *happens*. I'm a *person*."

Silence stretches on while I study my fingers entwined around my coffee cup in my lap. Then, abruptly, Wade exits the car. He walks quickly around to my side and opens my door. "Get out, please."

"Wade—" I try to take his hand, but he pulls back like I'm on fire.

"Get out. Please. I can't stay here with you." I've never seen him cry, but I'm betting that what I'm looking at is close to it. "Fuck it. Just leave my car at my house."

"Wade!" I'm horrified. Out of all the things I expected, this was not one of them. I told myself over and over again that no one was going to get hurt. But I was talking about myself, and about Dean. Wade was not even a consideration. It never occurred to me I was capable of hurting him. He's always been so laid-back, so steady, so ready to handle anything that came his way.

What have I done? What kind of animal am I?

I keep watching him, but he walks on, not looking back, until he's part of the snow.

I sit in the passenger seat for I don't know how long. Then I get behind the wheel. Instead of turning toward my mom's house, I go in the opposite direction, toward Danborn Square, taking the right down the hill. Conditions are already slick and I almost go off the road twice trying to find it. But I do. Still dressed for work, I kneel down on the cold ground, snow wetting my tights.

I knew they'd come today. It's his birthday. He'd be sixty-six. Marina and my mom have placed a new poinsettia arrangement and a tiny, tasteful evergreen wreath in front of the stone. At least it's not shaped like a cross.

Seven years ago, back from Thanksgiving break and on my way to history in McConnell Hall, I started wondering what I'd get my dad for his birthday. I'd already discarded two ideas and was searching for a third when I remembered he was dead. McConnell was behind the student union, on the other side of a ravine with a picturesque walking path and bridge through it. Thinking about his birthday, I stopped short in the middle of the bridge. "Whoa," a guy behind me said. "Careful there." He swung his backpack over his shoulder and threw an annoyed glance at me as he passed. I still didn't move.

People you love don't just die once. You keep losing them, over and over. Like when your sister breaks his heart. Or when you move back home and expect to see him still sitting in his chair, reading the paper and calling you Charlie Brown.

I wonder how he'd feel about me now. If he'd gotten to know me as an adult, a person who changed majors three times, but with opinions and criticisms, who made good decisions and treated people well, would he have liked me better? Would he have left the light on for me?

A small picture frame to the side of the headstone, new since the last time I was here, has to be my mother's handiwork. It's of her and Dad, probably the last picture ever taken of the two of them. I know because I took it. In her hand I can see the prayer book, the one he started asking us to read to him in those last few weeks.

That's how I knew he knew he was dying.

My mom had warned me that the pain medication had been affecting him, and when I came home from school that last weekend I saw what she meant: my dad was high. He was talking to the ceiling, to the closet. He called me Teresa, his sister's name. It was Saturday. I'd gotten in that morning and would go back the next night. I'd offered to spend the semester at home, but by then Marina was already there, and word had come down: I was to stay in school. The hospice nurse left the room and I took the chair next to his bed. He indicated his prayer book next to him. "Read," he said. My father was never a religious man—even when I'd gone to church as a kid, he never joined us—but he'd gone to Catholic school, and it was his choice to send Marina and me there. When we were forced to attend mass as a family, at weddings or on Easter, he always knew what to do, when to stand and sit and kneel and when to make that cross sign on his forehead and chin during the gospels. The book was small, pocket-sized, the size of a jumbo deck of cards.

He listened to me read, nodding along in rhythm, as if I were singing the words. He talked to his friends in the closet, raised his eyebrows at their questions. It was hilarious and heart-wrenching and hopeless.

I read until I saw his eyes close. I waited a few minutes to see if I could tell he was sleeping. Then I stood and asked softly, "Dad, do you need anything?"

He didn't answer.

I lowered my voice to a whisper. "I love you, Daddy."

He still didn't answer, nor did he open his eyes, but he stretched his mouth into something that could have been a smile. I replaced the prayer book and was almost at the door when his voice made me turn back. He was looking straight at me. "Charlie Brown," he said. "Happy boy, happy Charlie." He reached out to find my hand, squeezed it. "Happy with a good boy. Get married."

"Dad, Marina's the one getting married."

But he didn't seem to hear me. "Happy boy." He smiled at the ceiling.

Screw the snow. I sit down all the way, wetting everything, like a little kid. For the first time, I do what Marina would do. I talk to him.

"I figured it out, Daddy. Why you gave up, and why I couldn't find you anywhere anymore. You were letting me go. But then Dean brought you back in a way I couldn't. Remember? You saw me again. Remember how you started teasing me, the way you used to with Marina? Inviting Dean in for dinner and talking about the Bruins while I finished getting ready? You'd always ask about his dad, talk about what it was like to be a cop's son." I pause. "You knew he wouldn't take me from you."

In the distance, somewhere, someone is shoveling. The scrape of metal on asphalt scratches rhythmically through the snowy stillness. "And remember how when you were happy, Mom got happy, too? Our family was healing. But then you left again. For good. Forever. Maybe dying wasn't your fault, but it's still leaving. There are lots of ways to leave. You thought that leaving me before you had to would keep the pain at bay. But you were wrong, Dad. You were selfish. I know, because I went and did the same thing to Mom."

I don't know how long I've been sitting under the falling snow when I feel the glow of headlights. A car door shuts. The headlights go back the way they came. The lightest of footsteps skim the snow, and Wade's boots stop next to me on the ground.

"Left my phone in the car."

An app for everything.

"I'm so ashamed." I'm quiet enough that Wade has to kneel down to hear me. "I'm ashamed," I repeat, louder. "All this time, I thought they pushed me out, but the truth is I did that to them. All because he didn't like me."

I don't go on, and for a long while, we both say nothing. But then Wade's voice softens into the one I'm familiar with. "Charlie. Your dad loved you."

"He didn't. I was there. I saw it."

"Maybe he just stopped showing it," Wade suggests gently.

"But that's the same thing." Tears are falling down my face, but my voice is clear and true. "I've been so selfish, just like him."

Nothing I can say will make anything any better. So when Wade touches my arm in an offer to drive me home, I let him, and afterward, when he lifts his hand in a final wave and goes inside his house without looking back, I let him do that, too.

Sienna Cash

PART 3:
after

twenty-four

Boxes are everywhere in the front room of Dean's house. He holds the door open for me, then leads me into the kitchen. "Sorry for the mess. At least it's all concentrated in one place."

I sit at the kitchen table. His parents are in Florida, and they'll be driving down again in a couple weeks for good, right after Christmas, along with the moving van. "Do you think you'll miss them?"

"I've been gone so long I'm used to seeing them only on holidays. I may even see them *more* often now, now that I have somewhere to escape to in the winter." The way looks pointedly at me suggests that he means *we* have somewhere to escape to.

"Oh," I say, remembering. "I left it in the car. But my mom sent you bread."

"Seriously?"

"She was pretty excited to make some more for you."

She made some for Kendra, too, also a longtime fan. I told her I'd let Kendra know it was here for her, but who knows when that will be. We're not in a fight, exactly. But things aren't normal either. Kendra mourned the loss of Wade with me, even though I could tell she thought I was closing the door too quickly, not considering moving to Colorado at all. But she didn't want to press, and I appreciated that. When she found out I had officially gotten back together with Dean, however, she wasn't just annoyed. She was furious.

"What are you doing?" she asked me, after I'd confessed our reunion.

"I'm doing what I'm supposed to," I said calmly.

"According to whom?"

"Me. Everyone. Kendra, you have Patrick. This is the same thing. I finally have what I want."

"Do *not* compare Patrick to Dean." I thought she would apologize for that, but she didn't. "You had what you wanted. The best thing ever. And you threw it away for someone who threw *you* away."

So dramatic, as always. I hung up on her. We haven't spoken since.

"I bet she made it all the time when you were home," Dean says now.

"Sometimes. It was one of the good parts of living there."

"Just one?"

"Oh, I don't know," I say, relieved to take my mind off Kendra. I think a minute. "It was... weirdly nostalgic. Not necessarily in all the good ways. But"—and I realize this is true—"better than I expected, ultimately." I've thought about it the last few weeks, as I've gotten used to living alone again. It *was* much better than I expected, staying in the house I grew up in. That's kind of nice to realize.

"Is that because of Wade?"

I'm caught up thinking of Marina, and of dinners with my mom, and I don't quite hear Dean's question until I play it back mentally.

I snap my gaze to him, but his attention is on the open fridge. Was that an edge I heard in his voice? Is he jealous? "Dean. Let's not talk about him, all right?"

He smiles over his shoulder at me. "I can do that."

"He's moving back to Colorado anyway," I say. "It's a complete non-issue."

"Yeah, he left last week I think."

Dean's still searching through the fridge, so he doesn't see me react. I take a breath, and then another as I try to steady my voice.

"Didn't he... wasn't he leaving after Christmas?"

"I have no idea. All I know from Keith is that he's back there. Wanted to go skiing or something." He turns back to me. "I don't suppose you want a Bud Light?"

Somehow I've lost every mascara I own moving to Medford. I drive to CVS in Davis Square to replenish. I could probably find one that's closer, but I haven't learned my new neighborhood well enough yet.

251

I'm in the hair spray aisle—might as well get everything I need—when I feel rather than see someone staring at me.

"I thought that was you," Cam says, smiling shyly.

"Cam!" I give him a genuine hug. "It's so good to see you."

It really is. I can't keep myself from grinning as I take him in. He looks relaxed, almost disheveled. He's holding a CVS basket whose only contents are a box of Hot Tamales—his guilty-pleasure favorite—and a super-sized bottle of Pantene. Seeing me notice it, he explains sheepishly, "Katherine's out of conditioner."

"You're very helpful," I say magnanimously.

"That I am." He squints a little. I get the sense he's deciding whether to stay or go.

"So Katherine's good? You guys are doing well?"

He nods, seems to hesitate. "We're... we're getting married next June."

Whoa. For a hot second I think of Scarves. *The marrying age.* But as the news settles, it occurs to me that my primary emotion is happiness. For him. "Cam. I'm really happy for you," I tell him.

"Thanks. That means a lot to me."

We grin stupidly at each other. I want to ask him why he's so far from home, but somehow that feels too personal. This has the potential of getting awkward, especially since I know he's too polite to excuse himself prematurely. "So anyway—" I begin.

"How are you?" he asks at the same time.

"Me? I'm great."

"I saw Kendra a few weeks ago. Her boyfriend?"—he looks at me as if needing confirmation, and I nod—"works with Katherine, actually."

"I heard."

"She seems pretty happy."

"With Patrick? Oh yeah. They're, like, the real deal."

"So I hear. You think they'll get married?"

I shake my head. I can't picture Kendra married, even to Patrick, marrying age or not. "I doubt it, but stranger things have happened, I guess."

"And it sounds like you've got a... real deal of your own?"

He means Wade, I realize. "Actually, I'm back with my ex." He looks confused. As far as he knows, *he's* my ex. "Dean."

Cam's brows knit. "From high school?"

"Yes."

His eyes widen. "Seriously?"

God, him too? He never even *met* Dean. "Yes," I say shortly.

Perhaps detecting that I'm displeased, Cam backtracks. "I'm sorry, I didn't mean to sound like that."

"But?" I prompt, not exactly politely.

"It's just that... he seemed like someone who belonged in your past. For a reason." I'm about to respond, but he cuts me off, speaking rapidly. "Listen, Charlie, I know this is none of my business. And there's no reason you should listen to me, after how we ended."

"I was never mad about that, Cam."

"I know." He smiles. "That's why it's important that I say this. I really care about you, Charlie, and I probably always will. Hell, I hope you'll come to my wedding. You were good to me, and you let me go because you knew it was right for me."

I shrug, like *no big deal.*

"No, Charlie, that meant something to me. I've thought about this, and I owe you, big time. If you ever need anything... you call me, okay?" When I nod, he goes on. "Now I never met Dean, granted. But from what I heard from you, and from Kendra, and just your whole demeanor about him—that relationship wasn't easy for you."

"Cam, that was a while ago."

"I know. Just hear me out, please, okay? We may not have been soul mates, but I got to know you pretty well, I think. That relationship ultimately brought you a lot of pain. And two people rarely change so completely that they can get past something like that." He pauses, as if weighing whether to go on. "Kendra said you were really happy with your new guy."

"I was." I shrug. "But it didn't work out."

"I just..." Again his words come out in a rush. "I just don't want you to have a difficult time." He shrugs, a little helplessly. "Does that sound cheesy?"

"Relationships aren't easy, Cam."

He smiles faintly. "But they are." He steps closer to me, puts his hand on my shoulder, somehow more tender than he ever was as part of a couple. "That's what I didn't know, until I met Katherine. When it's right, it's not hard at all. It's not forced. It's like the flow of a river. It's easy."

twenty-five

I 'm still in bed Saturday morning when I get a text.
Brunch?
It's our ritual, mine and Kendra's, at least when I lived in Somerville: oversized pancakes (her) and stuffed omelets (me) at Jimmy B's. I'm glad to hear from her, but I have a feeling her displeasure with me about Dean is not over. We may as well get together in a public place where we're both forced to be civilized.

Cam's words reverberate in my head as I drive to the restaurant. He never met Dean, never even saw me with him. I like and respect Cam, but the more I think about it, the more I know he's off base. I think he is right, though, about things being easy. It hasn't always been easy with Dean, true—but it's getting there. Definitely.

The line for brunch is uncharacteristically short, and we're led to a table after only a ten-minute wait, which is all but unheard of. I take it as a good sign. Kendra, never much for beating around the bush, surprises me by talking about everything but Dean—and Wade, for that matter—throughout the meal. Her brother's thinking of buying a share in a house on Cape Cod, Patrick may start job-hunting, she's getting a hefty Christmas bonus and is considering blowing it on a trip to Whistler, Patrick's favorite place to ski.

I nod and smile politely, contributing to the conversation where I can. I tell her I'd like to have her over to help me hang things on the wall; we both know she's better at that kind of aesthetic decor than I am. She smiles and agrees, but I can tell she's nervous. She's usually Kendra on eleven, but today she's dialed back to four, maybe even three. It's disquieting. The way she's clearly avoiding what's really on her mind is crazymaking.

Finally I can't take it anymore. We've sent our credit cards off with the waitperson when I face her and cross my arms on the table.

"Kendra, just say it."

"Say what?"

"The fact that I'm back with Dean really bothers you."

"Well, there's nothing I can do about it, is there?"

"No, there isn't." I know my voice is defiant. "Kendra," I start again, as gently as I can, which probably isn't as gentle as it should be. "You're just going to have to get used to it. I want to be with him."

"But you *wanted* to be with Wade." Her tone is all sarcasm, and I mash my lips together as I sign the credit card receipt. I wait until we're out on the sidewalk to respond. I face her with purpose.

"Kendra, you don't get it. We are supposed to be together."

"Maybe in high school. Not now. Charlie, maybe if you talked to Wade—"

"Wade's gone."

"I mean, before he leaves for Colorado."

"That's what I'm saying. He's gone. Back to Colorado. He didn't even say goodbye."

Her look of surprise relaxes into something sorrowful. I can tell she doesn't know what to say. I can't stand her sadness. "You don't get it," I say again.

"You keep saying that, Charlie. What don't I get? Seriously, tell me."

God, she sounds like Wade. I put it in words she'll understand. "Dean is my person."

She looks stunned. Literally. Like I've zapped her. "Dean is your person," she repeats.

I shrug. Glare at her. "Yes."

She begins to speak, and as soon as she does, she's uncorked. Everything she's been holding in for the past forty-five minutes comes barreling out. "Charlie, I love you, but for someone so smart, you're a complete idiot. Dean is not your person. *I* am your person. Oh, not in a Xanna way, don't look at me like that. I'm serious. Do you even know what 'your person' is? Your person is the one who gets you, who has your back and keeps it real. Who you can call anytime you need to, no matter what you've done or where you are, no questions asked. They get you. That's me. That is not Dean Carson."

I think a minute. "Fine. Whatever you say. He's one of them, then, okay? Kendra, we are supposed to be together. That's how this ends."

"How what ends? Are you saying you think you and Dean are going to live happily ever after?"

"We never should have broken up. Don't you remember? I made him break up with me. It wasn't supposed to end!"

Kendra looks as if she's trying to decide what to say. She walks over to a bench, sits, and indicates that I should sit down, too. "Charlie, it wasn't just that semester. Don't *you* remember? How you complained about him all summer, when he lived in Cleveland Circle? He was distant. He wasn't around when you called him. And then he barely visited you when you went back to school."

He didn't visit me at all, is how I remember it. And he only let me come to B.C. once. I shake my head. "No. That was me. Kendra, that was right after my dad died—"

"I *know* when the fuck it was."

"—and he was trying to be there for me, but I was way too needy. I could hardly blame him for—"

"He was *not* there for you," she snaps.

"I know, because—"

"No, not because anything. He wasn't there for you because he just wasn't. He was cheating on you!"

I stare at her. "What?"

"Charlie." Kendra stoops in front of me, tears in her eyes. Kendra never cries. "I swear I never wanted to say this to you like this. But you can't go thinking that he was some sort of angel, blaming yourself. That whole semester—and probably even before that, over the summer—he was cheating on you. That's why he wasn't there. It had absolutely nothing to do with you. It was all him."

She found out the day my dad died. It was a Thursday in October, and I was at school. I had already been planning to come home that night, since he wasn't doing well. I just had one test to take and then I could take off for a few days. Dean, as it happened, was already home for his school's fall break. But once I got the news, I couldn't get in touch with him. I called and texted and heard nothing for hours.

"Remember how hysterical you were?" Kendra asks me. "I was so afraid you'd try to drive all the way home from New

Hampshire by yourself. I couldn't calm you down. I didn't think you'd wait for me to get there for you."

She thought I might listen to Dean, if only she could reach him. She called him and got nowhere, just like I did. So she went looking for him. At his parents' house his car was in the driveway, but no one answered her knock. The door was slightly ajar, though, so she stepped inside and called his name. Nothing. Then she heard voices, a sprinkling of laughter in the backyard. She found him outside the back door in his parents' hot tub, newly purchased the previous winter. A girl was in the water with him, in his arms. She had long, curly red hair, and they were both very much naked.

The girl saw Kendra first. She nudged him and nodded in Kendra's direction. "We have company," she said, not embarrassed at all. She eyed Kendra from her blonde curls, a mirror image of her own red ones, down to her high-heeled boots, and let go of Dean. Still in the water she moved toward Kendra, hooking her arms over the side of the hot tub, her breasts glistening through the steam in the cold November air. Her smile was seductive. "Want to join us?"

"No thank you, bitch," Kendra said to her. "Just tell that asshole his girlfriend's dad died."

"Ciara," I say.

"Yes. She was a year ahead of him at school. She's from Chicago."

"He followed her there."

"Yes."

"They just broke up."

"No. They only lasted a couple years. But he did just break up with someone, way more serious. Her name's Stacy. She's from Ohio. And Charlie—it was only a month ago. Just before Thanksgiving. And *she* dumped *him*, not the other way around. He kept trying to get her to move to Boston with him."

Stacy. It's an impressive level of detail. I don't even ask her how she knows. She has to be right. Kendra always is.

Just before Thanksgiving. After the bachelor party? After he saw me with Wade?

"Charlie, I'm sorry. I know it sucks to find out like this. But this is who he is." She touches my shoulder. "Are you okay? Can I do anything?"

I can't believe this. I shake her off, stand up. "The whole time?"

"I'm sorry?"

I get louder. "You knew he was cheating on me the whole time?"

"Just right before you broke up—"

"For two months! Almost a whole semester! And you didn't tell me!"

"Charlie, your dad had just *died*. What the hell was I supposed to do with that information? I wanted to tell you, I did. So many times. But why would I do that to you? You were going through so much already," she says, shaking her head in something like desperation. "But eventually it didn't matter. You broke up anyway."

"Like that *absolves* you?"

She looks at me as if I've slapped her. "No, it doesn't. But put yourself in my place, Charlie. You'd have done the same thing."

"No." I'm shaking my head, over and over. "No fucking way."

She starts to speak, but I cut her off. "No." I think back to that time, my mind spinning. He was sleeping with Ciara. Probably all fall semester, maybe even over the summer. And how long before that? I was on the pill! We didn't even use condoms anymore!

"I mean, Jesus, Kendra! You knew he was sleeping with both of us!"

Her eyes narrow. "I made the bastard fucking promise me he would not expose you to anything, Charlie. He swore he didn't. I would have killed him, and he knew it."

"So you just let me think he didn't want to be with me," I say slowly. "Over all that time."

She opens her mouth, then shuts it.

I stand up, walk away without saying a word. But then I think better of it and turn around. "Fuck you, Kendra."

Another car, another breakup. When I did see Dean that fall, before my dad died, we didn't have sex. It confused me. Why was he rejecting me? Did it have something to do with my dad being sick, like he felt wrong about sleeping with me or something? Like I couldn't take it? But it wasn't that. He was just pulling away, and I was flailing.

I got home the day before he did for Christmas break. I hadn't even seen him over Thanksgiving—he'd gone to see relatives in New Jersey—so when he drove straight to my house from school I naively thought that he must have just missed me *that* much.

He didn't come in, so I got in his car. He was wearing a sweater I'd never seen, green, of course, and I wanted to compliment him, but something in his face made me stay quiet. And then without moving or touching me or taking his eyes from the windshield he said, "The way you need me... " When I didn't respond, he added: "It's not good. We've both known it for a while."

"Known what?"

"That we're over."

"Vince."

"What?"

And I was suddenly remembering the party at Kelly's over Thanksgiving break, where Vince Pulinski—kind of a dick but mostly harmless—seemed to be making a move on me. When I delivered the standard *I have a boyfriend*, he looked confused. "Didn't you and Dean break up?" I chalked the mistake up to his idiocy, but it turns out Vince was smarter than I was.

A cocktail of bewilderment, shock, and devastation jumbled my thoughts. "We're already broken up?" I asked Dean, stupidly. "Or are you doing it now, in my driveway?"

He didn't answer and still wouldn't look at me, so I got out and didn't see him again for seven years.

That night, in my living room in my apartment, I steal a look at Dean's profile as we watch a movie I can't even remember the name of. Just as we've watched hundreds of movies and TV shows on this very couch. The corner sectional came from my parents' living room initially, bequeathed to me when my mom bought a new, smaller couch. Dean looks engrossed, but content. He senses me looking at him and adjusts so he's closer to me. Takes my hand, puts it in his lap.

It was seven years ago. It shouldn't matter anymore. We're all allowed to change, aren't we? If not, what's the point? I'm nothing like the person I was seven years ago. And despite what Kendra says, neither is Dean. I've seen it these past few months. He's different now. Matured. The man he hinted at being in college, the man he was at the wedding. He *is* a man now. He's not nineteen anymore.

A forgotten song lyric of Wade's pops into my head, about how nineteen isn't the age of reason. He laughed when he shared it, in Fort Collins, at the fire pit. So did his friends.

Next month, Dean will be twenty-eight. In fact, I'm on my laptop now, searching flights, because earlier he suggested going to Florida together for his birthday.

I'm ready, Dean told me at the wedding. *I know what I need.*

I remember another voice, a shrill one, from Xanna's living room: *When they're ready, they're ready.* And now I recall what came next: *And it doesn't matter who.*

The movie's almost over. I yawn without noticing I'm doing so. "Are you tired?" Dean asks me.

"I don't think so. Maybe a little."

"Maybe we should just... " He indicates my bedroom with a chin-lift and a suggestive grin.

All at once I know that I don't want him to stay the night. "Dean," I start, but his phone rings, interrupting me. Or a song plays, anyway. A ringtone. The phone is closest to me, so I pick it up to hand to him. He declines the call without looking at it, then silences it and places it on his other side. "I don't mind if you answer your phone," I tell him. "It's fine."

"I know." It rings again, buzzing this time. "I'm not answering it," he tells me, his face clouded over. I'm about to ask him why when my mind catches up with what I've heard. The ringtone. I recognize it. Fountains of Wayne, "Stacy's Mom."

"Don't worry about it," Dean's telling me, and I look at him, and he stares back at me, and all at once I see in his face the same lost longing that must be threaded all through mine.

I look at my lap, and I can't help it. I smile. A sad one. Because we're both idiots. We're both settling for something that we're supposed to want. Turning to the familiar instead of being ballsy enough to look outside ourselves for something that may be better.

Cam might have been my placeholder, but now I'm Dean's. Neither of us fits.

"Dean," I begin, and he sighs, because he knows. Things just got much harder than we want them to be.

When it's right, it's easy, Cam had said.

Like the flow of a river.

The days leading up to Christmas pass in a gray haze. It's freezing, but there's no more snow. At work I don't miss JJ's drama, but at least it would have distracted me from my own life. So I throw myself into work in a way I never have, even for JJ. Spencer, my new boss, compliments me on my industriousness, even to the point of delivering me lunch at my desk when he realizes I've skipped it without noticing. I even called in sick to work one morning when I had stomach pains, but I went in later when I realized I'd just forgotten to eat for a while. Some people stuff themselves when they're depressed, but I do the opposite. I've lost almost five pounds. Which could be looked at as the only positive in this situation, but I'd gladly go up a size in jeans if it meant zapping back to a time when Wade looked at me like I mattered.

I thought I knew heartbreak. I knew grief, but not heartbreak. Not like this. And I have no one to blame but myself.

With my first paycheck, I write Wade a check for $150 and send it to the same address I sent the thank-you card to. I buy Kendra a present, because the *Big Bang Theory* shot glasses I run across when shopping for my mom? I can't *not* buy them, even though I have no idea when I'll be able to give them to her. We haven't spoken since brunch. I also buy Xanna a stuffed cow, in homage to Bridey, but I haven't called her, either. Kendra's probably told her the whole story, and I'm not interested in hearing what she thinks. Not yet.

Marc has called me a few times. I hate shutting him out, but I don't know how to exist with him knowing that everyone who cared about me was right, and I didn't listen. I take a tiny bit of solace knowing that at least I have my own space to mope around in. And that no one has to see me feeling sorry for myself. I listen to the "Hunter" playlist on repeat. Every day, I think, *Today. This will be the day I stop crying.*

My favorite place to cry is the shower.

The day Wade and I moved me in to my apartment, he scrawled our takeout order on a random piece of paper. It's still on my fridge. Next to the music, and a photo Xanna took at Kendra's party, it's the only memento I have.

The day before Christmas Eve, I meet Nina in the city to go shopping. It's obvious she notices something's not quite right, but I tell her I'm fine every time she asks. When we sit down at Panera for lunch, she finally gives it to me straight. "Charlotte

Michaelsen, please spill on what your deal is or I will tell your mother."

"You've never met my mother."

"And that's a good way to meet her."

I smile faintly. "I'm fine, I told you. Just holiday blues."

"Holiday bullshit. Something is up with you. Way up. I'm worried, okay? You're not talking, you're not even smiling. What gives?"

"Nina, honestly. I'm okay. Come on, let's figure out what to get Tess." Nina's big quandary all day has been trying to decide what to get her sister, who, she says, does so much shopping for herself she makes her gift-giving life more difficult than dealing with JJ.

"No way. This is our lunch subject. And you know, I'm serious about telling your mom. I know where you live."

"I moved."

"But HR still has your old address."

I sigh.

"Charlie, pretend I'm, like, a stranger. You are the picture of someone who needs to unload. Anything you say will stay in the vault. Girl Scout's honor. I'll start, even. Get you going. Ready? Last month, before I got back together with Raj, I totally slept with a married man."

"Seriously?"

"Well, legally separated. But still, you know, married."

"How old is he?"

"Twenty-five. Got married too young. They might even get an annulment."

"Wow. Lucky they found out soon, you know? That's a tough thing, getting married really young, before you even know—"

"Next."

"What?"

"Your turn, Charlie Brown."

There's no way she could know my dad called me that. No way. But because I've been like a swollen dam for weeks, I burst into tears.

"I feel like I have been crying so much lately," I say through my hands. "I am so fucking sick of crying!"

"Tell Auntie Nina what happened."

So I do. Slowly at first, but as she hands me napkin after napkin and gives dirty looks to passersby who regard me with curiosity, it all comes out—Dean, my dad, Wade, even Marina. All of it.

"And now I have no one," I say. "And I deserve it. I have shit on everyone who cared about me, everyone who kept it real. I twisted everything around to fit what I wanted. Or what I thought I wanted. And as if all that isn't bad enough, I find out my best friend let my boyfriend cheat on me for months."

Nina sits back. "Hmmm." She twists her mouth over to the side.

I sniff. "That's all you've got?"

She twists it to the other side.

"Nina."

"You want it straight?"

"Would you give it to me any other way?"

"True, but will you take me seriously?"

"I have no idea."

She bursts out laughing. "Honesty! I love it. Okay, risks be damned. I'll tell you what I think. First of all, Wade? I'm sorry, but best I can tell, that ship has sailed. It's harder to screw that one up worse than you already did."

"Thank you."

She shrugs. "I'm sorry. Straight can suck. But for what it's worth? Total love of your life, that kid was."

I lower my eyes.

"Okay, before you start crying again, let's move on: Kendra. Your bestie. You gotta cut her some slack. No, for real. I know you're way wrapped up tight in the middle of this now, but when you can find it in your heart to get outside yourself for a damn minute, you'll see that she really did have no choice. Now, would I have done that? Hell no. But I don't think I've ever had a friend like you seem to have in Kendra. Girl would walk through fire for you, and probably already has."

"You got all that from what I just told you?"

"I told you, I'm good. And it's easy to recognize things when you don't have 'em in your own life."

I consider that. "I don't know. I mean, honestly, don't you think she should have just told me?"

"That situation is so historically shitty it's biblical. If a girl catches her friend's man stepping out on her, she's stuck. Ain't no good way out of that. Either way, she's screwed. So your friend, Kendra? She did what would hurt you the least, especially knowing how bad of a place you were in with your dad. Again, not what I would do, but I'm a bitch that way."

"You're not a bitch."

263

Nina smiles. "Thank you. But for real, you have some good forever-friends. If you kick them to the curb, it's your own damn fault. Now Marina? Hell, it sounds like things are okay with the two of you. Keep up on that therapy and I bet you'll even be able to talk about your dad."

"I actually agree with that."

"Good. Now, Dean. The chapter is over."

"I know."

"You did a good job."

I sigh. "Thanks. But it still doesn't feel...."

"What?" she prods. "You're second-guessing?"

"No, it's not that. It's just... it wasn't just me, you know? Everyone seemed to think we belonged together. Well, my family, anyway."

"But do you think you belong together?"

I shake my head, slowly.

We sit for a minute, then Nina says quietly, "Can I talk to you about your dad for a sec? Will you mind?"

"No, it's fine," I say, exhaling.

"Charlie, I can't tell you how it breaks my heart to hear you tell me how he made you feel, because my Daddy loves me something fierce, and I've always known it. But the math, as it were, just is not adding up. You know he really loved you, right? Not just when this guy was around?"

I take another shaky breath. "It was more than that. He just... came to life. And I think it was because he knew Dean and his family, and he knew Dean would never take me away like Steve did with Marina. That's my latest theory, anyway. I'll never know for sure."

"I guess not."

"I have no idea where to go from here," I admit.

"None of us does, Charlie Brown. But if we couldn't allow ourselves to change our damn mind once in a while, life would get pretty boring, don't you think?"

"I guess." I sigh and rub my eyes. "Jesus, Nina. Who knew? I actually feel better. Thank you—for listening and for being honest."

"Don't be so surprised. I told you. I'm good."

"You're a good friend, too."

She smiles thoughtfully, as if she's rolling the idea over in her head. "I am, aren't I? Maybe I'm not as much of a bitch as I think."

twenty-six

Marc's family's holiday party is in full swing. I can hear it from my living room—the friendly yelling, the Christmas music. Aunt Anita even invited me, but I begged off saying I had to leave for Danborn. Which is pretty much true. I'm starting to wonder if I'll make it out without Marc seeing me, and I don't know if I hope I will or I hope I won't.

He solves the problem for me by showing up. When I open the door he's looking dashing as always, holding two Solo cups.

He hands one to me. "Aunt Anita's famous Christmas Eve punch. Goes well with seven kinds of fish."

I accept the cup and take a sip. "You need a date tonight?" he asks me.

"Why, you free?"

"For you I am."

He nods toward me: *Can I come in?* We sit down on the sectional.

"So you should know, I'm just as guilty as she is," Marc says.

I stare at him. I am about to ask why, then I realize. "You knew too?"

"Kendra told me that day. Don't look at me like that. Or hell, do look at me like that if you want—I'm the one who told her not to tell you. She wanted to. She thought she owed it to you. But I told her not to. If you're going to hate anyone, hate me."

I sink into the seat. "Why would you do that?"

"Charlie, I know it's hard to turn this around right now, okay? But at some point you're going to be able to, and you'll realize what it looked like from our perspective. What would you have done if Kendra told you? With everything else you were going through?"

"I would have broken up with him." He doesn't respond to that. "What? You don't think I would have?" His silence makes the voice inside my head louder, and I let it out. "I would have! I would have broken up with him! Who stays with someone who cheats on them?"

He shrugs. "Lots of people, actually."

We both say nothing for a while. Did lots of people really do that? Would I have? A sea of faces in the funeral home. Me, watching the door, examining the line of people, hating myself for it. Dean came, someone told me later. It had been brief, and I missed him, out of the room somehow for those few minutes. Slowly I put the cup down on the coffee table. "Fine," I say. "So what? So what if I would have stayed with him? I needed him. I needed him in my life."

"That's probably true."

"And now I don't."

"You really think that?"

"I broke up with him."

He looks shocked but says nothing, just raises his cup to me. I meet it with my own, the gesture suggesting that I should feel something like pride. But I don't.

Then I get quiet. "Jesus. I told Kendra to fuck off."

"Actually, you said 'fuck you.'"

"Of course she told you."

Marc stands. "Listen, we're about to do our Yankee Swap and I have it on good authority I could go home with an Easy Bake Oven. But say you wanted to maybe call someone? Wish 'em a Happy Festivus one day late? She'd probably take your call." He kisses me on the cheek. "And I forgive you for ignoring me."

"I'm sorry."

"Just don't ever do it again."

I cross my heart. Marc leaves, but before he shuts the door, he sticks his head back in. "Charlie?"

"Marc?"

"I'm really sorry about Wade."

The kindness in his eyes makes me want to weep. I offer him a small smile. "Thanks. So am I."

I gather up the family's presents and load them into my car, along with my overnight bag. Now that I've got my own place, I actually don't mind spending the night at my mom's—especially a time like Christmas, when absences are felt.

It's got to be less than ten degrees. The car is going to take a little while to warm up. In the driver's seat I peel off my gloves, then pick up my phone. I slide it on, click to "Favorites" on my contacts and hit the top option.

"Thank God it's not yesterday," Kendra says. "I had so many grievances to air."

Christmas Eve twinkles at my mom's house in Danborn. Reflexively I glance over at Wade's as I leave my car to walk in the house; everything is dark.

We've had the same Christmas Eve snacks at our house since I was a kid: brie and crackers, sliced pepperoni and cheddar cheese (my personal favorite), and lasagna full of specialty sausage from my mom's favorite place in West Roxbury. This year Marina has shaken things up with a few new contributions: mulligatawny soup (Todd's family is half-Indian), corn fritters, and baked apples. It's an unlikely smorgasbord, and it's delicious.

The tree sits in the same corner of the living room it always has, adorned with the gold-trimmed, quilted tree skirt my grandmother made when Marina was a baby. The three of us—Marina, my mother, and I—helped decorate the tree together a few weeks ago, for the first time in years. As we'd done as kids, Marina and I saved my dad's hockey ornaments for last, including the three Bobby Orr ones—all of which are older than me—that Marina long-ago dubbed his Orr-naments.

"She's really going to like the frame," Marina says to me. From the couch we both glance over at my mom, running through old photo albums at the kitchen island with Todd, who looks dutifully interested. We've chipped in on a digital photo frame preloaded with hundreds of photos we've scanned from her collection.

"I think you're right."

"So how's the apartment?"

I search out coasters to rest our drinks on, Jack and Coke for me, San Pellegrino for her. "I love it. It's owned by my friend's aunt, actually."

"Right," Marina says, remembering. "Katelyn's mom. I work with her, remember?"

"Marc's cousin—that's right. Wow." Connections always sneak up on you that way, growing synapses when you're not looking. I watch Marina, staring into the fire we started earlier with the flick of a switch.

"You have some good friends, Charlie."

"I know." More than ever before, I know this now.

"They were there for you when Dad died, weren't they?"

"Well... yeah. Kendra and Marc, anyway. And Kelly."

She goes on, spinning her drink in her hands. "I remember when the group of them came in to the wake. And you started crying so hard, like you never had the whole time up till then." She turns to me. "I thought you were putting on a show."

"I know."

"Yeah, I told you." She looks away again. "I'm sorry about that. I know now that they were the people who knew you best, and that's why you lost it when you saw them. You could let your guard down."

I hadn't thought about it like that, but it sounds about right. It also sounds like something the therapist might have said.

"Thanks. But I don't really think about that, not anymore. It's the past."

"Still." She takes a sip. "I wanted to apologize. It was a cruel thing to say."

We sit in silence for a while. Marina's likely moving on to other things in her head, but I'm dumbfounded. I'd conveniently forgotten how Marina had called me fake, and a drama queen, for crying that way at the funeral home. At one time, I knew, it had upset me. Tremendously. But I put it out of my mind, because it was easier that way. Never in a million did I expect I'd get an admission that she'd done it, never mind an apology.

She sighs, glancing over at my mom and Todd. A wistful smile grows on her face as she watches them. "Sometimes I miss Dad so much it hurts. Like, physical pain."

"I know what you mean."

"Do you?" But her question's not a dare. "Sometimes I think we had different fathers, you know? I was five when you were born. You were barely in middle school when I graduated." She shakes her head. "No offense, but if I have more than one"—she looks down at her still-flat midsection—"they're going to be close in age."

268

"That sounds… admirable."

"Todd comes from a big family. If he had his way, we'd have five. But I think two is going to be my limit." She turns to me. "Do you ever think about having kids?"

"Never."

She smiles, like she's not surprised. "I was that way for a long time. I'm not saying you're going to change your mind, but if you do, it may well be because of a guy. Who are you dating, anyway? I know you went to the wedding with Dean, but Mom thinks you had something going on with the kid next door. Wade?"

This is news to me. "She does?"

Marina shrugs. "I think that's what she said."

That's all she says, and I realize that to Marina, her question was completely casual. She has no idea of the firestorm I've just gone through. "I'm not dating anyone. I was dating Dean, and I was—before that—actually dating Wade." It feels good to say this. It should never have been a secret in the first place. "But it didn't work out."

"Because of his age?"

"No. Yes. Sort of."

"Eh. Age ain't nothing but a number."

"He moved anyway. Back to Colorado."

"Oh, that's right. He said he was going to." I stare at her. She and Wade *talked*? But then she smiles, like she's remembering something. "Dad was so sad when he moved."

"What?"

"I think I remember it so well because it was right before he was diagnosed. I was gone, you were gone… he seemed to like having a little boy around." She sighs, then turns her nose toward the kitchen. "Hey, I think the apples are done. What a perfect Christmas Eve smell, don't you think?"

I'm going up to bed when my mom hands me a stack of envelopes. "Make sure to change your address," she reminds me.

"I did last week."

I scan through the mail going up the stairs. There's an insurance bill I'm expecting, one that may have gotten lost in the shuffle of the move, plus a few Christmas cards. Mostly I'm flipping past junk, credit-card applications and marketing mailers from Danborn businesses who think I'm new to the neighborhood.

One handwritten envelope stops me. On the front is the same handwriting as the paper on the fridge in my apartment. It's postmarked Denver, Colorado.

I shut my bedroom door and sit on the bed. With shaking fingers I open the envelope, where I find two smaller envelopes labeled *Read first* and *Read when you're done* in the same handwriting. I open the first one.

I left you something.

That's all it says. And it's enough. If he's left me something and he's not telling me where, I know exactly where it is.

I wait until everyone's asleep before going outside. It's freezing. But I don't think about the cold as I climb up to the treehouse with my phone. A scan of the empty floor with my flashlight app reveals nothing out of the ordinary. But there's a storage compartment in one corner, originally designed for tools, where we'd store our snacks. I lift the hinged lid and see a lump. It's a small fleece blanket. Wrapped inside of it is a padded envelope, and inside of that is something small and hard. A flash drive.

Back in my room, I plug the drive into my laptop and locate the file: CHARLIE. It opens in iTunes, and I click on "play."

I don't know what I'm expecting exactly, but I'm guessing I might hear Wade's voice. Or a song—something related to the two of us. But what I actually hear makes me gasp, and my hand flies to my mouth.

Okay, are we ready? Got ya machine all working?

It's my dad's voice.

I think so, sir.

So do you have a list of questions, or do you want me to just talk?

We were supposed to prepare a list of questions. It's part of the assignment.

It's my dad and, from what it sounds like, a much younger Wade. He has a school assignment to interview someone about their profession. I feel a glow thinking of Wade choosing my dad. I'm sure proximity played a role, because the details of his career—industrial engineer—probably didn't breathe life into the interview the way, say, a firefighter's would have.

I listen to them talk about my dad's hours and commute, and the reports he prepared and the projects he oversaw. His voice assumes the same slightly nasal tone I remember, and I'm overjoyed to hear his Boston accent again. He was born and raised in Danborn—unlike my mother, from southern California—and dropped his R's with ferocity. It's all very straightforward but with bursts of humor, like Wade's insistence on calling my dad "sir." I stop and rewind certain parts to hear them again, hear my dad come to life. I could listen to it all day. I watch the status bar get closer and closer to the end, and I dread its finish.

Then the conversation is interrupted.

That ya phone?

Yes, sir. I'm sorry, I should have turned it off.

Oh. Well, you could have answered it if you needed to.

That's okay. I'll call them back.

What was that when it rang? Was that a song?

You mean my ringtone?

A what?

A ringtone.

So you can have any song play when your phone rings?

Yes, sir.

Huh. And what song is that?

My ringtone?

Yes.

A song my dad likes. My real dad. He used to play it for me a long time ago.

Can I hear it?

The ringtone?

Or does someone have to call you?

No, I can play it.

I hear a song, faintly—nothing I've ever heard before, with a lot of funny sounds and what sounds like exaggerated laughter.

Huh. I like it. You say your dad plays the song?

He just likes it. He's crazy about music. Taught me a lot.

That's great, son. Your dad, he live in Colorado now?

Yes.

You see him much?

Not as much as I'd like to.

You get to visit?

Some. [Then, quickly:] *I'm thinking of moving there, actually. I have a little sister there. She's almost two.*

Oh, two. My Charlie—she's in college now, but she used to get into so much trouble when she was about that age. Maybe three, now that I think. Found her down the street one time, almost all the way to where the Radmans live now. And it was summer. They always had that pool. Yours wasn't built yet, I don't think. [Laughs.] We hadn't even woken up yet.

Really?

Her big sister was the one who found her. Marina. She must have been around eight or nine. But she loved taking care of Charlie. Thought it was her solemn big-sister duty. Now Marina's in law school down in Philadelphia, Charlie's in college up north. What's your sister's name?

Fiona.

Bet she'll love having her big brother around. You really want to move all the way there? Won't it break your mother's heart?

That's why I haven't gone.

Huh. Well, if it's something you really want, maybe she'll understand.

I don't know. I hope so. Would you?

Would I what?

If your kid wanted to move away? Would you understand?

[Long pause.]

Son, I don't know. That's an honest answer. The one time it did happen, I didn't handle it well. It was a little different than your situation, though. My older girl ran away. Don't run away!

My dad laughs, and my hand flutters to my mouth. I realize my face is wet.

I won't.

[Another pause.]

We lost Marina for almost a year because of it. Got involved with some lowlife who convinced her to run away. And I didn't understand that at all. Thought it was something I did, that maybe we were too close. But I was dead wrong.

So why did she go?

She went because she's Marina. It had nothing to do with me. Or her mother. But for a long time I thought the opposite, that I'd done something to make her leave.

[Unintelligible.]

What's that, son?

Do you think my mom will think that she's done something to make me leave?

Well, I can't say for sure. I can say that if you do go, you can make sure to tell her that's not the case. In the absence of an explanation, people will make up all kinds of crazy things, not a one of them usually true.

The pause is so long I check the iTunes file to see if I've hit the end. Then my dad goes on:

I learned something from my big girl running away, but not soon enough. Wade, my boy, this isn't anything you asked for, but I'll give you something more valuable than the ins and outs of industrial engineering. Adults can make mistakes. Don't ever forget that. When you're grown, you'll make your share. And don't be afraid of them. Make 'em in style. Trying to avoid making any mistakes at all only guarantees that you'll make bigger ones.

My parents made a big mistake in getting married.

Well, I don't know as I'd say that. You're here, aren't you? And your brother? And you both seem like fine young men. I bet your mom tells you that all the time.

She does, actually.

She's a smart woman. I always liked Marla. Liked your dad, too, when he lived here. A mountain man, he was.

You knew him?

Sure I did. He was my next-door neighbor. My point is, maybe your parents did make some kind of a mistake somewhere down the line, but they weren't afraid to do right by it. Fear's a funny thing. It'll bite you in the ass when you're not looking. Huh. I was so afraid to lose my little girl the way I did my big one that … ah… it doesn't matter. But I figured I'd make it better when she was older, the way my big girl and I did, and I'd be able to let her know how proud I am of the beautiful, unique woman she's become. But I'm a fool, son. We don't always have all the time we want.

[Long pause.]

Sir?

Eh. Now as far as moving to live with your mountain man dad, I'm not going to tell you what to do—your decision has to be yours. But if you do go to Colorado, you love on that little sister of yours, okay? Promise? Little girls need lots of love, lots more than us boneheads think they do.

[Laugh.] *I'll try.*

And you make sure she knows every day that no matter what, you'll still always love her more than words will let you say.

Yes, sir.

Oh, stop with the "sir." I know, I know, it's how you were raised. There's that song again!

I'm sorry. I really thought I turned my phone off that time.

I distracted you. I guess you can turn off your recorder though. Neat little machine. Tiny. There a name for that song, son? Maybe you can get me a copy. What am I hearing—happy something? Who sings it?

It's the Beat Farmers. It's called "Happy Boy."

Well, I like it. Maybe—

And that's the end of the file.

I open the next piece of paper, a letter from Wade. Handwritten.

Dear Charlie,

I always knew I was going to give you that. I figured the right time would come. It didn't, but I couldn't keep it from you. It's like having a beautiful photograph of someone who doesn't know it exists. They need to see that image of themselves. And no matter how I felt or what happened between us, if I were you, I knew I'd want that.

So I'm sorry. Sorry sounds a lot like an apology, doesn't it? It's not. I'm just saying I'm sorry about everything that happened. Well, not everything I guess. Just the end. There's been a lot of snow so far here, and the guys were taking some ski days in Crested Butte (that's pronounced byoot, like in beautiful), so I decided to go along. Sometimes I think I should have said goodbye, but mostly I'm glad I didn't.

I never told you why I was back in Danborn. Maybe I will someday. But it had to do with trust. You may have gathered that trust is something I don't mess around with. But I'm good now. My time in Danborn was up.

So now you know that your dad helped me with my move to Colorado. I'm not sure I would have done it without him. I think about that a lot. And about how you and I come into play in that. But I don't take it too seriously. Our lives are our own, all the better to make our mistakes in style. A very smart man told me that.

Merry Christmas.

Wade

It's the day after Christmas, the holiday mood relaxing into just another day. I have the day off, but the trash people don't. I'm dragging the trash bin and recycling container out to the curb when I hear someone calling my name.

Keith's on the Hunters' front lawn. He's coming towards me with purpose, like he saw me and came out specifically to talk to me.

"Hey," I say guardedly.

We stand there, facing one another.

275

"How was your holiday?" he asks me.

"Good," I say. "Yours?"

"Pretty good."

We're both quiet, until he says, "I heard you and Dean broke up."

I study him. He doesn't look or sound accusatory. "We didn't even get it started, really."

He nods. I wait. I can't imagine what Keith wants to say to me. But I know that whatever it is, I will have to handle it on my own. No one will rescue me. I cross my arms.

"Charlie, I want to say that ... " He looks away, almost laughs. "I never thought that would be so hard to say, but it is, every time." He looks back at me. "You probably won't be surprised to hear that I actually don't remember what I said to you at the bachelor party. But enough people told me. So I wanted to say... I'm sorry."

Of all the things I expected from him, an apology wasn't one of them. He looks off down the street, sliding his hands in his pockets. And then he turns back to me and says something I expect even less. "You want to go get a coffee?"

We go to Java Jones, where there are tables. He asks me what I want, and I tell him a dirty chai. "Chai tea with a shot of espresso," I explain when he looks confused.

"Have you ever thought," he begins when we sit down with our drinks, "that for being so close when we were little, we ended up not knowing each other at all?"

So he does remember. He had me fooled, all these years. "I suppose that's true. We did have a lot of fun, at one time."

"Remember hide and seek in my house?"

"I do," I say, smiling at the memory. "We grew up, I guess."

"That makes it sound simpler than it was." His returning smile looks like an apology. His eyes flit around the shop, as if he wants to look everywhere but across the little table where I'm sitting. Finally his gaze lights on me, and I notice for the first time how similar his eyes are to Wade's. Not the color—Keith's are darkest-brown—but the shape. "The thing is, Charlie, I always thought you knew."

I'm not following. "Knew what?"

He doesn't answer, just looks more and more uncomfortable. He takes a sip of his coffee, puts the cup down. Looks away again. Then, finally, his eyes meet mine, the smallest of requests for understanding.

No. That can't be.

His face changes as he sees what's dawning on mine. Realization. Shock. Denial.

"Remember I asked you to the semi?" he says.

"But your mom made you!"

He looks genuinely perplexed. "Why would you think that?"

I swallow. I remember him at my door, shuffling his feet on a Thursday night, asking me to a dance happening only two days later. I didn't go to Danborn High, but even I knew you got dates to these things sooner than that. And then my mom, smiling as if she already knew, telling me there was a dress sale she knew about. And the night itself, when we stood off to the side, awkward and alone, except for the solitary time we danced. None of his friends were there, because the dance was only for juniors and seniors, unless you were a varsity athlete for Danborn High. Keith was the only freshman to make varsity soccer that year. He introduced me to his upperclassmen teammates, but they all had their own social circles.

"I... I thought your date had backed out or something, since it was so late. I figured you were desperate."

"No, not desperate. Just shy. I wasn't going to go at all. So in that sense, my mom did make me. But she didn't make me ask you. That was my choice."

"Slightly painful night," I say.

He winces. "I know, right?" He folds a napkin over and over on the table. "I couldn't figure out how to relate to you, anymore. Now that it mattered. It was a lot easier when we were nine."

I run my finger on the rim of my cup. "And then when Dean and I..."

He shrugs, like out of everything, this should be what's most understandable. "He was my best friend."

"But you *weren't* shy." I think of all the double dates we went on. "You had girlfriends."

He shakes his head and smiles. "Only later on. And that was Dean. I never had to work at it. Being around him, it was easy for things to just fall into place."

I nod. I knew all about that.

The moment feels like it deserves an apology. But from and to whom, and for exactly what, I can't say.

"I'm not telling you this to make you feel bad, Charlie." Keith shifts in his seat, and I suck in my breath involuntarily as I see another flash of Wade in, of all things, an uncomfortable expression. "I've done enough of that. I really just wanted to apologize. I... I don't drink anymore. I quit once before. It was a bad idea to start again." He pauses. Looks right at me. "I just wanted to explain. Where it came from, that night. Jealousy. A whole lot of history."

"Protectiveness," I say softly, wondering if he'll get it.

He does. "Yeah."

We're both quiet, and I can tell he's not done. I sip my coffee and wait.

"I talked to my parents," he says finally. Then, clarifying: "All four of them."

My grip tightens on my cup. "You went to Colorado?"

"No. But I'm going in a couple weeks."

I smile in spite of myself. "I'm glad to hear that. They miss you there."

He looks at me, as if trying to deduce how much I know. "Yeah, well. They all had things to say. About you. And my brother."

There it is. The elephant in the room. *Good things?* I wonder. But I don't think I deserve to know. He doesn't volunteer any more. I take a breath, brace myself to speak, hoping my words will dam any tears. "I'm sorry." This. This should be the apology. I say it again. "I'm sorry. I didn't mean to hurt him." I think of Wade's face, the car windows beginning to fog behind him, him saying *I'm a person*. I reach under my glasses, swipe at the wetness with my fingers.

"I didn't mean it," I say again. "I should have been stronger. I should have recognized it better. I was a coward, too scared to believe... I didn't know."

Outside, a woman wearing a bright green, Christmasy scarf walks up to the door, then looks around expectantly. Suddenly her entire being lights up and she's being hugged by a figure in a long brown coat. A woman. They both turn and walk in, red with cold and post-Christmas joy. The brown coated-woman pulls her hat off, revealing a shaved head. Green scarf pulls her closer with a linked arm. Besties. Lovers. Either. Both.

"I just didn't know," I say again, my eyes following the women.

"Didn't know what?" Keith asks me.

"What it was."

twenty-seven

A few days later I come down with the virus that has seemed to plague everyone over the holidays, if my Facebook feed is to be believed. The first hours of January 1 find me like so many others across the city: on the floor of my bathroom. Only I haven't consumed a drop of alcohol.

The new year skates in while I try not to notice. I spend New Year's Day with a bottle of Gatorade and not much else, dozing on and off, barely moving from the sectional. Kendra and my mom separately threaten to come over, but I talk them both out of it. It doesn't seem to be anything that fluids and proximity to a bathroom can't solve.

Late that night I'm flipping the channels when I come across a stupid movie from the '80s, *American Anthem*. Something about gymnastics. I notice it because it stars Janet Jones, whom I recognize from my mom's DVD copy of *A Chorus Line*, and whom I also happen to know is married to Wayne Gretzky, the famous hockey player (thanks Dad). Janet is practically a teenager in the movie, playing an even-younger high-school gymnast.

The plot line is so silly that even watching it ironically isn't that entertaining. Twenty minutes in I'm about to change the channel when the token hot guy—a male gymnast who seems to be squandering his talent, with already-squandered acting skills—takes Janet Jones, the new girl at the gym, for a ride in his Jeep. The wind whips through their hair, their conversation happening in voiceover as the Jeep races along the dirt road to a song I don't recognize outright, but I know I've heard before.

"You leave anybody behind?" the hot guy asks Janet.

"*What?*"

"You have a boyfriend?" he clarifies.

"No."

"You want one?"

She doesn't answer. The Jeep carries them bumpily along, windblown and smiling in that '80s teen romance way.

I rewind and watch it again, twice. I think of effortless conversations, of evocative smiles and comfortable silences. Sandy, unruly hair, and a question under a snowy streetlight. I stick with the rest of the movie, but he's right. It's seriously the only good line.

Sienna Cash

Acknowledgments

Like everything else in my life, I wrote this book the hard way, learning as I went over five years. Sincere, prayer-hands thanks to:

Alex Dezen for eleventh-hour permission and lyrics that ignite.

Jena Barchas-Lichtenstein for ace copyediting.

Jenn and Jamie for heroic proofreading.

Readers from draft one to draft gazillion Denise, Deirdre, Kirsten, Jesse, Ellen, Carrie, Danielle, Kayt, and Amy.

Kirsten, Ellen, and Jesse for inspiring playlists.

Nancy for the opportunity to not bore her.

Jeff for priceless male perspective and efforts to keep me honest.

Julie for detailed feedback not once, not twice, but three times, and for fearless cover design.

The Wreckers, for modeling good music taste for a decade and a half, even when I've been too crazed to follow up.

I could not and would not have done any of this without Johannah.

To my kids: this is what following a dream looks like. Can't wait to watch you do the same.

Eternal gratitude and love to Matt, for always giving me the reason.

About the Author

Sienna Cash grew up in the suburbs of Boston and lives in Colorado with her family. Like Wade, she believes that there is a song lyric equal to every occasion in life. And possibly a movie quote. *Worst-Kept Secret* is her first novel.

To be kept informed of any updates *Worst-Kept Secret* or news about Sienna Cash, please add your email address to our list at siennacash.com.

COMING in 2017

Sneak preview of the next book in the Charlie-and-Wade saga...

Marina was quiet for a minute, frowning. Did I say something wrong?

"Was Wade the reason you and Jake broke up?"

Jesus Christ. "He said that?" Sometimes I forgot that Marina and Jake were friends. Which was crazy, since she was the whole reason we met in the first place.

"No, no. Just that you broke up. But he did imply that there was some sort of ex-boyfriend problem."

I didn't answer. What else did he tell her?

"So was it him?"

"Was what him?"

"Was Wade the ex-boyfriend?"

"Wade wasn't really my boyfriend."

Marina the lawyer heard what I didn't say more than what I said. "But he's the reason?"

Thanks, Jake. "Part of it, I guess."

She was confused. "So are you moving to Colorado too?"

"Me? No. I mean, Kendra and I were—I'm staying here."

"But if he's—" She stopped, started again. "Aren't you getting back together?"

"It's not that simple." This came out more sharply than I intended. I did not need to explain Wade to Marina. But she was Marina, so she couldn't let it go.

"I'm sorry, maybe I'm dense. But you broke up with a great guy because you can't get over another one. Right?"

Yes, counselor.

"And you're not going to pursue him."

I sighed. Of course, to Marina it would be that simple. The girl who runs away from home at eighteen, screwing up what should have been her first year of college, yet somehow manages to become a PhD *and* a lawyer by age thirty. Never had a muddled thought in her life.

"Oh," she said, like it was just dawning on her. "Does he not feel the same?"

"He *does*." Now I was defensive. Great. I took a breath. "I mean, he did. I have no idea how he feels now." For a tiny, glorious little second, I felt like bragging. "But he did want me to move with him." Before she could ask why I didn't, I just offered it, straight out. "There's a big age difference."

"He can't be that much younger than you."

"Seven years."

"Hmmm." Was that judgment in her tone? I gritted my teeth waiting for what she'd say next.

"Does he have a girlfriend?"

"What, now? I have no idea—"

But she was already interrupting me. "Fuck it."

"Marina!" In front of the *baby*!

She laughed. "Fine. *Frick* it. Even so. I think you should go."

I blinked at her. "You think I—what?"

"Should go. To Colorado."

Did I ask you? I wanted to say. And perhaps she knew what I was thinking, because she said: "You need someone to tell you to go."

How was it that she could do this to me? I tried not to let myself crumble, concentrating on the cut of Sierra's chin, the curve of her nose. "I'm fine here," I said quietly. "My life is here."

"What life?" She shook her head abruptly, like she couldn't believe she said that. Her voice softened. "I'm sorry. That's not what I mean."

It was time to be the bigger person here. "Marina. You just had a baby. You don't have to say anything. You should be resting. We can talk another—"

"No," she cuts me off. "I want to say this. And I feel great, actually. Charlie, you're twenty-six." I give her a look. "Twenty-seven? Sorry. You're not married. You don't have any kids. You don't even have a boyfriend now. You have no responsibilities, nothing tying you down at all. If there's ever a time in your life that you can sprint across the country to chase a guy you know is in love with you, you're sitting smack in the middle of it."

I was speechless. I grasped for something to say, but all I could think of is *I don't know if he's in love with me.* I did not say this.

"I'm jealous, a little," she went on, laying back, arms behind her head. "That time when you have no baggage? It's the best time in life."

To be alerted when this title is released, please add your email address to our list at <u>siennacash.com</u>.

Made in the USA
Middletown, DE
16 August 2020